Lindsey Barron Series Volume 8 Down the Dragon Hole

Vic Broquard

Lindsey Barron Series Volume 8
Down the Dragon Hole
First Edition
Copyrighted © 2013, 2015 by Vic Broquard
ISBN: 978-1-941415-81-8

Published by:
http://www.Broquard-ebooks.com
Broquard eBooks
103 Timberlane
East Peoria, IL 61611
author@Broquard-eBooks.com

Artwork by Crooked Willow Studios.

For Morgan and L. Ron Hubbard

Table of Contents

Chapter 1—Formation

June 10, 2200, two Stratospheres, the latest in luxury airliners, touched down at Lambert Field, St. Louis, Missouri. One displayed the stars and stripes of Air Force One. The other, black and non-descript, had only the tiny logo of the Homeland Defense Force-World Investigation Team on its tail, HDF-WIT. President Billy Bob Becker stepped down the ramp, surrounded by a dozen Secret Service agents, dressed in black, as had been their custom as far back as anyone could remember. All were heavily armed, as were the local police and the group of St. Louis FBI personnel, who had cordoned off this portion of the field. Both planes had circled the airport before landing, but for two different reasons.

President Billy Bob wanted to inspect the damage yesterday's terrorist bombing had done to the giant airport—a political necessity, considering the terrible loss of life—at least a hundred killed, though the recovery process had just begun—and significant destruction. Half of the main concourse was smoldering rubble. However, he also had a secondary agenda, one that involved those on the other airliner, which had flown in from Chicago. Across the tarmac, a wall of reporters and cameras waited his anticipated speech, but they would have to wait a bit longer. He spotted General Franco Porti stepping down from the other plane. The rotund President in his expensive suit, polished shoes, and slicked-backed hair, waddled over to the uniformed man, who saluted. He headed the Homeland Defense Force, the HDF, more specifically the subsection called the World Investigation Team or WIT.

"Ah, General Franco Porti, thank you for responding so quickly. Times like these demand swift and significant action," President Billy Bob declared, a bit too pompously for the general's taste. However, he accepted the president's handshake, limp and moist. That General

Franco didn't like the president was a well-known fact around Washington. Nevertheless, he was his commander-in-chief and he had to obey. The general had a deep bass voice, was six-one, and appeared to be quite handsome, perhaps in his late thirties.

"I've assembled the team as you ordered. Mr. President, it is our best WIT team, run by field agent, Lead Detective Alan Bergson," the general introduced the man slightly behind him and to his left. "He's got the best case closing record in the entire department. I'm confident he and his team will apprehend those responsible for this terrible bombing in short order, Mr. President."

President Billy Bob barely glanced at Alan, who was six-three and two hundred pounds of solid muscle. The thirty-year-old, brown haired man, nodded towards his president, though he clearly didn't think much of the man. He hadn't voted for the weasel. Billy Bob was just another brilliant talker who told the people what they wanted to hear, but subsequently did nothing useful. No, Alan was rough and tough, a no-nonsense detective who closed cases that others could not. Hard evidence always wins the day—that was his motto and how he approached cases. This one would be no different. Someone or someones had deliberately blown up half the busy airport. There were clues to be discovered, which would inevitably lead him to the perp, one way or another. Always had, always would.

His two team members for the last three years stood a step behind him. Twenty-five-year-old Chrissy Miller was his communications expert and profiler. Rather short, she had shoulder length blonde hair, but was quiet and soft-spoken. Alan often said, "Don't let her appearance fool you." She held two black belts in two forms of martial arts and often bested Alan in practice sessions. Alan greatly respected Chrissy, ever since he'd made the mistake of teasing her about being half his weight, after which she promptly threw him flat on his back onto the mat and didn't say a word while doing so.

Twenty-nine-year-old Arnold Kelly stood at her side. He brought keen weapons and explosives knowledge to the team. One would be hard-pressed to find a better sharpshooter and demolitions expert than Arnold. On the other hand, his personality was opposite of Chrissy's. Opinionated and something of a jokester, he loved to play pranks on others. As the President turned away from the trio, Arnold spoke up, "Ah, Mr. President, you've lost some weight since taking office." He meant it as a sarcastic joke, since Billy Bob had in fact put on another twenty pounds.

President Billy Bob ignored the man, since he was of no real importance. Instead, he said, "General, you have my orders. See that they are followed or there will be hell to pay. I want action yesterday. Now, if you will excuse me, I have the cameras waiting and you have your job to do. Get started on it. Where's my damned speech?"

"Right here," an aide said, rushing up papers in hand. Surrounded by men in black, the two headed to the waiting reporters, out of hearing from the four.

General Franco Porti turned to Alan, "Okay. You heard the president. I've given you his direct orders. Carry them out." By that, he meant the President's special request to have a witch on his team, namely a female wizard. He expected to hear flak and wasn't disappointed. *Amazing how easy it's been to influence Billy Bob.*

In the Old Age, wizards and witches lived in secret, and many were burned at the stake, but nearly two hundred years ago, the Wizard Board of Review approved the New Age. Magic users openly joined the world, establishing schools of magic in which they were drilled in the four inviolate laws binding all those who used magic.

1. Thou shalt not use magic to injure or harm another unjustly.

2. Thou shalt not use magic to kill another unjustly.

3. Thou shalt not use magic to steal from another that which is not yours.

4. Thou shalt not use magic to force another to do something against their will unjustly.

Violations of these rules brought swift and just punishment.

Alan protested as much as he dared, "General, you

can't be kidding? Are you? You, you mean we have to have one of those damned witches with us? Can't you just put her somewhere else? You know me and my team. No magic! Not ever! Ruins cases! You can't do this to us! We won't stand for those damned magic users making a mess of our work. Assign her to another team. Hell, put her anywhere but with us—not if you want us to be able to solve this case." Perhaps, he went a bit too far, he thought, seeing the cold, return stare on his boss's face, a stare that might chill anyone but Bergson.

Arnold butted in with his opinion, which differed none from his boss's, "Yeah, we don't want meddling witches messing up our investigation. Besides, she'll just be in the way and probably get herself killed. These are terrorist bombers we're talking about, not meddling spell casters with their illusions and such."

Chrissy kept silent, but her cold expression indicated that she was in complete agreement with Alan.

"You have her file. You have your orders. Carry on, Bergson. That will be all," the general barked as though Bergson was in the army, which of course he wasn't. He turned and strutted towards the waiting cameras to help protect the President.

"We're screwed," Chrissy commented too softly to be heard by the departing general.

"You can say that again," Arnold declared rather testily. She did so, causing Arnold to chuckle.

Even Alan smiled. "Okay, we're screwed, but we've a job to do, meddling or no meddling, so let's get on it," he ordered. "We'll set up a base of operations in the downtown FBI office. They've arranged a suite for us. Pack your gear into the Rover and we'll head there first. Can't do any prelim work on the site. Too hot. Still smoldering. Besides, we have to discover what the Feds have found out, but I bet that's not much or we wouldn't be here." The two acknowledged his orders with head nods and headed back into the Black Bird.

Several minutes later, a black, armored van drove down the back ramp of the luxury liner and headed off

downtown. Kelly drove, while Miller called out directions from the onboard nav system. Still fuming over the direct order to include a civilian and a wizard no less, Bergson sat in the backseat looking over the file he'd been given on this annoying, unneeded, unwanted, useless wizard person.
***

Governor Lindsey Barron-Cross ran the premier Bradbury's School of Magic in Colorado. She'd ascended to this position because she and her husband Deiter had been instrumental in capturing the world's most evil and powerful wizard, Dominus Malefic back in 2183. Dominus very nearly conquered the world, but after his capture he was assassinated by the sister of one of his many victims before he could stand trial for his voluminous crimes, many involving mutilation of women of whom he had low respect.

One of his supporters, Thaddeus Black, dug up his grave and cast Cause Life. With this spell, the caster had no control over what form the new life would take, other than it would be human. Through a comedy of errors, Dominus returned to life as a twelve-year-old girl! Unable to undo the mixup, Dominus assumed the identity of Monica Nicole Black and enrolled in the St. Louis School of Magic with the intent to learn the Full Wish spell in her sixth year, which she hoped she could then use to undo the sex mess.

However, by experiencing life as the opposite sex, Monica's entire personality began to slowly change. When she graduated six years later and a full archmage, she was determined to do good this lifetime. With her close school friends, she established a magic store called Protections, Investigations, Wands, Items, and Potions or PIWIP.

Then came the invasion of the demons from the Abyss. Monica and her friends were instrumental in dealing with that terrible situation, earning her the title Demon Hunter. In fact, of all the wizards and witches in the world, only archmages Monica and Lindsey could cast all of their spells without the use of the usual power-amplification wand and without vocalizing the words.

Thirty-year-old Archmage Monica Nicole Black reread for the tenth time the Presidential Order she'd received the day before the planes landed. President Billy Bob requested her to lend her unique talents to the Homeland Defense Force, specifically joining their best detective squad to help solve the recent terrorist bombing. *Why? Why does the President want me on this? A terrorist bombing? The team is all normals.*

What was her problem with President Billy Bob's request? As the evil wizard Dominus, he had detested norms, the head blind (a derogatory term), that is, those without any magical skills. He had even attempted to turn norms into second-class citizens and walking automatons during his National Health Care program.

In this new lifetime and until now, Monica had managed to make peace with many of those magic users whom she'd harmed during her lifetime as Dominus, but she still pretty much ignored norms. She had worked well with other magic users, particularly those in the Department of Magical Misuse and others departments to eliminate the invading demons. She'd even become friendly with the normal who led the St. Louis FBI office, Oliver Easton, helping him with the nasty demon problem nine years ago, though a few powerful demons escaped the dragnet.

If she accepted Billy Bob's request, she would be working with nothing but norms, people with no magical skills at all. But her dislike of norms went deeper. During the fourth month of her pregnancy nine years ago, she'd gone out to grab a box of ice cream treats for her husband, Rob. During those ten minutes, a bomb exploded in her home, killing Rob and injuring many others who lived in the complex located in the hilly bluffs just north of the city, close to the river. Though Monica was convinced the demons who had escaped had tried to kill her in revenge, sadly the FBI's full investigation turned up nothing at all. The norms simply never solved her case. Who was responsible for the bombing that killed her husband?

While she had planned on naming her son

6

Diancecht, she decided to name him after her loving husband. Rob was now nine and going into the fourth grade this fall, along with several other children of her dear friends. In fact, twelve children lived and played at the complex.

For the last nine years, she and her best friend Crystal had argued to anyone who would listen that the demons who had escaped the roundup must be located and dispatched. But those demons had simply vanished or were being highly successful at eluding detection. With no demon sightings or attacks during these past nine years, everyone believed they had returned to the Abyss. Even Crystal had at last given up trying to convince others to keep a vigilant watch, and now many others called Monica "the Demon Hunter," meant derogatorily.

Hence, Monica didn't trust or like most norms, but President Billy Bob had requested her aid and personally to boot. She knew she couldn't refuse him, but still. . . With a sigh, she reluctantly sent the president her agreement to do as he wished. Others here could watch Rob for her during her absence, for there was no shortage of babysitters at the complex. She headed off to tell the others the news and to prepare herself for the meeting the following day.

The next morning, she checked her appearance in her full-length mirror. Satisfied, she silently cast her Teleport spell, arriving at the FBI office in downtown St. Louis, where she was widely known and respected. "Good to see you, Miss Black," the receptionist said, handing her a visitor's pass. "They are expecting you in Suite 401. Between you and me, I'm glad that the president brought in the top Homeland Defense Force's WIT investigation team. From what little I've heard, no one's got a clue about the attack. It's just awful. Do you suppose the demons are back or was it a terrorist attack? My money is on terrorists."

Monica smiled. "I've no idea, Jean, only what I've seen on the news, which wasn't much. Guess I'll find out. Want me to let you know?"

"Oh would you? That would be wonderful," the

receptionist replied with a big smile that flashed her bleached teeth, compliments of her latest dental visit. Monica took the elevator up to the fourth floor and walked into Suite 401, somewhat reluctantly, more than a little worried about working with norms. Could she even do it?

As she entered, she caught the tail end of Oliver's briefing. "So that's what we've got so far. Nothing. Survivors first. Victims identified. Ah, here is Miss Black now." He turned and motioned for her to enter. "Monica, this is Lead Detective Alan Bergson of the HDF's WIT team. Alan, Miss Monica Nicole Black. I'll leave you to it. We've still got fourteen bodies or parts of them to identify. Pressure is really on us this time." He turned and left, leaving Monica feeling very ill. She sensed hostility directed towards herself.

The three saw a thirty-year-old, extremely attractive woman, dressed for a very formal affair. She wore a red satin pencil dress, hemmed just below her knees, allowing her expensive fully-fashioned black nylons to show. Her six-inch, red patent heels matched her gown; likewise, her lipstick. Her rich, slightly wavy, raven hair flowed down her back, reaching her curvaceous hips, though the men's eyes did focus on her extremely well endowed bosom, a fact she didn't miss.

Alan Bergson declared, "Looks like we pulled you away from an important meeting. It's fine with us if you go back to it. Probably preferable, too, since we've got an investigation to conduct."

"Oh, I always dress like this, unless I have to be in the field," Monica replied casually.

Bergson frowned, "Look, Miss Black, this is serious business—terrorist attack—hundreds killed. This is no place for you."

"Try a beauty pageant. That would fit you better," Arnold Kelly insinuated, his eyes sweeping up and down her very shapely form.

Monica fought down the surge of anger that threatened to explode out through her mouth. She swallowed and replied while controlling the tone of her voice making it sound far more pleasant than she felt, "The President requested that I join your team. I'm here. Shouldn't we get to work?"

"Guys, stop staring at her boobs," Chrissy interrupted, annoyed with the two men.

Kelly snickered, "Jesus, Miller, how can we? When she's wearing that 'come do me' outfit, what'd ya expect?"

Miller smiled, sensing the tension between the men and Miss Black. Wisely, she decided to change the topic. "I'm Miller, communications and profiler. He's Kelly, weapons and demolitions. He's Bergson, Lead Detective. We call each other by our last names, usually." Her frankness lessened the tenseness, but only slightly.

"Look, Miss Black," Bergson barked, "let's get one thing straight from the start. We three don't like magic, wizards, or witches—particularly so in our investigations. We want none of your magic messing up our case. We don't care about silly titles: Order of Merlin, Knights of Truth. We close cases based on hard, physical, irrefutable evidence, all done up proper like so it can't be challenged in the courts. So no magic is wanted or needed. Besides, this was obviously a terrorist attack, not a demon attack, Miss Demon Hunter. I know—read your file—Demon Hunter extraordinary. Well, no demons involved, so you might as well go home now and save us all a lot of trouble. Besides, we're dealing with deadly terrorists who will think nothing about killing you. We can't be responsible for you or your safety. They have my back and I, theirs. We can't do our job while we play nursemaid to a Barbie Doll."

"Hard evidence. I'll keep that in mind, Bergson," Monica countered, adding, "but I look after myself rather well, if I do say so myself. I dress like this for two reasons. One, I enjoy how I appear. Two, it disarms others, like you two, giving me the advantage, particularly so with men. I could have killed all three of you while you were distracted by my boobs. I certainly don't want you watching my back, but I will do my best to watch yours, since you're far more likely to need it than I do. Can we get down to business? Besides, I've already signed all the waivers of responsibility. I'm here of my own volition, and the HDF takes no responsibility for my safety. I signed your forms last night."

"Good. At least we understand that part," Bergson barked. "Since we can't get rid of you, let's get started. Have a seat."

Kelly motioned for her to take a specific seat.

Monica smiled, thankful that she was being observant. "I think I'll take this one, Kelly. You can have that one. Careful. A leg is about to fall off of it."

Kelly flushed, caught in his practical joke. "You were supposed to sit in it and fall over, Miss Black—could have been a nice laugh. How'd you know?"

"The nut is on the floor—pretty obvious, Kelly. Have to try harder, unless you want me to have a go at it for you," she replied, a coy smile on her red lips.

Miller broke into a broad grin. She commented, "Pretty cool, Kelly. She didn't fall for your joke. We've a sharp one here."

"All right, enough. We've a job to do. Here's what the FBI has so far," Bergson began, slapping a small folder on the conference room table. "Yesterday at 2 pm, a bomb exploded in the western half of the main concourse. Near total destruction there, but the eastern half is largely untouched. One hundred six dead. One hundred forty-one being treated at local hospitals. No one's claimed responsibility for the attack, at least not yet."

Kelly interrupted, "Hey, isn't that a bit weird? Usually some blokes claim they did it."

Bergson nodded, "Should have by now. Agents have been taking victim statements, but so far, they've only been able to talk to the less injured folks. They were quite a distance from the blast center. I've just gotten word that the more critically injured survivors, those who were closer to the origin point, are now out of surgery. We have doctors' permissions to interview them. So if Miss Black will escort us to the hospitals, we'll find out what they have to say about the bomber. After that, we'll visit the site and see what we can discover there. Remember, no demons here, just an insane bomber and his backers. We want hard evidence to throw them into jail for life."

Three hours later, the four finished the interviews and met in one hospital's cafeteria to exchange what they had found. Miller went first, "Miss Black and I had—well let's just say we had a batch of really bad cases. Most lost one or more limbs. God, I've not seen so many who are in such bad shape. She took the time to cast a spell of some sort on them. Claims it will help them get better, but honestly, how can it ever be better if they've lost arms and legs?"

"Hey, I told you, Black, no spells," Bergson barked, noticing Monica gulping down her third sandwich.

"Regeneration of lost limbs," she muttered with her mouth half full. She took a drink of coffee and added, "I couldn't sit there and not do that, Bergson. In a few days, their lost limbs will have regenerated. They'll make a full recovery and have their lives back."

"Oh," Bergson muttered, wishing he hadn't been so gruff. "Guess that's good for the victims, but what did you learn about our bomber?" He wanted the topic changed at once. No way was he going to thank Black for what she had done. That would be an acknowledgment of magic's usefulness.

Miller continued her report, occasionally glancing at her notes. "We've had five victims comment that they saw a ghostly form in the smoke, right where the bomb exploded. None claims to have seen the bomber, but they did see the ghost. Weird, isn't it? Absolutely nothing useful, but then that's what I'd expect from traumatized victims."

Kelly broke in, "Talk about weird! We got something similar four times as well, but like you said, nothing else useful at all. Those who saw the bomber were too close and blown to bits."

"Probably just hallucinating or an after image," Bergson retook control of the brief meeting. "Well, I didn't expect we'd get anything useful from the survivors. Now if Miss Black is done gorging herself, let's head out to Lambert and see for ourselves."

"Sorry. I used up a bit too much energy with my spells. I'm done. Give me a minute to change," Monica replied.

"Ladies room for me, too," Miller added. "Meet at the Rover."

Five minutes later, Chrissy and Monica joined the men at their armored vehicle. Monica now wore work boots, pants, and a blouse. She had her hair out of the way, tied in a bun. She also wore gloves. Noticing the men observing her, she commented, "Can't dig around the rubble in heels, fellows." Kelly chuckled.

A few minutes later, their armored Rover pulled up at the airport, where swarms of personnel sifted through the rubble. A thin, plastic barrier now separated the relatively undamaged half of the concourse from the destroyed side, allowing normal operations to resume at the airport. Planes were taking off and landing, adding their roar to the disparate conversations among the personnel. Some were medical examiners; some, FBI crime scene agents collecting evidence. Into the assemblage went the WIT team.

"Okay, Kelly, this is your area of expertise. You lead," Bergson barked, though he need not have, since Arnold had already moved ahead of the three.

"What are we supposed to be doing?" Monica whispered to Miller.

"Looking for clues, but mostly we're just letting Kelly do his thing," she replied.

"Ah ha," exclaimed a jovial Kelly, holding up a charred finger, "Buffalo fingers here." He'd moved a pile of debris and found several detached fingers. Miller smiled at his jest, but Bergson wasn't pleased with his remark.

"Kelly, show some respect for the dead. Others are here. ME, over here! Body parts," he called out to a nearby man who responded, collecting the three charred fingers that Kelly had found.

"Well, here's the point of origin, Bergson," Kelly stated as though he'd been here and seen it happen firsthand. "This exact spot, about fifty feet from what were the entrance doors. Boom. Right here. See how the blast radiates outward?"

"But what about that fire damage yonder, where the planes were?" Monica asked. Certainly over there the fire had caused extensive damage.

"Secondary. Blast took out that wall and ignited the planes' jet refueling trucks, which then took out the two planes," Kelly explained, somewhat pleased that Miss Black needed his opinion and observations. He continued, "Given the structural damage and the designs which we looked at on the flight to St. Louis, the bomber probably used C-4 and somewhere around a hundred pounds of it. I'd say he probably wore part of it in a body suit, but more must have been in a bag, perhaps one on rollers, given this secondary blast oval here." He pointed to two patterns barely noticeable in the rubble, but once pointed out, they seemed obvious to Monica.

"Crap! A hundred pounds?" Bergson bellowed.

"At least that, Bergson," Kelly replied. "Severe structural damage. Why didn't the bomber detonate it over there, right in the middle of the entire facility? Makes no sense. If he had, there wouldn't be any airport left. It's almost as though he wanted to send a message or something by not totally destroying Lambert Field."

"Key point. Why didn't he walk another hundred feet or so before triggering the bomb?" Bergson asked. "I see what you mean. If he had, this whole place would be rubble, planes and all."

"I got to get down below, boss. Look; the blast knocked a hole in the floor. I see baggage down there," Kelly continued. "I bet I'll be able to identify the C-4 he used. With luck, I'll know where it came from, thanks to the blast hole. It's highly likely to have preserved telltale traces. Catch you later."

Miller spoke up, "Based on that, I'll go back to the Rover and see what I can get from the digital video feeds. They had surveillance cams everywhere, according to the specs they gave us. Each sends its feed through the wireless network to an off-site server. I'll access it and trace it back.

My assumption: the bomber walked into the concourse and over to that spot where he detonated his bomb. Took perhaps ten seconds after he entered to get to that location. I should be able to zero in on our bomber."

"Excellent. Go find us a face. We'll hunt for more clues here," Bergson replied. Kelly had already disappeared, presumably finding a way into the damaged section of the baggage handling system.

Monica had no idea what to look for. Besides, she felt overwhelmed with the extent of the destruction and the fact that workers around her were still pulling bits of body parts from the rubble. Bergson seemed detached from the gruesome details, rummaging through debris like a rat searching for a prized "find." Periodically, he stuck a small wire with a yellow flag on it into the debris, marking another body part. Shortly, others came and carefully retrieved them. Before long, Monica noticed that he was collecting other things and joined him, curious about what he had in his plastic bags.

"Ah, this one is full. Miss Black, take this to Miller in the Rover. Cell phones. Evidence. Hey, no damned magic. Walk it out to her. Chain of evidence," he explained.

"I don't understand why I can't just use magic to deposit the bag with her," Monica asked.

"This is physical evidence found at the scene. In court, we have to be able to document the chain of custody of the evidence. We have to swear what condition it was in when we got it, from whom we got it, and so on. If not, the defending lawyers can have the evidence tossed out of the trial. So Miller has to see you bringing the bag to her. She'll seal it with crime tape and log it. Evidence can't ever be out of our sight, unless it's locked up in a crime lab vault. Rules are rules. So take this physically to Miller, Miss Black."

"Got it. I think I understand. Sorry, I've never been involved with court cases," Monica explained, thankful he'd told her the "why," although he'd talked to her as though she were a child.

She found Miller sitting in the middle of six large monitors, each one displaying surveillance videos.

"Evidence bag. Cell phones," Monica said, interrupting the young woman.

Mechanically, Miller took the bag from her, sealed it with red tape, and logged it into a book, before sitting back before her screens. "I'm on to the bomber, I think. What do you think? Here, bomb went off at this point. I'm backing up that cam feed. You can see one older man walking into the right doors, maybe twenty seconds before the explosion. Assuming the bomber merely walked in and triggered the bomb, then that has to be him. Of course, that's not necessarily a correct assumption. For all we know, he could have arrived two hours early and merely sat around for two hours."

Monica nodded. That also seemed reasonable, but Miller went on, "That's not too likely though. The bomber isn't going to stand around for very long because security could well discover him. So I'm pretty certain this man is our bomber. I'm working on getting better views of him—his face would be great. Then, I'll back track and see how he got here."

"Mind if I watch?" Monica asked. "I'm useless out there."

Miller chuckled, "Figured you would be. Honestly, Miss Black, I couldn't imagine why fat Billy Bob and General Franco insisted we bring you with us. It makes no sense at all, unless as Kelly suggested, he wants us to somehow fail to find the bomber. You know, 'witch messes up the investigation' and all that."

"I'm not about to knowingly mess this up," Monica countered, "but then I admit I don't know all the rules you have to follow, like with this evidence stuff."

Miller cracked a smile. *She's not a know it all.* "Cool. Yes, lend me a hand. He's wearing a gray raincoat. You take the front cams there, while I take the side ones. I suspect he got here via a car or truck, which either he parked in the lot, if we're lucky, or someone dropped him off here."

Monica sat down before the sophisticated computer controls and began running the feeds in reverse. A half hour later, she called Miller's attention to her screen. "Hey, check this out. Isn't this the bomber?"

"Bingo, Miss Black. Yep, that's him. Taxi. Great break for us," Miller replied enthusiastically.

Confused, Monica asked, "How so?"

"Cause now we can track that taxi back to where it picked up the bomber! Read off the time tag on the screen—there at the bottom. I'll cue up the city surveillance system and start at that time, going backwards," Miller explained for her benefit. "While I'm doing this, you see if you can go frame by frame and get a close shot of his face."

A half hour later, Monica looked at the two printouts of the bomber that she'd made. One showed his face fairly well, enough to see that he appeared to be an older man, perhaps in his sixties. The other showed him pulling a bag on wheels behind him as he walked towards the entrance to this part of the concourse. A successful smile on her face, she turned to greet Bergson and Kelly who were just entering, carrying several more evidence bags with them. While Kelly taped and logged them in, Bergson asked for a report.

Miller replied, though Monica handed him the printouts. "We found the man we think is the bomber. Sixties—pulling a bag on wheels—came by taxi. Am following the taxi back to where it picked him up."

"Good work. We'll let the FBI run image enhancement on these. I concur. Wait! He's too broad around for a man that size—wrong proportions. Must be wearing a vest of C-4 beneath that raincoat to hide it. People get fat around their waist and hips, not their chests. His chest is too big for his body size, Miss Black. We've got our bomber for sure. Now who the hell is he and who put him up to it?"

Kelly joined them and looked over the photos. "So that's what he looks like. Doesn't explain what we found, Bergson."

"I know," Bergson growled, clearly annoyed by something. Even Miller looked up at Kelly. Seeing her glance at Kelly, Bergson barked, "Anomaly. Another damned anomaly. It's what Kelly didn't find. No skull. No body parts. He found a good deal of the raincoat down in the baggage area, which backs up your findings that this is the man we're after. But Kelly claims we should have found his skull and feet and hands. The rest would have been either incinerated or turned into a fine mushy spray. No feet. No hands. No skull. No spray. Anomaly."

"You mean the bomber isn't dead?" broke in Miller, clearly startled to hear this bit of news. "Crap!"

"Interesting. Maybe those witnesses who said they saw a ghostly shape near the center of the blast shortly after it went off weren't imagining it. Maybe it was the bomber standing there," Monica suggested. "Ah, but that means we've a far bigger problem on our hands."

Bergson grumbled, but said, "Quite possibly he was their ghostly figure."

"How? How could he be alive?" asked Miller.

Obviously Bergson was loathed to reply with what was plain to her, so Monica offered, "We can cast magic spells on our bodies, spells that would allow us to be unharmed by a bomb exploding. It's a higher level spell, but one that many of us use on a routine basis. Either the bomber is a wizard or someone else cast the spell on him. Of course, there are other possibilities as well." *I'd best not mention demons.*

"Darn it, Miss Black, don't start in on your demons!" Bergson growled. "Magic is more than enough right now. Darn magic users can't ever be trusted. Here's a clear example, if ever there was one."

"But we don't know that for sure yet," Miller cautioned him. "Like you keep telling us, don't get ahead of the evidence."

He smiled, "Right Miller. I'm getting ahead of it. Come on; let's find this man. Kelly wants his stuff analyzed right away, so I'll drive us back to the FBI office and labs. You two, keep on it. Find this man."

An hour later, Miller finished up, just as Kelly brought in Chinese takeout for supper. Excitedly, she announced, "Eat up. I found the place where the taxi picked him up from: the Majestic Motel."

"Where is that?" Kelly asked.

Monica replied, "North Hanley and 115—seedy area these days—not far from the university, too."

"Eat fast! If the bomber is still alive, we have a chance at catching him!" Bergson barked, downing his food rapidly.

Half an hour later, surrounded by an FBI bomb squad and a SWAT team, the group descended on the seedy motel, taking the manager by surprise. "This man here— what room is he in?" Bergson barked at the bespectacled young man who was just eating his own supper.

Quite nervous and looking over his records, he replied, "114. Down on your left. Paid up for a week. Why? What's this all about?"

While Bergson and Kelly headed off to the find the room bringing the other teams with them, Miller and Monica stayed behind.

Miller asked softly, "What is his name? When did he register? How did he pay for the room?"

Even more nervously, the manager fumbled to answer her questions. "Er. Well, he registered two days ago, paying for a week at the bargain rate. He still has five days left. Cash. He paid in cash, one hundred forty. Mr. James Smith."

"Car? Type of car? License plate?" Miller asked coolly, jotting down the information.

"None. From the records, none. Must have come by other means," he replied, his hands shaking slightly. "What's this all about?"

"Need to know and you don't," she replied coldly. "Form of ID?"

"Isn't any logged. We, we don't ask for ID here. You know, some come for a good time," he tried to explain, pointing to the large sign advertising their rates. Large print indicated their hourly rate and Miller got the picture.

Closing her notebook and dropping it into her purse, she nodded to Monica and headed out to join the others. Just outside the office, she whispered, "It should be safe enough for us now because they've probably already entered. Come on. Let's find out if they got him."

The two found disappointed men milling around the opened door of the room. Bergson barked, "Cleared out. Gone. No trace of him. No bags, no clothes. Nothing. I've sent for the FBI forensics team to scour the room for anything. At least we ought to get a DNA sample. A box of partially eaten pizza and coke cans are in the wastebaskets, along with two coffee cups. So we're going to have to wait for forensics to catch up to us. SWAT will keep watch on this place, just in case the bomber comes back, but he's probably flown the coup by now. You get a name and ID, Miller?" he asked, ignoring Monica.

"Mr. James Smith. Probably fake. No ID, no car. Paid for a week in cash. I got nothing, boss," she said softly.

"Figures," Bergson grumbled. "Well, we've done all we can here. Back to the plane. Get some sleep. Hopefully, the labs will have something for us by morning. They are supposed to call me whenever they find out anything."

"What about her, boss? She coming with us?" Kelly asked, referring to Monica.

"Hell, I don't care. Miss Black, we stay on our plane at night. You can come too or you can go home to your kid. Your choice."

"I'm supposed to be on your team, so I best tag along with you. Maybe the lab will come up with something soon," Monica replied.

Miller led Monica into a small sleeping room onboard their large airliner, next to hers. "Our guest room," she explained. "I'm going to be in my comm center for a while yet. I've got ideas to explore."

"Want some company?" Monica asked. It was far too early to sleep and she was quite bored. Miller really didn't, but nodded affirmatively anyway. The comm center had more monitors and computers in it than Monica had ever seen in one place. Wisely, she sat quietly in the back, watching the blonde woman work her magic at the controls.

Soon, Monica guessed what she was doing. She hacked into the St. Louis Surveillance System and queued up cam footage from around the motel on the day that Mr. James Smith arrived at the Majestic Motel. Minutes later, she had him walking into the motel's office, pulling that same bag on wheels behind him, but he wasn't wearing the raincoat and was not as large as he had been in the airport footage. "Gotcha," Miller whispered to herself.

Now she began backtracking, switching from street feed to street feed. Monica found it unnerving to watch everything moving backwards, cars, people, and dogs, though dogs walking backwards did seem rather funny to her. She followed Mr. Smith back to Kendale Drive, in a wooded residential section of the city and then to Lake Drive. She lost track of him by the tennis court. Dense trees hid him from the cams. Miller cursed softly, but didn't quit.

Further on down the street, he'd become visible again. Unfortunately, he didn't reappear walking backwards! She cursed again and went back to the tennis court. After logging back into the system's main console, she found another cam near the court and brought its video onscreen. It took a while for the software to bring up the proper date and time. A few minutes later, Miller whispered, "Gotcha, Mr. Smith." She had him walking on the grass beside the court on out onto the street, dragging his bag behind him.

Once more, she reversed the feed's direction and watched him moving backwards along the court. Then, he simply vanished from sight! "Whoa! What the heck?" she exclaimed. "Magic for sure. Miss Black, come take a look." She replayed the video. Suddenly, Mr. Smith appeared, paused a moment looking about, and then headed off along the side of the court to the street.

"Teleport spell most likely," Monica explained. "We use it all the time. Our Mr. Smith teleported to that spot. Still doesn't prove he is a wizard. Someone could have teleported him there."

"But I don't see anyone else, just him," she protested.

"Could be invisible," Monica explained.

"Well, I'm not satisfied. Let me see what else has

been observing here," she countered and began typing again.

"What else could be observing?" asked a curious Monica.

"Surveillance Drones," Miller answered in her soft voice, as though Monica was stupid.

"Sorry, I didn't know we had such things."

"You are ignorant of Homeland Defense aren't you? Well, nearly every big city has armed drones flying over them 24/7. Most are armed, too, just in case. God, Detroit has twenty of them overhead at all times. Nothing there but drug-infested gangs, shooting it out with each other daily. There's an armed cordon around that entire city—has been for fifty years. I've heard it once was the motor capital of the country, but that's ancient history. Now it's nothing but the worst slum zone in the country. When the fighting there gets too bad, they drop a bomb on the perps. No one dares go in there without wearing full armor. St. Louis has six drones overhead at all times. Now let's check their flight paths and connect them to the right day and time."

It was midnight before Miller got a usable video from one of the drones. "Now Mr. Smith, let's see how you got there," she muttered. "Gotta switch over to IR feed."

"What?" asked Monica, just getting oriented to the fuzzy images on the screen.

"We know he magically appeared there. So I'm switching to the Infrared—the IR view. The spy cams also record a parallel stream in the infrared. Your invisible person will show up this way. Might be optically invisible, but they'll have a heat signature and that will show up on the screen. Let's see what we have."

"Darn! You're right. Someone teleported him there!" Both women spotted two fuzzy, reddish images appearing, and then one promptly vanished while the other began moving. "Conspiracy. The boys will love this. Best let them sleep for now. Nothing more we can do tonight."

The next morning proved more than frustrating. Impressed with what Miller had found out, Bergson and Kelly had grim faces. Bergson declared, "Conspiracy! I knew it. Bomber wasn't acting alone. We've got our hands full on this one!" He added, "Cursed wizards and witches!"

A call to the FBI labs yielded more frustrating results. Facial recognition software didn't find a match in any known database. Fingerprints were a bust. The motel room had been wiped clean. DNA results came back, but there wasn't any match anywhere. However, Kelly's collected bits of evidence yielded unexpected information. The bit of the raincoat was of Iranian origin. The tiny chunk of C-4 that didn't detonate, probably having broken off the main body, was also manufactured in Iran.

Reluctantly, Bergson placed a secure call to President Billy Bob and General Franco Porti. He outlined what had been uncovered thus far. In all likelihood, the bomber came from Iran. Magic had been used probably to disguise the man and to drop him off close to his target. "How far do you want us to carry this?" he asked.

"You are clear to follow it to the only acceptable conclusion. I want the perps captured or killed," General Franco replied.

Chapter 2—Following Leads

Bergson stood before the whiteboard just outside the comm center of the airliner. Monica observed that he'd carefully arranged images and notes on the board. In the center middle was the image of Mr. James Smith. Beside him was a blank silhouette, like those web pages on which the person forgot to upload their photo. Its label was "Wizard Transporter." A diagonal line down and to the left of Mr. Smith led to a note declaring: Apparel and explosives of Iranian origin.

"Okay everyone. Check over The Board and see if I've missed anything. Any other questions I've overlooked?"

Everyone gathered around and Monica did as asked. She read the enumerated list of questions, noticing that Bergson only mentioned magic use with the wizard who teleported the bomber to St. Louis. There were no sign of demons anywhere.

Bombing of Lambert Field Concourse at 2 pm on June 9, 2200

1. Did the bomber perish in the blast?
2. Or did the bomber survive the blast?
   3. If he survived, where did he go?
   4. How did he survive the blast?
   5. Will he bomb again and, when, where and why?
6. What is the true identity of the bomber?
   7. Is Mr. James Smith an alias?
8. What was Mr. James Smith's motive for attacking Lambert Field?
   9. Why St. Louis?
   10. Why this date and time?
11. Did the bomber act alone, perhaps hiring a wizard to transport him to StL?
   12. If so, who did he hire?
   13. What is the identity of the wizard who brought him to StL and was he involved in the plot?
14. If not, what group is the bomber and wizard working for?
   15. What are the group's future plans? Past actions?
16. Did the bomber make his own bomb?
   17. If not, who did?

18. If so, how did he learn to make the bomb?
18. Who provided the bomb making supplies, since the
     C-4 came from Iran?
19. Was the bomber's target only half of the airport?
20. If so, why? What message is he sending?
21. If not, why didn't he take out the entire airport?

Knowing how these three felt about even mentioning magic, Monica ventured a question. "Bergson, would it be permissible for me to use magical spells to help give us some answer clues? Not hard evidence, just a direction to pursue?" She saw his face muscles tense up at the mere mention of the word "magic," but the reaction softened as he grasped her addendum.

"I suppose so, as long as you realize that nothing turned up by magical means can be used in evidence in the bomber's trial," he reminded her.

"I understand, Bergson," Monica replied and then ventured further afield. "Look, you've not entertained the question: was Mr. James Smith a wizard himself?"

Bergson's face tightened hard. "Obviously, Miss Black. If, as you suggest, Mr. Smith turns out to be one of those kind, then obviously we will be removed from the case. Your kind will take over and have jurisdiction, Magical Misuse or some such nonsense. And we all know what that means!"

Monica didn't and seeing her confused expression, Bergson added, "He'll not get proper justice. Wizards take care of their own. Here, normal people were brutally slain by this insane bomber. We and the victims demand proper justice. So no, we aren't turning this case over to let the perp get away with slaughtering innocent people. Enough said."

From his tone, Monica suspected that in his past, he must have had a terrible interaction with magic users, but she had no idea what that had been. However, her curiosity was roused, and she decided that it was worth looking into when she had the chance.

"Boss," Miller spoke up softly, "I might be able to answer Numbers 1 and 2 and maybe 3. Plus, we might get a clue from the SIMM cards of the partially destroyed cell phones the FBI recovered."

Bergson barked, "Good, Miller. You follow up on those. Kelly, you go to work on sixteen through eighteen. Figure out how they made the bomb. I'll see what I can do to identify this Mr. Smith and who he works for. Time is pressing. Let's get to work."

Monica couldn't help but notice he didn't give her an assignment and looked questioningly at him. He was observant and added, "I don't care what you do; just stay out of our way, Miss Black."

She had no real position on the team; he'd made that perfectly clear. Monica decided to see what she could discover on her own. Nodding to Miller, who was heading back to her comm center, Monica stepped out of the airliner and promptly teleported to Bradbury's School of Magic in Colorado, arriving before the main gates. There, she sent a message to the school's Governor Lindsey Barron, asking for permission to enter and chat with her.

"Tea?" Governor Lindsey asked, as Monica took a seat before the mahogany desk.

"Please. It's a bit of a rough patch for me. I've been asked by President Billy Bob Becker to aid the Homeland Defense Force's World Investigation Team. The team is supposed to be the country's top case solver, but they are hard-nosed normals who detest magic and everything having to do with it. We're investigating the St. Louis Lambert Field bombing."

"Ah, interesting, Monica. It's been on the news. Lots of speculation. What have you found so far?" Governor Lindsey asked, hoping to hear inside news. Monica didn't hesitate; after all, Bergson hadn't told her not to discuss the case with anyone. She outlined what they'd uncovered so far.

"So I suspect strongly that either a group of wizards or perhaps even demons are behind the attack, but I've no proof. Obviously, a mage teleported the bomber to St. Louis, that much is certain," Monica suggested.

"Ah, I get it. Just don't rule out the possibility that it wasn't a Teleport spell as we cast, but one more like what you and your late husband Rob can do," Governor Lindsey pointed out. By that she meant their ability to use their minds to power a Shadow Walk or stepping as she called it.

"I haven't, but honestly, we're so rare that it's more likely a Teleport spell. I was wondering if Professor Betts might be able to shed some light on the events. Or perhaps there's still enough magical energy trails left for Amanda to sense," Monica finally asked what she'd come to the magic school to discover.

Just then, a magical door appeared in Lindsey's office and Professor Betts stepped out into the room. "Hi, Monica. Got your message, Lindsey. What's up? I've five minutes before my next class."

Hastily, Monica relayed the basic facts. "So any chance you could still detect anything at the site?" she asked the Sleuth.

"It's been three days, but I can try." Glancing at her watch, she added, "Be free in an hour. Lunch time, that is, if it's okay with Governor Lindsey," Pam added.

Lindsey grinned, "Pam, when could I ever stop you from investigating anything?" Both women chuckled. "I'll keep Monica entertained until you can join her at noon, Pam."

"Way cool! Haven't had a really good mystery to solve in just ages!" Pam declared and promptly vanished through her magical door once more.

"Let me see if Amanda is available," Lindsey said. "She's been on a rock band tour, the last I heard." Silently, she Messaged the Apache Tracker. Shortly, a message scrolled before her eyes and Lindsey smiled. "She'll drop by around noon. So we've an hour to kill. How's Rob doing? Third grade?"

Monica smiled. "Fourth this fall. Three more years and I'll be sending him here, if you'll have him." She then became serious. "You know, just when I thought I had handled everything from my lifetime as Dominus, this comes up: norms. I'd forgotten how badly I had mistreated them, how I used to loath them. Now, I find myself working for normals and not just any normals, but ones who loath and detest magic and anything having to do with it."

Lindsey smiled. "Karma perhaps. Well, it certainly appears that magic is involved in the bombing. Still, do your best with these normals. After all, normal humans greatly outnumber us. Say, what about the demons? Any signs of them? I know you've beaten it to death, Demon Hunter and all that. Still, we both know that several escaped and went somewhere."

Monica sighed. "It's been nine years, Lindsey, and not a single sign, not a hint of their activities. I know, most think they headed back to the Abyss. But you and I both know better. Those were mighty powerful demons who escaped, and they likely want revenge. Still, no signs. I've been diligently looking every day, but nothing so far, unless this attack turns out to involve them." The two chatted and sipped their tea.

Precisely at noon, Professor Pam Betts joined Monica just outside the gates at the school, since Teleport spells could not be used while on the premises. Seconds later, the long black haired Apache arrived, via her own Teleport spell. She wore shorts and a tee shirt, quite different from the professional woman's appearance of Professor Betts and Monica's Barbie Doll look. "Hi, all. Long time no see. I might be a bit rusty. Been mostly playing rock shows of late."

"Hi, Amanda. Glad you could come," Monica greeted the Tracker. "We best hurry, since Professor Betts must be back in an hour. I'll take us to the site." The three joined hands and Monica stepped them to Lambert Field, preferring this to using her Teleport spell.

"Your stepping sure is different from our Teleport spells," Amanda declared.

"Safer, too," Professor Betts pointed out the obvious. "Gosh, it looks worse than what we've seen on the news." They stood before the destroyed entrance of the left half of the concourse.

"Follow me. We've identified the precise location of the bomb's detonation. At least we know that much information," Monica said, instantly changing her shoes into more practical tennis shoes. "Here we are. The bomb shot a hole downwards into the baggage claim area. I haven't been down, but Kelly found lots of bomb fragments there. I know it's been three days and that there has been a large amount of other magic in use around here, but please, anything you can sense will be valuable."

"Holy molly! Look at all the magical energy trails!" Amanda gushed as she focused and expanded her senses. "It's like a Christmas tree!"

"Focus on this precise spot," Monica suggested. "We know he detonated the bomb here. We suspect he survived. Almost a dozen witnesses said they spotted a ghostly figure standing here amid the smoke and dust right after the explosion."

"Ah, got it," Professor Betts declared. "Monica, you're right. Something really, really strange happened here. Give me a minute."

"Hey, weird!" Amanda spoke up, ending her focused concentration. "Absolutely no Teleport spell. I can tell you that much, but there was some other type of magic used here, but I've never seen it before. Sorry that I'm not all that helpful."

Professor Betts studied the scene, looking at the residual magical energies around this tiny space and over the hole in the floor. Five minutes passed before she broke her focus and her eyes returned to the present. Her face had turned slightly whitish though. She swallowed before speaking, "Well, Monica, this is the weirdest site I've yet studied. I expected to see traces of our protection spell Skin of Stone around the blast site, activated of course when it absorbed the blast. But it's not here! There's no hint of it and yet, something else is at work here. I see the residual energies of a spell though. Here, let me show you." She picked up a twisted piece of metal and sketched in the filthy debris.

"Oh my god! That's a Gate pentagram! Demons!" Monica gushed.

"That's what I'm thinking," Professor Betts declared.

"I believe your perp was a demon in disguise and that it Gated out of here after the bomb exploded. Obviously, a bomb isn't going to harm a demon, which can only be hurt by magical weapons and sometimes magical spells."

"A Gate spell? Wow!" said Amanda, growing excited. "Let me look again!" She focused for several minutes before speaking. "Now it makes sense. Yes, it went that way," she declared, pointing north. "Long way. Too faint to follow, though. Too much time's passed since its casting. Still, it didn't Gate to the Abyss. I'm sure of that detail. Wow, so the demons are still here! Wait till the others hear about this!"

She had to return to her band and Monica thanked her for coming on such short notice. Amanda added, "Hey, call me sooner next time. Perhaps I can follow their Gate! How cool is this!" She teleported away.

Exercising great care, Professor Betts and Monica stepped over the debris and stopped on the undamaged walkway near the front. To their left, many other passengers came and went, and planes roared while taking off or landing behind them. Professor Betts declared, "Monica, you be careful. These norms that you are working with haven't got the slightest chance if demons are involved. We both know that."

Monica sighed. "I know and yet these three are totally against anything magical and detest us, as though we've got the plague or something."

"How strange. Another mystery, Monica," Pam said. "There must be a reason why they so hate us and magic, and I'm going to find out why. Best get back and grab a bite before classes. Don't hesitate to call when you need assistance. I love a good mystery and this one certainly is that!"

With that, she promptly teleported back to Bradbury's School of Magic in Colorado, leaving Monica with a very serious problem on her hands, as she left the area, walking out onto the tarmac where the giant airliner stood. How did she tell her team members that the perp was a demon in disguise? They'd never believe her, not remotely.

While what Amanda and Pam had told her was "hard evidence" in any magic trial, it wasn't the type of hard evidence the WIT team could accept. Monica bit her lip and walked into the airliner, stopping to pick up a foot-long from their refrigerator along with a Coke. She found the others at the giant whiteboard and noticed that more questions had answers beside them. Monica paid close attention.

"Ah here you are, Miss Black," Bergson barked crudely. "While you've been out, we've obtained hard evidence and gotten several of the questions answered. The bomber didn't die!"

"Right," Miller interrupted him, since this was her contribution. "I accessed satellite IR scans and got lucky." She posted another image on the board beside the photo of Mr. James Smith. "Here he is just after the explosion, as close to the actual detonation as I could get. The explosion recorded as a giant ball of white. He stood beside the blast hole in the floor for ten seconds before vanishing. I got the precise time from the satellite images."

Bergson pointed out, "So did the bomber perish in the blast? No." He'd added that annotation to the list of questions. "Or did the bomber survive the blast? Yes." He'd added that next to the question. "He left, unfortunately via magical means. We don't know where he went yet and are looking into how he could survive that blast."

Kelly spoke up, "And I've answered a couple more of them. I did some checking into the C-4's origin. While the plastic definitely is of Iranian origin, it was imported into the states. It came through the Port of Chicago last month and from there shipped to Detroit. Acme Building Demolitions was the recipient of the shipment. Five hundred pounds of it to be precise, enough for four more huge bombs! Company's apparently legitimate. They've a federal permit to have and use explosives. Until now, according to the FBI, they aren't associated with any terrorist organization. Anyone could have made the bomb. It's a very simple procedure requiring minimal knowledge to make it. So I can't really say yet if the bomber made his own. But it's highly likely that he will bomb again. Heck, he could bomb four more targets at least!"

Monica noted Bergson had made these entries beside Number 18 on the board. Bergson added, "I checked on that company in Detroit. None of their employees is our Mr. Smith, unfortunately. Half of their employees are of Iranian origin; some are here on Green Cards. So I've added another question to the board.

18A. Are we dealing with an Iranian backed terrorist organization?

It sure looks that way to me. Considering the facts so far, I'm going to alert HDF and the White House," Bergson declared. "I've also added to '4. How did he survive the blast?' Probably by use of a magical spell. So I will give you that much, Miss Black. Probable use of magic. Not confirmed, mind you, just probable."

Miller spoke, "Boss, are we flying to Detroit next? If so, can we request a SWAT team to escort us to the Acme place? No one goes into Detroit proper unless they have a death wish!" Miller was frightened over where this investigation was heading, for her fingers had a nervous twitch in them and her eyes glanced about.

"Haven't decided, Miller. I know, Detroit isn't safe but we ought to take a closer look at this Acme Building Demolitions company and its employees," Bergson admitted. "Let's see what this afternoon uncovers first. I'll let the HDF and the White House know what we've got so far."

He turned and left to make the calls. Kelly cursed silently and left the room to track down more information on this company, leaving Monica standing beside the petite Miller.

"Good work on getting those IR images, Miller," Monica alleviated the tension. *How the devil can I hope to convince these people they're likely dealing with a demon perpetrator? They'll think I'm nuts.* She stared at the IR image. Then, it struck her. The image appeared to have four arms! An idea jelled. "Miller, can you enhance that image some? Can you possibly get a size reference scale on it?"

"Maybe. Why? All you can observe is the reddish form," she replied, but Monica detected a hint of curiosity in her voice tone.

"Humor me, Miller. Let's get it enlarged and cleaned up and get a way to measure the size of the perp. How do we do that?" she asked, knowing that this was Miller's specialty.

She followed the silent Miller out of the room and into her comm center. Monica saw Miller's profile in progress on the large monitor, outlining possible motives and mind-set, and she guessed that was what Miller was exploring, working up a perp profile. Clearly, she was lacking key data: that the perp was a demon.

Miller brought up the overall satellite image from which she'd made the blowup of the perp right after the explosion occurred. Together, the two studied the image. "I can use the tail section of that burning plane, if we can identify it and get its dimensions."

"Okay, leave that to me," Monica advised. "You see if you can find a way to enhance the image and get the tail section and perp together."

"K, but I don't see why," Miller protested slightly, annoyed with herself for not having already done that— getting a guess at the perp's height. Monica sat down at a terminal and began doing what she did best, internet searching. A half hour later, she had what she wanted.

"Okay, it was a Stratosphere 737. The tail section is six feet six inches, from there to there," she pointed out on the screen's overall image.

"Okay, it's already overlaid. Now we can estimate the perp's height to within a couple inches. That should help. Now to enhance it a bit further with Skylar's Algorithm. I know. It's a new one, but it applies mostly to IR images. Let's see what we can do," she said, her voice hardly above a whisper. Monica wondered if she ever raised her voice.

A few minutes later, the revised dual image finally

appeared on the monitor. "Crap. Something's wrong with it. Like I said, it's a new algorithm—probably very buggy at this point. I best try another approach," Miller lamented.

"No wait. Save that one!" Monica declared.

"Okay, but it's obviously not right," Miller protested as she saved the image and printed it out for Monica.

"I'll be back in a minute. I need to fetch a book," Monica declared, trying hard to hide her rising emotions.

When she returned Kelly was excited. "Hey gang, I've got my bombing simulation done. It proves my theory on the point of origin. I've entered the specs of the Lambert Concourse. Watch the simulation," he declared, proud of his work. "Bingo, it replicates the damage, confirming a hundred pounds of C-4 was used and at that location where we found the hole in the floor. No doubts about any of that now. Conclusive. Look here, I've a second demo. I've planted the charge in the center of the concourse. See, it would have destroyed the entire airport and most of the nearby planes as well. So either he goofed and detonated his bomb prematurely or he was just plain stupid or he didn't intend to totally wipe out this airport."

"Well done," Bergson complimented Kelly.

"Monica, I've got another enhancement image done. The resolution isn't as good, but it still isn't perfect. Rather strange yet—probably because it's an IR image. They aren't all that good anyway," Miller justified.

Monica looked at her second try. The woman was right; it was far fuzzier. Still, seeing what she needed to see in the image, Monica decided to at least break the news to these people. They'd likely not believe her, but if they ran into this Mr. Smith—well, at least she had warned them.

"Miller, put up both of those images. Yes, I know the first one looks strange," she requested. Reluctantly, Miller pasted both images on the whiteboard, just to the right of the image of Mr. Smith.

"Now then, please look carefully. I want you to estimate the perp's height first," Monica requested, trying a backdoor approach. *Let them get its height worked out.*

Miller produced a ruler and walked the two men

through the calculation. The rough result was ten feet.

"But that's impossible, Miller!" Bergson barked. "No one is ten feet tall!"

"I know, but I get nearly the same result on both images, so there must be something wrong with the images," Miller hedged.

"No, they're fine," Monica interrupted the two. "Now, look closely. How many arm-like appendages do you see?"

"Four, but that's not possible," Miller answered before the men could. "I told you the process was an experimental one. The second one here is better."

"And how many arm-like appendages do you see in that one, Miller?" Monica persisted.

"Darn it, Miss Black. People don't have four arms, not even you stupid wizards and witches," Bergson barked loudly.

Displaying another point of view, Kelly grinned and said, "Four arms. All the better to grab you with, my dear." That brought smiles to all faces. "Seriously, four arms? Must be an image distortion. Wouldn't two heads be more practical? You could think twice as much or twice as fast. Hey, multitasking gone bonkers," he added in jest.

Monica decided now was the time, if there was going to be one. "Now look at this image I brought along with me." She held up a page from one of her leather-bound, ancient volumes, though hiding the caption with her hands. "Notice the resemblance?"

"Well sort of," Miller conceded, "but it's just image distortion."

"So what is this a drawing of—one of your demon fiends?" Bergson correctly guessed.

She showed the caption as she answered, "Yes. It is a Type 10 demon, commonly known as a Wrestler. It's pretty dumb, very low IQ, but they are known to hang around certain other more powerful demons."

Bergson broke into a howling laugh. "Leave it to Miss Black, the Demon Hunter, to find demons in a terrorist bombing!" Even Kelly laughed heartily. Miller, however, didn't. She looked worried.

"But what if she's right?" she said quietly, but with intention, causing both men to stop laughing.

"Image distortion, that's all. She's seeing demons in distorted images, Miller. We're dealing with a perp here, the human kind," Bergson dismissed Monica's suggestion. Miller still wasn't satisfied and continued to fidget with her blouse. "Look, no hard evidence. That's our motto, hard evidence. I'm not about to go to the idiot President or General Franco and tell them we're hunting a demon based on one lousy, fuzzy IR image, which in all likelihood is just image distortion. No, let's not be silly about this. If and only if we get hard evidence of Miss Black's demon will we take it to the President and General Franco. Is that clear?" he barked again. Everyone nodded.

Monica refused to let this lie. "I brought in two of the best witches in the world. Both have confirmed my findings. In fact, the demon used a Gate spell to vanish after the explosion. My Tracker was able to determine that it headed north. So perhaps this Detroit connection is worth checking out."

"Hold on, Miss Black," Bergson interrupted her. "Did you tell them about our investigation without my permission? Heck, you obviously did. Do you realize that this could compromise our entire investigation? Now all we need is the wizard world complaining about this supposed demon of yours to President Billy Bob or worse, taking it to the press. Having you along is proving to be a very bad idea!"

"So what do we do about it?" Miller broke in, softly as always. "What if she's right? We can't fight demons, can we boss?"

"I tell you this perp ain't no demon. Can't imagine a demon needing Iranian C-4," Kelly protested as well. "Just a bunch of 'witch speculation.' No hard evidence, Miller, none except for that distorted image of yours. So forget about demons."

Monica's ire rose with each passing minute. *No wonder I used to hate and despise norms! Ignorant, stupid—heck, they can't even see what's right before their very eyes!* "You're blind idiots!" Monica burst out, finally unable to contain her outrage at their condemnation of her. "I'm trying to help you and this is the thanks I get. I'm out of here. Find your perp on your own. Mind you, when you get your selves killed, don't blame me! It's a demon you're dealing with, and all your stupid guns aren't going to scratch it, let alone harm it. Idiots. You norms are all just a bunch of big-headed, opinionated nincompoops!" With that, she stormed out of the airliner and teleported back to her estate on the far north of St. Louis.

She didn't hear Bergson yell after her, "And good riddance!"

"Aye, exit one Barbie Doll," Kelly smirked.

Miller alone looked pale. *What if Miss Black is right and it's a demon? From the accounts I read, they can't be harmed by our weapons. Crap! I best do more research. It's my ass Bergson is messing with!* Silently, she turned and headed back to her comm center, fired up her computer and began searching the online archives from nine years ago. She recalled that one of the largest groups of demons had been here in St. Louis, so she focused on this city. A minute later, she found the extensive archival listings and began reading in earnest. The more she read, the paler her complexion became and the more her stomach knotted. Only now did she finally begin to see the role that Miss Black had played, and it was a gigantic one at that! For a time, she toyed with sending these links to Bergson and Kelly, but decided against that just now.
***

"I tell you these norms are just a bunch of blind morons!" Monica fumed. Crystal, her closest friend, had suggested that she pay a visit to Governor Lindsey and Professor Betts. She took her best friend's advice and teleported to Bradbury's around seven that night. She found Professor Cho Lin was there as well as Professor Pam Betts in Governor Lindsey's office.

Cho Lin said calmly, "Tell us about it, will you dear?" She purposely sipped tea, as though there was nothing that could upset her, which was far from the truth. Already Governor Lindsey had issued a school-wide warning to the professors to be alert for signs of the demons, that at least one had made its appearance known. Monica sighed, took a deep breath, and related everything to the three women, who listened patiently.

"So they have an IR image of the demon and it has four arms?" Professor Betts asked.

"Precisely. Has to be a Type 10, which makes sense because we know several of the succubus demons escaped our dragnet at the last second," Monica explained. "Type 10's often work for succubuses.

"What I don't get is why after nine years of hiding have they surfaced and blown up a section of St. Louis' airport? Makes no sense," Professor Cho Lin asked.

"Demons are chaotic, unpredictable in many ways, but yet predictable in others, such as holding a grudge for millennia," Monica pointed out what she'd learned from Crystal and from her own experiences.

"It's a shame these three World Investigation Team members are so pigheaded," Professor Cho Lin stated.

Governor Lindsey added, "And it's equally a shame that Monica lost her temper, shot back at them, and departed their team. I know norms can be stupid, pigheaded, and bullies, but there are always reasons why a person acts and thinks as they do."

"Point taken, Governor Lindsey," Professor Cho Lin agreed.

"Yes, I'm sorry I got so upset. I can see I still have to face things from my past lifetime," Monica declared. "I guess the question for me is how to I undo what I've done to the team?"

Professor Betts decided now was the time to speak up. "Understand where they are coming from, Monica, especially their leader, this Alan Bergson. I couldn't help but do a bit of research on him after I returned this afternoon. Here's a URL for you to look up when you get home. I think much will become clear to you. As far as their fears that we will broadcast dire warnings about demons, you can relax. Until we have hard evidence of demon involvement, irrefutable evidence, no one is likely going to believe us anyway. We're just on guard here, that's all, though perhaps Governor Lindsey is being a bit paranoid about demons wanting to attack this magic school, what with all of its protections and such."

"Thanks, Pam. I owe you one. I feel better now and I best get back home. Have to tuck Rob in and read him a story, though I suspect those days are rapidly coming to an end. My, how fast boys grow up," Monica replied.

Pam giggled, adding, "And girls, too!" That brought more smiles and Monica promptly departed.

Once home, motherly duties handled and Rob safely asleep, she headed to her computer to see what Pam had found out. As she read the official reports, she began to understand why Bergson so hated magic. Nine years ago, Alan had just gotten married to his childhood sweetheart, one Amy Brown. They were on their honeymoon at Niagara Falls when disaster struck them. A drunk wizard accosted them, paralyzed him, raped Amy, and then tossed her over the falls. Alan was helpless to protect Amy. When his paralysis wore off the next day, Amy's body had been recovered below the falls. Because the perp was a wizard, the case went before the Department of Magical Misuse and the wizard received only seven years in prison.

At the sentencing, Alan went ballistic! The man had murdered his wife and raped her, and in Alan's eyes, the man just received a slight slap on his wrist. Alan didn't understand the rest of the wizard's sentence—that they cast an Idiot Mind spell on the wizard, followed by a Make Permanent spell, thereby ensuring that he'd never be able to cast even a Grade 0 Clean spell again. In effect, that stripped the wizard of his magical abilities, a far greater punishment than life in prison. Reading this, Monica realized Bergson had no idea how terrible that wizard's punishment had been. Not only had he lost his ability to cast spells, but as a norm, he had an IQ of barely 60, just enough to barely function!

"Darn, I wish I'd known that," she muttered to her

laptop. "Well, Monica, you sure put your big mouth in this one. Now how do I make amends? Considering how Bergson reacted with me, I best not let on that I know what happened to his wife. Get some sleep. Perhaps an idea will come to me."
***

Monica awoke, startled by the phone ringing at seven in the morning. No one called this early! "Hello," she said sleepily, slowly getting up out of bed. "Yes, Mr. President, I will join them shortly. Thank you. Goodbye."

"Who was that, mom," Rob said, getting up himself. "Why call so early? It's summer vacation."

"That was President Billy Bob. He begged me to go back and help out the World Investigation Team," she answered. Inwardly, she rejoiced. He'd given her a reasonable excuse to head back to the team.

"Cool mom. Can I sleep in?"

"Sure, but I best get up and get ready. I think Ericka will be looking after you today."

Hastily, she rose and dressed, grabbing a quick breakfast from the Yellow Arches. Then, she ordered three more to go, before heading to the airport and the giant Stratosphere.
***

"Darn it!" Bergson swore. He'd just hung up on a conference call with President Billy Bob and General Franco. It had not gone at all well, from his point of view. First, he'd very carefully outlined just where they were in the investigation, that they had made progress, but somehow General Franco found a different meaning in what Bergson had said.

General Franco had asked, "So we have at least one wizard involved and the possibility that the perp was also a wizard. Heck, he must be, if he wasn't harmed in the explosion and somehow vanished moments later. Thank goodness for satellite and IR coverage. So what does Miss Black think? What's her take?"

"She blew up at us and left, sir," Bergson had to reply. He wasn't one to lie, though sometimes he didn't tell everything, not until he had hard evidence to back his suspicions.

"What? Left? Bergson, what the devil is going on? What aren't you telling me? What did she say about the perp?" General Franco demanded in no uncertain terms.

"Darn it; it's not hard evidence, sir."

"Out with it!"

"Okay, okay. Miller got an enhanced IR image, and with Miss Black's suggestion she was able to get a height estimate on the figure standing at the blast sight moments after the bomb exploded. Mind you, Miller believes that there are glitches in the enhancement software and the image is damned fuzzy."

"And?" the general probed.

"And the perp's height is around ten feet and it shows he has four arms. We all know that's impossible— just glitchy, buggy software, sir."

"And what did Miss Black say?" General Franco probed.

"She showed us an infernal drawing she had in a book, claiming it was a demon—right height and four arms—used something called a Gate, whatever that is. I told her that was nonsense. No hard evidence and she blew up and flew the coup. Best thing for us, sir. We don't need her messing up our investigations, sir," Bergson finally answered the general's question. He heard gasps from President Billy Bob and what was likely a curse from General Franco, though likely muffled by his hand.

"Darn it, Bergson. I ordered you to have Miss Black on your team on this one, and I meant it. Either you get her back with you tomorrow or I'll replace you and your team!" General Franco ordered so loudly that even Kelly and Miller heard him over the phone from three feet away! After that, he heard the general slam the phone down, breaking the connection.

"We're screwed!" Miller said, uncharacteristically loudly.

Kelly couldn't resist. "I'll gladly do you, Miller, but you can't do me. Sorry, that's how it works." Miller slammed him in his groin, but that didn't stop Kelly from laughing, though he did double over for a minute.

"Crap, how am I supposed to get her back? I don't want her back, especially after her mouthing her stupid demon theory," Bergson asked more or less rhetorically, since he was the Lead Detective.

"Man, I'm glad I'm not in your shoes, boss," Kelly replied.

"Just ask her politely," Miller suggested. "I think tempers got raised on all sides yesterday. Maybe she'll have cooled off by morning."

Grumbling, Bergson nodded and headed to his private room.

"I take it no screwing around tonight?" Kelly continued baiting Miller. She ignored his crassness, turned, and headed to her own room, rather sick of the testosterone this day had brought out. What if Black was right? Were they facing a demon? If so, her life wasn't worth a nickel if they caught up with this perp! That worried Miller considerably.

***

Around seven-thirty the morning that Monica received the call from the President, Monica stepped up to the entrance ramp and called out politely, "Hey, anyone for coffee and sausage and egg biscuits? I brought them with me."

"Come on in, Miss Black," Miller called. She'd just arisen and was fixing a pot of coffee for the team. Long ago she'd learned the hard way not to let the men make it, for it was undrinkable, unless one had a cast iron stomach, which she didn't. "Hey, thanks. Been a while since I had one of these from the Yellow Arches. Thanks. Glad you're back."

"Me, too. Sorry about blowing up last night," Monica replied, setting the bags down just as Kelly and Bergson came out of their quarters, rubbing their faces.

"Oh. You're back. Good," Bergson said as politely as he could muster, which was saying something Monica thought.

"Yes, General Franco and President Billy Bob called me early this morning, insisting that I put my feelings aside and return to help out, if that's okay with you. Brought some breakfast and coffee," she replied.

"Just between us, it's not okay, but I will follow orders. General Franco insisted that I get you back on the team," Bergson said dryly. "Just remember, we want hard evidence, Miss Black."

"Yes sir," Monica replied, sensing this would help defuse the rather embarrassing situation for both herself and Bergson. She was right. Both men dove into the peace offering and began discussing what to do next in the investigation. Kelly was all for taking a trip to Detroit, though Miller physically cringed when she heard him make that suggestion.

"I agree. We best check out this Acme Building Demolitions company and its employees. As soon as we can, let's get airborne. I'll file a flight plan with the tower," Bergson declared.

"I have to pop home and pack a bag," Monica stated. Bergson nodded and she teleported off to do just that, along with making arrangements for Rob.

She returned in a half hour, just as the engines started to rev. After she got onboard, wiggling around their armored Rover now parked where the rear ramp entrance had been, she asked Kelly, "So who is flying us? Who's the pilot?"

"It flies itself," he answered.

"Huh? Flies itself?" Monica asked somewhat confused.

Kelly guffawed. "Pulling your leg. Miller's the crack pilot. Come on. Let's get up front where there are windows. This way." Kelly lent her an arm. In her tall stilettos, walking was proving challenging on the moving, bouncing plane.

Chapter 3—Windy City

Monica had never been on an airplane trip before and spent a few minutes looking out of the windows of the giant Stratosphere. "Nice view, eh?" Bergson said, finally coming over to her row and taking a seat beside her, but keeping one empty seat between them.

"Yes, impressive. I've never been on a plane." Monica decided now was the time, if ever there was going to be one. "Say, I ought to tell you that I now understand you better. I mean a friend of mine showed me that online case file. I'm so sorry that your new bride was so savagely mistreated and murdered by that wizard—and on your honeymoon no less." *How's he going to react? God, I hope I've not opened Pandora's Box.*

Bergson flinched, deep, old wounds opened. Although it had been nine years, a loss such as that was still very fresh in the back of his mind. How could it not be? "Yeah, well that despicable man got away with rape and murder, and your kind supported him!" Anger arose once more, an anger that simply refused to ever be satiated.

Monica saw that and took a different approach. "I know. I lost my husband when I was four months pregnant, but you know that from my file. At least I have my son, so I guess you can say I'm better off than you after the murder of our spouses."

He nodded, giving her that point. Since he didn't react further, Monica decided to press on. "You know, from what I read in the case report, those in charge of the trial and sentencing really goofed."

"Yeah, you can say that again and again and again! The creep should have been executed on the spot or at least locked up for the rest of his miserable life!" Bergson barked, venting his pent-up anger. *Maybe she understands,* he thought.

"No, Bergson, a death sentence or life imprisonment would have been far, far too good for that creep! What he did is unforgivable!"

She saw Bergson finally relaxing his taught muscles and knew he was listening to her, presuming that she was on his side, probably the only wizard or witch who ever had been. She proceeded very carefully, knowing she had this one, and probably only one, chance to reach the man.

"Bergson, the judges knew that too and gave him a far, far worse sentence. Let me explain before you react. You're the best detective in the entire country, at least that's what I've been told by General Franco."

He nodded, but kept a cold, alert eye on her, suddenly not trusting her in the slightest.

"What would happen to you and your life if suddenly you had an IQ of say 60? That's the moronic idiot category, barely able to function in life, if at all? Wouldn't that end everything for you?"

"Heck yes, devastating, but what's this got to do with that vile murdering wizard?" he replied.

"With magic users, casting spells is the most important part of our lives, just as being a super detective is for you. It's everything. What the judges did to that wizard was give him a punishment far worse than death or life in a prison somewhere. They cast a spell on him—Idiot Mind we call it. His IQ dropped to barely 60! Since the effects of that spell can be undone, they went further and cast one of the more powerful spells in the magic world, a Make It Permanent spell, making that Idiot Mind spell un-removable by all normal methods. How is that worse than death? Simple. With an IQ of 60, that man will never, ever be able to cast any spell, not even the most basic, beginning Clean Up Dirt spell that children learn to cast. In short, Bergson, they took away from him forever the one thing he prized most in this world and in his life, his ability to use magic. Further, he now has such a low IQ that he can barely survive in the world. He gets to live out the rest of his life knowing each and every hour of each and every day just what he has lost and will never get back. My god, Bergson, that man probably wishes he was dead every day, but now he doesn't even have enough intelligence to figure out a way to kill himself. If that isn't worse than death, then I don't know what is." As she talked, she began to see the dark, black mass around his head thinning and slowly vanishing. She finished, "The judges should have taken you aside and explained this to you back then."

"My god, I had no idea. You mean he's not only a moron but can't cast any spells?" Bergson probed a bit, still slightly uncertain that this was real.

"Yes, a moron who probably bawls about what he's lost every day, knowing there's no way he can ever regain what he's lost," she added.

"Miss Black, I—I didn't know all this. So he's not a wizard any longer? He can't do what he did to Amy and me to anyone else? It can't possibly be undone?" he asked. She noticed that his complexion had lightened noticeably.

"Hardly. Wizards by definition cast spells. He probably can't even tie his own shoe laces, Bergson. No, if he wants to be a criminal, he'll have to do it the way ordinary criminals do, but with an IQ of 60, he probably won't even be able to do that!"

Bergson laughed. "That's unreal, the bastard."

"True. However, I should also say that there is one and only one way that all that could ever be undone—a Full Wish spell. There are only a handful of wizards in the entire world who can cast that spell, and the cost to them to cast is terrible. One Wish spell cast ages their bodies an entire year! Cast ten Wish spells and you are ten years older! I doubt if you could even buy a Wish spell for less than several million dollars. So having that sentence undone is highly, highly remote. He'd have to come into many millions of dollars and be able to convince one of a handful of wizards who can cast that spell to give him a Wish. With an IQ of 60, that's never going to happen. No, he's facing a lifetime of eternal torment for his actions against you and particularly Amy. I can't imagine a crueler punishment for such a wicked crime."

For the first time since she met Bergson, the man actually smiled. "Incredible. I feel—well I don't know how I feel. Good—no, relieved. Yes, relieved. Thank you for telling me this. No one ever did. I'm—I'm sorry about your husband. A bomb wasn't it?"

"Thanks. Like I said, the judges should have explained all this to you and they didn't. We make mistakes, too. Yes, it was a bomb, but I don't want to talk about it. Too painful," Monica twisted about in her seat, hoping that he would drop the topic. Nine years and the pain and loss hadn't entirely gone. Rob was the only man she'd ever loved and probably could love. She wasn't about to share such intimate feelings with Bergson or any normal person. They simply couldn't understand.

"Never caught the bomber?" he asked politely, though he already knew the answer from her file.

"No," she replied and looked out the window to avoid meeting his eyes. Grief swelled; she might lose control if she met his gaze just now. Wisely, he suggested they get coffee and left to do just that.

He returned with two cups. "That's Chicago coming up down there," he explained, handing her a black cup with the WIT logo on it.

Just then, Miller's voice broke in over the intercom system. "Bergson, top priority call is coming in; relaying it to you now. On speaker phone," she said.

"Bergson?" the deep bass voice of General Franco echoed through the small passenger compartment of the giant Stratosphere.

"Here, general. What's up?" Bergson replied.

"Turn on the news, Channel 9. I'm diverting your flight. You'll be landing at New O'Hare in three minutes. I want you on the scene as fast as you can get your team there! Got to run. Bye." He hung up, but Kelly got up and flipped on the TV system. An overhead big screen came to life and he switched to Channel 9.

"Oh wow!" Kelly exclaimed, sitting back down, staring at the screen, while the giant plane began banking for the emergency landing. Another bombing had just occurred, this one at Lake Land Mall in Franklin Park, just a couple miles south of New O'Hare! On the scene cameras and reporters streamed live video of the carnage site.

Rescue teams were just arriving. Bloody survivors could be seen stumbling about just beyond the near total destruction zone of the huge shopping mall, half of which was now rubble.

"Get the Rover ready, Kelly," Bergson barked. "Miller, to the Rover as fast as you can. I think we have found more of that C-4, Kelly. May they rot in Hell! We have to get these bastards!"

His anger seethed once more. A wave of anger swept over Monica as well. Mentally, she correctly presumed that this attack would prove more deadly than the one at Lambert Field.

A minute later, Miller sat the giant plane down and followed the tower's orders. They had her parked in less than a minute, surprising her. Once she powered down, Miller headed back to join the others.

"Wow, Bergson, they bumped us ahead of all the dozens of other planes wanting to land and stopped everything on the ground to get us parked as fast as possible. General Franco Porti really pulled some strings on this one. Is it as bad as I was hearing?"

"Probably worse," Monica answered, since Bergson merely nodded and began racing to the rear cargo bay where the Rover was being prepped by Kelly. The two women followed him. Three minutes from touchdown, Kelly roared down the cargo bay ramp and saw airport security stopping all traffic so they could get off the tarmac and onto the interstate as fast as possible. With a broad smile on his face, Kelly turned on their sirens and flashing emergency lights, before putting his foot down on the gas pedal.

As they hit the congested interstate, already CP had begun clearing an emergency traffic lane, and Kelly made good use of it, racing the couple miles, flying past the columns of halted traffic. Monica held her breath, hoping they wouldn't crash into anything! As they neared the mall, he had to slow down. A veritable wall of emergency response vehicles slowed their progress, frustrating Bergson. Then, his cell phone rang. He put it on speaker phone.

"Franco here. Bergson, first action, get to the Channel 9 crew and confiscate their streaming video taken moments after the explosion went off. Cite national security if you have to, Billy Bob's orders!"

"Okay, but the press isn't going to want to go along with this," Bergson replied.

"You'll know why when you see the video they shot. Key to your investigations. Miss Black may have been correct. Got to go. Bye." He hung up.

"Crap is hitting the fans on this one," Kelly barked. "Big time," he added. "Franco's never asked us to confiscate a reporter's video before."

"Hope you aren't squeamish, Miss Black," Bergson hinted, "because this one is going to be really messy."

"Hope you don't mind my casting a spell here in the back seat," Monica countered with her own tease. "Gotta change clothes."

"Can I watch?" Kelly asked with a straight face.

"Best keep your eyes on the road," Monica countered. Miller roared with laughter, but she did look at Monica beside her and saw nothing but an instantaneous clothing change. In an instant, a blouse and jeans replaced the red satin dress, which she usually wore, being partial to red. Her tall heels became work boots. Plus, her hair was now tied up in a tight bun.

"Now that would be a useful thing to be able to do," Miller said in her soft voice, while her face displayed a broad smile.

Monica smiled back. "All set. Can't we get there any faster?"

"Want me to drive overland?" Kelly teased her.

"Where do you want the Rover parked?" Monica asked.

Bergson answered because Kelly had to maneuver to avoid running into the back of an EMT vehicle. "By the Channel 9 van, the one with the extended satellite dish hook up, way over there."

"Your wish is my command," Monica teased him

and silently cast her spell. Instantly, Kelly found the Rover precisely where Bergson wanted him to go. He slammed on the brakes, though he need not have, because Monica took that into consideration when she cast the spell. "Now let's get that video," she added.

"How the heck? What? Crap! We're there," Bergson struggled to grasp what had happened.

"Time is of the essence. So let's get cracking," Monica called out, opening her door and stepping out into the chaotic scene. An acrid smell assaulted her nose, along with concrete dust and of course human remains. Around her some distance ahead lay the smoldering remains of half of what had once been a very large shopping mall. At least this time there were not huge fires to extinguish, but the human toll was far greater. She saw dozens of wounded victims sitting or lying around the outer perimeter of the rubble. Even as she looked, EMTs dashed towards them, carrying stretchers and bags of equipment. To her right, the police lined up rows upon rows of ambulances of all types. Amid the carnage and chaos, a live Channel 9 reporter was doing his best to describe the situation to his audience. Idiot, Monica thought, the video says it all; you don't need to say anything.

Bergson strode up to the reporter, while Kelly moved beside the camera crew and motioned for them to cut the live feed. "Stop your live coverage for a minute. HDF orders," Bergson barked, showing the pale-faced reporter his large badge.

They stopped the live feed. "What's this all about? You have no right to interfere. Freedom of the press," the reporter declared, somewhat nervously, Monica noted as she watched Bergson in action.

"We need to see the video you shot right after the explosion went off," Miller said in her soft, but commanding tone.

"Sure. Let me cue it up," a crewman said, growing even more nervous than the protesting reporter.

"We, we were here doing a live report on the growth of Lake Land Mall when we heard a huge explosion and filmed it. What's this got to do with national security?" the reporter inquired. Monica smiled. The man had guts, she thought, standing up for his rights as a reporter.

Bergson didn't answer but moved back to review the video with the rest of his team. The reporter was right. He was doing a human interest piece on the remodeled mall when the camera captured a huge explosion. Instinctively, the cameraman turned away from the reporter and zoomed in on the explosion, which mushroomed upwards and outwards, the noise drowning out all commentary and explicatives from the reporter.

They watched for a minute as the explosion turned into a dust cloud and began dissipating. Then they saw it! Likely standing at the center of the explosion was a ten-foot tall creature that had four distinct arms. It looked more like a pale, grayish ghost amid the still flying dust and debris, but it was definitely there for all of ten seconds before it vanished completely.

"What was that?" the crewman asked.

"We need to confiscate this video. National security," Bergson declared.

"You can have a copy," the reporter butted in, "but freedom of the press will require you to get a court order to take away our video. Besides, it's already gone live, and my editor says that video snippet has already gone viral on the Internet."

Monica burst out laughing. Her team members stared harshly at her. "Look, the general wanted it to keep it from doing just that, going viral. Now that it has, there's no point in confiscating the video. Once something reaches the Internet, there's no stopping it."

Miller defended her, "She's right boss. If it's gone viral already, there's no point in confiscating the video. A copy will do fine. I'll hook into their digital stream now and get it."

"Crap! Okay, do it. I'll talk to the general now," Bergson barked, but he understood the significance of the video having gone viral. He suspected that was behind Franco's orders and a minute later had that confirmed.

"Okay, Miller, you are on the video. Kelly, you look for bomb evidence. Miss Black and I will search for other clues," Bergson ordered, and the group set off into the chaotic scene.

Shortly, Monica found herself alone with Bergson, stepping carefully over the debris field, littered with human body parts. "Say, this just happened. The magic energy trails are still hot. I can bring in a Tracker. She might be able to follow the bomber and see where he went. We might have a chance at catching him this time. What do you say to using a bit of magic to catch this beast?"

"I'm not sure what you are saying or suggesting, Miss Black. We need evidence."

"In simple terms, I know someone who stands a very good chance of being able to follow where that bomber went. She can track magical energy trails. With luck, she can lead us to where it is at now. We might be able to stop him from carrying out further bombing attacks, especially if it still has more C-4," Monica explained. "I know you want to apprehend those responsible. This might get us there really fast this time. It can't hurt. Besides, we don't try demons. We kill them."

Bergson looked around at the carnage and destruction. "All right. Do what you think necessary. I'll fetch our guns. This demon creature has to be stopped now."

"Thanks." Monica focused and sent a hasty message to Amanda, hoping that she'd be able to respond at once. Meanwhile, Bergson rounded up Kelly and Miller, both protesting at being interrupted in their work. By the time that the three had donned their body armor and multitude of weapons, Amanda and her powerful wizard staff arrived. As usual, the Apache was wearing a tee shirt and jeans.

"I saw it on the news, Monica. But it's worse in person!" Amanda exclaimed.

"We're working with norms, so be careful what you say. Here they come now. They really don't know that all those weapons of theirs aren't going to do anything to the demon, but I'll kill it, if you can find it. Ah, Bergson, this is a very good friend of mine, Amanda Whitewater-Orondarka. Amanda, this is Lead Detective Bergson, Kelly, and Miller. They saw a long, raven haired Apache Indian wearing jeans and a rock band tee shirt standing before them, approximately their own age, and holding onto a strange wooden stick.

"Hi, all. Best get to work. Let's see where this demon went," she said, closing her eyes and focusing her attention onto the Gate spell. After a minute, she opened her eyes. "Coolest! This time, he didn't go very far away, just a ways that way. Monica, how are we going to take them there? I mean we usually use our Fly spells on the group."

While Amanda was focusing, Monica worked out this detail. "You go Invisible and follow the trail to where it ends. I'll Watch Through Your Eyes. Once you land, I'll teleport them to you. This is our fight, so you stay hidden. Lindsey will have my hide if I let anything bad happen to you. Okay?"

Amanda laughed. "Aye, she'd do that, Monica. Okay. It's not far."

Bergson and the others saw her simply vanish from sight, rather unnerving the three.

"Okay, hold on to my hands. Don't worry; I won't let anything bad happen to you three either. We need to stop this demon before he can bomb again!" Monica declared.

She felt their hands clutching hers, rather hard. Well, these three had never experienced magic before, and she took that into account, though her hands throbbed in their vice grips. "Okay, here we go."

Monica cast her spell silently, and they arrived before an abandoned, rundown warehouse. Around them were many other warehouses, but all looked in disrepair. "We're about ten miles east of New O'Hare," Monica whispered as the three struggled to get their bearings. Amanda canceled her spell and appeared beside the group.

"The demon is inside that warehouse," she pointed straight ahead. "I think it's abandoned. What's the plan, Monica?"

"You stay here and keep out of sight. We'll go in and

see what's what," Monica suggested.

"Hadn't we better cast defensive spells on them?" Amanda asked.

"Gang, we should do that for your own safety," Monica hinted, uncertain whether they would agree.

"Hey, I'll take anything to keep me alive," Miller said softly, but sincerely. Of the three, she was the most worried about this assault on a demon.

"As long as it doesn't interfere with our fighting abilities," Bergson reluctantly agreed.

"That tingles," whispered Miller, when Amanda touched her shoulder.

"Good. When it stops tingling, you're no longer being protected," Amanda explained, watching Monica casting the Skin of Stone spell on Bergson and Kelly.

"So what's this gonna do for us?" Kelly asked, more than a little curious.

"As long as the spell lasts, the demon can't hurt you. Bullets will bounce off of you. That sort of thing," Monica replied.

"Like our vests?" Kelly asked.

"Yes, but the vests aren't protecting your face and hands or legs. This spell is. Come on; let's get this bomber!" Monica declared.

Bergson took the lead, breaking the rusted lock on the door and sliding it open, removing any chance of taking the demon by surprise. The warehouse was huge and quite open, probably once housing rather large machinery. Pigeon dung littered the floor as well as bits of down here and there. Standing in the middle of the giant space stood the ten foot tall demon, currently giving itself a bath, washing off the filth from the explosion. Seeing them enter, it roared something like a lion and charged at them, flailing its four arms before it. Each hand held giant claws, capable of slicing through human torsos like butter! It needed no other weapons!

Gunfire erupted! Bergson and Kelly blasted away at the demon with very large caliber rifles, while Miller emptied her 9mm clip at the demon. Only a hundred feet away, they couldn't miss, but as Monica expected, their bullets merely bounced off of its still mostly filthy body, though it reacted, lurching backwards slightly with each hit. Nevertheless, it continued charging the three. Monica anticipated this and quietly went invisible. She opened a magical door near the back of the demon's head and stepped into it. Carefully, she prepared her next spell, hoping that by taking the demon by total surprise, she could cut through its magical resistance. If her ancient volume was correct, this Type 10 demon was particularly vulnerable to electrical forms of attack. Thus, she chose to hit it with a massive lightning strike.

The demon had already gotten close to the firing trio who continued to back up, frantically reloading and emptying clip after clip into this beast. Just as Monica stepped out of the magical door behind its head, the demon's hands reached the trio. Bergson felt the massive claws strike him. The next instant, his body went flying across the warehouse, smashing into a far wall. Kelly's body flew in the opposite direction, meeting the same fate. Miller ducked and dodged the swinging arm, and then rolled out of its reach, at least temporarily.

Monica's spell detonated. All four saw enormous bolts of lightning arcing down onto the demon's head, forming a connection with the rusted steel beams far overhead and the slightly damp concrete floor. As they watched, the demon's body writhed, twisted, and finally slumped to the ground. The arcing electricity ended as suddenly as it had come. Monica stepped out of the magical door and back onto the floor and walked up to the demon. "It's dead. Are you all right? Miller?"

"Fine here. Got out of the way," she exclaimed, far louder than she normally spoke. "Boss? Kelly?"

Both men got up slowly. "Darn! It threw me clear over here!" Kelly yelled. "Don't think anything is broken."

"Incredible, that thing had supernatural strength! Is it really dead?" Bergson barked. "Why didn't our bullets harm it? Heck, I dumped enough lead into it to bring down a charging rhino!"

"You get it? You all right?" Amanda called out from the opened doors.

"Got it, Amanda. Everyone's okay. Thanks a million!" Monica called out.

Bergson got to his feet and took charge again. "Thanks Amanda, but you best stay outside. This is now an active crime scene. That thing—it's huge and disgusting!"

Kelly came up and gave it a kick, just to make sure it was dead. "Thought I was a goner. Tossed me like a carrot or something."

"These demons are strong, but this type here is pretty stupid, too," Monica explained. "I wonder what we've stumbled into here?" She began looking around the warehouse.

"Hey, over here," Kelly called. "C-4. Probably a couple hundred pounds of the stuff!

"We need our Rover here. That's the trouble with magic. Leaves you in the lurch," Bergson barked. He didn't even have a collection bag on him.

"Leave that to me, fellows, back shortly with the Rover. You see what hard evidence we've got here," Monica replied. She walked out of the warehouse, joining a smiling Amanda. After exchanging hugs, Amanda teleported back to her band, while Monica teleported to their Rover. While the vehicle was incredibly heavy, she was just barely able to use her mental powers to move it the few miles across town to the warehouse. She walked back inside, bringing their evidence collection bags with her.

"Ah there you are. We've hit the mother lode! Evidence galore," Kelly remarked. "C-4, detonators, plans for more bombings, the works."

Miller added, "We've certainly prevented other bombings!"

Bergson barked, "Hey, keep looking. This was supposed to be a dumb demon. So someone else had to put together the bombs and make all the plans." He looked at Monica and added, "Right?"

"Right. This type of demon just follows orders. Someone or someones were just using the demon," Monica added.

Bergson explained, "While you were gone, I made some calls. I managed to pull one forensic team off the mall to process this site. Also, I got an army platoon coming to guard the warehouse as well. Don't want those behind these bombings to return to get the rest of their C-4."

"Excellent, Bergson. Let me take a look around here," Monica replied. She had other things to hunt for besides explosives. A few minutes later, she called, "Bergson, over here. Bingo." He strode over to her location squarely in the middle of the giant, open warehouse. She stood beside a ten-foot pentagram etched into the concrete.

"This is a permanent Gate for the demons. That's real silver outlining the pentagram. This is an operational Gate. At any time, more demons could come pouring through this portal," she explained.

"Can you somehow make it not work?" Bergson asked the key question.

"Absolutely. One only has to break the silver outline."

"Here, will this work?" Bergson asked, handing her a large hunting knife with an eight inch blade.

Monica smiled. "Yep. Watch. Just pry the soft silver out of the etching, like so." She dug and pried. Soon she had a break in the pentagram. "There, now it is inoperable. When the forensic team gets here, it would be wise of them to remove all the silver."

Just then, magical energies began to illuminate and radiate around the center of the pentagram. Someone or something was trying to activate the Gate spell! "Holy crap!" cried Bergson. Monica backed up, readying spells. "What's happening?"

"Someone is trying to use the Gate. I hope I removed enough silver or we're screwed!" Monica replied, frightened for the first time in a long time. Taking on one lower-cast demon by herself was acceptable, but if a group of stronger demons gated here, she'd be grossly outnumbered and had no way to protect her team members.

As all four stared at the glowing, yellowish energy, they saw the outline of a woman, a very strange looking woman at that, beginning to appear in the center of the pentagram. Then, sparks flew, shorting out the gate. The energy dissipated rapidly, leaving no trace that it had been there.

"Well, we just got lucky, fellows," Monica breathed a huge sigh of relief. "Just to be safe, I'm going to remove more silver. That was too close for comfort."

"What the heck was that woman-like thing?" asked Miller.

"That, Miller, was a succubus, probably one of those that escaped our dragnet nine years ago. I assure you I don't want to go up against one of those by myself. I rather like being alive," Monica said, half in jest, half serious.

"We've got serious problems, don't we?" Bergson remarked, still a bit shocked by what he'd just seen with his own eyes. This was not the kind of day he'd imagined having.

"Very. But we need to find hard evidence, as you keep telling me, Bergson. Let's get to it," Monica carefully changed the topic back to something with which these three could deal. A few minutes later, the platoon of soldiers arrived, and the three began to relax, believing help had arrived. Monica, however, knew better, but kept silent.

"Hey, over here, I've got something. Documents," Miller called out.

The three gathered around the petite woman, who held up two envelops. "They are marked: To be delivered to the press. Both are interesting." She was wearing gloves to avoid contaminating the evidence. "Looks like we know the group behind the Lambert Field bombing, because this one by one Al Zwarih claims the ILF was behind it."

"What the heck is the ILF?" asked Kelly.

"The Iranian Liberation Front," Bergson answered before Miller could. "Supposed to be an inactive terrorist group, but I guess they've surfaced again. What's the other one say?"

Miller answered, "Lake Land Mall bombing brought to you by Hezbollah II. That's supposed to be a defunct terrorist group as well. Guess they've been lying low."

She went on, "That's not all that's here, fellows—plans to blow up Grand Central Station in New York and the huge Hurst Building in Los Angeles. I think we prevented two more bombings by these fiends. Most of the writing is in Arabic or something, and I can't read it, not without my translation program. This will give forensics something to do."

"What have you got for us? Oh wow!" The team of three forensic men arrived and walked into the warehouse. One spoke up, but became quite startled as he spotted the demon carcass on the floor.

"We've killed the bomber of Lake Land Mall," Bergson pointed to the carcass, "and prevented two more planned bombing attacks. Plenty here for you boys to analyze."

"Right," Kelly added. "Check that C-4. I'm certain it's of Iranian origin and the same that was used in the St. Louis bombing, if I'm not mistaken."

"Bergson, thank you for pulling us off the mall scene. That one is beyond horrid! They'll be weeks recovering all the body bits, let alone identifying them. Hundreds dead. Even more wounded. Never saw so many detached arms and legs lying around in my life. Glad you got the fiend that did it," the lead forensics expert declared.

Monica added, "Guys, make sure you remove all the silver from that pentagram. We don't want the demons ever reusing it." One walked over to it and nodded that he understood.

"Okay team. We should head back to the bomb scene and see what assistance we can be," Bergson barked. With little else they could do just now, the team followed him out to the Rover.

They had been gone from the bomb scene for several hours. When they returned, at least the survivors had been evacuated. The responders now carried out the grizzly work of recovering body parts.

Monica suggested, "Bergson, I'd like to go to the hospitals and see what healing I can do for the worst victims."

"Sure thing, kid. This isn't a task for a woman," Bergson declared.

Monica replied, "Or a man either."

Miller cracked a smile, as Monica teleported away.

Later when they were out of earshot from Miller, Kelly admitted, "Boss, Miss Black—she saved our bacon today. We wouldn't have made this much progress without her, magic or not."

"I know, Kelly. I know, but don't tell her that. She's already got too big an ego as it is," Bergson replied. "Now I'm just hoping they don't cut us off from this investigation and give it to one of those damned wizard departments. It's our case, Kelly, ours. Like Black said, someone is behind it, and I aim to bring them to justice."

"I'm with ya. Hey, more Buffalo Fingers," he joked, picking up several burned finger bits, adding them to his collection bag. Bergson gave him a cold stare, but didn't chastise him. He thought collecting the body parts was enough to drive any man nuts. So give Kelly his outlet.

From time to time, Monica checked in with her team to see if they needed her back at the sight. Meanwhile, she visited two of the local hospitals where the injured survivors had been brought. It took a bit of doing, but at last she got the administration to allow her to visit those who had lost one or more limbs and cast her Regeneration spell on them. Monica had never been to Chicago and, for her references, wisely referred the administrators to St. Anne's Hospital in St. Louis. Drained and exhausted from having cast many complex Regeneration spells, Monica joined the others around six at the Rover. The Red Cross had kindly brought in a hearty supper for the hundreds of rescue workers, quite welcomed by all.

After eating, Bergson asked, "So how did it go at the hospitals? All done?"

"I've only scratched the surface. I got to some who lost limbs today. Those should make a full recovery, but there are so many more of them. I may be days at it," she replied with a sigh.

"Aren't there others who could do that?" Bergson asked, curious about why Miss Black took it upon herself to do this for complete strangers.

"I supposed that somewhere in the wide world there might be someone else who could cast this complex spell. Certainly, a few magical rings exist, which when worn for about a week, accomplishes the spell, but those cost a fortune, millions. There might be a dozen such rings still in existence. No, Bergson, as far as I know, I'm the only wizard or witch who can cast this obviously enormously powerful spell. With that kind of power comes the responsibility to use it. Heck, Bergson, my file probably also tells you that I lost my arms once to demons from the Abyss, so I know just what these victims are going through. I've the power to help, and so I must, but casting such powerful spells does drain me. If you don't mind, I'm hitting the sack now."

"Would you mind waiting a minute or two? I've got to make my evening report to Franco and Billy Bob. Now that we have hard evidence that your demons are involved, they could well take us off this case. I don't know—giving it to your kind," Bergson explained. For once, he wasn't barking, but talking in a normal tone.

"Would they do that? Just because there was a demon involved?" she asked and then realized why he'd suggested it. "Oh, I see what you mean. Normal weapons can't harm demons. It takes magical items or sometimes spells to do that. It would certainly be safer for you three to have wizards take over, but you three are like me. When you start something, you want to see it through to the end."

"Er, exactly. Okay, I'll make the call and put it on speaker phone," Bergson said, doing just that. A bit later, he finished his report, "So with the help of that Apache woman, Amanda Whitewater, we killed the Lake Land Mall bomber, prevented at least two more bombings, and uncovered two potential terrorist organizations that might be behind these bombings. We'll pursue those leads in the next few days, once we finish up helping here, sir." *There, I've finished. I wonder how fast he transfers us off this case?*

"Amanda Whitewater? Yes, I know of her. Another of those incredibly powerful wizards and witches, out of Bradbury's if I'm not mistaken. Superlative job, Bergson. Tell your team very well done," General Franco replied. He sounded calm for once, or so Bergson sensed.

"So now I suppose you want us off the case," he added. *No sense waiting for the bomb to land on us. Since he didn't say so directly, I might as well force him to say it and be done with it.*

"You've got the notorious Demon Hunter with your team. Unless you don't want to pursue this case, Bergson, it's still yours. I'm sure that Miss Black will call in others to help when and if needed," General Franco replied. "You haven't fired her again, have you?"

"Er. No. We are working out our differences sir. Thank you. We will pursue more leads in the morning," Bergson replied, greatly relieved. However, he began to wonder if all along General Franco had known that demons were involved. Had he some inside information to that effect? Had that been why he and the President had assigned Miss Black to his team? Bergson had many questions to ponder when he hung up.

"Okay all. You heard the general. Get some sleep. We're still on this one, and we've got to find those who are pulling the strings before they can recover and carry out more attacks," Bergson barked.

Half in jest, Monica saluted him. Kelly roared with laughter, adding his salute to hers. Miller merely cracked a smile and quietly retired, just as exhausted as the others, emotionally more so than physically.

Chapter 4—Washington

The brief meeting broke up and a tired Monica headed back to their private quarters. Miller followed behind her. "Say, I'd love to have a hot, soaking bath. Don't suppose we have a tub on this plane, do we?" she asked.

Miller chuckled. "I requested one, but it got rejected by the fellows. Got one shower—a rather large one to accommodate the fellows. We can share it, if you like. I'll never get that horrid stench off me. I've been to a lot of crime scenes, but nothing was ever as bad as this one is. So many dead."

"Sure. Let's. I feel incredibly dirty, too," Monica admitted, thankful for Chrissy Miller's company.

A bit later, Chrissy said, "Can I ask you a personal question? Monica nodded. "Your file said you lost your husband shortly after you were married and that you have a son. How come you haven't remarried? It's been nine years."

Monica laughed. "Chrissy, if you must know, I love women, but Rob was the only man that I could ever allow in my bed with me. He was—well one of a kind. I doubt that I'll ever meet someone like him again. I certainly haven't yet."

Chrissy laughed. "I know what you mean about men. It's all wham, bang, thank you ma'am. They haven't a clue."

It was Monica's turn to laugh. "Chrissy, you can say that again! Only don't!" Both women laughed, knowing that she meant Kelly, who would have done just that.

Chrissy then asked, "Is sex any different for witches than it is for us normal women?"

Monica smiled. Apparently, this was what Chrissy really wanted to know. "I've nothing to compare it with, but from all that I know, I don't think it is any different just because of magic. Now with Rob, it was different, but then he was different. Oops, the water is cooling off. I think the boys are going to have to have cold showers!" Both laughed and ended their shower.

The next day, Monica headed off to the hospitals to continue working her magic on the many victims. Meanwhile, Miller stayed on the plane, researching the two potential terrorist organizations, while the two men headed out to help others collect remains, though they kept their eyes opened for more clues. This time, the Chicago FBI conducted the interviews with the survivors, for which both men were thankful.

Around noon, Monica returned, joining them for lunch, provided by the Red Cross volunteers. As they ate, Bergson's cell phone rang. After answering it, he quickly put it on speaker phone. The general's voice was speaking, "fly to DC immediately!"

"Could you repeat that for the rest of the team, sir?"

"The Pentagon has just been bombed! Fly to DC immediately. I'll handle the arrangements! What the hell is going on? Another call. Hurry up!" He hung up.

"To the Rover," Bergson barked.

As they drove back the short distance to New O'Hare, Miller commented, "But I thought we stopped two more scheduled bombings."

With a steeled face, Bergson answered, "We did, but obviously others were planned. It's an epidemic. Has the world gone insane? Three bombings in less than a week!"

Miller was impressed. As they reached the airport, the general again had the security personnel escorting them to their plane. The tower stopped all traffic, allowing her to taxi and take off just as fast as she could handle the process! Similarly, they had top priority once they reached the DC area.

"So how could they bomb the Pentagon?" asked Kelly. "They have that place locked up tighter than a drum!"

"Don't know, Kelly, that's our job. Find out how and who," Bergson answered.

Monica added, "Well, I know for a fact that their security is tops. Anyone carrying C-4 and walking close to the Pentagon would be identified in seconds. The bomber simply couldn't just walk on in like they did at the mall and the airport. Even if they used a Morph spell to make themselves appear like a Pentagon employee, they couldn't get the bomb past security. Further, I know for a fact that Teleport and similar spells won't work either. You have to land outside the Pentagon on the arrival pad and be subject to a search."

"We're just theorizing. We're going to have to see for ourselves," Bergson countered. "Hard evidence."

Monica smiled and made a valuable suggestion. "Say, could we get permission to fly over the Pentagon and see the damage from above? Is that possible?"

"Hey boss, she's got a good idea there. I can get a far better grasp on what happened that way," Kelly supported her.

"Okay, I'll make the call, but I don't know if they'll let us."

Later on and escorted by two jet fighters, the giant Stratosphere flew over the Pentagon, rather surprising Miller, who enjoyed the attention of the jet pilots. As they made their low altitude pass, Kelly used streaming video to record what he was seeing for future reference. Monica and Kelly ignored the many emergency vehicles on the ground and all the "ants" moving about, focusing instead on the bomb's damage, quite visible from the air.

"Now this is a good one!" Kelly commented as their fly over ended and Miller headed in for a landing.

"Huh? What do you mean?" Bergson barked.

"Someone dropped the bomb on the Pentagon—from the air, boss. That's a typical bomb crater you see after an air strike on a target. Vastly different result on the ground. My guess: a thousand pounder. Why does it look so funny though?"

As Dominus and when he was buddy-buddy with President Missy Snow, he learned all about the precautions being taken at the Pentagon and other key sites. Hence, Monica answered, "The bomb knocked off some of the building's concrete structure. However, long ago wizards erected Walls of Force inside the building to prevent any internal damage. The bomb merely wiped out some of the outer shell. I doubt that we will find any casualties on the ground, unless someone got hit by falling chunks of concrete."

"That's why it looks so weird, like we're Superman using X-ray vision to look inside at the zillions of offices," Kelly commented.

"Precisely. With all the security, how did they allow a plane to fly over and drop the bomb?" Monica asked.

"That's what we're here for, Miss Black," Bergson barked, but more gently than normal.

After landing, NCIS and FBI security surrounded them and issued the four their temporary ID badges, and whisked then off to the site, where they were escorted through tight security, all before finally entering the Pentagon proper. There, they met with numerous other investigators and were briefed on the event.

"Look, it's no secret that someone dropped a bomb on us," one official explained. "And yes, Mr. Kelly, we believe it was a thousand pound bomb. Worse, we've identified fragments. It was one of our own bombs."

Kelly replied, "Then, the answer is simple. Someone hijacked one of your surveillance drones, drove it over the Pentagon, and dropped its bomb on you."

Several men protested that was impossible. Just then, General Franco Porti walked in, along with several other high ranking officials, including the Secretary of Defense. He spoke up, "Mr. Kelly is correct. Someone hijacked Drone 1456 and dropped its bomb on the Pentagon before releasing control of the drone. I've just come from Drone Command. Now then, the question we should be asking is just who hijacked our drone and how did they do that? I've ordered all armed drones to land until we work out how they were able to break drone security, hijack one, and take control of it. Until we have the answers to that, everyone here will give Mr. Bergson and his WIT team total and complete access to anything they desire. Am I clear on this point?" Heads nodded, though many were reluctant to do so.

The long afternoon passed swiftly and hectically, as the group was escorted from location to location. First, they needed to completely understand the security arrangements surrounding the drone program and how it operated. Next, they had to visit each site and see for themselves firsthand, sifting through the myriad denials and protests this just couldn't happen.

Around six that night, the team met back on their Stratosphere, where Bergson hastily constructed a whiteboard layout while they dined on catered food, compliments of the Navy in this case. Kelly commented while staring at the results, "This is hopeless. Everyone says it can't happen, yet it did. Someone is lying."

"Please don't ask me to hack another system today," Miller protested, "I'm utterly exhausted. I hate having ten guys watching my every keystroke over my shoulder. I'm a nervous wreck tonight. I need that bathtub you fellows rejected!"

Ignoring the two, Monica and Bergson stared at all the facts arrayed on his whiteboard. "The answer lies here, I'm sure of it," Bergson said calmly.

"We're missing something, and it's probably right here before our noses," Monica replied. He cracked a rare smile. Both continued to stare.

After a time, Monica commented, "Impersonation. That's all that's left." Suddenly, the solution flashed in her mind, just as it did in Bergson's. Simultaneously, they both said, "The drone operator was an imposter!" Startled, the two stared at each other. Of course, their sudden conclusion roused both Kelly and Miller.

"You go," Bergson said.

"No, this is your operation. You go," Monica wisely insisted.

He smiled and explained, "The drone operator is the only possible person who could have flown the drone over the Pentagon and released the bomb. Everything else checks out, so it had to be that man. But everyone knows him well, so it had to be someone pretending to be him, an imposter."

"But how?" Kelly grumbled, not seeing how this could be the answer.

Monica took over. "There are lots of ways. The absolute simplest is for someone to cast a Morph Self spell. There is also the potion method, where one obtains a sample of the target DNA and brews that into a potion, which when drunk changes him or her into a replica of the target person. There are more ways, but the key point is that Mr. Dirk Derringer wasn't the real Dirk Derringer, but an imposter, a good one mind you. Probably stole his ID card as well, maybe even mind-linked to the real Dirk, forcing him to tell the perp the special codes to enter."

"Gear up! We're raiding this Dirk's home now. I'm calling it in now," Bergson barked. Kelly and Miller leapt into action, adrenaline flowing once more.

A half hour later, a swarm of police from many departments surrounded the apartment complex where Dirk lived. Armed to the teeth and wearing all manner of protections, Bergson led the raid, as a SWAT team busted down the man's door. Men raced from room to room, calling out "clear," as the seconds passed. Then, one yelled, "in here." Bergson and his team followed the voice into Dirk's bedroom.

Dirk lay bound and gagged, unconscious on his bed. His ID card was missing as were his wallet and other personal effects. When the EMTs arrived, they suggested that he was probably drugged and whisked him off to a local hospital. After they left, Bergson summoned an FBI forensics team to the apartment with orders to go over it with a fine tooth comb. "Clues. We need clues about who his abductors were."

Meanwhile, Miller sat in their Rover hacking into the local surveillance cameras, which were on nearly every block. She focused on four that were closest to this apartment and began to run the footage in reverse. By the time the ambulance whisked Dirk away, she had spotted the imposter leaving Dirk's apartment. The man looked identical to what little she'd seen of Dirk. Now she continued to watch as the early morning turned into the previous night. Later on, the rest of her team joined her, having found no clues as yet.

As the frames swept past on the monitor, Miller commented, "God is watching you."

Kelly laughed. "Good one, Miller, good one."

"Hey, God is watching you, too, Kelly," she added.

"Ah, here we go!" she interrupted the others who were now fixing a late night snack. "Look, he's going into his apartment with another man. Time reading is 7 pm. Is that a gun in his back?" She backed it up and played it running forward, pausing here and there. "Guess I will have to go frame by frame for positive proof, boss, but I'm thinking he has a gun poked in his back. Okay, backing up. Let's see where this assailant came from. Might take some time."

Monica learned something about Chrissy Miller that night. By midnight, the men had gone to bed, but Miller was still at her post, running through six different video feeds simultaneously, attempting to backtrack the perp. She brought the comm expert coffee and later some donuts. By one o'clock, Monica brought her a decent meal, which Miller ate rather ravenously. "Thanks! I needed that." Once Chrissy got on the trail of a perp, she had the tenacity of a bull dog!

"Gotcha!" Miller exclaimed, rousing Monica who had drifted into a light sleep. Monica had refused to go to bed and leave Chrissy working all by herself.

"Found him?" she asked, sleepy-eyed.

"Yep. The perp took a cab, following Dirk home from work. Two blocks away, he approached him. There's a printout showing the gun in Dirk's back. More importantly, I found where he caught the cab and got the cab's number as well. Even better, I've tracked the perp back to where he was staying. That motel there. Wake the fellows. We ought to strike as soon as possible, in case the perp is still there!"

"Well done, Chrissy! Okay. I'll wake them," Monica praised Miller and headed off to do just that. Chrissy smiled broadly, glancing at Monica's back.

When she knocked on Kelly's door, he said, "Hey Barbie Doll. Come on in. Bed's all warmed up for you."

"Not a chance, Kelly. Get up. Miller's located where the perp was staying. Says we need to raid the place right away," Monica countered.

"All work and no play makes Kelly a dull boy," he argued back.

"Guess you have to resign yourself to being a dull boy, little fellow," she retorted, bringing a laugh to his face.

"Well, you're no fun," he replied, pulling on a shirt.

By the time Kelly finally joined them in the comm center, Miller had finished briefing Bergson. "Now if you don't mind, I'm getting some sleep. Monica, too, since she was up all night with me."

"Okay. We'll take care of this one, Miller. Great job," Bergson complimented her, and Monica didn't miss that fact. Whatever else Bergson was, he gave praise where it was deserved. Both women headed to bed, asleep before the two men departed. Bergson placed a number of calls before he and Kelly drove their Rover off into the early morning twilight light.

Around noon, the two men returned looking tired. "Well?" Miller said as they climbed out of the Rover.

"You were dead on, only the perp had already fled the room. Forensics is going over it now, but we did find out quite a bit. Iran Jihad was behind this attack. Found incriminating documents and the man's passport, probably fake, but his picture matches the description the manager gave. Plus the manager identified him from the photo. FBI and CIA are now working on getting a true id on the perp. His image is out on all media. He can't get on a plane, train, or bus without being discovered," Bergson reported.

"Today, Miller, you and Monica see if you can discover how he got here in the DC area: plane, train, car, whatever." He nodded to Monica and added, "Of course, if he's a wizard, you might not find anything, but look anyway. This is our best lead yet. We're heading to bed now." The women smiled and headed to the comm center.

"So Monica, if this perp is a wizard, how could we

possibly track his arrival in the DC area?" Miller asked.

"That's a very good question, Chrissy," Monica explained. "If he can use the Teleport spell, it's virtually impossible to trace, except if he cast the spell recently and we know where he cast it from or where he arrived, in which case Amanda could tell us the rest. Not all wizards can cast that spell so he might have come here by other means. However, if he is an Iranian citizen, then. . ."

"If he came by normal means, I can find his entry, but if someone teleported him here, then nada. Right?" Chrissy said, grinning.

Monica nodded and together they began reviewing video streams from customs. Chrissy had a special program that she fired up. Inputting the man's image, she had the program search all customs entry stations on the east coast during the last month. Meanwhile, she launched a second instance of the program and helped Monica get it running on city-wide live video feeds. "If we are very lucky, we might locate him somewhere in DC right now."

Enthused with that possibility, Monica paid close attention to the work, boring as it was. "I don't know how you can do this all the time," Monica admitted an hour later. "My eyes are starting to see things that aren't there!"

Miller chuckled. "And I don't know how you can do what you do either. So I guess we're even there." Monica returned her smiles.

Around four that afternoon, Miller exclaimed, "Gotcha again, Mr. Perp! Monica, rouse the guys; we have him at last!"

Monica dashed off to do as asked, wishing they were wizards so she could just Message them instead of darting through the giant plane.

Five minutes later, both men watched a monitor as Miller replayed the video. "He boarded flight 1123 to London's Heathrow at 1 pm our time. Too late to have them intercept him, but he couldn't go too far around London. They've more spy cams around than we do. What's the plan, boss?"

"I could kiss you, Miller! Great job. You too,

Monica!" Bergson exclaimed.

"Better not, if you know what's good for you," Miller replied softly, but firmly.

Kelly commented, "Lighten up, Miller, or I'll kiss you, too."

"Get the plane ready to take off. If I know General Franco, he'll order us to go after the man. I'll phone him now," Bergson declared, his voice sounding more hopeful than Monica could ever recall before now.

As Bergson predicted, they were ordered to go to London immediately. General Franco promised they would have the full support of the British authorities. An hour later, the giant Stratosphere was once more airborne, heading across the Pond. Partway through the trip, Bergson received another call. The FBI had managed to get the man's true identity, via the Department of Magical Misuse. He was Al Rumati, a low level wizard closely associated with the Iranian Jihad movement. By the time that they landed at Heathrow, their British counterparts were already on the case.

No sooner had they been briefed at Heathrow when the calls came in. The game was over. Via their CCT system, they'd tracked him to an apartment where he spent less than thirty minutes. He'd just departed when the authorities arrived there, but they soon picked up his trail as he headed for their subway system. He'd been cornered before he could get to the Underground and had blown himself up as they moved in. Only the wizard was harmed. However, they also raided the apartment and found more bomb making supplies, arresting two other men. Case closed, except for the lengthy interrogations that followed. After visually verifying the remains of the man, Bergson had no choice but to head back to DC, though the British authorities promised to relay any thing further that the two prisoners might divulge.

They spent the night on the plane, giving Miller time to sleep, before letting her fly the Stratosphere back stateside. When they arrived in DC, General Franco was there to meet them. "Good news. Forensics has turned up some additional clues. It seems the same person wrote both of those documents claiming responsibility for the two bombings. They are almost certain, 95%, that the Hezbollah II document is a fake, probably written by the ILF group. Their conclusion is that the ILF was behind both bombings and had planned at least two more. They got three excellent DNA samples as well. Unfortunately, the three individuals, all men, do not match anyone in any system. Still, in time, I'm sure we'll get them."

He went on, "One positive action has resulted though. The HDF has ordered all the armed drones to now be completely controlled by remote control, removing any opportunity for anyone to impersonate a drone operator and hijack another drone. Actually, this was always an option called Alert Level Red. So no more drone attacks are possible."

Miller groaned. "What's wrong?" Monica whispered.

"The fools! Now it will be even easier to launch a drone attack. Computer systems can be hacked. All you need now is a hacker and someone who can fly a drone. Idiots," Miller whispered back. In a flash, Monica realized that Miller was probably correct. Professor Betts was proof enough of that!

General Franco ignored the whispering women and continued, "President Billy Bob is considering launching a drone attack on the Iranian headquarters of the ILF in Tehran. I'll keep you posted. Excellent work. Now take a day off and catch up on your sleep. We have things well in hand." The men saluted and the general departed.

"Sleep. What's that?" Kelly commented, then added, "anyone want to share my bed?"

"Dream on!" Miller responded softly.

"I can loan you my dog, if you need company," Monica teased him back.

Bergson broke in, "Hey, your file didn't say that you had a dog."

Monica broke into a laugh. In point of fact, she didn't have a pet. Rob did. Miller headed to the shower, while Kelly rounded up some beers and popped in a DVD to watch.

Meanwhile Monica and Bergson decided to brew a pot of coffee. In the galley, he said, "You know, something doesn't feel right about all this."

"You have that feeling, too?" Monica asked, her eyes rising. *Perhaps he is smarter than I give him credit for.* "I do, too. A couple of things are bothering me."

Surprising them both, simultaneously, they said, "What if this ILF is a ruse?" Both stopped a second and broke into grins. "Okay, you first," Monica assented.

"My thought precisely. President or not, Billy Bob is an idiot, a political puppet. If he goes ahead and attacks the ILF in Tehran, Iran has no other option but to retaliate. Escalation follows. What if someone is trying to set up a confrontation between us and Iran? What better way than this? Heck, at this point, the country is up in arms over the senseless bombings and would readily back an attack on Iran. Say, is that what you were thinking?"

"More or less, but from a different angle. Demons. This could well be part of their plot against us. Throw suspicion elsewhere than on them. Even though we killed the demon actually carrying out the bombings, we really don't know yet who was behind the demon or what their true objectives might be. Whatever they are, it can't be good. Instigating a conflict between us and Iran is a creative way to create all kinds of world chaos, hiding further their true plans from us," Monica explained her feelings. She added, "Honestly, Bergson, my hunch is that we haven't remotely seen what they have planned for us and that, my friend, scares the crap out of me."

"Say, is there such a place as the Abyss? It was mentioned in your file," he asked.

"Yes, but it's not a place anyone in their right mind would want to visit—makes Detroit look like a very comfy home. Evil incarnate might be a good description. Let's hope that you never meet its denizens. That Type 10 was sufficient."

"Hey, if you're right and there's a bunch of these

powerful demons behind all this, what can I do to fight them? How can I protect my team?" Bergson asked.

Monica chuckled. "Bergson, ever since Miller showed me her enhanced image of the perp with four arms, I have been asking myself that very question. As a power witch, it is my responsibility and duty to protect others, particularly you three. As you've experienced, I can put the Skin of Stone on each of you. That protects you from their blows, bites, and clawing, at least as long as the spell lasts, though they can still pound you nearly senseless. However, some of the more powerful demons can also cast spells to which you three are quite vulnerable. Again, there are some protection spells that I can cast to prevent that from happening for a short time. Just remember, there's a limit to just how many of these spells I can manage in a day. Spell casting can be nearly as demanding as physical fighting."

Since Bergson was actually listening to her and paying attention, Monica continued. "About your abilities to harm or kill demons, now that's quite another matter entirely. I believe a bit of history will help you understand the entire situation better. You see, the first known record of demons appearing on our world was back in ancient times, in Mesopotamia, Babylon in particular. Archaeology gives us that glimpse into the distant past. At that time and for centuries after that, demons were fought by using magically enchanted weapons, usually some form of sword, reaching its pinnacle during the iron age when master craftsmen made mighty swords."

"Most demons can only be harmed by use of magically enchanted weapons or specific magic spells, but which spells harm them are dependent upon the specific type of demon. Some are allergic to electrical energies, some to fire, and so on. So my first thought was to see if we couldn't acquire some of those ancient enchanted weapons, assuming you three could learn how to fight with swords."

Bergson commented, "I can see how that might work. Are such weapons available?"

Sighing, Monica answered, "For the most part, no. Only a few have survived all these centuries. Some are in private collections, some are in museums. I found a couple being offered for sale on the Internet, but the sellers are asking monumental prices, particularly so since the demon attacks nine years ago. Realistically, we haven't any hope of buying such weapons. I don't know of any expert sword maker. That art died out centuries ago. One of my dearest friends has her own business manufacturing and selling magically enchanted items. So I've chatted with her a bit about this. There might be another way to go about this."

Bergson chuckled. "I doubt that I could convince the general to part with millions of dollars to buy some ancient sword. Okay, Miss Black, I'll bite. What's this other way?"

Monica grinned. "Enchant the bullets you use in your guns."

Bergson roared. "You mean like making silver bullets to kill werewolves and all that malarkey?"

"Yep, right on," Monica smiled. "If you can give me a handful of your best quality bullets for the guns you want to use, I'll take them to Ericka and see what she can do. I believe it is worth trying. Nine years ago, the FBI in St. Louis used massive amounts of fifty caliber shells on some of the lesser demons. Heck, the shell casings literally filled the street when they finally downed one of the demons. Probably a thousand rounds hit the demon, maybe less. I sure didn't count them."

"Hey, so they can be killed with large enough shells? That's encouraging," he replied.

"To be honest with you, it was we wizards and witches that eliminated most of the demons during the battles. The FBI and National Guard men merely kept the demons' attention focused on them, giving us a chance to take them by surprise with our spells. Still, if Ericka can enchant your bullets, you've got a fighting chance. Of course, there's no telling how many hits it will take to bring one of them down. They are hardier than humans."

"Hey," Bergson declared, "everyone that we kill is never coming back here!"

"Er, not exactly true, Bergson. You see, if you kill a demon while it is here on Earth, it is immediately sent back to its home in the Abyss. After that, magic prevents it from returning to Earth for around seventeen years, when it can come back if it has a way and so desires. Worse, evil wizards and witches are able to Gate demons here to our world. Such actions are extreme crimes and very heavily punished by our kind. I'm telling you this so you have a better picture of the problems we're facing, Bergson. You have to know what we are up against."

"Miss Black, you've told me more valuable information just now than all others of your kind put together have in my entire life! I do appreciate it and you're right. I need to know." Bergson gave her a compliment of sorts. "I'll collect up ammunition samples for you. Thanks, Miss Black."

An hour later, Monica teleported home, carrying a large bag of various caliber ammunition in hopes that Ericka could somehow enchant the lead slugs in them. Without it, she knew her team had very little chance if they ran into more demons.

***

"Wake up, Monica! It's all over the news," Miller jostled Monica awake. They were still hold up in their giant Stratosphere plane, but Monica had had a long night with Ericka and Crystal, discussing the situation. Hastily, she rose, donned a nightgown and joined the others, who also weren't fully dressed, only Miller was, their early riser.

"Well, Billy Bob has gone and done it now," Bergson grumbled. "Acting on unverified evidence is a recipe for major trouble. Politicians. Can't stand them."

Kelly remarked, "Escalation can be fun! Get into the spirit, Bergson. Whee, watch us bomb Iran. Watch Iran bomb us. Now we won't have to worry about job security, Bergson. Soon we will have more bombings to investigate. I like job security."

"Are all politicians idiots?" asked Miller in her usual soft voice.

Kelly answered her, "Look Miller, everyone knows

that if you have more than one brain cell, you can't be President." She grinned.

Bergson growled, "Cool it. He's only bombed the known headquarters of the ILF in Tehran. God, I hope that's all he's bombed. Anyway, today, we need to focus our efforts on finding clues. We need to find out just who was really behind the bombings in St. Louis and Chicago. We'll let the Pentagon folks deal with their attack. So get dressed and get to work. We need real answers, not theoretical ones."

"What can we track?" asked Monica, who was used to solving mysteries. "We have the paper on which the two documents we found were written, and we've not followed the trail on the imported C-4."

"Hey, I'll deal with the C-4," Kelly broke in.

"Monica and I will visit the forensics labs and see if they've uncovered anything that might be useful. Miller, you do your thing," Bergson ordered.

He and Monica headed to the whiteboard room, and he handed her the number for the Chicago lab, while he took the St. Louis lab. Both made their calls and began taking notes, knowing that somehow they desperately needed clues to follow. An hour later, both finished their extensive follow up calls.

Simultaneously, both said, "I might have something here." Instantly, both laughed. Bergson commented, "We're going to have to stop saying the same thing." Then, he grinned, which Monica appreciated. He was finally beginning to accept her. Wisely, she let him talk first.

"They reconstructed the last seconds before the blast from a number of SIMM cards in the cell phones we recovered. Long story short, that didn't tell us anything we didn't already know. He walked straight to the spot and detonated the bomb without any hesitation. So we know conclusively he did not intend to wipe out the entire airport."

He went on, "What is curious though is the analysis of the bits of the jacket that he was wearing. True, the fibers are of Iranian origin as we originally thought, but it was distributed by Kellog's Coats, a company based in Rolla, North Dakota. Further, we got lucky. They found a bit of paper fused in one of the pockets of the jacket. It was a receipt from that company. We're going to have to check this company out. So what did you discover?" he asked, feeling relieved that he had some new avenue to pursue.

"How curious, Bergson. Rolla, North Dakota has come up in the Chicago labs. The paper that the documents were written on came from the Rollette County Courthouse in Rolla. It had their watermark on it. Whoever wrote those documents somehow had this paper at their disposal. Rolla is just a dot on the map in farm country. It's close to the Canadian border and basically in the middle of nowhere. Population is barely a thousand. I've brought up a map on my laptop here: a one block main street plus a lot of grain elevators for the farmers. There can't be much there, but I am going to look into it," she explained.

"Okay, you take Rolla. I'll go see how Kelly is making out. We'll probably have to make a trip to Detroit, but we'll go in with a SWAT team protecting us," Bergson declared and left her to continue her explorations.

Shopping. If there was one thing that Monica excelled at, besides making large sums of money from wise investments, it was shopping. She loved to shop, but did most of it online, though she wasn't above popping in to a store to see something firsthand. Hence, knowing the population was so small, she decided to see shopping records that involved Rolla.

If they were hiding numerous demons there, she anticipated discovering far more grocery deliveries than one would expect for a thousand or so people. Unfortunately, nothing seemed unusual there. Kellog's Coats had imported a batch of Iranian made jackets, mostly a drab gray, but the reason was soon apparent. They were extremely cheap. More significantly, they dealt with heavy winter clothing, for the winters there were long and brutally cold. So that lead seemed to go nowhere.

Then while going down the list of apparel purchases, something caught her eye. Women's heels—specifically the same maker of the expensive, leather pumps that she always purchased. They were classified as fetish heels, just as hers were. Upon a closer inspection, she saw that only six-inch, spiked heels like she wore were ever ordered. This was unusual. Six hundred pairs? Presuming that half the population of Rolla were women, did this mean that every woman in Rolla wore fetish heels? She looked further and found no resales of these heels to other cities. So they weren't a reseller. How very strange.

Curious, she drilled down further. Most of the heels had ankle straps, unlike her easy slip-on pumps. Further, there were also an equal number of knee-high, high quality leather boots, again with six-inch spiked heels, similar to those she sometimes wore in the winter, fleece-lined for warmth. Speculation: did every woman in Rolla have a pair of dress pumps and boots? This, too, Monica found quite strange.

She looked deeper but discovered they weren't importing the fancy silk and satin gowns that she preferred to wear. Nothing erotic about their apparel, on the contrary, it appeared they wore practical, if not drab, clothing. Well, it was a rural farming community, she thought.

Having found one anomaly, Monica continued her search of shopping and purchase records. A half hour later, she came across another curious set of purchases. The town had one dentist, according to Rolla's Internet web page. However, during the past few years, he had ordered over six hundred full sets of dentures. Had half the town lost all their teeth? This too seemed odd to Monica, who made careful note of this as well.

Next, she looked into the grain elevator businesses, since those were prominent on their nearly perfectly flat landscape. Once more, she began to find small anomalies here as well. Bringing up the company records for the last twenty years, she plotted the elevators' intake and outflow of grain. For years, the graph was fairly level. However, nine years ago, changes began. At first, the outflow of grain lessened, though the intake remained fairly constant. Then four years ago, the intake began lessening as well, while the outgo dropped even further. This past year, the outgo was about a tenth of what it once had been. Also, the intake was half of what it once had been. Conclusion: there was a huge amount of grain being stored and not sold at a later date, while farmers must not be bringing their harvests to these elevators as they once had. Why? Obsolete storage bins?

Monica used her computer savvy to make a stab at just how much grain ought to be now stored in these elevators. When she finished and looked at the elevator capacity, she knew that she had another anomaly. The amount of grain that should still be there was five times the maximum capacity of all the grain silos in Rolla! Were they piling it up on the ground and covering it up with a tarp? This made no sense, but she wasn't a farmer and had no idea what this could mean, other than it was an anomaly.

Although she looked further, she found nothing else noteworthy and decided to join the others. As she rose, they came to her, or rather joined her by the whiteboard. Bergson looked pleased and Miller was smiling. Monica concluded they must have gotten some clues as well.

Kelly's face was gloomy. "Don't get to kick butt in Detroit," he grumbled and took a seat in the back of the small room.

Bergson began by saying, "Now you can see why I demanded that Miller was on my team. Go ahead. Tell Miss Black what you've uncovered. There's no better hacker anywhere."

Still smiling, Miller's soft voice said, "Orders can be traced. We knew that the C-4 came from a company in Iran and was shipped to a company in Detroit. What I wanted to know was just who ordered it and who paid for it. You know, follow the money trail. So while they were looking into the Detroit connection, I went my own way."

She continued, "The order was apparently placed online by some computer at Acme Building Demolitions. However, I noticed that the IP address was goofy, spoofed. So I did some backtracking and database searching and found that original online order. From there with some cool hacking, I found the real IP address of the person who placed the order. It came from Wes Sporting Goods in Rolla, North Dakota, of all places! But that's not all.

"I like money trails. So I hacked into Acme Building Demolitions' bank records. Guess what? Someone deposited the precise amount of the order for the C-4 and then used the funds to pay the Iranian company. Now I was interested. Where did that deposit come from? More hacking. Caymans Islands bank. Well, I won't tell you how I did it, but the funds were deposited in the Caymans from an account in Prague, but someone at Wes Sporting Goods then transferred it to Acme Building Demolitions' bank account. Clever scheme, but they didn't count on Miller being on their trail."

Monica exclaimed, "Wow, Chrissy. That's really good detective work! Dove tails with what I've found out, though mine is really, really weird." Quickly, she explained about the fetish heels and boots, the huge number of full dentures, and the severe grain anomaly.

When she finished, Kelly commented, "Hey, I can appreciate women in the heels that you wear. Sexy and inviting! So the women of Rolla are all looking good!"

"Not if you look at their clothes, hot shot," Monica countered him. "Besides, half the population has false teeth. That can't be sexy."

"Ah, why did you have to burst my bubble?" he teased back.

Annoyed with Kelly's banter, Bergson took charge, "Okay. We have enough anomalies and hard evidence that something connected to the bombings is going on in Rolla. So tomorrow, we are going to pay this town a visit. Miller, figure out a flight plan. I doubt there is any airport that can handle a Stratosphere anywhere near there, so we'll take the Rover from wherever you can land us. Just get us as close as possible. I don't relish driving across vast flat farmlands."

"On it already, boss," she said softly, but resolutely. "Minot is about as close as we can get. We'll take US 2 to US 281 north and then State 5 west to Rolla. It's about a hundred fifty mile drive, unless you want to gamble on back country roads. I'll file the flight plan now before I turn in for the night."

"Excellent. Let's get some sleep. I've called General Franco with our latest findings and he insists that we check out Rolla. Tomorrow should prove to be an interesting day," Bergson declared. He had no idea how prophetic his statement would prove.

Chapter 5—Road Trip to Rolla

"Welcome to the boondocks of nowhere," Kelly grumbled. They'd landed at the airfield in Minot, where the Air Force had built runway extensions capable of handling these giant Stratosphere planes. With their gear stuffed into the Rover, the four headed off overland. "Flat as a pancake," he added, looking out at the seemingly endless fields of grain, waving in the breeze. "Windy Land. If there's a Windy City, this should be Windy Land. America's breadbasket," he added.

Bergson was driving, Miller coordinating with the onboard nav system. He commented, "Hey Kelly, sit back and enjoy the ride. We don't often get to go on such long Rover trips. You know, I read once that a century ago, these cars had some kind of engines that burned some kind of oil or petroleum products and that they'd have to stop every so often and put more of the fuel into the cars. I can't imagine how annoying that must have been to be a driver back then."

Monica smiled. "See, that's one big benefit we wizards and witches have done for the world, given them clean, cheap power for vehicles. We got rid of a lot of pollution as well."

Miller chuckled. "She's got you there, boss."

Feeling particularly jovial, Bergson uncharacteristically replied, "I'll give your kind that one, Miss Black."

Monica returned their smiles, "Hate to correct you, *boss*," emphasizing the word, "but there isn't really your kind and my kind. We're all humans—same species. It's just that some of us have other abilities. We all have different personalities, different skills, different likes and dislikes. I once made a horrible mistake thinking that there really was a fundamental difference between us—that normals were an entirely different species, but I learned my lesson the hard way. Look, Miller has skills I can't begin to duplicate. Kelly knows more about guns and explosives than I'll ever know. We each know things the others don't."

Kelly laughed, "Only what you know is so much more powerful than what we know. You gotta say it like it is, Miss Black. Compared to wizards and witches, we're second class people."

Clearly, he had a substantial bias, Monica noted. "Darn it, Kelly," Monica countered growing a bit annoyed with him, "I once thought like you are doing. But you know, in the final analysis, the only one who can make you be a second class citizen is yourself! Besides, if I truly felt that way, I certainly wouldn't have accepted this job with your team. However, I will admit our team is a bit out gunned by our opponents, assuming there are more demons involved. None of us knew that demons were involved when I joined your team."

"Hey, we should be thankful that she's with us, considering everything," Miller said softly, but pointedly.

"Okay, okay, point taken. Only get me some bullets that'll take these nasty fiends out," Kelly conceded. "Are we there yet? How much longer?"

Miller chuckled. "We've gone ten miles, Kelly. Another hundred forty to go."

"Man, this is going to be a boring trip!" Kelly countered.

Bergson agreed, "Miller, find us some music or something. We're supposed to have Satellite Radio in this thing, though we've never driven the Rover long enough to use it."

Miller turned it on, bewildered by the hundreds of stations to choose from. "Country and Western, Rock, Classical, Jazz, whatever that is?" she asked.

Simultaneously, Bergson and Monica suggested, "Antique Rock." Both burst out laughing. "Good taste in music," Monica teased him.

"I was going to say the same thing about you," he teased her back. The old rock sounds began echoing through the super sound system of the Rover, pleasing everyone. After a time, Bergson got bored driving and Kelly took over. He lasted thirty miles before he gave it up, allowing Miller to take the wheel. Some three hours passed before she finally called out, "Rolla ahead. Keep a sharp eye out for troubles and such." That brought all four back to the present and the tasks at hand.

"Let's get a feel for the town," Bergson ordered. "Drive through slowly. Keep your eyes peeled." A moment later, he added, "Darn, this is a very small town!"

They had driven through the heart of the town, hardly more than a block long. At the main crossroad intersection, a rest station stood, though the building still had some of the ancient gas station artifacts and signs on display. Most of the buildings looked quite old and weather-beaten, though the courthouse appeared to be modern and well kept.

A few cars were parked on the wide streets, and several had more than a few dents in their fenders. Two cars sat parked partway up on the curb. Several men sat on lawn chairs out in front of a few stores, one being the barber and another being the dentist office. While they were observing, two men went into the local grocery store, and one man with two bags came out. In the distance, tall grain elevators towered over the trees. Although early summer, brisk winds swept down the street.

The four got out and three checked their guns. Monica simply stretched and suggested, "I'm all cramped up. What say we go over to the rest station first, and then check out the suspicious businesses?"

"I'm with her. I gotta use their bathroom," Miller said quietly, but flashed a thank you to Monica. She didn't need to make that suggestion. Bergson agreed and the four walked the short distance across the empty street to the rest station, which sold candy, sodas, beer, and snack foods.

Upon entering, they spotted a young man sitting behind the counter. "Bathrooms?" Bergson inquired politely.

"New people. Aren't you? Think so. Maybe. Not see before. Bathroom? You dirty? I'm not dirty. Dirty not good," the man replied and asked.

"We need to use your restrooms," Bergson added, growing slightly annoyed with the young man, though he couldn't quite put his finger on just what bothered him.

"Restrooms. We have restrooms. Nice restrooms. Pretty ones. Candy is pretty, too. You want pretty candy? Candy worked here once. Not now. I work. Clean floors. Feed Candy. Feed birds, too. Like birds. You like birds? Bob no like birds."

"Yes, restrooms. Where are they?" Bergson repeated his question, growing more annoyed.

Miller whispered, "He must be autistic. Go easy on him, boss."

"Can - you - point - to - where - the - restrooms - are - located?" Bergson said slowly, deliberately pausing between each word.

"Back here, boss," Kelly interrupted the exchange. All four headed to the back of the store. "Must be autistic. Probably can't really run the store."

A few minutes later, the four felt refreshed. Monica had also adjusted her makeup and looked presentable. "Anyone want anything?" she asked. "I want a Coke." The others headed for the coffee machine, but she saw the sodas lined up behind the counter and went up to the young man. "I'll take a Coke, please."

"Coke bad. Do coke. Get arrested. Bad coke. Bad lady."

"A soda then. The one with the red can there," she pointed to the cans of Coke.

"Okay. Soda. Have lots soda. Red one. Good one."

"Could I have one, please?" she asked.

"Sure. Good soda. Have soda. Not for baking. Sally said. Not for baking. I no bake. I no worry."

"Can you hand it to me?" she asked, growing even more annoyed. How could this place ever make any sales with this man running the counter? She looked around for anyone else, but only he was present.

"Hand. See. I have hand." Exasperated, Monica turned on her heels and headed back to the others, opting for a coffee instead.

"Don't bother! It tastes beyond awful!" Bergson stopped her from pouring a cup. "Come on; let's get going. This place gives me the creeps!"

The four left the rest station, but the young man kept waving at them and saying, "Bye, bye. Bye, bye."

"Look, the dentist office is on our way. Let's stop there first. I want to find out how come he's ordered nearly six hundred full dentures," Monica suggested.

"Might as well. After that, it's going to be more exciting. That's the clothes store," Bergson barked, still annoyed with the rest station attendant.

The dentist was indeed sitting on a chair in front of his office. He appeared to be in his fifties and wore warm but drab clothing. "Howdy. Windy day. Fine day," he greeted them as they walked up.

"Excuse me," Monica said politely, "we're looking for the dentist."

"Dentist? Me dentist. You don't need teeth. You don't, too," he said pointing to Miller.

"I noticed you ordered six hundred dentures these past few years," Monica struck up a conversation with him, or thought she was.

"Big number. More than two?" he asked, raising ten fingers. "I get mixed up. Women need teeth. Men don't. You woman. Look like woman. Strange. Well, howdy. Windy day. No snow. Snow gone. Snow come again. Later. Just wind. Always windy. Keeps road clean. Don't like to clean. Have to. Gets dirty. Have a seat. Pretty day. You sit. Watch pretty day, too. Me dentist here."

Bergson tugged at her arm, pulling her away from the man and on down the street. He whispered, "One autistic man, okay, but two? Something's not right here. Let's check Kellog's Coats. Looks like Wes Sporting Goods is just a building beyond them on the other side of the street. Ah, and beyond them is the courthouse where the paper came from."

Dutifully, the four entered the coat store. The smell of leather and new jeans struck their nostrils. The left side held shelves of men's pants and shoes, while racks held various kinds of shirts. The right side held women's apparel, all pretty much everyday styles. What caught Monica's eyes were the women's shoes and boots. Here were the very brand of expensive leather fetish heels that she loved to wear. Every one of them had a six-inch spiked heel with an ankle strap, but came in many colors and styles. None were the simple slip on pumps that Monica preferred. Above them were rows of knee-high boots with the same tall heels. These were mostly black suede leather, fleece lined. From her experience, Monica knew all these were very expensive shoes. Very.

Near the rear, a young man sat beside a cash register. He looked up and smiled at them as they entered. "Howdy. New people. Fine clothes. Women. Men." He pointed to the two sides of the store in turn. He added, "I man," confusing all four.

"You have an incredible selection of women's fetish heels," Monica took charge, while Miller went over to look at them, grimacing at their extreme heel heights.

"Huh? Lots heels. Women wear. You like. You have. Choose. Supposed to choose. I told that. Men, too. You pick. Picked corn once. Hard work. Tassels no good. Pull tassels. You pull tassels, too?"

"How much are your heels?" Monica asked, thinking that she might find a bargain here, if nothing else. And what was wrong with this man? Autistic?

"You like. You take."

"No, I mean how much do I pay for them? Do you take charge cards?" she asked.

"Huh? Pay? I like Payday. Good candy. Get rest station. No candy here. No cards. Try courthouse. They, cards. Picture cards. Pretty cards. Pretty women."

"I want to buy a pair of your fine heels. How much do I owe you?" Monica continued to pester the man.

"Oh. You choose. You take. No pay. No owe. You take," the man insisted.

"We're getting nowhere," Bergson whispered to Monica. "Let's move on. This is beyond creepy!"

After they stepped outside, Miller whispered, "I

don't see how women can even walk in them, but you do, so I suppose it's possible. What's with all these men anyway?"

Kelly suggested, "Hey, we're in Rolla Nowhere. What did ya expect? No rocket scientists here. Probably our perps are just using these dopes to carry out their orders. Bet we don't find a single valuable clue here."

"Wes Sporting Goods looks promising. Lots of gear in their window," Bergson suggested as they approached the next store, passing by the beauty parlor, which was deserted. "Remember, this place handled the C-4 purchases. Caution. We don't want to get ourselves blown up!"

He entered first, but Kelly, his hand on his pistol, was right behind him. Monica chose to guard the rear, along with Miller. A minute later, Bergson stuck his head out, "All clear. No one is inside. Come in and have a look." The two women headed inside as well. "Look at the sign on the counter there by the register."

Monica read: Help yourself. Gone fishing. Love fish. Back sometime. Wes.

"I checked the cash register. It's completely empty," Bergson declared.

Miller poked around and added, "Their charge card swipe machine isn't working either. They must not have much business around here. Gang, what the heck is wrong with this town? What have we stumbled into?"

"Dunno, but let's try the courthouse. That's the only 'official' building we've seen. Besides, the perps wrote the notes on their watermarked paper," Bergson ordered.

As they four paused before its door, they glanced in all directions. The same men still sat on their chairs. Another man was just leaving the grocery store, a bag in his hand. Two other men were trying to open a car's door, but were having a very hard time with that, even though it was an old convertible!

Shaking his head, Bergson opened the door, and they went inside the nicest looking building in Rolla. Off to one side, a sign read: Courtroom. Another sign pointed towards the basement steps and read: Clerk and Records. A third sign pointed to their right and read: Mayor. Bergson headed to the right, bound and determined to get some straight answers. This was beyond unbelievable!

The office, as you might expect, was quite plush. Four guest chairs were top-quality leather and the carpeting, a dark maroon and thick. A large desk sat towards the rear; a bespectacled man in his thirties sat behind it. He was perhaps six feet tall and wore a western style suit of brown swede. His hair was black and nicely oiled. He looked pleasant enough.

"Welcome to Rolla. We've been expecting you. I'm Mayor Sam Westerbrock, but my friends call me Sammy. You should, too. Please have a seat. It's not often we have such distinguished guests as yourselves. Oh, I'm forgetting my duties. I'm also the sheriff of Rolla. Can you show me your badges, please? Must keep up formalities, mustn't we?"

Bergson flashed his badge, as did the others and each sat down on one of the very expensive chairs. "Now we can forget all the formalities around here. Just call me Sammy. What can I do for you law enforcement folks from the big cities?"

"Well, for starters, where are all your people? We've seen some of the store owners. Does Rolla have an outbreak of autism? And where are all the women? We expected to see some in the apparel store," Bergson began, avoiding outright asking about the perp situation.

"Oh, the women are in their homes. Most of the men are there looking after their women folk, as is our custom here in Rolla. Now Bobby down at the rest station, he doesn't have a woman in his life, not yet anyway, so he minds the rest station. Harry's wife died some years back, so our dentist often sits outside his office, that is, until someone needs his help." Sammy continued to droll on.

Monica sensed something wasn't right the instant she entered the mayor's office. Hence, she kept all her senses wide open, eyes darting around the room. She smelled something in the air, and it wasn't the mayor's hair. It smelled a bit repugnant, but she couldn't put her finger on it. Finally, she silently cast her See True spell and inhaled sharply.

"It's a trap! He's a demon in disguise!" she yelled, rising to her feet and casting a Dispel Magic spell at "Sammy." Instantly, the demon's illusion vanished. The four saw a black-skinned demon, whose form was mostly human, but with a very angular head. His hair came down his forehead forming a sharp point, V-shaped. His canines were overly large and his grin, wicked. Monica yelled, "Cambion demon!" Then the room went utterly black!

Curses flew from Bergson, Kelly, and Miller. Kelly even got off three rounds, firing in the general direction where the mayor had last been seen behind his desk. Sammy's voice now came from behind them. "Tsk, tsk. You'll soon fall unconscious. But don't worry; you'll be well taken care of. We've plenty of fine homes here in Rolla for you. Please don't put more holes in my fine furniture. Besides, your puny guns can't possibly harm me."

Thump. Monica heard someone falling onto the floor, guessing it was Miller. "One down. See you when you wake up," Sammy added. Thump. Thump. These were much heavier noises, and Monica knew Bergson and Kelly were down. She tried to teleport away, but for some reason her mind stopped working. Then, she realized she too had fallen unconscious! However, she could still hear voices, at least for a short while.

"Take them to the preparation room. In four days, you can measure them and get the necessary things from the stores. Oh, and find them a vacant home. They'll be our guests for a long time. See, Rolla's population is growing again." She decided that must be Sammy talking. Then, all went black.

Chapter 6—The Dragon Hole

Nine years ago just after the massive downfall of Prince Graz'zt of the Abyss and his Grand Plan to take over total control of the Earth, the few demon survivors still on Earth met in secret. Moving on was precisely what General Franco Porti, the powerful Cambion demon leader, suggested to the small group. He was tall, very well-muscled, a powerful fighter, a deadly assassin, but just a mediocre magic user. His skin was a dark gray and his black hair, wiry and quite pointed in the front, formed a V over his brow and between his horns. Until now, only Prince Graz'zt held more power than this marquis, his top general. With Franco were the three succubi, namely Gisella Harmoni, Bella Zaronetti, and Donatella Ratini. Each had stunningly beautiful human features, if one ignored their large bat-like wings and horns. Nowhere near as powerful as the general, they were clever and cunning, but their kisses could kill. They had been in charge of the Prince's outposts on Earth, before the fall. Of the three, Gisella held the most power. All four of them used Morph spells to appear human.

With them was a human clone, the lone remaining Dr. Menninger. He was rather thin and only five-eight with brown hair and strange, oval glasses that would have been popular in say 1940. But back then, his original body had been a key SS doctor, performing deadly experiments on captives. Miraculously, he'd been whisked off to the Abyss and over the years, cloned many times by Prince Graz'zt. His comment spoke volumes to the small group of survivors here on Earth. "What the heck am I to do now? It's all been destroyed—millennia worth of work—gone—destroyed. Those painstakingly accumulated DNA samples—my work—gone!"

Discussing their situation, they knew they couldn't go back to the defeated Prince Graz'zt. He'd likely execute them. Further, they couldn't join up with the victorious demon lords. They'd never be accepted or trusted and would likely find themselves spending the rest of their lives in the backwaters of the Abyss.

"So what do we do?" Donatella asked.

Gisella took charge, pointing out just how Prince Graz'zt have been doomed to failure for many reasons. His notions of Earth were over two thousand years old, antiquated; he didn't listen to the reports from his agents, the succubuses; he completely misjudged the current Earth technology and weaponry, sending in his Cambion soldiers to fight with swords instead of guns, tanks, artillery, guided missiles, and drones. The only aspect that had not changed in the millennia since the Prince was on Earth were the magic spells. Gisella declared, "We should have been acquiring their weapons for our own use, not kidnaping young normal women. Our defeated prince failed to know what the enemy leaders were planning, and we ourselves paid dearly for that mistake."

General Franco spoke up, "She's right. We should have known about those things. If we had, we could have taken countermeasures and avoided the disasters."

"Talk, talk, talk," growled Donatella. "Piss over the pond. Dung in the field. So what? Hindsight is perfect. Everyone knows that. So what? Where does that get us now?"

Gisella grinned evilly, "Everywhere. We know what should have been done. What's to prevent us from starting over and doing it properly? Eh? Nothing at all. We're here. We're powerful. Why can't we take over this world? Yes, us. We won't make the same stupid mistakes the prince did. We shall arm our soldiers with modern weapons. We will have top intelligence and so know what they are planning even as they make their plans. They won't make any move that we don't know about ahead of time."

"Yes, yes, yes. Sounds good but you're leaving out the *how*, Gisella. Just how do you propose that we do all this?" Bella barked sarcastically.

Gisella laughed and cut her down, "When you get as old as I am, Bella, you will have finally gotten some intelligence. We already possess what's needed to do all that, only we've not been able to use our skills, our powers. We figure out just who the key people actually are—say here in this country. We swap them out with some of us; we use our own Morph spells to become them and take their roles in the running of the country. We steal the weapons we need or even better get one of us Morphed into one of their leaders and have them to send them to us—so simple a child could have thought of it."

"Oh I like it, Gisella!" Donatella spoke up, growing excited about the possibilities. "Instead of chasing around after pathetic human females, we can *become* their rulers and *dictate* what we want them to do! Oh I do like it!"

Dr. Menninger spoke up, "All well and good, but what am I supposed to do in all this?"

"Anything your little heart desires," Gisella replied. "Collect more DNA samples. Work on new experimental tortures that can't be undone. Hell, I don't know. Put your brain to work on that one. Sky's the limit, doctor. Incinerate that Monica woman's legs; turn her into a head and torso for all I care. We need to get into their electronic age. They do everything via electronics: cell phones that surf their Internet, take photos, make purchases, organize their days—shoot, these humans do everything with those tiny devices. Be inventive, doctor."

She went on, "We know what to expect from the wizards and witches and know how to combat that. It's the normal human's technology that we need to learn, steal, and use to bring this world to our knees."

Dr. Menninger spoke up, "Okay then, I must have a new, modern laboratory. You need me to invent a way to keep the men and women as restrained captives so you can replace them. These humans have made some startling advances in genetics. They've sequenced the whole genetic makeup of humans. This may well open some vast new doors for us. My researches must be done before you can get on with your plans. Thus, my needs must come first," he declared. "I noticed that they have an advanced college of medicine in the small town that we visited, Peoria. I should be able to fit my facilities in there nicely and not attract undo attention to us. So get me set up, and I'll soon have answers and solutions for you." He laughed wickedly.

Armed with his own covert research knowledge and back on his home world, Earth would once more learn of the genius that was Dr. Menninger. Gisella didn't like this insane man, but then perhaps, he might yet be useful. Besides, he was their most powerful wizard at the moment, since Benedetta departed.

Bella complained, "The only flaw in your plan, Gisella, is that some of these top leaders are wizards and witches. How can we hope to impersonate them? They know zillions of spells that we don't! I think we need a different plan."

"Hey, I never said this was going to be easy, Bella. Lots of them are just normal humans. We have to be picky about just whom we replace. Unless you have a better idea," Gisella tossed it back into Bella's lap, knowing full well that she didn't have an alternative.

"I can take over the Secretary of Defense or maybe the head of the Joint Chiefs of Staff," General Franco Porti suggested. "Funnel some good new weapons our way and figure out how they were able to find our facilities."

Dr. Menninger agreed with the general, pleasing the man, but he needed a bit more time to incorporate all these modern genetic methods into his own discoveries. He'd perfected his own non-magical methods for making clones and felt confident that at long last he would be able to create the promised race of super-men, among many other alterations of which his diabolical mind had long conceived.

However, he had one remaining problem that simply had to be solved: the demons. Unpredictable and chaotic, the demons seldom stuck to the "plan" at hand. Prince Graz'zt had been the exception to the rule. He was the man in power, driven by his own personal goals, sticking steadfastly to them for at least two centuries as far as Dr. Menninger knew. Yet, his minions seldom followed his orders, at least not completely. Turn a demon loose on this world and it would soon forget its original mission, following its own notions of what ought to be done. This, Dr. Menninger believed, had led to the total failure of the Prince's Grand Plan and would likely interfere with his own new plans as well. He had to find a solution before he went much farther. Gisella was being very thoughtful and quite reasonable at the moment, but he knew that wouldn't last for long. He'd need his own backup plan.

***

"Welcome to the Dragon Hole," Sammy said some nine years after Gisella's planning meeting. "You four are finally awake from your genetic modification comas, compliments of the good Dr. Menninger here. Doctor, they are yours. I better get back to Rolla. Bye." He vanished.

Monica struggled to get her eyes opened, but everything was utterly black. She tried to rub her eyes, but found her lower arms and hands were somehow missing. She tried to call out, but no sounds came from her mouth. Then, she noticed that her teeth were missing. Slowly, fear seeped into her very being, particularly when the doctor began speaking, for she recognized his voice.

"Welcome to our new Paradise Fortress in the Abyss—well technically it is just barely in the Abyss. We finally meet again, Miss Monica Nicole Black. Unlike last time, I am fully prepared for you. Don't worry, your three friends are right here with you. I should explain the situation, though I'm afraid the two men will not understand anything I'm going to say.

"I should start at the beginning, I suppose. You see, some years ago, we discovered the ancient Dragon Hole, a portal to the Abyss built by Babylonian priests at the height of their power and influence in the ancient world. Although you will not be able to see it any longer, we have restored it to its once incredible beauty. The oasis pool otherwise known as the Dragon Hole is the permanent portal to Paradise Fortress.

"Being the genius that I am, I've perfected a number of simply incredible genetic biological agents that completely alter human genetic makeup and their bodies. One of these causes a body to age prematurely. A sixteen year old man wakes up in a few days to find that his body is now eighty years old—a wonderful way to eliminate potential human opponents. I really don't like to just kill them, unlike the demons that I'm forced to work with.

"But we need human workers. Hence, Agent One, administered to your two male companions here. It does not age them. No, it simply destroys brain cells, reducing their IQ levels to around 50 at most. You met a number of such men in Rolla. In fact, all the men in Rolla have been so treated, though an IQ of 50 might be a bit generous. It's tough to measure humans with such low IQs. They are still functional men, capable of following orders, more or less."

He went on, "Now I could have applied that Agent One to you women, but I didn't. Women bring forth new life, you see. So we can't have moronic women—not safe for their children. Instead, I developed Agent Two for you women. Since you can't see, Monica, I'll tell you what Agent Two does to female genetic structure, which after a few days' time in a coma, forces the human body to conform to the new genetic makeup.

"First, lower arms and hands fall off. This will prevent women from making any kind of trouble for the moronic men who look after them. Second, your bodies no longer have voice boxes. Women don't need to speak, just perform their wifely duties. Third, to do that and create new life, you will find you now have powerful sexual urges that must be satisfied. We encourage women to have many babies. Of course, their daughters will be like they are, just as their sons will be like their male donors. Fourth, women have no teeth. We don't want them using their teeth to bite or harm their donor men. Don't worry; you'll soon be provided with a fine set of dentures.

"So you see, you women still retain your full intelligence, but you're physically helpless and utterly dependent upon your male companions to survive, which is as God intended the Ideal Woman to be, not like Eve who brought the downfall of man. Fifth, we don't want you women running away or fleeing your moronic men, so your legs and feet have been slightly genetically altered as well.

You can no longer place your feet flat on the floor. If you do, you will tear up your leg muscles. Women now must wear the exotic fetish six-inch heels. We've seen that the men do enjoy seeing you wearing them so that helps breeding as well.

"Sixth, I've observed that modern women are enamored of longer hair, much like I'm told it was millennia ago, so you will find that yours grows substantially faster than normal. Plus, so many women are getting breast enhancements. I don't believe that is a healthy way to go, so seventh, I've used genetics to naturally enhance your breasts. However, Monica Nicole, we know that you enjoy them on the very large size, so I enlarged yours even more than your blonde friend here. I do so hope that you enjoy them to their fullest.

"However, Monica Nicole, I also know you are one powerful spell caster. So I removed your eye balls, replacing them with rather fine looking glass eyes that match your former eyes. Now that you can't see or speak or use your hands, you won't be able to cast spells. In these new heels, you can't move fast and thereby cause your moronic men trouble.

"Although you can't see them, let me assure you that they both are standing here completely confused by all this talk. I'm sure they haven't understood any of this. Instead, my assistant will take them aside and instruct them in very simple words. They will be your caretakers and your male donors. Don't complain about their cooking. Most men aren't chefs. As soon as they get trained, they will put your new dentures in for you and put your new heels on your feet. We use ankle strap styles so you can't accidentally take them off and be unable to walk. So just sit there and be patient until your men are ready to help you. Yes, take the men away now, please.

"Where was I? Oh yes. For a couple of days, you will remain here in the Paradise Fortress so that we can make sure your men have learned to care for your needs. After they satisfy us that they can, you will be taken back to Rolla and given a new home in which to live out the rest of your long lives and raise large families for us. For that, I do thank you both. That is all. Please remain seated until your men return. I must be off now. I've so many things to attend to these days. My plan is working to perfection, but the pace will now be quite rapid indeed. Much work to be done. Perhaps, I will drop by Rolla later on and tell you about my many successes, Monica Nicole. Goodbye for now." She heard footsteps departing, then utter silence.

For a minute, Monica fought hard to control her nervous stomach, which threatened to knot into a tight ball. Breathing in and out, she finally calmed down enough to cast spells. Blinded—she had to be able to see, so she cast See Through Another's Eyes. The utter blackness instantly gave way to a brilliantly lit room, as seen by Chrissy. Chrissy's vision was slightly blurred. Then, Monica realized why. She was sobbing silently. Nevertheless, she took what she could. There wasn't anyone else around to use just now.

They were sitting on nice chairs, rather similar to those in the mayor's office. However, the smell of the room was awful, akin to a dead, rotting rat. Well, this was the Abyss, or so Dr. Menninger claimed. Chrissy sat at an angle and could see Monica, who now got a good look at herself. All that the mad doctor had told her seemed to be true. Her raven hair seemed much longer now, but until she stood up, she couldn't be certain of that. Chrissy's hair was noticeably longer, probably falling to her lower back, Monica estimated. *Well, Chrissy's bosom is now as large as mine used to be so she might like that tiny change. But my goodness, what did he do to mine? They are twice the size of my head! Hell, my back is aching already. They are too big and way, way too heavy! Oh darn! We're both totally naked!*

After staring at herself for a few minutes, Monica desperately wanted to examine the room, but she had no way to tell Chrissy to focus her eyes on the room. The poor woman was emotionally too far gone to even try sending her a Message, assuming a normal could even be the recipient of a Message spell. Monica had never tried sending one to a normal. All she could really do just now was to wait for the men to return. Besides, she was starving and dehydrated, in desperate need of a drink.

Eventually, the men returned, carrying bags. Bergson came up to Monica, while Kelly stood in front of Miller. Bergson said, "Monica mine. Monica beautiful. Monica dress. Oh teeth. So pretty. Fine teeth." He retrieved the new dentures out of the bag first, staring at them. "So pretty." In an effort to try to get him on track, Monica opened her mouth as wide as she could. "Oh. Teeth. Me have teeth. Put in. Now." Clumsily, Bergson managed to get them into her mouth, but not before trying to put the upper plate on her lower gums. "Not right," he grumbled before he finally figured out this one was the upper plate.

That done, he seemed very pleased with himself. "Good job." He pulled out a pair of heels next and struggled, trying to figure out how to put them on her feet. The ankle strap gave him a good deal of trouble, frustrating him, and he muttered nonsense to himself all the while. After yet another annoying round, he got her into a loose fitting dress, but had enormous difficulty getting it on her. Monica also felt frustrated because she couldn't talk to tell him how to do it or even help him with it. She nearly panicked before he got it zipped up, but realized that with practice, he would improve. At least she hoped so.

Nearby, Kelly was having just as many problems handling Miller as Bergson was, but he finally managed to get her dressed and ready to go. A pleasant looking man entered and told the men, "Help woman up. Hold her. Walk to your room."

Bergson struggled with this simple task. As Monica stood, her hair slipped down to nearly her ankles. However, she felt perfectly at ease in the heels, wholly unlike Chrissy, who teetered and wobbled, frantically moving her arms about, trying in vain to hold onto Kelly, who seemed oblivious to her panic. The man repeated his orders and Kelly finally did put a steadying arm around Miller. As they began walking, the world went utterly black for Monica. Her spell expired. Hastily, she recast it and began looking through Bergson's eyes. Now she had much better vision, un-blurred by tears.

Ah, she noted, the floor was wavering in colors, grays, browns, and blacks, typical of the Abyss. Leaving the waiting room, the rotten stench grew stronger. While Chrissy noticed it, the men seemed oblivious to the foul odor, though eventually Kelly said, "Smell bad."

They arrived in what appeared to be a small kitchen with attached dining room. Someone had brought Earth appliances here along with Earth food and water. Monica realized why. The men had to fix the meals and thus had to have facilities with which they were familiar. Even so, after helping the women drink a glass of water, the two men had a terrible time trying to prepare a meal. If the circumstances were different, Monica would have roared with laughter at their comic attempts to make bacon, eggs, and pancakes. Ordinarily, she expected that both could have fixed the meal without much trouble, but with their dismal IQs, every action seemed utterly confusing. Plus, they constantly got distracted, often admiring some new thing in the kitchen. At least the Abyss man stuck around and kept getting them back on track. If he hadn't, the food would have been inedible.

Another whole new arena of difficulties soon arouse for the two women: trying to eat for the first time with dentures. Frustrations mounted not only with the women struggling to get by, but also with the men, who simply couldn't figure out what needed to be done or how, ignoring the fact that they constantly got distracted by what the women saw as utter trivia.

Finally thirst quenched and stomach full, Monica began to relax and think about what she could to do get them away from here and back to the safety of her own home, where she hoped and prayed her friends could help find cures for the four. It didn't help that her See Through Another's Eyes spell was short lived, often plunging her into utter blackness at most inopportune times. Her mind wandered.

Genetic mutations. *What did Dr. Menninger mean*

by this? I've tried Dispel Magic, but nothing happened. When I'm alone, I'll try a Morph spell, but that's not going to help me see. If he did all this to us via genetic mutations and not spells, will we even be able to undo it or cure it? Will my Regeneration spell work on us now? Oh no!

Suddenly, she began wiggling about. I'm getting horny! Chrissy is as well. Wait a second!

What will the men do? I really don't want to have sex, and Chrissy doesn't either. Will this brain alteration of Dr. Menninger's also affect their moral judgments? I know both men wouldn't normally bed us, but will that be wiped out, too? Will they have no social inhibitions? Will their entire personalities be altered? If it's the last thing I do, I'm going to eliminate the Dr. Menninger clone!

Now this is hilarious! Monica, via Chrissy, saw one grand comedy of goofs by the two men, who were making a complete disaster out of washing the few dishes in the sink! If someone could video them doing this and post it on the web, the video would go viral in no time.

By the time the men got them to their temporary bedrooms, again filled with beds brought here from Earth, and had the women undressed and their dentures out, both were so exhausted that they fell onto the beds asleep at once. However, both women were now desperate for sexual relief. Something fundamental in their bodies had definitely been altered, of that Monica and Chrissy were convinced. Neither had ever felt this frantic for any kind of sexual relief before, but the men were sound asleep.

Chrissy was so desperate that she got up on her own. Wiggling her upper arms for balance, she walked on her toes into Monica's bedroom, not knowing what else to do to suppress this almost overwhelming urge. She sat beside Monica who had already gotten herself into a sitting position and hesitantly tried to kiss her. Their lips met, but without teeth, their lips pushed back inside their mouths, surprising both women. Soon, they worked out ways and means. An hour later, they, too, were sleeping soundly.

The next morning, the comedy of errors continued, providing humor for the two women. However, after they were dressed and fed, the same man returned. "Okay. Men. Time to go home." He issued other simple commands, and soon both men kept an arm around their "woman," as they followed the man through the Abyss fortress. Monica did her best to "see" what she could, in case she needed to return here.

In the center of the courtyard of the complex was what appeared to be the bottom of a watery pool. The viewpoint was totally disorienting. They looked up at the underside of the pool, though they themselves were not in the water. Sunbeams filtered down through the water, and the two men gawked and stared, constantly saying how pretty it was. The man explained primarily for the women, "You will now be taken up the Dragon Hole, a portal back to your world. There, a wizard will teleport you to your new home in Rolla." Instinctively, Monica nodded that she understood. Chrissy just began crying again.

"Tripping. I tripping," declared Bergson, as his body moved through the magical space of the Gate from the Abyss fortress up the Dragon Hole and out into the small, restored, and quite beautiful oasis. Kelly made similar comments. Again, Monica had to recast her spell and paid close attention to the details of the oasis, hoping that would be enough to allow her to return here later and somehow destroy it. While the two men tried to grasp where they were, Monica saw three dozen demon fighters, Cambions, also arriving nearby. The fighters teleported away, before a new man appeared. He didn't say much, except to get the men to hold onto their woman's arm and then his hand. Confusion reigned. They were now in Rolla in the mayor's office! Both men nearly fell down, wholly unable to grasp what was happening to them.

"Ah back at last," declared Mayor Sammy. "This way. We have a fine new home for you four. Slowly. Walk slowly, fellows. That's it. Yes, it is windy. Pretty day." He chatted mostly for the benefit of the two men, keeping them on track. If he hadn't, they would have stopped innumerable times to admire this and that along the way. For that, both women were grateful.

Their house was an old one, but it had been refurbished recently. It had two adjacent bedrooms, a living room with a big screen and nice sound system, a small kitchen and dining room. At least it had a bathtub. Monica sensed how much Chrissy appreciated seeing it as they passed by the bathroom. Once there, Sammy ordered the men to get groceries and get more clothing and shoes for the women. He wrote down the two orders using two words each and gave the papers to the men. They seemed to understand, at least Monica hoped so. The men left to run the errands, and the women remained sitting on the couch watching the news channel, probably a tease by Sammy.

Soon, Monica saw that they'd been gone for a week. The White House had been bombed during this past week; President Billy Bob had declared war on Iran, but that country probably had nothing to do with the bombing. Hearing Billy Bob making his announcement, Monica gasped silently, her face taut. He was talking just as the men did here in Rolla. Somehow the President of the United States had been genetically modified into a super low IQ man.

As she watched more of the news, she calmed down. Surely, she thought, the Congress will veto his war plans. A bit later, she began hearing congressmen talking, which dashed all such hopes. They were now morons. Much had happened during the past week, none good. Then, she realized why. Bergson's boss was General Franco Porti, the Cambion general. Her screeching curse would have been heard all around Rolla had she a voice. Chrissy, too, suddenly recognized the general was actually a demon, and she tried to scream in recognition of that very fact. Her face twisted and her mouth opened wide.

The men did not return for many hours. Monica suspected they had gotten distracted many, many times while running the two errands. For groceries, they brought back coffee, donuts, and boxes of macaroni and cheese, hardly a suitable diet. At least Kelly had also brought along two pizzas, though they were frozen and had to be cooked in the oven, assuming the men could figure out how to do that. Looking at the very haggard men, Monica realized they were incredibly frustrated—dealing poorly with their new situation, and it was just noon. Trying to handle life with such low mental skills might well drive both men insane, if they weren't there already. She knew she needed to act and soon. But how? Where to take everyone?

She decided to answer the second question first. While she'd prefer to go to Bradbury's School of Magic simply because if anyone could help her and the others it was them, she decided against that because three were normals. She needed to ask Lindsey about this first. Hence, the destination had to be her own home on the very northern edge of St. Louis. The how was simple in theory, a Teleport spell. The complication was how to manage it. She needed a firm grasp of all three, but without hands, she and Chrissy couldn't do that. It had to be the men who did all the holding, but there wasn't any way to really get them to understand what she needed from them. If they let go— well she'd rather not think of that disaster.

I need another way, she thought. Then, she remembered their Rover and a new idea formed. *Can I use my PSI skills? I know I can 'walk' them back home, but can I actually 'drive' the Rover there with my PSI powers? Hell, if I can't, then I can just drive us back to Minot somehow*. Utter darkness returned, scaring her once more. Again, she cast her spell and continued looking through Chrissy's eyes. Both men sat on chairs, leaning over, their heads in their hands, beyond depressed.

Monica acted. She cast a Morph Self spell, turning herself into what she looked like last week. Now she had arms once more, at least as long as the spell lasted, but she continued to need to "see" via the others. Chrissy looked shocked, but accepted her hand with her upper arm stump and rose. Monica then gently touched and roused the two men, who looked shocked to see that she had arms again. Although she couldn't speak, by pulling on their arms, she got them up. After a bit more physical handling, she had Bergson's arm around her waist and Kelly's around

Chrissy's. Out the front door they went.

"Walk? Beautiful day. Windy. Fine day," Bergson began his moronic chatting and Kelly added his own as well. Gritting her non-existent teeth, Monica moved them on down the street, hoping their Rover was still parked where they'd left it. In a flash, she realized that no one living in Rolla could actually drive a car. No wonder they had dents in their sides and were parked askew here and there. Walking was challenging for Chrissy, who'd never worn heels above an inch before, so Monica took it slow and easy, constantly holding the men back. They wanted to "move out," an impossibility for the two women.

Her heart skipped a beat. The Rover was right where they left it. Minutes later, the men opened the doors, admiring the wonderful machine, but they had no idea what it was or how to drive it. Either that knowledge was gone from their minds or perhaps their brains could no longer translate their thoughts into proper actions. She hoped it was the latter. She took the driver's seat. Fortunately, like all modern cars and vehicles, a key wasn't needed, only the presence of the electronic lock in the vicinity of the car. She pressed Start and the magical engine came to life. Without any hesitation, she drove off down the street,

She got the Rover turned around and headed back the way they had come. Then the utter blackness returned. Frantically, she recast her spell, just in time as she nearly drove off the road. Her heart finally stopped pounding. *Look I can't keep this up. It took us hours to get here from Minot. Next time the spell drops, I might crash us. I have to do something soon.*

Well rested, Monica's mental powers that her deceased husband Rob had helped her develop were at their peak. Pretending that she was walking, she began Shadow Walking, pulling the car and everyone with her. The world shifted and blurred, then slowly began clearing as she saw her own long driveway ahead. She slowed down and entered their circular drive by their main entrance. Their store sign was very visible: PIWIP—Protections,

Investigations, Wands, Items, Potions—your one-stop magic store. She stopped the car just as total blackness reappeared. She didn't see Chrissy blinking madly and rubbing her eyes with her two short stumps. The men were completely confused, and soon began talking about the "pretty flowers." Instead, she sent a Help Message to Crystal and Ericka, then silently sighed and waited, wondering how she could communicate all that she needed to tell them.

Chapter 7—Genetics Versus Magic

"Now we're being effective," Monica typed on her laptop, while Ericka and Crystal looked on, particularly Ericka from whose eyes Monica was now viewing. They had worked out a way to communicate. Crystal cast a Morph spell on Monica, turning her into a Crystal look-alike, while Monica continued to cast See Through Another's Eyes. With the new arms of the Crystal morph, she could type. Monica's fingers flew over the keyboard, outlining what had happened to them.

They finished some ten re-castings later. Using this unorthodox method, Monica related every detail, outlining in detail precisely what the Dr. Menninger clone had told her about his genetic modifications to the men and women. Monica could only wait and see what her dearest friends could do, though Crystal assured Monica and Chrissy that everyone at PIWIP was working flat out on cures.

Already, Monica had cast her Regeneration spell on herself. According to Ericka, who removed Monica's glass eye balls, something was happening. If the spell worked, her new eyes would regenerate and thus needed that space in which to re-grow. Although Chrissy's vision was perfect, in her almost helpless state, she was terrified and refused to be separated from Monica.

Rather, the men posed the greatest problem for everyone at the estate. In their near moronic state, they had to be constantly watched and given specific orders or they'd wander off looking at flowers or test tubes or wands. Thanks to Crystal's clever use of the Morph spell, Monica's friends knew what was wrong with the men, but they continued to closely watch the two men.

At this point in time besides Monica and her son, four couples lived at the mansion complex. The shy, short brown haired Enya Homes-Scorsky and her husband, Brad Scorsky, were very competent potion makers. The blonde, conservative Misty Worth-Williams and her husband,

Jasper Williams, made and sold magic wands, now a lucrative business, providing a goodly number each year to the new students at the St. Louis School of Magic. Long black haired Crystal Holliday-Mac Pheerson and her husband, Gregor Mac Pheerson, specialized in arcane knowledge, focusing on demons. The long blonde haired Ericka Van Nie-Green and her husband, Tyler Green, made magical items of all kinds. All the others who had lived here nine years ago had either died in the bombing along with Monica's husband Rob or had moved away, taking advantage of new and lucrative positions elsewhere.

When the group finally fully understood what had happened to the four, Misty and Jasper volunteered to look after all the children. "Look," Misty explained, "we are wand makers and realistically haven't anything that we can offer in the way of cures. At least if we're manning the stores and watching the kids, you six are all free to help cure them."

As usual, Crystal took charge. "Excellent. Enya and Brad—you look into every conceivable potion possibility. Meanwhile, Ericka, Tyler, Gregor, and I will investigate every possible magical spell. Let's get cracking before the world goes down that Dragon Hole! We'll meet after suppers to go over anything we've discovered."

By the end of the first full day of research, glum faces told all. "Doesn't seem to be any potion anywhere that would help," Brad pointed out.

"Nor spell," Ericka added in a depressed tone. "But we'll keep at it."

By the fourth day, Monica's eyes had developed sufficiently that she could partially see out of them, giving her some hope for the future. The others began to lose all hope. That's when Enya and Brad suggested that they take a blood sample from all four to study. Enya hinted, "It would help if we had lab equipment to do a full gene study."

Monica sent her a Message to buy what she needed using Monica's bank account. At great expense, she did just that, paying top dollar for immediate delivery and setup aid. Using the new equipment, she and Brad dove into their studies of Monica's altered DNA as well as Bergson's.

Meanwhile, Crystal insisted the men get complete medical checkups. It took all four of them to get the two moronic men through that trip to St. Anne's! Not only did the men not grasp what was wanted, they continually got distracted by what they saw. Later that day, the doctors outlined their findings. One doctor explained, "Whatever Dr. Menninger did to their DNA, the result is simple. Their brains are now well over a hundred years old. Ninety percent of their "gray matter" has atrophied, which causes this massive disconnection between what they think in their minds and their brains' signals to their physical bodies. It is almost as though they are suffering from advanced dementia. They must find this terribly depressing. Be alert for suicides."

This, everyone found sobering, but at least they had some clues with which to work. The real breakthrough came when Enya made a startling discovery in her lab. She was studying Monica's new DNA via her blood sample when she noticed that parts of the genetic strands carried traces of magical energies. The new equipment allowed her to see these tiny effects. Emboldened, she began casting Dispel Magic spells on the sample and had Brad come and cast some as well. After each cast, she re-examined the sample. Sometimes their spells did nothing at all, but other times, part of the magically altered DNA strands changed. "We've got to tell Monica what we've found!" Enya declared, rushing off to do just that.

Enya explained, "So if we can dispel all the magical DNA changes Dr. Menninger made to your DNA, then perhaps your Regeneration spell will finally work. It's worth a shot, don't you think?" Monica nodded vigorously.

Crystal, Ericka, Enya, Brad, and Monica began casting Dispel Magic spells on her, one after the other. Not only did they not know just how many actual spells Dr. Menninger had used to make his genetic alterations, but there was no easy way to tell if one particular spell worked or not. To be on the safe side, they cast fifty such spells before Enya took another blood sample. This time, she just needed a pin-prick to analyze the results. Ten anxious minutes passed before she got the sample examined with the new equipment.

"We did it. Monica, you have no more traces of magical energy in your DNA. Try your Regeneration spell now," Enya announced, keeping her fingers crossed. After all, she wasn't an Archmage, merely a very competent potion maker, which was where her interests lay.

Silent Monica cast her power spell on herself. While the others began discussing just how Dr. Menninger had done what he'd done, Monica began to feel sleepy. She was sitting in a chair, thankfully. Noticing Monica's body slumped in the chair, Enya spoke up, "Hey, she's unconscious! Something must be happening. She's in a coma. That's good, isn't it?" she asked, growing worried that perhaps they'd only made things worse for Monica.

Crystal took charge. "We best get her to St. Anne's. Let the doctors monitor her. If her body is regenerating all those things, she might need special care. I'll take her. You go tell Chrissy what's happening and even start working on her as well."

Monica's mind drifted. For a time, she believed that she was once more Shadow Walking on another plain. *Is Rob here? Can I find him? No, he's dead*, she reminded herself. Still, the gray plain refused to vanish. *Am I lost now? Without Rob, I'm lost. Am I lost out here? Which way is back?* Monica began to panic.

Just then, she felt the contact of Rob's mind. *Mom, this way. You're slipping away. Your body is regenerating and is in a coma. You shouldn't be leaving it like this. Come on. I'll show you the way back.*

Rob! Is this really you? I thought you were dead.

My body was, but you provided me with a new one. Why do you think you named him Rob, eh? My doing, mom. This way. See, there's your body. Now stick around it please. Cya when you wake up. Rob's presence vanished, leaving Monica speechless. Her Rob was her son.

Six days later, Monica came out of her coma. "Oh,

I'm thirsty. Starving, too. Oh! I can speak again. Oh, arms, hands. It worked!"

A nurse helped her sit up and allowed her to sip water. "If that stays down, I'll bring you some solid food. Your friends are waiting to see you now. Just don't overdo it."

A tearful reunion followed, with Monica thanking them repeatedly. Then, Crystal brought Chrissy in to see her. Chrissy's eyes opened wide when she saw Monica looked completely whole again.

"I'll cast my spell on you now, Chrissy. When you wake up, you should be whole again, too," Monica declared. "It's so wonderful to be able to speak again. You don't know how much I depend on talking."

"Yes we do!" Ericka teased her. Everyone chuckled. Before long, the doctors took Chrissy to another room, just before she slipped into her recovery coma.

"Well, now we have a way to rescue all the women Dr. Menninger has altered," Monica declared. "We just have to get to them. So how about the men? Any breakthroughs with them?" Sad faces told all.

Once released from St. Anne's the following day, Monica decided to experiment on Bergson. After all, it couldn't be any worse for him. Based on the doctors' analysis, she chose to cast her Rejuvenate spell, hoping that by restoring his brain cells, he would recover. By the next day, Bergson was feeling better, but that was about all. His responses were still just as goofy as Kelly's.

"Conference time," Monica ordered, and gathered all her friends together to discuss the situation with the two men. Once more, they went over everything they had discovered.

Crystal suggested, "You know, we should take Bergson back for another medical scan and see if your spell really did alter his brain cells. If it didn't, then we know this approach isn't going to work."

Lacking any other plausible idea, Monica did just that. She was just as frustrated with Bergson's antics as the others had been. "No. Keep walking," she insisted a hundred times on the way there. He kept getting totally distracted by nearly everything he saw, particularly so once they entered St. Anne's.

"Pretty wall. Nice thing. Sit on it now." On it went, as they passed the entrance where some comfortable chairs for registration lined the wall, on which they'd hung a mural of the founders of the hospital centuries ago.

A frustrated Monica finally got Bergson back to her complex, along with the new scan results. "His brain cells are completely restored, perhaps even better than before. The doctor said he has the brain of a twenty-one year old man now. But he still isn't right."

Crystal put her hands on her hips. "Well, the spell worked, Monica. Somehow, he isn't. Let me cast an informatory spell on him, do a bit of mind probing. I doubt the he'll mind at all."

Monica shrugged and gave her permission for the mind probe, an action that would violate him, highly illegal under normal circumstances. She figured it would be acceptable in this situation, since nothing else was working.

Crystal waved her wand, and her eyes glazed over as she focused on and penetrated Bergson's mind. All his personal, private thoughts were laid bare before her, akin to mental rape. After a few minutes, she canceled her spell. "Well?" Monica asked.

Crystal wanted to say that Bergson liked Monica, but decided that wasn't to be shared. "It's most peculiar. It's as though he has totally given up on making his body respond to his thoughts and wishes. He's disconnected himself from his body."

"Wow. How can we reconnect him?" she asked.

"Dunno, but perhaps a shock would get through to him. You know, have his body send something shocking to him, causing him to reconnect with it," Crystal suggested.

"Won't that harm him further?" Monica asked, growing a bit worried that they might cause irreparable harm to the normal.

Crystal shrugged her shoulders. Sighing, she said,

"At this point, it can't hurt. He's useless as he is."

"Okay then, what kind of shock will we need?" Monica decided that perhaps this approach might work. She had nothing else to try.

"Well, it's got to be big, impressive, and something guaranteed to get through to him," Crystal said thoughtfully, biting her lip. "I know. Here goes nothing or everything." She waved her wand and cast another spell on Bergson, barking sharply, "Morph into Monica as she appeared last week." Magical energies flashed.

Even Monica was startled to see herself sitting on the chair in front of her. She had no lower arms and hands. Poor Bergson, until this instant, he was off in his own mental world, barricaded against the awful physical shape in which his body had been. Suddenly, he had Monica's body! Worse, he had no hands! From his barricaded mind, he was thrust into his new physical body. He screamed shrilly! Satisfied, Crystal canceled her spell, returning him back to his own body.

"What? What just happened? Where am I? Monica, you—you're all right now? General Franco! He's one of them! Traitor! We've been played!" Bergson screamed in alarm and shock.

"Bergson. Welcome back to the land of the living," Monica said, keeping her voice calm and soft. "My friends and I have been working for weeks on cures for Chrissy and me and for you two men. I think we've finally got you fixed up. How do you feel?"

Bergson ran his hands over his body, touching this and that as though they might have gone missing. "I, I think fine. I'm all here now. God, that was hideous!" He flushed, adding, "I mean it was even worse for you and Chrissy. Where's Miller? Kelly?"

"Chrissy is at St. Anne's healing up. Kelly is in another room. He's still messed up. I'll get him cured now that we know how to do it. Welcome back. And yes, it was hideous for you men and very trying for my friends trying to help you both with life."

"Er. Sorry about that. Was I you? I mean a moment

ago, I thought that I was somehow you, Miss Black," he asked.

"Well, you were. Your brain cells atrophied to that of a hundred year old man who had severe dementia. I rejuvenated your brain cells, but it took more than that to sort of restart you. Crystal did morph you into me for a moment, long enough for you to reconnect to your body. Sorry that we had to do that," Monica explained.

"Well, thanks. Thank you both. I think I'm back now. Best get Kelly fixed up. We need to get to Minot and retrieve our Stratosphere. All our things are on it. We've a war to fight!" he barked in his usual way.

"That we certainly do, Bergson, but let's get everyone healed up first. Then, we need to find out all that has happened. We've been out of touch with events for nearly a month now. A lot of bad has happened," Monica suggested.

"Well, I do feel incredibly tired. I hope we've not been imposing on you and your friends," he admitted politely.

Crystal chuckled, "You've no idea how bad it was. Then again, perhaps you do. Still, that is of little importance. As you said, we have a war to fight now. Come on. I'll take you to the room you've been staying in. Monica can go work her spell on Kelly."

***

By August 1, 2200, the four had recovered from their ordeals. Bergson, Kelly, and Miller must have thanked everyone a dozen times. "Look, you saved our lives. We owe you. You ever need anything, and I do mean anything, you just let us know," Bergson insisted.

"I'll hold you to that," Crystal teased him, but was appreciative of his offer. "Now, let's get your big plane back. We'll teleport you to Minot and you can fly it back to St. Louis yet today. Then, we all need to make serious plans, though I suppose many others are doing the same thing. This situation is already far out of hand and only promises to get worse."

Monica stayed behind, since she had to get Rob

setup for fourth grade and his books purchased. Crystal teleported them to the airbase and returned home.

As the three flew the giant Stratosphere back, Bergson said, "We should do something for Monica. After all, she didn't have to save us. We're not wizards."

Kelly replied, far more seriously than he'd ever been before, "Right boss. I don't think I'll ever crack another joke or play any pranks! After what we've been through, I don't think I can. But what can we do for her?" This whole episode had thoroughly shaken him up, and he doubted that he would ever be the same man again.

Miller looked up from the plane's controls and suggested, "Well, the FBI never did solve her case—you know, who bombed their place and killed her husband and the others. Maybe we can, do you suppose? It's a very cold case now, though."

"Brilliant, Miller! Let's. But don't tell her anything. Don't even let on that we're looking into it," Bergson insisted. "Lots of reasons," he added, though he didn't mention them. It wasn't necessary. For one thing, they might not find out any more than the FBI had.

Chapter 8—Executing the Plan

"See, I told you we would get her," General Franco boasted to his inner circle. "My plan worked to perfection. Sammy reports they're modified and are now down the Dragon Hole. They'll be brought up and taken to Rolla in a few days, and he'll keep an eye on them. So now we are free of that meddling witch and the best detectives the US has. We're free to continue with the plan, Gisella."

The succubus gave the general an appreciative nod before speaking. "Excellent work. Dr. Menninger, are you ready for the next phase of my Grand Plan? I remind you, we have one chance at the White House and the Congress." She detested this vile human man with his stupid looking black-rimmed glasses. And yet, for her plan to have any chance, she needed him—well, for now. Once they moved into the last part of her plan, she had a surprise waiting for him.

"All is and has been ready for some time now. General, just don't mess this up," he snickered. *Monica Nicole, dear me, now I've got you this time. No more meddling in my affairs. I must pay you a visit soon.*

"I assure you all is ready. When do we do it?" General Franco replied, very willing to move along this plan. He'd been lucky for nine years now, far too long a wait as far as he was concerned. "Is tomorrow acceptable?"

"I'm more than ready," grumbled Gisella. "Bella Zaronetti is with the Iranians and has been griping that she can't hold them back much longer. Donatella Ratini is in Detroit and has them ready for action. But I'm still concerned about the human female congresswomen, Dr. Menninger. If they end up with your Modification #2, they may not be able to cast their necessary votes when Congress meets."

Dr. Menninger dare not say what he believed, that women are and should be the sex objects of men—not with Gisella here. Surely she would object. Well, time enough to handle her later on. "They only push buttons to vote. They can use their pretty arm stumps to vote if they want to. Stop worrying. Everything will work out according to your Grand Plan, Gisella." She looked pleased, and he smiled politely, but thought, just you wait succubus, just you wait.

"Good. Then tomorrow at ten it will happen," General Franco declared. "Just make darn sure that the right ideas are spread in the news and among the Congress. I'll handle Billy Bob."

***

At ten the next morning, Drone 9 veered out of orbit and positioned itself to acquire its target. Right on schedule, it released its thousand pound bomb. Seconds later, it detonated above the left wing of the White House. Long ago, wizards had set up permanent Force Walls within the building for just such an eventuality. While the outer walls shattered and crumbled, the inner walls held, though in the aftermath, the White House looked very strange with a see-through left wing!

"This way—this way to the bunker!" General Franco ordered, ushering the President, Vice-president, and their staff, along with dozens of Secret Service personnel down into the bomb-proof bunker and safety. Five harried minutes passed before everyone was sealed in and safe, at which point, he released Dr. Menninger's special biological agent gas. It, of course, did not affect General Franco in any way; he wasn't human, but everyone else present, including the wizards and witches, quickly slumped over in comas. Once everyone was unconscious, General Franco unsealed the bunker and headed off for the next part of the plan.

The giant explosion echoed all over Washington, D.C. Naturally, other agents rushed all the many Senators and Representatives and their staff to safety in the Congressional bunkers below ground. There, other morphed demons released the gas into the sealed rooms as well.

Right on schedule, Bella, who was in Tehran, had those there finally release their long suppressed declaration of war. "You bombed us, so now we've bombed you." That was the essence of the message sent to Washington. Bella wanted to launch an all-out war immediately and would have done so had not Gisella been keeping a close watch on her via several of her loyal Cambions. Bella thought, well if Gisella is right, we'll have war in a few days, but I'd rather have it now! *Darn, nine years is way too long to wait!* Seeing one of the Cambion spies watching her closely, she didn't say anything further.

Meanwhile, in Detroit, Donatella Ratini had a wonderful time stirring up troubles, which was the essence of simplicity, considering the state of that city. Centuries ago, it had been the automobile capital of the US, raking in billions, but as costs rose and corporate greed escalated, the manufacturers slowly moved their factories to other places, even overseas. The corrupt city politicians, facing declining revenues, continued to dole out money they didn't have while raising taxes on the few who remained. That led ultimately to financial ruin and bankruptcy. Street gang leaders and drug dealers ran the city, which was now home to the poorest who had no means to move elsewhere. Crime was everywhere. In fact, "non-crime" was non-existent. The situation got so bad that the federal government setup an outer perimeter around the city to prevent its wild violence from going beyond the crumbling city. Thus, Donatella found an audience eager for her vitriolic messages.

But like Bella, Gisella's minions kept a sharp watch on Donatella's activities. Although she was more than prepared to launch her attacks, she had to wait on Gisella's orders, something that constantly ate at her. One day, one day, she swore, Gisella will get hers!

The day after the bombing of the White House, General Franco held a news conference, since he was now the highest ranking official not in a coma. For the last twenty-four hours, the many news organizations scrambled for official word on what had happened, why, and how many were injured. Unfortunately for them, their usual contacts in Washington, DC, had no answers. All high officials were locked away in their bomb-proof bunkers. Thus, when General Franco made the announcement that he would hold a press conference, all major news outlets were present.

"Hello my fellow Americans. Today is a sad day for us all. As you know, yesterday, the White House was attacked and the left wing destroyed. At this time, I am here to assure you that the President, Vice-president, all members of Congress, and many of their closest aides are completely safe and secure. I've been instructed by the President to address you at this time. Why?

"We've traced the bombing back to Iran. At this time, we are anticipating further terrorist attacks. Hence, in an abundance of caution, our elected officials are staying at undisclosed, bomb-proof bunkers. If no further attacks occur, they will emerge in a few days. President Billy Bob assures me that he has the situation under control and will be addressing the nation at that time. Expect a full report from President Billy Bob in a few days. In the meantime, know that all safety precautions are being taken around our country, which is now on the highest alert. That is all. No questions at this time, please." He turned to leave the wall of microphones, but the reporters screamed out many questions, all of which he completely ignored.

Once inside the White House, General Franco placed a call on his cell phone. He said only one word, "Now," and hung up. Three hours later, all power to New York City was cut off. The city went dark. Mass panic ensued, once more covered intensively by the press, who brought in portable generators to provide the electricity they needed to broadcast, though only those outside the affected area could view their reports. Many hours later, the mayor held a brief news conference, telling the world that their main power grid had been damaged by a terrorist bomb and that repairs were underway. Power would be restored, but several locations didn't have power for over four days. Naturally, this took everyone's attention off the missing government officials, giving them time to come out of their comas.

Four days later, President Billy Bob held his first press conference since the bombing. Of course, he and all the others had recovered from their comas, if that is the correct representation. The males now had IQs of barely fifty, while the women could no longer speak, lacking teeth, a voice box, and their lower arms and hands. However, since many of these women held positions in Congress, General Franco gave them a pep talk, insisting that they continue to represent their constituents during this time of national crisis. Further, the men were coached on what they needed to do, in very short sentences, naturally.

"Hi. Everyone, so pretty," President Bill Bob said. Bad thing. Very bad. Iran did. War on Iran. Fight back. We fight. All okay. Congress approval. Needed." General Franco worked long and hard to get him to memorize those last three words! "I good. All good. Women pretty. Have to fight. Bye." President Billy Bob smiled and waved, wondering if he had remembered everything he was supposed to say. The flowers on the lawn looked so interesting to him as did the many women around him.

General Franco stepped before him at the wall of microphones. "As President Billy Bob has just said, he is asking Congress for a declaration of war against Iran at this time. The attack wasn't just a bomb, but a bio-genetic weapon of terror. The congresswomen who were affected are insisting that they continue to represent their constituents during this time of national crisis, despite their crippling mutations from the bio-genetic agent. We will have more to report once Congress has met and authorized a war on Iran. Thank you. Please, no questions at this time. The President has many critical decisions and plans to attend to right now, just as do your Congress men and women. Let them do their job. More, later on." As before, he abruptly ended the conference without allowing any questions.

While there were some wizards and witches in Congress, either senators or representatives, they could no longer cast their spells. The men's IQ prohibited the casting any magic spells and the women couldn't speak or hold a wand. Hence, Dr. Menninger's bio-genetic agents had completely nullified their use of magical spells, about the only thing that could harm the demons.

Yet this public display of the results of the bio-genetic agent on wizards and witches served another even more important purpose. Users of magic worldwide saw they were in real danger. Simple exposure to this new diabolical gas would end their entire careers as wizards and witches. As Gisella hoped, spell casters of the world would think long and hard about getting involved in the coming conflicts, since the gas was very easily released.

Later that day, Congress, coached along by disguised Cambions, officially passed a declaration of war against Iran. Word of their action spread rapidly around the entire world. Many held their breaths, wondering what would happen next? Another world war? At this point in time, General Franco placed another call, this time to Bella in Iran. He spoke only one word, "Now," and hung up.

Pleased that her time had finally come, Bella issued her orders. For years, she'd been building up the Iranian army, supplying them with automatic weapons, ammunition, and more. Plus, she'd been providing them with "un-killable" Cambion fighters disguised as human soldiers and brought up from the Abyss through the Dragon Hole. At long last, her mighty army poured out of the country, attacking on two fronts. One half of the army swept through Iraq and Syria, adding many recruits along the way, before attacking Turkey. Their path was always northwest, with France and Germany as their ultimate target. The second half swept towards Israel, effectively blocking the Israelis in, before sweeping across North Africa and then across the Mediterranean Sea to Italy. Ultimately, they were to join forces with the other half of their army and together attack France and Germany.

By August, their plans became clear to many world leaders, including Pope Pius and the Israelis. Thus, on August 1, the Pope and the President of Israel held a joint press conference. Their message was a simple one: they called for a Holy War to exterminate all Muslims throughout the world! The Pope christened the Crusade, giving the Holy War his highest blessing, further inciting worldwide hatred.

With their announcement making world headlines, General Franco gave the okay to Donatella to begin her attack. Long had she prepared for this day. She'd brought in automatic weapons and ammunition for the gang lords, along with Cambion demons, again disguised as African-American men. She promised the drug and gang lords revenge against both the greedy corporations and the super-wealthy top one percent of the country, who's combined wealth allowed them to control nearly everything. Thus, on August 1, an army of angry men stormed out of Detroit, easily breaking through the protective barriers that had previously prevented them from leaving Detroit. They had broadcast their campaign from stations within Detroit, calling them the CACG and the CAGW—Citizens Against Corporate Greed and Citizens Against the Greedy Wealth.

As they swept across Michigan, they attacked anyone who looked wealthy and all larger companies, spreading death and destruction in their path. Naturally, this diverted the US's armed forces from their planned attacks against Iran, all according to Gisella's Grand Plan. Further, it soon became obvious to everyone that there had to be demons in disguise among them, since direct gunfire did not harm them. Panic spread out in front of these thugs from Detroit, resulting in mass evacuations further tying up valuable resources, spreading chaos more broadly.

Just as Gisella and General Franco had predicted, with so much worldwide chaos happening, the world's wizards and witches could not unite into a single fighting force to repel the demons. Instead, they were needed locally to combat the chaos there, particularly in the US and in Western Europe. Unable to unite, the mages would not be an effective fighting force against the demon hordes. Victory was certain.

***

"Good grief! All this has happened while we were out of it!" exclaimed Bergson.

"Has the world gone insane?" Kelly cried.

"Traitor General Franco must be terminated," Miller said softly but with a ferociousness Monica had never heard from her. She left to visit Ericka, hoping and praying that she had invented magic bullets!

Ericka looked up from her workbench and noticed Chrissy's face was twisted and red. She didn't need an Empathy spell to sense the young woman's rage. She also knew why she was here. It could only be to find out if she'd developed a way for normals to kill demons.

"Hi Chrissy. I believe I have some ammunition enchanted sufficiently to kill a demon, if you can hit it in a vulnerable spot or pepper it with enough wounds."

Chrissy managed a reactive smile. "Read my mind. Yes, thank you, thank you. Let's see what you have. I need to kill that vile traitor General Franco!"

"Well, it has to be these larger rounds. I believe they go to your automatic rifles. I had to create special platinum bullets, replacing the lead and copper ones. It's a time consuming process, but I've got about a thousand rounds prepared. Come on. I'll show you."

"Now you *are* talking! Thank you!" exclaimed Chrissy. Her face regained its normal color and the tenseness vanished. Franco could be killed. That was all that mattered to her.

Lugging the bags of ammunition back with her, she walked in on her team and said, "Here we go—demon-killing bullets. Ericka succeeded. For our big guns only. Now we have to get to Franco and kill that bastard demon before he can do more harm! He's mine to kill, you hear me? Mine!"

Never had Monica heard such a vitriolic outburst from this usually soft-spoken woman. Monica thought she certainly was more than justified.

Chrissy plopped the bag down and said, "I know how we can do it! Listen up."

Bergson, Kelly, and Monica did just that. When

Chrissy finished, Monica said, "I can make that even more believable with a suitable illusion, Chrissy. One way or another, it will work. Let's do this!"

"Darn it, Miller," Kelly exclaimed, "remind me never to get on your bad side!" He meant it.

Two hours later, their preparations made, Bergson picked up his cell phone and placed the call. "Boss. Nice Boss. Me here. Ah, Bergson. Yes, Bergson. Escaped. Know Dragon Hole. Pretty water. Got blow up. Can't. Crashed plane. Nice plane. Broken now. Can you come? Help make bomb. Blow up water."

"Bergson? Is that you?" General Franco replied, startled to hear Bergson's voice. The last he word he'd had that fool of a demon, Sammy, had let them all escape. "Where are you?"

"Bergson. Me. St. Louis. Crashed. Plane can't fly."

"You're in St. Louis? Okay. Who is with you?"

"Me St. Louis. Kelly. Miller. No Monica. Dead. No Miller. She no hands. No talk. Pretty. She pretty. You like her. Very pretty. You come?"

"Okay. You at the airport?"

"Yes. Pretty airport. Plane not pretty. No more."

"Okay. You stay there. I'll be there in say twenty minutes. You know where the Dragon Hole is located?"

"Yes. Blow up. Soon. Big boom. Kelly make boom. You take us. Make boom. Stop demons."

"All right. Stay put. Be there in twenty minutes, Bergson. Stay there. Got that?"

"Stay there. We stay. Pretty airport. Pretty Miller. Want make boom. Stop demons."

"Good. Stay there. Goodbye." The line went dead.

"All right, I think he bought it. Lord knows how many others he'll bring with him. We best be prepared," Bergson barked.

Monica positioned her mage friends at key locations around the giant plane's exterior. "Remember, stay hidden unless it looks like we can't handle the situation."

"Naturally," Crystal teased her, but they all knew how much this meant to the three normals, who took a huge risk to kill this demon that had betrayed them and probably the whole country and perhaps the world. Ericka kept her fingers crossed that her enchanted platinum slugs would actually penetrate demon flesh. If not, she and the others would cast any number of power spells to kill this demon. She swore Franco would not leave here alive.

Bergson positioned himself to the right side of the cargo ramp with Kelly on the left side. In the middle, Miller stood with one of their automatic, high caliber rifles with silencer, loaded with Ericka's new ammunition. Monica had cast an illusion over the woman so that she appeared the way that she had been after the bio-agent attack. She looked pathetic and helpless, but in fact held the large rifle at the ready. Monica, satisfied all was arranged according to plan, cast Invisibility on herself and moved behind Chrissy, ready to intervene if the magic slugs failed. Now they waited.

General Franco was taken by surprise when Bergson called him. *The fool doesn't even realize that I set him and his team up. I can't let him spread the word about the Dragon Hole, let alone its location or bomb it. I best see to this myself. He's obviously still an idiot and Miller is helpless. This should be easy. I'll just teleport them back to the Dragon Hole and stuff them back into the Abyss. Good thing that witch is dead and out of the picture, though for the life of me, I don't see why Dr. Menninger was so worried about her of all people!* He checked his gun and spare ammo clips. Satisfied, he cast his Teleport spell, arriving at Lambert Field. Glancing around, he spotted the giant Stratosphere parked way off to one side, out of the way. *Well, if Bergson crash landed here, it makes sense to move it way out of the way of other traffic.*

He strode confidently across the tarmac, occasionally flashing his badge to airport security personnel. A minute later, he reached the plane and headed up the cargo bay ramp, where he saw the pathetic looking Miller standing in the middle, with Bergson and Kelly off a few feet to either side of her. "Well done, Bergson," he said.

126

Chrissy wasted no time. As soon as the demon set foot on the ramp, she opened fire with her automatic rifle. The silencer worked perfectly, emitting only faint popping sounds. She watched, as did many other eyes, as the bullets struck his chest and penetrated, coming out his backside. Shock and utter disbelief shown from his eyes as dozens of rounds ripped his chest to shreds. Then, the life went out of his Earthly form, ripping Franco back into the Abyss, where he'd be unable to return to this world for at least seventeen or more years. Some kind of goo now lay inside his uniform on the ramp of the plane.

Spells canceled, and cries and cheers went up all around. Ericka's magically enchanted bullets worked. "Take that, you beast!" Chrissy yelled above the others, rather wishing she'd said it before she killed the demon.

Crystal said, "Monica, I'll relay this bit of good news to other key wizards and witches. You've definitely put a gaping hole in the demon leadership, Chrissy. Well done!

At the same time, Gisella sensed her General Franco had been killed. As a succubus and his superior, she had a loose connection with him. "Well, so the fool has gotten himself killed. Too bad, but he served his purpose. I no longer need him in the slightest. All is going according to my Grand Plan. Nothing can stop me now. I must remember to look him up the next time I'm in the Abyss, which may never be. There's too much to like in this world!" She laughed heartily.

Chapter 9—Escalation Can Be Fun

"Things are getting out of hand, even here in St. Louis," the local FBI director Oliver Easton explained to the rather large gathering of wizards, witches, and key normal figures. He had summed everyone to this War Council Meeting, and Monica's group had to come, long with the WIT team, who of necessity stayed in St. Louis. The entire HDF had been compromised by General Franco. Today, no one trusted that department, let alone the elected government officials, who now were either silent helpless women or moronic men.

Monica had also asked Governor Lindsey if she could send a representative to this meeting, though she knew that Colorado had their own mounting problems. Still, she hoped they could arrange joint forces to combat the rising chaos and demon armies. Lindsey sent her husband, Deiter Cross, who was now one of the directors of the federal Department of Law and Justice. Leslie Traub, head of the Missouri Department of Magical Misuse, was also present, along with Herb Jackson, a normal and the head of the Missouri Department of Defense.

Deiter spoke up, "I guess I'm here representing the federal government as well as Colorado. I can tell you the situation is deteriorating rapidly. We've had a few raids, particularly around the Denver area, but local forces have fought them off. It is much worse closer to Michigan. The trouble is that the enemy wizards, witches, and demons are teleporting raiding parties nearly anywhere. Fortunately, those have thus far tended to be small enough that local defenses are able to hold them off. But there is a big however involved." He knew they weren't going to like what he had to say next.

"Go on, Mr. Cross, we have to hear it," Leslie demanded. Herbert nodded his agreement.

"Well, it's that damnable biological-genetic agent gas of theirs. They've begun to use it in their attacks." He waited for the anticipated gasps and wasn't disappointed. "I know, it turns men into babbling idiots and women, well I don't have to tell you about that. I'll give the demons credit; taking out the entire elected government officials of both branches was a brilliant move. Bottom line: at the federal level, chaos reigns. No one is in charge of more than their own areas, and they're not working together, which only makes things worse."

He went on, "Since I'm still at the federal level, I can relay more information to you. Since the mobs are now beginning to use that the biological-genetic agent gas in their attacks, people are scared out of their pants, wizards, witches, and normals alike. Heck, who wants to risk becoming a moron or even worse a helpless woman? Brilliant tactic, nevertheless. We're starting to see far fewer individuals responding to the attacks. Frankly, that's one of the reasons I'm here today. It's very risky to offer resistance to the attacking mobs. The second reason is to see with my own eyes that there really are cures for both these genetic mutations."

"Well there sure are cures!" Bergson barked, standing up for Monica, though he need not have. "My whole team is proof enough of that."

Deiter smiled, "You can say that again. I'll be spreading the word about the cures. That alone should help convince those who can fight back to do so. However, from the federal level, how are we going to handle those of us who get gassed and mutated?"

He went on, "While there are several dozen wizards and witches who are registered as official casters of the Rejuvenate spell, only one person in the world can cast the Regeneration spell, and there are about five available magical Regeneration Rings whose owners might be persuaded to loan them to the victims. What I'm saying is that Miss Monica Nicole Black here is *the* most important person in the world at this moment. She alone can cast the spell needed to restore the women. If I had my way, I'd lock her away somewhere safe and bring the lines of women desperate for the cure to her. I doubt she'll see it that way though. I know Monica." Several chuckled, knowing Monica would never go along with that approach.

Monica decided to speak her mind. "Look, Deiter, I'm always willing to cast my spells to heal those who need it, but I can and must fight back. Perhaps the best way to approach this is to set up St. Louis as the national healing center. Bring those who need the cures here, and we'll see they get them. Besides, Deiter, you know there's no place you could put me that I couldn't escape from." Several grinned. Those who knew her past knew precisely what she was hinting at, hence their response.

"Right, we did just that nine years ago," Leslie backed her up. "I'll handle the coordination with St. Anne's."

Crystal added, "Plus, I will help out with my Rejuvenation spell as well. We can't make Monica do all the healing. I'm afraid there's going to be a huge number needing it."

"Excellent. I'll spread the word," Deiter promised. "I'm sure those who were hesitant about responding because of the terrible gas will now join in the fight when needed. Ericka, I've heard you have developed magic bullets. True?"

"Yes, I replaced the lead slugs with platinum, which then hold the magical enchantment, but I can't promise you how long they will hold their magical energies. That arena is wholly untested."

"Still," Miller spoke up softly as usual, "they worked. I was able to kill General Franco with them."

Oliver added, "Now we normals have an effective way to fight back. Ericka, how soon can you get us a whole lot more?"

Tyler answered instead of his wife, Ericka. "We're working flat out on it. Only the large caliber automatic rifles have a large enough slug to hold the enchantment. We've another thousand about ready to go. What's slowing us down is that we have to manually and carefully remove the lead slug, make platinum slugs, and install them first. That's what is taking us forever to do. If we had some helpers who could do that, allowing us to focus on the enchanting part, we could produce far more."

Herb Jackson spoke, "Son, let me see what I can do. I should be able to get you quite a few competent ammo makers. We'll discuss details after the meeting is done. And yes, Mr. Cross, as soon as we can, we'll make the ammo available for others besides those of us in Missouri."

Deiter smiled, for that was precisely what he wanted to hear. That ammo would enable many normals to enter the fight as well as wizards and witches.

"Next question," Deiter continued to dominate the meeting, and it wasn't even his meeting, but that was Deiter Cross, "will gas masks provide sufficient protection during one of those gas attacks? Does anyone know?" Unfortunately, no one had any idea. He'd have to experiment on his own to answer his question.

Oliver attempted to regain control of his meeting, "Now then, we need to arrange a mutual aid system. If we get attacked here in St. Louis, we need a fast way to let all others know to come at once and join our defense."

Leslie volunteered, "I can arrange for the St. Louis School of Magic to have their students send a message to specific other wizards and witches around the country. We need a list of whom to contact and just what that message should be. If we're attacked, someone can send that info to the school's governor, and the governor can have her students send it to their designated recipients. Word can spread rapidly that way."

Deiter answered, "Excellent. I'll provide you with a list of contact names by tomorrow. Let's keep it simple. Send: Help. Demon attack. Followed by the city or location."

"I get it," Bergson declared, "an emergency response team. Count us in on that, Mr. Cross. If someone can get us to the battle, we'll come guns blazing!"

"Wouldn't think of leaving you out, Bergson," Deiter replied with a wry smile.

"Can I ask a question?" ventured Miller. Her voice was quite soft compared to Bergson and Deiter, but Oliver heard her and nodded her way.

"What are we to do about the Holy Crusade that Israel and the Pope have begun? People are going around killing all the Muslims they can find, even here in St. Louis. What are we supposed to do if we see someone doing that? All Muslims aren't terrorists."

"Quite true. Most aren't," Leslie pointed out. "But right now, President Billy Bob, Israel, and the Pope have really stirred up a hornet's nest with their call for a Holy Crusade. If you recall your ancient history, it's Nazi Germany and the Jews all over again. My advice, do what you need to do to prevent senseless murders."

Deiter added, "Look, some are always going to sympathize with the Israelis and the Pope, going on a crusade to murder innocent people because of their religious beliefs and how they dress. Right now, we can't do anything about those people. We've demons and criminals to handle first. But once we win this war, I'll do all I can to bring those who have murdered innocent people to justice."

"But what is going on over in Europe and North Africa, Deiter? We've had spotty reports and the news isn't very clear," Leslie decided to ask this federal agent. She might not have many other opportunities.

Deiter rubbed his hands through his hair and then down his face. "Not good. Our information is still sketchy— just what our wizard and witch friends are telling us. The Israelis are holding their own, even with the chaotic and suicidal attacks from the northern Iranian army and demons, who have left millions dead or gassed in their wake, particularly in Syria and now Turkey. Part of their group seems headed towards Greece. North Africa is a butchering ground. Most Muslim radicals are joining the attacking army and taking this opportunity to slaughter all those that don't join. There have been mass evacuations from Cairo and other major cities. At least Italy is holding them off from crossing the Mediterranean Sea to their boot. Some reports suggest this southern army is now pushing westward in hopes of crossing at Gibraltar. Spain is likely to attempt to hold them off as Israel is doing, but no guarantees. Bottom line, mass slaughter is going on over there, whereas over here, we're getting far more of the biological-genetic agent attacks.

"What has many of us at the federal level very worried is what happens if and when these two armies break through into Central Europe. The whole continent could fall in short order. Plus, right now, there well could be more demons on earth than magic users! So we need that magic ammo! I'll spread the word on how you two are doing it, though I expect lots of other powerful wizards and witches are also working on that challenge as well— necessity and all that. Of course, our big barrier is that damnable gas they're using. If they take too many of us out, there'll be nothing to stop them."

"Deiter, everyone, I've an idea that might work," Monica suggested. "We know that the part of the biological agent that harms women is magical in nature. The cure involved dispelling all the magical genetic modifications in their modified bodies. My idea is that when a gas attack comes, cast as many Dispel Magic spells as you can. Perhaps that will help nullify the gas attack, at least on the women. Won't work for the men, at least I don't think so. Deiter, if you can, spread the word as widely as possible among all your connections. Leslie, do the same thing. If nothing else, it might abate some of the awful body modifications on women."

"Brilliant, Monica. I'll tell them your suggestion along with your cures. See, by working together, we are coming up with solutions. I just have to get them spread far and wide," Deiter exclaimed, rather excited about her idea, for he could offer some hope to the others at the federal level.

"Might I ask a question?" Bergson said, far more politely than normal. His voice was nearly as soft as Miller's usually was and his eyes seemed very large and moved from person to person.

"Sure, Bergson, ask away," Deiter replied, once more usurping Oliver's control of the meeting. The mild-mannered director smiled and nodded to Deiter.

"The Israelis. They are holding the swarm off. Might I ask just how they are managing to do that? If there's a hundred thousand in that army, how are they able to stop them?"

Deiter flinched visibly and then sighed. "Okay, I guess there's no reason not to tell you what I've heard. When a bunch of the enemy swarms to attack a location, they simply drop a huge amount of bombs on them, butchering all the humans in the party. Those that survive are the demons, and their wizards and witches deal with them as best they can. From what I've heard, it's more like a slaughter than a battle, but it does mostly prevent suicide bombers and being overwhelmed by sheer numbers. I hope it doesn't come to that here in the US. Personally, I think their approach stinks, but I can also see their point of view."

"Why? Aren't those Iranians just normals?" Bergson probed, curious about Deiter's response and reactions to his question.

"Yes, they are normals, but they are humans. I think it's a crime to murder and kill humans. Demons? Heck yes. Stop the terrorists, yes, but not wholesale battlefield slaughtering. Unfortunately, I don't have any other answer for them. Wish I did," Deiter replied.

"How curious," Bergson commented. "I was under the impression that you wizards and witches thought we normals were rather like sub-humans or something."

Monica flushed. He hit too close to home for her. Deiter smiled and explained, "There are some bad lots among us, just as there are among you normals. We do our best to apprehend those who break the Laws of Magic, but sometimes catching them can be incredibly challenging, especially if they are really powerful wizards. That kind of thinking was fostered by a really bad, now dead, wizard some dozen years back." He looked at Monica and added, "Some crazy ideas can take forever to vanish from the scene." Little else transpired, though they talked for another hour before breaking up.

Bergson pulled Oliver aside for a private chat. He said, "Would you mind if my team took a look at your file on the bombing of Monica's home that killed her husband? I know it's a cold case, but fresh eyes might turn up something."

"Sure. Be my guest. Heartbreaking case—she's never recovered from that loss, not really. I always felt we let her down on this one, after all she's done to help us, the city, and world. Does she know you are looking into it?" Oliver asked.

"No, and I think it best that she doesn't know. No sense in giving her false hopes and bringing back all that pain and loss for her. We might not find anything more than your people did. I don't want her to feel that tragic loss all over—not with everything that's going on now," Bergson explained.

"Very wise move. She was an emotional wreck for months after the bombing—in here every day asking what we had. Come on. I'll take you to the file," Oliver volunteered.

Leslie explained, "Monica, with raids happening in random cities at unpredictable times, I think it best if we keep all schools in Missouri closed or rather not open them in late August like normal. Keep the children safe at home. I fear these mobs and demons might well attack a school. Besides, if and when the mobs attack, parents first actions will be to get their kids out of the schools and to safety instead of dealing with the mob and demons. What do you think as a mother?"

Monica chuckled. "You got that one right. Yes, we'd be torn between making sure our families are safe and fighting back. Rob won't mind having a long summer vacation. I think you've made the right decision, Leslie."

"Thanks. I plan on making the announcement later today. With luck, the Detroit mess will not get to Missouri," Leslie said in a hopeful tone, masking that she didn't truly believe that would happen.

***

Three days later, the action came to St. Louis.

Without any warning, a group of heavily armed Detroit thugs and disguised Cambion demons arrived via a mass Teleport spell on the rolling green fairways of Westborough Country Club, mere blocks from the Kirkwood Industrial area and Kirkwood Public Library. Security guards at the club made the emergency call to the FBI Notification Center, seconds before they were gunned down by the rioters. In a wild and reckless abandon, the group fanned out in all directions, smashing into homes and shooting the occupants.

The demons quickly disregarded all the previously made plans. Blood lust took over. The drive to kill as many humans as possible and as brutally as they could took over what little reasoning ability these demons had, quite unlike the organized Detroit mob, whose goal was to get to the Franklin Diamond Exchange several blocks away in Kirkwood, there to confiscate one hundred million worth of uncut diamonds recently delivered from Africa.

With guns mowing down any people in their way, some fifty humans charged down the street heading single-mindedly towards their goal, confident that the utter chaos the demons were sewing would allow them to achieve their objective.

Oliver's FBI organizational skills once more paid off. Previous newscasts disseminated the action which anyone spotting the mobs or demons should take: call the FBI Notification Center. He had people manning these dedicated lines every hour of every day. Giant "call lists" were plastered on the walls in front of the people manning the phones. Thus, seconds after the security guards reported the invasion, hundreds of key personnel around the greater St. Louis area were notified.

When the call came in to Monica's mansion, she immediately teleported to FBI headquarters where her WIT team was working, leaving Crystal to organize the others. She found the three suiting up, putting on their bullet proof vests. Bergson tossed her one. "Put it on. There's hundreds of them."

Monica did as asked, knowing that her defensive

Skin of Stone spell would only protect her from a few gunshots, not a wall them. Still, before she took the heavily armed group into the combat zone, she did cast that spell on each of the three, along with one that protected them from lower grade spells. Then, she teleported them to the general location, arriving on the country club greens.

Overhead, three helicopters scouted the action below. Obviously, a large mob had gone nearly due southwest, thanks to the trampled grass. However, many footsteps headed off in all other directions, particularly west and north.

"Oh crap!" yelled Kelly, pointing up to one of the helicopters. Gazing upwards, Monica saw three demons had somehow gotten up there and were ripping the doors off to get to the men inside. The helicopter came down, exploding in a ball of flames. Aghast, Bergson watched the three demons get up and walk away from the carnage they'd just caused. Kelly's rifle jarred Monica alert. Miller's gun echoed his, and the three demons' bodies jerked wildly as the enchanted platinum slugs ripped into them, killing their physical forms on Earth.

"We go that way," Bergson indicated the north and westerly routes.

"Right," Monica yelled, "let the FBI handle the organized mob. We've demons to slay!" The four raced after the trail of the demons, though soon they had to pick specific ones to follow, since almost at once, the demons broke up into groups of no more than three. A Message scrolled by Monica's eyes.

Crystal and friends arrived, flying above the area. Enya remained in the skies, directing the wizards, witches, and the WIT team to the small groups of rampaging demons. In the distance, massive gunfire erupted. Monica recognized the sound and smiled. That had to be the FBI and their automatics having at the mob.

The team of four closed in on three demons, which were covered in blood as they smashed their way back out of a home, disregarding the doors. One was chewing on a dismembered arm. Through the hole in the wall, they saw the revolting aftermath. A family of four were dead, their arms and legs had been ripped off. What remained of the once huddled group lay in a giant mass of blood. Monica fought down the urge to vomit and pulled the trigger, holding it back, allowing her weapon to fire as rapidly as it could. Close by, Bergson, Kelly, and Miller did the same thing, as dozens of the enchanted slugs ripped into the demons.

"Cease fire! Cease fire, Monica. Save this precious ammo!" yelled Bergson.

Monica flushed. "Oh. They're dead. Sorry."

"This way," Bergson ordered, and the team ran down the block after three more demons. Monica realized Bergson was not easily riled, that he really was a superb leader in a crisis. She'd not seen this side of him before. While Kelly was deadly and enjoyed his work, he needed direction, as did Miller, who was nearly as shocked at the horrific sights as Monica was.

As they shot and exterminated this next group of three demons, another two came charging up from behind them. One reached Monica, who suddenly felt powerful arms nearly crushing her shoulder. The next thing she knew, her body was flying across the street. Before she could react, her body slammed into an oak tree. Fortunately, her protective spells prevented more than a severe jarring.

At point blank range, an unflinching Bergson and Kelly opened fire, ripping gaping holes in the two demons' bellies, dropping them a fraction of a second before they could latch onto Miller and toss her as one had done to Monica. The two shocked, gray, wicked looking faces changed into gray ooze, slumping into a puddle of slime on the black asphalt of the street.

"Miller, check on Monica," Bergson ordered, while he and Kelly pressed their backs against each other so they could cover all directions at the same time.

Miller took Monica's hand and pulled her back onto her feet. "You okay?"

"Shook up a bit, but yeah, I'm okay. Spells worked.

Come on. There are more to get," Monica replied, as the two ran back over to the two men.

Bergson nodded to Monica and led them on down the street. Enya shot another flash of magical energies, pointing out the location of more demons, and Bergson headed that way.

An hour later, the relatively large group met on the greens of the nearby Algonquin Golf Club. The last of the demons had been dispatched, and the group met to check on each other. Crystal, who had been in charge of the magic user pack, declared, "Well, we got twelve of them, but damn it Monica, Bergson, you guys got four times that number. Looks like your enchanted bullets are superior, Ericka. Perhaps we need to follow their example, if we're going to be more effective."

"Don't rush to conclusions," Monica offered, bloody bits of human remains dripping off of her, as it was from her three team members, "your spells would have been needed if there had been other kinds of demons with them. I'm a little surprised there were only relatively weak Cambions in this party and no Type I's or IV's."

"It's carnage back there. These demons are insane savages!" Bergson called out. "Worse than a battlefield!"

"We should go back and see if there are any survivors," Enya suggested.

Grimly, the group fanned out, retracing the bloody path of destruction the demons left. "Ghastly! Never seen anything like this before," Bergson said, as they entered yet another home only to find the occupants dead, their bodies ripped apart and limbs torn off.

"Hey, over here!" yelled Miller. "This woman's alive, sort of."

Monica dashed over to the young blonde woman. Only a head and torso remained, and she'd lost a good deal of blood, but she was still breathing. "Do we try to save her? What kind of life could she have if we do?" she whispered to Monica.

Monica didn't answer. Quickly, she pulled out an Enya flask and poured its contents into the woman's mouth, forcing her to swallow some of it. Then, she produced another flask and poured it in down her throat as well. "Healing potion," she explained to Miller, who stood beside her watching Monica's actions. Miller saw the horrific wounds suddenly closing, the seeping blood flow cease, the woman's breathing becoming easier.

"Good going, Miller. We've saved her life," Monica pointed out.

"Kill me," the wounded woman whispered, barely audible. "Kill me."

"Heck, Monica. You've saved her, but what kind of life can she have now? She knows it, too," Miller whispered, staring into the pleading eyes of the blonde woman.

"Give me an uninterrupted minute, Miller," Monica ordered, "and call for an EMT team." She focused and cast her Regenerate spell.

A couple minutes later, she looked up and saw her team members staring down at her and the young woman. To the woman, she said, "Your body will be regenerating your lost arms and legs. Give it a week or so and you'll be back to normal."

Just then, the emergence team arrived with a stretcher and blankets, along with their bag of equipment.

"Take her to St. Anne's. Tell them her arms and legs are regenerating," Monica told the two medical responders. Monica finally got back on her feet.

"Well, that's a miracle if I ever saw one," Bergson spoke up. "Good going, Miller, Monica. Come on; we've more houses to check out. Might save another one."
***

"They were going after the diamond exchange in Kirkwood," Oliver explained. Three hours later, he had everyone who participated attend a debriefing at his headquarters in downtown St. Louis. "My forces got between them and the Kirkwood business district and mowed them down. Fifty mobsters dead. Five of my people were wounded, none seriously. The demon horde is another story. One hundred sixteen dead, brutally so. One survivor, thanks to Miller and Monica. No biological-genetic gas was found on their remains, so we lucked out this time. On behalf of all St. Louis, I want to extend my heart-felt thank you to each of you who dropped everything and responded to the call. Well done, all of you. I hope we never have to face this again. Now go home, clean up, and get some sleep."

Monica looked at her fellow team members, covered in dried blood. "Dibs on the bath first." All four laughed.

Bergson looked at his three team members and said, "Well done, WIT team. I'm proud of you three. We proved that we are an effective force against the demons, thanks to Ericka's bullets. Monica, you go home to your son. Oliver's letting us stay here. See you in the morning."

Monica didn't need to be told twice. Grinning, she gave him a mock salute and cast her spell, vanishing before their eyes.

***

The next day, Monica and her group received a summons to meet at the FBI headquarters at noon. When they arrived, Oliver did the introduction, "I'd like you to meet Mr. Fred Delius, head of the States Defense Force. He's replacing the HDF for now. He wants to address you all, especially Ericka and Tyler." He sat down.

Delius was a tall, thin wizard, but one used to positions of power and authority. He had once served under the Idaho Red Brigade that had fought against Dominus and his Death Stalkers. "Ericka, Tyler, on behalf of the entire country, I want to thank you personally for developing the enchanted slugs which have become a proven technique to exterminate these demons. That said, I've ordered a massive operation to manufacture as much of this ammunition as possible. As I speak, fifty of the best munitions experts in the US are flying here to set up shop. They will be processing the platinum slugs that are needed, removing and installing them. Ericka, Tyler, assemble all those who can properly execute the enchantments that you do and let's get a production line going. We must create enough ammunition to supply the country!"

Ericka said, "Wow. Thanks. That will help lots. Two spells are needed: Enchant Object and Make Permanent. Not all wizards and witches know both spells. There's a dozen of us that I know of in and around St. Louis who know both."

"Excellent. I figured those would be the spells. I'll assemble a team of fifty who can do this in the next day or so. Oliver here has made the St. Louis National Armory at our disposal. We'll be setting up shop there today. Thanks to you and the top WIT team, we now have a fighting chance against this demonic invasion," Delius declared, bringing smiles to everyone's faces. "Let's get cracking!"

As the brief meeting broke up, Bergson said, "Monica, we'll lend you folks a hand getting things setup."

"Okay, but first I have to pay a visit to St. Anne's. I need to see that blonde woman that Miller and I saved last night," she replied.

"Why? Isn't she going to recover?" he asked.

Miller moved up and paid close attention to what Monica answered.

"Physically, yes, in about a week or so, but she's also got a huge emotional trauma sitting there. I need to also run that out of her mind, sort of erasing it. Otherwise, she'll continually re-live that night over and over," Monica explained.

"You can do that?" he asked.

"Yes, another spell that I once learned."

"Can I tag along and watch?" asked Miller, her curiosity roused.

"Sure. We'll join you in about an hour or so."

The doctors at St. Anne's knew about Monica and her trauma erasing spell from all the activities there some nine years ago. Thus, they weren't too surprised when she and Miller arrived and told them what she wanted to do for the young woman, Mrs. Shelly Kettlebaum. They found her in a private room lying on a bed. She looked alert, but Miller gagged, seeing her laying there, just a head and torso.

"I'm going to help you erase that horrible trauma,

Shelly. It's okay to scream all you want. I'm putting a silence spell on the room so no one outside can hear us," Monica explained.

Before she could actually do it, a nurse entered. "Excuse me, Archmage Monica, I'm witch Glenda. I've trained to be able to cast this Erase Trauma spell, but I've never had a real chance to cast it. Would you mind if I watch you and pick up any tips? I hope to be able to provide this service for all trauma victims here at St. Anne's."

"Sure. This is my WIT team member, Chrissy Miller. Let's get started.

"Wow! You're famous, Miss Miller. Everyone's talking about how you and your WIT team saved countless lives last night—the demons and all that. Wow!"

Chrissy looked very surprised, and the shy woman didn't know what to say. Fortunately, Monica went ahead and cast the spell on Shelly.

"We are watching TV. The side wall—it's shattering, bursting. Ugly demons. Gray-black skin. Pointed, weird hair. Horns. Ugly. Rush in. Tom, he stands up. Oh god! They are pulling his arms off! I scream. Protect my babies. I run to them. No, not my babies. I'm screaming, holding them. Feel their cold arms on my arms. Pulling. No, I can't take it. Pain! Shooting pain!"

Shelly began shrieking at the top of her lungs, terrifying Chrissy who'd never heard such blood-curling screams before and with such volume, though Monica and Glenda didn't seem to be bothered by it.

Bit by bit, the ghastly scene replayed itself out before Chrissy and the others. Over and over, Shelly went, adding new details each time, but her screams died down, until at last, she had no reactions while describing that awful night and scene. Monica then canceled the spell.

"Thanks Monica. I feel better. Still completely helpless here."

"Well done, Shelly. Don't worry; your arms and legs will be back as good as new. Just give the process time to work. I've got to run now. Demons to fight and all that,"

Monica advised her. The three left Shelly alone in her room.

Outside, Glenda said, "That was a bit more than I anticipated. Now I understand the spell and how it works so much better. Thanks for letting me watch. I promise to give this kind of relief to as many victims as I can."

"Thanks, Glenda. It's good that others can do it, too. I'm afraid many are going to need it before this mess is done," Monica said.

After Glenda headed off on her rounds, Miller whispered, "Would that work on us? I mean we both did suffer a lot when we got genetically gassed and modified."

"Sure. I was planning to give it to you and the guys later on. It's just that we've too much to handle right now to worry about that. We didn't suffer like that poor woman did. I can't imagine the pain she felt when they literally ripped her arms and legs off. Savages," Monica declared, "but then that's what demons love and thrive on. Come on; we've got work to do. We've not even seen the really powerful demons yet, Chrissy. The worst is yet to come."

Chapter 10—Win Some, Lose Some

September 1, the threat funneling out of Detroit was terminated, though those in St. Louis played no role in it and were generally thankful they did not. As Deiter put it when he again met with the large St. Louis group, "It was just that many people got too fed up with the raids from those in the Detroit slums." That was his summation of what happened there. Even the newscasts were a bit ambivalent about the action taken by the States Defense Force.

What did they do? Simple. They dropped enough bombs on the city to completely level every last building in Detroit. With the city reduced to rubble, all the humans who lived there were basically exterminated, leaving only the demons surviving. With clear targets plainly visible, a host of wizards and witches, primarily from Michigan and nearby states that had been attacked often by the rampaging demons, attacked, unleashing a storm of deadly magical spells never seen in one location in the history of the world.

Donatella Ratini, the succubus in charge there, didn't go down without an impressive fight. Survivors reported Donatella alone Gated in dozens of powerful demon allies, each impossibly hard to kill. Worse, she also unleashed another bio-genetic agent gas attack, downing nearly thirty wizards and witches, who ultimately ended up at St. Anne's in St. Louis for Monica's cures. However, against nearly two hundred wizards and witches, some armed with the automatic firing weapons spewing forth the newly enchanted platinum slugs, the Detroit demon threat and Donatella's reign came to an end. There was no accurate human death toll, for no one actually knew how many lived in the Detroit slums, but estimates suggested a million. This was hard to stomach by many people, including Bergson.

The WIT leader commented, "I understand why they

did it, but surely not everyone in Detroit was a drug lord or criminal. How many were just impoverished humans trying to survive as best they could?"

"Wars always have collateral damage," Deiter justified. "Look at the damage they did to our country? They murdered one hundred sixty-five thousand, nine hundred six men, women, and children, including babies. Perhaps even worse, we've got nearly one million three hundred thousand genetic mutations on our hands, many of which are, or were I should say, our elected federal officials and their staff. Monica, I don't see how you could possible handle that many victims. The men are morons and the women, helpless. Also, a surprising number of those victims are the wealthiest men and women in the US and their families. This time, their vast wealth isn't going to do them much good at all. At least those are the latest figures that I was able to get. If that isn't enough for you, one of the captured drug thugs reports that Donatella, one of the three succubus demons, recruited perhaps as many as a hundred thousand men and women from Detroit and sent them down the Dragon Hole, promising them undefeatable, powerful demon bodies. We don't know whether to believe him, though."

Monica sighed, "Deiter, the thug is probably right. Nine years ago, they did the same thing, promising the fools unlimited power if they went into the Abyss and got new bodies. But 1.3 million? Dieter, I can't deal with that many. No one can. If I push myself, I can maybe do eight per day. It's going to take me nearly five hundred years to fix that many up."

Deiter smiled, "We know, Monica, we know. Even if we somehow got our hands on the few available rings, it will still take half a millennium to regenerate their lost limbs and voices. There's a new group in the States Justice Department looking into it. Last I heard, their best guess was that the women's genetic mutations would be passed on down to their daughters, perhaps not to their sons. So their thinking right now is to dispel all the magical genetic modifications, hoping their future children will be normal.

Between you and me, I'm not holding out much real hope for those million."

Bergson spoke up, "Don't be so hasty, Deiter. This isn't over yet. If I understand it right, these demons can still appear anywhere in the country. What's to keep them from appearing and unleashing more of that bio agent gas stuff? Nada. I think this is just the beginning. There is likely to be far more victims. Mark my words."

"Deiter," Monica backed him up, "he's right. While they've eliminated the obvious and real threat here in the US, the demons aren't going to forget about us. Wiping out the Detroit group will only incite them further. Demons hold grudges for very long times. It wouldn't surprise me in the least to see them dropping by with special delivery 'presents' of that terrible gas stuff. If you have any pull at the federal level, get everyone working on finding alternate cures and to expect more victims. This isn't over, not by a mile."

Her pronouncement sobered the entire group, primarily because she had been so right for so long. Many wished they'd listened to this Demon Hunter's rants over the last nine years, when she claimed the demons were still around and plotting. She'd been right and many knew it, though they dared not say such.

Oliver took control of his meeting once more. "Look. While Bergson and Monica are likely right, let's not forget we've won a victory. We should be thankful we don't have to worry about the Detroit mobs any longer. That is something positive."

Just then, a Message scrolled past Deiter's eyes. His face grimace. "Gotta go. Just got word that Israel has just nuked Iran! Crap! That's going to have all kinds of repercussions. Gotta run." He waved his wand and vanished from the room.

Hastily, Oliver turned on the giant monitor in this conference room. All eyes watched the unfolding news. ". . . has unilaterally taken action early this evening, launching a massive nuclear attack on key installations inside Iran and on the horde on their borders. Initial reports from the Sinai region and the borders with Jordan, Syria, and Lebanon indicate the attacks were successful. The invading army from Iran surrounding Israel has been pretty much annihilated. Only a handful of demons survived. Pundits are suggesting that most of the demons with this northern Iranian army are now pushing through Bosnia, heading for the heartland of Europe. Our reporters in Rabat, Morocco are reporting the southern army of Iran has halted their march towards Gibraltar and are now being transported by magical means northward. Speculation suggests that having increased the number of jihadists from across North Africa, they are planning to join the northern army in preparation for attacking Central Europe.

"This just in. The President of Russia released a brief announcement that they will not allow Iran to counterstrike Israel with nuclear warheads. Finally, someone is using their brains, at least that's what I think, but perhaps it is all talk, since the Israelis probably targeted Iran's weapons in their attacks, and they now have no means to launch such a counterstrike. The question on everyone's mind is where will this demon horde strike? Looking at the map on your screen, the key location is Slovenia. Once they get there, will they strike Austria, Italy, or Hungary? Let's bring in retired General Hamilton and get his professional opinion. General Hamilton."

The gray haired general wore his dress uniform, filled with medals, looking impressive, but overweight. "Thank you. Yes, there are three routes they could take, once they assemble in Slovenia. It is only a short distance across Austria before they are in the heartland of Germany, a vital target. Of course, they could go west, ravaging northern Italy, but that puts them a goodly distance from France. On the other hand, the third route open to them is to go north and east into the Ukraine and ultimately Russia itself."

He went on and the map zoomed out. "Further to the east and south, India and China have already gone on record stating that they would fully back the Holy Crusade to eliminate all Muslims should their lands be attacked.

148

However, my own suspicion is that they are using this as an excuse to exterminate the Muslim population in their lands. We do know that there have been a few demon attacks in those countries, made particularly deadly by the release of the biological agent gas. Neither country has released actual casualty figures as of this morning.

"At this time, I understand that a number of other countries are exploring the solution we've taken with Detroit, seeing that as perhaps the only solution possible. We've seen mass evacuations from towns and cities as the Iranian hordes approach. We can expect far more in the future—"

Since the general continued to droll on, the reporter abruptly cut him off. "The Slovenian government has asked the international community for assistance. Already, we are seeing mass evacuations there. Both Austrian and Italian border crossings are now wide open, and reports suggests thousands are crossing into Austria and Italy every hour. Of course, what happens next is anyone's guess.

"We do know that a number of Schools of Magic in the Balkan lands have already evacuated their students to the safety of other such schools, primarily in France, Italy, and Romania. What of the Armed Forces of these countries? To answer that, let's go to Armando in Paris. Armando, what can you tell our viewers about the mobilization of the French army?"

"Well, Sam, just today, the President of France had ordered a full-scale mobilization of their nation's armed forces. While their actual deployment is top secret, it's reasonable to presume they are setting up along their border with Italy. I spoke with the Italian ambassador earlier today. He hinted that perhaps his country's much smaller army may join with the French. If so, then perhaps the deployment will be in northern Italy. One thing is certain, the arrival of the demons has certainly jelled all the various Islamic jihadist fractions into one united fighting force! Makes me wonder just where they were able to get the arms and munitions for so many fighters. Back to you,

Sam."

Oliver had seen enough. "Well, it's bad over there, but we best get on with our duties here. The meeting is dismissed, by the way." Several chuckled and the group dispersed.

Bergson nodded to Monica, who responded by joining him off to one side, while the others vacated the room, though Kelly and Miller stayed behind, but in the back of the room. "Thanks for sticking around, Miss Black. I know in the past that you made it perfectly clear to us that your private life was your own business, particularly so with the unsolved bombing nine years ago."

"Quite right, Bergson. I've spent nine years trying to put that behind me and move on," she said didactically.

"Well, considering all you've done for us and for so many others, well, we just couldn't let it lie, not like that, unsolved, a cold case. So we asked Oliver if we could look at his files on it."

"Sure hope he told you no," Monica barked reactively. She didn't want old wounds opened.

"Well, he did and we've uncovered some very interesting details the FBI missed. Please, hear us out."

Since he was being polite, Monica resisted the temptation to slap his face and make a hasty exit. He took her silence as her response.

"Kelly made the first discovery. Miss Black, that wasn't a suicide or package bombing as the FBI believed. He found unmistakable traces. The explosion was caused by a US 1,000 pound bomb! From the images of the destruction, it was dropped on your mansion complex from at least ten thousand feet above it."

"What?" Monica shrieked. Images of that day, images that she'd worked hard to suppress, came flooding into her conscious mind.

"Yes, a thousand pounder dropped from at least ten thousand feet. Miller looked into the government's logs— all right, hacked into the logs, and found that an armed drone was indeed over St. Louis on the day of the attack. Further, it was carrying a thousand pounder when it took off in the early morning, but landed that night minus the bomb. She and I did some further checking, calling in a few favors. The men running the flights over Missouri that month were under the control of General Franco. That strike was carried out just like the strike on the Pentagon and on the White House. I believe it was General Franco who ordered that strike, hoping to kill you in your own home when you least expected an attack. After that failed, he had to invent another way to get to you, and I believe that he used us, me and my team, to do just that, eventually getting us to find out about Rolla, knowing we'd go there to investigate. Again, he didn't count on you being able to rescue us and even cure us. Doesn't this make the whole attack make sense now?"

"So my Rob and the others were killed because of me and my attacks on those demons back then? They were killed because of me? It should have been me, not Rob. I was the one who insisted on going out to get the ice cream," Monica wailed in protest, fighting back tears. "Now" was "then" in her mind. "Excuse me, gotta go." Hastily, she teleported to the safety and quite of her own bedroom.

"Boss, I think we've blown it with her," Kelly suggested.

Running his hands through his hair, Bergson said, "Maybe you're right. We should have left it alone. Me and my bright ideas."

Miller spoke up, "I think you stirred up too many emotions, and she needed to be alone, boss. She thinks it was her fault that her husband got killed. That's a lot to take in. Give her some time, some space."

"Miller, I hope you are right. Come on. Work to be done," Bergson declared, still upset that Monica didn't react the way he'd anticipated. No "well done," "good job," "incredible discovery," "makes perfect sense now." Not even a thank you.
***

Ericka Van Nie-Green's ancestors immigrated to the US from Germany over two hundred years ago. However, she still had some distant relatives of the Van Nie lineage living primarily in Bonn, Germany. Some of these were users of magic as well, and they tended to keep in touch. The date was September 15, 2200, the day Monica learned the truth about how Rob had been killed. Ericka was working on enchanting more platinum slugs with Tyler when a message scrolled past her eyes, distracting her from the spell.

"Rats. That one fizzled. Tyler, take over for me for a bit. A cousin in Germany wants a word with me," Ericka explained her rare fumble and headed into the hallway, thankful that she could still work in her lab and not on that stale factory floor where so many volunteers toiled, removing, forming, and replacing the platinum slugs. At least once each day, Tyler made a trip there returning the enchanted ammo they'd made and bringing home more to do. They found this method far less disruptive of their family, especially since their children weren't in school. All schools were still closed indefinitely. Ericka waved her wand and sent back a Message. It was from the middle aged Katarine Van Nie-Stossel, who taught Grade 0 and 1 spells at the Bonn School of Magic.

Magic flashed and the blonde Katarine apparated beside her distant cousin. She was thirty-five years old, relatively attractive, despite having had two daughters and teaching full time at the Bonn School of Magic. However, her eyes were bloodshot and she looked miserable. "Hi Katarine. You look awful. What's happened?" Ericka said. "Come; let's get some tea."

"Thank you for seeing me, Ericka. I just don't know what to do. Adler, he's dead. The demons got him during the last raid. Now they've closed the school and told the parents to flee to safety somewhere. I just don't know what to do," she repeated herself, thankful for a place to sit down.

Making the tea, Ericka said, "Katarine, that's terrible! I liked Adler. He was a good man, able wizard, good with kids. Cursed demons anyway! Honey in your tea?" Katarine pulled out a handkerchief and dabbed her eyes, nodding that she did.

Sipping the brew, she said, "I'm sorry for barging in on you like this, cousin, but I didn't know where else to turn. Germany is in complete chaos right now. I don't think anyplace is safe. Have you seen vat happens to de men und women when they suffer dat biological attack?" she asked, her English slipping slightly. She was terribly upset.

"Yes, we are well acquainted with that. Monica and Chrissy were victims, as were the two male members of her team. However, we were able to get all four cured. You've heard that both mutations can be cured? Just not easily," Ericka asked, hoping to instill a bit of relief in her cousin.

"Ya, ve heard dat der vas some kind of cure, but most hard to do. I'm sorry. I'm not always this upset," Katarine said, still dabbing at her eyes before going on. "Vell, they got our Math Professor and History Professor during one of the random raids. She can't even talk, almost completely helpless and he, vell, he can't even remember his name now. They put both of them in an assisted living complex just at the edge of Bonn. Terrible, just terrible. So she closed the school. I just don't know where to go now."

"Katarine, you come here and stay with us. That's an order, cousin. Come on. I'll go back with you and help you pack and bring your girls. Our kids will enjoy meeting and playing together. Ben is a first year student—well he will be once they open the magic school for the fall term or should I say if and when they do so. I think it's a wise idea to keep the schools closed—too easy a target for the demons. Kids are safer with their families. Come on; drink up. We'll go get your daughters."

"Ve don't vant to impose on you," Katarine protested slightly, trying to at least be a bit polite.

"No imposition, cousin. We've tons of unused bedrooms here and a well-stocked kitchen. We used to have a lot more families staying with us, but that was nine years ago before the place got bombed and Monica's husband and some others were killed. Now we've rebuilt, and I've inserted permanent Force Walls around the whole place. If a bomb goes off, we'll all be safe in here. Come on. Let's get your girls."

Katarine took Ericka's hand and teleported them to her small apartment complex at the Bonn School of Magic, where Mitzi and Nadja, twelve and thirteen respectively, huddled in a bedroom. Both were blondes like their mother.

"You're back. We're hiding. Someone said the school was being attacked so we hid," the older Nadja explained. She was ready for her second year at the school, a proud caster of Grade 0 and 1 spells and now looking after her younger sister.

"Ve saw no signs of an attack. Never mind. Pack your bags. We're going to stay with Cousin Ericka Van Nie-Green in America. St. Louis," Katarine explained, bringing smiles to her daughters' faces.

Eagerly, they began stuffing clothes into bags, though occasionally, Katarine or Ericka cast necessary Shrink spells so they could get everything in them.

As they packed, Nadja pulled on Ericka's dress. She looked down and the young teen whispered, "Are we going to get turned into one of those helpless women with no arms and who can't speak? Me and Mitzi are really scared of that. Mom is too, but she won't say anything about it."

"Not a chance. Even if the demons do it to you, my dear friend who lives with us, Monica, she can undo it and make you all fine again. She and Chrissy were modified by the demons, and she found a way to undo it. So you're more than safe with us," Ericka whispered back, though Mitzi listened to her every word.

An hour later, the girls met the many other children running around the mansion complex and skipped off to play with them. Katarine finally relaxed and volunteered to help with kitchen duties, something that pleased Ericka, who was second only to Monica in finding ways of getting out of her turn cooking group meals.

"So you are Ericka's cousin, pleased to meet you," Monica greeted the new arrival, though Ericka had already notified everyone about Katarine and her daughters. "Welcome. I wish the circumstances were better though. She said that you're a professor at Bonn School of Magic.

What do you teach?"

"Grade 0 and 1 spell casting. I love to work with the beginners and see their potential develop. Say, can I ask all you something? In Bonn, we heard rumors that the demons were recruiting humans and taking them to something called the Dragon Hole. Is there anything to all that? And what is the Dragon Hole anyway?" Now that she was relaxed, her English improved.

Monica answered for her group. "That's correct. You see, the demons are always trying to recruit human beings to turn them into more demons in the Abyss. So are the devils for that matter, only they usually make better offers for your soul, that is, for you, the person. The Abyss offers you powerful bodies that are nearly immune to human attacks, but what they don't tell the recruits is that in their new demon bodies, they aren't likely to be brought back to Earth anytime soon."

She went on, "And the Dragon Hole is real. We, my WIT team and I, have been through it. Millennia ago, there were permanent gates between the Abyss and the Earth, primarily in and around Babylon and perhaps Persia, as Iran was called back then. Long ago, most all these permanent portals between the worlds were destroyed. However, we were told that during the nine years of silence, the demons found one of them and managed to restore it. It looks like a fabulously beautiful oasis in the desert, grasses, trees, and a pond. But if you dive into the pond, the Dragon Hole, you end up in the Abyss, a top level mind you, but still the Abyss, and it stinks horribly."

"Incredible," exclaimed Katarine. "Someone should find it and destroy it. Stop the demons from coming here."

Monica felt rather silly. She should have gotten onto this very project long ago. She and her team were probably the only ones who knew approximately where it was. "We'll look into it," she said. "We really should do that pronto."
***

The next day, Monica sighed, took a deep breath, and headed into FBI headquarters. She knew she had to face Bergson and the others and that she'd reacted badly to their very valuable contribution. They'd solved the nine year old mystery, even if it had upset her. Pride can be a killer, she admitted, and headed to their usual meeting room. She wasn't disappointed. All three were present, discussing something.

Monica interrupted them. "Hi, everyone. Sorry for becoming so emotional yesterday. Thank you all for solving that mystery. I can sleep easier now."

"I'm glad we could do that for you," Chrissy spoke before the others could find a way to blow Monica's arrival.

"Yeah right," Kelly added. "We owe you."

"Well, you might not want to hear what I have to say now," Monica teased all three.

Bergson finally said something, but in an uncharacteristic playful mood, "Just what are you going to get us into this time, Miss Black?"

"The Dragon Hole. Someone has to destroy it, to stop the demons from having a highway to our world, from being able to funnel millions of human recruits down to the Abyss. Look, as far as I know, only we four have been through it and have any idea where it is at. So, gang, it's up to us to find it and blow it up."

"Blow it up?" Kelly perked up. "Now you are talking, Miss Black. That's something I haven't had any chance to do for a long time. Count me in!"

"Can we find it? Is it possible to destroy it?" asked Bergson, somewhat hesitantly. He didn't want to commit his team to a futile exercise.

"If we can find it, then we can destroy it with explosives. If nothing else, we can bury it deep beneath desert sands where it will be useless for a darn long time. The real hurdle is our finding it. I'm going to see about getting some advice on that detail. You all work up the demolitions and supplies we'll need for a desert excursion," Monica suggested.

"Okay then," Bergson declared, "count us in. Let's get cracking. We've a portal to destroy. That should set the demons back some."

Monica knew that since she was there once, she

could simply gamble on a simple Teleport spell. However, once they arrived, how heavily would the Dragon Hole be guarded? If there were a dozen demons on duty, they could well be outgunned. This time, she needed a goodly measure of safety, and thus she contacted Deiter, who Teleported to St. Louis a half hour later.

"So what's this you're talking about?" he asked. "You can get us to this Dragon Hole?"

"Yes, we four were there once, so I can gamble on a Teleport spell. As long as we arrive high we should be okay. Of course, I'll need others to help me with my three team members if we arrive high. Plus the place could well be very heavily guarded. So can you arrange a number of powerful wizards and witches who are willing to lend us a hand? It could well be very, very dangerous. Lord knows how heavily guarded it'll be. If I was in charge, I'd have an army guarding it," Monica explained.

"Great. We could arrive invisible and scout it out, but then the demons can see in the infrared, so that might not work so well. Still, we have to do it. Give me a day to round up a bunch of us. Don't worry. I'll handle Lindsey, who isn't going to like this one little bit. She's still not gone along with the Regent's orders to keep Bradbury's closed. Of course, she's got every protection known to man on the place now."

"Thanks, Deiter. If we're successful, this should put a crimp in the demons' plans, maybe take the pressure off Europe," she suggested.

That night, Deiter Messaged Monica, telling her the attack would take place on September 20 and that his group would arrive at the FBI headquarters around eight that morning.

Chapter 11—The Battle for the Dragon Hole

"Wow Deiter!" exclaimed Monica. He'd arrived bringing fifty others. The entire Rodent Pack was present along with many, many others, primarily from the western states. Everyone carried staves of power or automatic rifles and carried small packs with healing potions in them. Monica gave up on the introductions, simply introducing Bergson, Kelly, and Miller to the large assemblage of wizards and witches. Five minutes passed while they cast many protection spells on everyone present, including the three normals. Kelly and Bergson moved slowly, weighed down with huge backpacks filled with explosives. Miller also carried one, but hers was not as heavy as theirs.

Naturally, Deiter took charge. "Now here's how it will go. Monica will Teleport me and five others there first. As soon as we land, the five will Teleport back here. Since they will then know the location, they'll assist the rest of you to Teleport there. Monica and I will hold them off until you can get there. It shouldn't take all that long, since a Teleport takes only seconds. Bergson, your crew will arrive last, after we engage the guards—can't have our explosive folks getting hurt. We're counting on you being able to blow the Dragon Hole sky high. Okay, let's do this!"

Lindsey, Pam, Amanda, Ashley, and Jim took a hold of Deiter, who latched onto Monica. Lindsey gave Monica a stare that said, "You better not screw this up!" Monica took a deep breath, brought the images she had of the Dragon Hole firmly into her mind, set her arrival point ten feet above the sands, and cast her Teleport spell, dragging the others along with her. Instinctively, she knew why Deiter had chosen them. Ashley was a Class IV Diviner. If anything was going to go terribly wrong, she could warn them. Amanda was a powerful Tracker, so if something did go wrong, she could always find the Dragon Hole on her own, back-tracking the spells. Lindsey wasn't about to let Deiter out of her sight, likewise Jim with Ashley.

Heat. Stifling desert heat stung their faces as their Fly spells detonated. Monica arrived ten feet above the desert floor, some distance from the trees that marked the edge of the oasis. Hovering, Deiter called out, "Bring the others. Monica, go invisible now. Let's scout out the place."

"Deiter, you wait for the rest of us!" Lindsey ordered her husband.

"All right, all right," he exclaimed, clearly frustrated with Lindsey.

After the five left, Monica said, "It will only be a minute or so, Deiter. As I remember it, the Dragon Hole is right in the middle of those dense trees. Grass covers the sands near the pool. Whatever you do, don't go into the water or you'll be sucked down into the Abyss!"

No sooner had she said this than another ten arrived, and then twenty. Within a minute, Bergson, Kelly, and Miller arrived, bringing up the rear. "Crap! I forgot how hot it was," he grumbled, already sweating beneath his heavy load and protective vest.

"You ten, arc around to the rear; you ten, come at them from the right; you ten, the left. Bergson, you keep your group back until we call. The rest, head straight in. No holds barred!" Deiter ordered, and the small army of wizards and witches flew into action.

As soon as they moved out, Bergson barked, "The hell we're going to stay put. Guns armed. Let's head there on foot!"

The trio began trudging across the hot sands. All around them, they could see nothing other than distorted heat rays radiating from the desert. Where were they? They had no idea, but it certainly was remote.

As Deiter closed in and finally entered the oasis, he spotted the guards. Monica was once more dead on. It was heavily guarded, though for a time he didn't realize just how heavily guarded it was! Laying back among the palm trees and positioned to form a giant triangle around the entire oasis were three Type I demons, each nearly nine feet tall, each with a vicious looking bird-like beak that could tear flesh from bone, each with long arms ending in wicked claws larger than a man's head. From the attacks nine years ago and via Monica, Deiter knew that these were the kind that had plagued St. Louis, but were not overly powerful and were rather stupid.

Three strange looking demons perched atop three other palms, looking something akin to a four foot fly. The demons had massive eyes with a long snout. Their front arms ended in claws, but they had four rear legs and strong wings. They were the lookouts that spotted the incoming party as they flew into the oasis, despite everyone being invisible! So much for invisibility and surprise, Deiter thought when these fly demons sounded the alarm. He had no idea what these Chasme demons could do.

Rather, he focused his attention to the three demons he saw close to the edge of the black pool of water, the actual Dragon Hole itself. Thus, he missed spotting yet another deadly demon hiding among the trees. He recognized the three guardian demons at the edge of the pool from Monica's detailed descriptions of the demons that had once plagued St. Louis nine years ago.

One ten-foot tall monster had four arm-like appendages. Two looked like well-muscled human hands, powerful enough to rip off human arms. Two ended in enormous half-ring claws, more than capable of ripping through steel. His head looked more like that of a giant hyena but with overly large teeth. Plus, he had two large horns protruding from the dog-like head. This was a Type III demon. The second demon was a foot taller, but it was positively huge, built more like a sumo wrestler, but with wings and bat-like ears. It stood on cloven hooves, much like giant pig's feet. No doubt about it, this demon could deliver enormously powerful punches.

The third demon by the pool was another tall Cambion, with gray-black skin, oily hair that looked more like punk spikes. His face was sharply angular and V-shaped. Even his ears were V-shaped, as were his eyes, giving it a ferocious appearance. He towered over Deiter at nearly seven feet tall. He wore strange armor plates, carried several swords, but more significantly, he held an automatic rifle.

Topping off the scene, Dieter saw a beautiful, naked woman with long blonde hair swimming in the cool waters of the pool, as though she was merely relaxing and enjoying the day. Oh how Deiter wanted to rescue that beautiful damsel. But first, he knew that he had to take out the Cambion with the rifle, for that alone posed the most serious threat to all the wizards.

With surprise gone, the demons reacted. The Cambion immediately took charge and the others obeyed him. This was Baron Jamal's show. If he performed well here, Gisella promised to promote him to her top general's position. Armed with the latest in human killing weapons, he couldn't fail. He began firing a deadly stream of bullets towards the attackers. Because they were still invisible and flying about, he hit nothing, but his mere automatic fire alarmed every one of the magic users! Their protection spells could handle a couple of bullet hits, but not a stream of them! They were vulnerable to his gunfire.

All manner of spells erupted from both sides, akin to a 4th of July celebration! The three fly-like demons took flight and began attacking the wizards as though they were quite visible. Three veered off and began to duel the Chasme demons, who countered by making a weird noise with their wings, somewhat like cicadas. Pam fell victim to the noise; she ceased flying, landing on the soft sand and grass, sound asleep. One of the Chasme demons landed beside her and tried to insert its long snout into her body, ready to suck her delicious blood. Its nose bounced off of her skin, nearly breaking it. The demon howled in pain and tried to insert its snout again, with no better success. She had her Skin of Stone spell on her, which was saving her, at least for a very short while.

A nearby wizard shot a bolt of lightning onto the Chasme demon, temporarily knocking it off Pam. These demons were quite resistant to magic. It got to its feet, shook itself off, and headed back to suck Pam's blood. *Conk.* Lindsey swooped down, landing a heavy blow to its head from her Staff of Power. As she swooped back up, she shot a very powerful bolt of lightning at the demon. This time, her spell worked. The fly demon shook wildly and collapsed dead on the ground, its remains sizzling from the electrical energy still surging through its body. She then landed by Pam slapping her face to wake her up. "Er, what happened? Thanks, I think," Pam muttered, getting to her feet.

At the same time as the fly demons made their attacks, Deiter and six others saw Baron Jamal as the most serious threat and shot bolts of lightning or balls of fire at the Cambion demon. The baron was powerful and was quite able at resisting the effects of magic, which was one of the reasons he'd risen so rapidly among the ranks of Cambion demons in the outer layers of the Abyss. However, he could not handle six powerful spells at the same time. His still firing rifle managed to wound two of the attacking wizards, but three of their spells affected him. Surrounded by a massive ball of flames, his body jerking wildly from two enormous bolts of lightning, Baron Jamal took the only action possible for him. Writhing in pain and with his body jerking wildly, he managed to dive into the waters of the Dragon Hole, vanishing from sight. In fact, he landed back in the Abyss, specifically at Paradise Fortress, where hundreds of other Cambion demons waited their turn to be taken to Earth to join the glorious battles being fought in Europe. He managed to deliver a final order before he passed out from his injuries, "Under attack. Charge!"

As the baron dove into the waters of the pool, gallantly, Deiter offered his hand to the gorgeous young woman in the pool. "I've come to rescue you. Let me help you out. There's a demon in these waters now."

Simultaneously to these, other attacks happened as well. Esnee, the Type IV demon, bellowed and flew into a pack of flying wizards, swinging his powerful fists, knocking two out and sending them flying off at crazy angles, eventually smashing into the soft sandy ground. Others hovering nearby fired off their power spells at this brutish demon. His resistance to magic was phenomenal.

Ten power spells struck him, but only three actually worked and of those, two he managed to partially nullify their effects on him. He wasn't expecting the acid-like magical arrows and for several more minutes, they continued to eat into his flesh, further wounding him.

Esnee bellowed, lashing out at another pair of flying opponents, both of whom dodged out of the way, but as a result were unable to unleash any spells at him. Eight others fired again. One more spell connected and partially wounded the monster. Their battle waged on for minutes.

Simultaneously, another group of witches took on the Type III demon, being careful to stay well out of range of its four arms. Highly resistant to magic, only four of their initial volley of ten spells had any impact on the demon, who howled from two balls of fire that hit him. However, like most demons, fire damage caused far less than the anticipated damage to the demon. Acids, poisons, and magical missiles were the only forms that were likely to cause the expected range of damage to demons, not electrical based or fire based or even freezing cold based spells. At least these clever witches managed to not get themselves hurt during their first contact with this demon.

The three bird-like Type I demons came charging out of the palm trees, but without Baron Jamal's orders, they didn't know what to do. Hence, their basic instincts took over: kill and devour humans. They darted this way and that trying to grab onto a flying human, but were quite unsuccessful. Shortly after, another group of wizards descended upon them, blasting away at them with numerous bolts of lightning. One succumbed during that initial round.

As Bergson, Kelly, and Miller ran towards the oasis, they heard the sound of automatic gunfire. Bergson knew what that meant and urged his team on at top speed. When they entered the oasis proper and saw the Dragon Hole again, the entire area was lit up like the fireworks finale. For a moment, they stood there trying to grasp the situation.

They saw Deiter apparently helping a beautiful, but

naked woman with long blonde hair get out of the Dragon Hole's waters. The two were off on the left side of the pool from where the trio of normals stood. They saw several of the demons using some form of magical force to literally toss two flying wizards and a witch off like flies, their bodies arcing off and thudding hard against palm trees, knocked out. Those were to their right. They recognized the witch as Amanda Whitewater.

Even more frightening, an unseen until now demon slipped out from the trees where it was hiding, moving swiftly to the fallen Apache. The seven foot tall demon had huge wings, as big as he was tall, with scrawny arms and legs. Its eyes were brilliant and his demeanor, devilishly cunning, glowing reddish as it approached Amanda's body. Further, an eerie, spooky form of not-quite darkness surrounded the demon. As they watched, it looked as if it was bending over to kiss her.

Simultaneously, the gorgeous young woman whom Deiter rescued transformed into her true form, one that Monica recognized instantly. The naked woman in the pool wasn't a damsel in distress. She was Jonellith. The Type V demon, who had once abducted Rob, was seven feet tall. Her upper half looked like a beautiful woman with long blonde hair, except that she had six arms, all wielding various kinds of magical edged weapons, swords, axes, and wicked looking knives! Worse, below her torso, she had a long snake body. Already, its coils wrapped around Deiter's body, while her six arms embraced his body, making him immobile. In seconds, Monica knew that she'd begin constricting the life out of Deiter.

At the same time, Bergson and the others noticed a wave of Cambion demons rising up out of the still waters of the Dragon Hole. Lindsey and Monica both saw that Amanda was in serious trouble as well as Deiter. Monica acted, knowing that Lindsey would never, ever forgive her if anything bad happened to Deiter, though the mess he was in was his own fault. Instantly, Monica opened a Magical Door, stepping out on the back of Jonellith and wrapped her arms around the demon woman's neck, hoping to strangle her or get her to release her hold on Deiter.

Bergson ordered, "Miller, to Amanda. Kelly, open fire. We can't let those demons in the pool get into the battle or it's over!" Both opened fire, raining a hail of enchanted platinum, large caliber bullets at the Cambion demons rising from the pool. Slugs ripped into their bodies, which recoiled this way and that from the heavy impacts. As the arriving demons died, their bodies turned into greenish goo and slowly slipped back into the dark waters, while other Cambion demons moved past their fallen comrades, eager to get to Earth and join the glorious battle, which must be transpiring above. Bergson and Kelly continued firing, loading clip after clip.

Meanwhile, Miller opened fire on the Nabassu demon trying to suck the life out of Amanda via its kiss of death. The shocked demon recoiled wildly from Miller's slugs that tore gaping holes through its body. After taking an entire clip from her automatic rifle, the Nabassu demon took flight, dripping what appeared to be something akin to blood. It swooped and dove into the pool, vanishing from sight, the only demon known to have survived the attack, beyond Baron Jamal and Jonellith. As soon as the demon flew away from Amanda, Miller loaded another clip and joined her team, firing nearly continuously at the arriving Cambion demons.

With the life being squeezed out of him, Deiter realized his folly, but way too late. With the demon wrapped around him, there wasn't any way for Bergson to shoot the bitch without killing him in the process. Lindsey couldn't shoot her spells at Jonellith either, unless she shot magical missiles only, which wouldn't likely do much to this powerful demon woman. He knew that he'd lose consciousness in a few more seconds. She'd already crushed the air out of his lungs. Deiter did the only thing he could think of doing: a half-teleport, taking Jonellith with him to that strange place outside the known universe. Suddenly, Deiter was there, standing on the gray, endless plane outside the universe. The move took Jonellith by complete surprise. She'd never see this place before and had never done a half-teleport. This had been Deiter's secret weapon that had allowed him to capture Dominus and the many Death Stalkers years ago.

On this plane of existence, all motion was done by thought. Here, intelligence mattered. Those with a normal IQ would be transfixed to the spot, unable to even move. Jonellith, however, was a genius, and thus could take full advantage of the strange plane. Unknown to Deiter, he'd also brought Monica with them, since she was holding onto Jonellith's back trying to strangle her.

"Deiter, what is going on? Where are we?" Monica called out, stepping back from the very surprised Jonellith, who had temporarily released her grip on Deiter and was looking around trying to also grasp where she was at.

Deiter didn't want to give anything away to Jonellith. Hence, he sent a Message to Monica: *Move by thinking in this realm.*

Monica was always quick to grasp new situations, always had been, particularly so as Dominus. Wherever Deiter had brought them, here, things worked by thought and intelligence, she thought. *Jonellith is brilliant, too. Well, let's see just how.* Silently and without words to give her away, she cast the Idiot Mind, touching Jonellith on her shoulder.

Suddenly, Monica found herself on a gray, featureless plane facing Jonellith herself. Jonellith was very nearly immune to magical spells, so great was her resistance to them. Thus, a battle of wills ensued, as the two women stared each other down. Jonellith realized Monica was vastly more powerful that her "hero" Deiter, and thus a far more formidable opponent. Rare was the day when she had to have these confrontations of will power.

You cannot win. I am far more powerful than you are, Jonellith thought towards Monica.

While she'd never experienced such a battle of wills before, she grasped what was going on. She thought towards the demon, *Correction. You are about to lose this one. I am the Demon Hunter. You have messed with the wrong woman this time.*

The phrase, Demon Hunter, struck a chord of recognition in Jonellith's mind. For an instant, she recalled helping Donatella once, when she coiled a man called Rob. Ah, Monica. Now she recognized her and knew who Monica actually was. She was the woman who had escaped from Graz'zt's clutches and Rob, hers. That instant, she felt a slight doubt, an infinitesimal break in her confidence. Magic flashed. The void gray plane vanished for both women, who found themselves back with Deiter in this strange location. However, Jonellith stood there utterly motionless. She'd lost the battle with Monica, whose spell activated. Now with a moron's IQ, Jonellith was unable to function at all in this environment.

What the hell did you do to her? Deiter sent, then sent, *Oh, Idiot Mind. Damn, Monica, you are good, far better than I ever gave you credit for. It's the prefect spell to use in this place. Of course, now what do we do with her? I suppose I should use one of her swords and cut her head off.*

Don't you dare, Deiter Cross! We don't murder unnecessarily. Jonellith is defeated. Toss her back into the Dragon Hole, send her back to where she belongs, Monica sent.

Deiter gave Monica a strange look but complied. In the next instant, Monica, Jonellith, and Deiter appeared above the Dragon Hole. He dropped the shocked demon down into the waters. Her body sunk below the waters and did not resurface. Meanwhile, the two landed near the water's edge trying to grasp the current situation.

The battle for the Dragon Hole ended. Wounded men and women sat around pouring healing potions down each other like water, while Kelly and Bergson scampered about, setting their numerous charges, and Miller stood by, her automatic rifle pointing at the pool in case more Cambions appeared.

Lindsey spotted Deiter and rushed over to him. "Are you all right?" she yelled as she ran to him. "You fool. You scared me out of my wits! Monica, are you okay?"

Flushing, Deiter said, "Yes, I'm okay, thanks to Monica here. Did a half-teleport. Monica figured it all out and cast Idiot Mind on Jonellith. How she was able to do that is beyond me. That Jonellith is almost immune to magical spells."

"Monica, again, I thank you for saving my silly husband. Honestly, Deiter, what were you thinking? A naked maiden in distress? Here? Among the demons? Honestly, Deiter Cross, we're going to have to have a very long talk when we get home!"

Monica suppressed a chuckle and didn't want to be in his shoes when they got home.

She turned to Monica. "Your team saved our butts. This certainly is a portal. Numerous Cambions came sweeping up from the pool to join the battle, but your team mowed them down with gunfire before they could get out of the pool. Saved our collective butts. Well done. They're setting up the explosives now. None of our party is seriously hurt, few broken bones and concussions. Healing potions are handling everyone's injuries. Get ready to evacuate. Kelly says he'll be set in a couple of minutes."

Deiter asked, "So Monica, mind telling me how you managed to best Jonellith?"

Monica smiled, "I'll tell you if you will tell me where the heck you took us?"

Deiter laughed. "You want to know my secret weapon, eh, the one that captured you and the Death Stalkers, eh?" He purposely kept his voice down so that no one overheard him.

"Sounds like a fair trade to me," Monica teased, smiling broadly, knowing that she'd get the better deal this time, if he would actually tell her.

Deiter looked at her silently for a moment. "Well, you've saved my butt several times now, so I suppose you aren't Dominus any longer. Okay, I'll bite. You tell me and I'll tell you."

"Okay. It was a battle of wills, Deiter, something that I excel in," Monica began.

The two talked in hushed tones for several minutes

before Kelly was ready to blow the hole. Lindsey moved everyone back to the safe distance that Kelly suggested. To be safer, several wizards threw up walls of force. Proudly, Kelly pressed his igniter button, triggering the explosion of nearly four hundred pounds of C-4.

The massive explosion shook the earth beneath their feet, but numerous Silence spells dampened the sound. Kelly had also given the Abyss a bit of a surprise. He'd attached some C-4 to a long wire, lowering it far down into the pool. Thus when the explosion occurred, it also took part of the Paradise Fortress with it. The dust cloud was enormous. "Wonder if we used a bit too much?" Kelly teased Bergson.

Bergson stared at Kelly before breaking into a laugh. "Kelly, never is too much too much for you!" Both men laughed.

A half hour passed before enough dust and sand settled so that they could inspect the damage and see if they'd actually destroyed this ancient, but restored, portal to the Abyss. As the large group stepped gingerly around the area, they saw nothing but the reddish sands of the vast desert region. The Dragon Hole was either destroyed or at least buried beneath tons of sand.

Standing approximately where the portal used to be, Deiter declared, "Well, that should put a damper on more demons coming into our world. Now they will be forced to use Gate spells. Well done, everyone, well done."
***

At her hiding place somewhere in Washington, DC, Gisella fumed when she learned of the destruction of her Dragon Hole. Stomping around her apartment, she swore to get even. Things were definitely not working out as she'd so carefully planned. General Franco had served his purpose, but the loss of Detroit and all those demons, to say nothing of her fellow succubus was a severe blow to her plans for the US. However, she still felt confident of overall victory. The war over in Europe was rapidly advancing, faster than she'd even anticipated. Soon, Europe would be under her control. Time enough to go after the US then, she thought. Besides, Bella could open Gates and bring up more reinforcements as she needed. This was merely a minor setback.

Chapter 12—The Rise of the Reich

Something Katarine mentioned bothered Ericka. A new group calling themselves the Schutzstaffel or Protection Squadron was claiming to have a way to stop and destroy the Iranian horde and the demons. She didn't know much more, only that their abbreviation, SS, struck a chord in many Germans. "Times are getting desperate and people will grasp at anything that offers them safety and security," Katarine stated. Thus, while Monica was off with Deiter attempting to destroy the Dragon Hole, Ericka decided to investigate the Schutzstaffel group. She doubted that they could offer the type of protection that Katarine suggested they could.

***

In his new and secure quarters in the heart of Spandau, just west of Berlin proper, Dr. Hans Menninger set up his new organization in total secrecy from his demon allies. While Prince Graz'zt had had his plans and now Gisella had hers, they never considered just what Dr. Menninger desired. No, they'd used him and his genetics research and experimentation for their own ends. Now at last, he was going to execute his own plan and those did include the demons and the jihadists, just not the way that they believed. His friend many centuries ago, Adolf, had the right ideas, but the fool didn't carry them out. He, Dr. Hans Menninger, would not fail, for the time was right, the world, primed and ready to accept the Fourth Reich.

It had taken him nine long years to cultivate and find just the right three top men to aid him in his quest. These included General Berend Bettingdorf, who led his newly formed Schutzstaffel, Propaganda Minister Dirk Nordstrom, a wealthy man who knew how to manipulate people to obtain what he desired, often their support and funds, and Dr. Fritz Bielfeld, who owned the largest pharmaceutical company in Germany and who was independently wealthy as well. All three men were also wizards, though nowhere near as accomplished as Dr. Menninger.

Phase I, recruitment, was checked off as completed by late May. His Schutzstaffel then boasted a thousand followers. Phase II was carried out by his SS men during the summer of 2200 and was checked off as done just before the first word of the demons became public knowledge. Dr. Menninger now had a complete listing of all those influential men in Germany and their political leanings. A second list contained the names of those men and women who were certain to oppose Dr. Menninger and his plans for the Fourth Reich. These would have to be handled when the time came.

Also during this period, Fritz began preparations for mass production of several of Dr. Menninger's new formulas. These were, in point of fact, a pill formulation of his biological-genetic agents, specially crafted for his new Reich. There were two different pills to be given to the women. Both pills would genetically modify the woman into Dr. Menninger's ideal form for the woman objects of his new Fourth Reich. One aspect of the twenty-first century that irritated the doctor more than almost anything else was the idiotic notion that women were equal to men. The women's liberation, he found beyond disgusting and as a result built up strong allies in Saudi Arabia, where the wealthy oil magnates were increasingly desperate, since no vehicles now used gasoline. Demand for their sole resource had become as dry as their desert sands. Hence, the ideal woman object for his new Fourth Reich was much like the women now living in Rolla, North Dakota. No lower arms and hands. That was mandatory to keep women in their proper roles in the Reich. To compensate them for that loss and to keep men pleased, their bosoms had to be at least that of an H-cup in size. Plus, he found women wearing very high stilettos enchanting. Thus, their feet and legs had to be altered such that they couldn't wear anything lower than a six-inch heel, preferably a seven-inch heel. What was the difference between the women's red pill and their pink pill? Simple. The red pill was for those who would likely oppose him and his Reich. Like the women of Rolla, they had no voice boxes and thus couldn't speak out their condemnations. The other pill had no such impact, for the women who got this pill would be supportive of the new Fourth Reich.

Pills for the men came in three varieties. The blue pill would be handed out to those who actively opposed him and his Reich, aging their brains to that of a hundred-year-old man while dropping their IQ levels to the moron range, ending their ability to effectively oppose him, presuming they could realistically function in the new Reich society. The brown pill was designed for his supporters. The genetic modifications lowered their IQ levels somewhat, but also increased their stamina and physical strength. These men would form the backbone of his Schutzstaffel, his Protection Squadron. The green pills would be given to his loyal followers and apparently did nothing physically to the men. However, carefully crafted into all three types of men's pills was a subtle enforcer that made it very hard for the pill-taker to disobey any order given by himself, his staff, or his SS men, akin to a Mass Charm spell.

Further, all five pills had an additional component, an anti-demon-killing compound—essentially an anti-radiation dose, which would neutralize the effects of his coming "bomb" that would terminate demons and the human jihadists with them. He had long ago found the Achilles heel of the demons among which he'd lived with for so long. They couldn't tolerate high levels of gamma radiation. It had something to do with the makeup of the Abyss and its basic particles of matter.

When the demons broke onto the international arena in the late summer, Dr. Menninger was prepared. His thousand-man Schutzstaffel were given their monthly supply of their green pills and Phase III began. Propaganda Minister Dirk took center stage. The SS rounded up likely supporters for a meeting to discuss the demon problem. While Dirk did discuss the problem, outlining how events would likely play out and to everyone's total surprise, predicting the total downfall the US government, he also encouraged them to join the Schutzstaffel and help support the new leader, Der Führer, who alone would lead everyone to victory over the demon hordes. The men and few women who attended these first meetings were those already selected as being likely to support Dr. Menninger and the new Reich. During his speeches, Dirk used a Mass Charm-like spell on the gathering, but unlike the casting of the spell, which would be readily detected by the wizards and witches in attendance, his use was far more subtle, woven into the fabric of his speeches and thus undetectable as a "spell."

Thus, during July and August, the numbers in the Schutzstaffel grew to nearly a hundred thousand. Still Dr. Menninger hung back, waiting for the precise time to make his appearance known. When Israel bombed Tehran and the Holy Crusade announced, followed by the counterattacks out of Iran and as the demon led hordes began making their incredibly rapid advances, Dr. Menninger finally entered the picture and began Phase IV.

Chaos reigned. The Board of Regents closed all schools of magic around the world, unwilling to have these random and horribly debilitating attacks harm the young and future wizards and witches. That only fueled the fires. According to Gisella's plan, a few random demon raids took place throughout Germany as well as other key countries. It likewise strengthened Dr. Menninger's hand, for President Maud Schmidt was seen as being a wholly ineffective leader. She had no way to predict these attacks or protect German citizens, much less undo the horrific aftereffects of the bio-genetic agent attacks that left men as morons and women unable to speak and virtually helpless.

During the entire late winter and spring, General Berend's task was to ramp up production of women's quality high heels, the kind that they'd have to wear once genetically modified, women's blouses, tops, and dresses that supported H-cup bosoms, and even production of full dentures in commonly needed sizes. Thus, when the first bio-genetic agent attacks occurred and Schmidt's government was wholly unable to handle the victims, members of the Schutzstaffel stepped in, providing the women the items that they needed to survive, further embarrassing the government and gaining more support from the average German citizen. The stage was now set for Dr. Menninger's Phase IV. People were scared; many were terrified and would listen to his words.

His timing was impeccable. The very day when Gisella's forces launched a surprise bio-genetic agent gas attack on the key government officials, including President Maud Schmidt, he activated Phase IV. His Schutzstaffel drove around the streets of Spandau announcing a huge public meeting that evening in the old Olympia Stadium, where Der Führer himself would address those in attendance, promising them safety and protection from the demonic hordes.

The stadium was packed that night. As usual, Dirk spoke first, priming the overflowing crowd of very desperate, worried men and women. "And now it is my greatest pleasure to introduce to you our savior, the man who is bringing the Fourth Reich into being, our leader, Der Führer himself. Please welcome Hans Gotthilf!"

Dr. Menninger had very carefully chosen his new alias. God Help. Yes, it was subtle, but had a remarkable impact on the masses. Wearing his new uniform, dark gray with a black armband indicating he was a member of the SS, Dr. Menninger took the stage in the first of many, many such speeches throughout Germany during late August and all of September. There was quite a lot of wild cheering at various times during his speeches, but for clarity, those will not be so indicated.

"Welcome one and all. I am so glad to see that you, the elite of all Germany, have come out tonight to see what can be done to protect your selves, your families, and your loved ones. Our government has failed to do so and has failed to even protect themselves from this demonic horde. Yes, it is true. Our President Schmidt is herself a tragic victim, unable to speak and virtually helpless.

"You, my friends, you have the vision to look for real

answers, real help. For that, I am truly impressed with each one of you here tonight. Unlike our corrupt and ineffective elected officials have told you, there is hope for the future. These demons can be stopped. Long have I known of their existence on our world and long have I labored to develop a foolproof and certain way to stop the demons.

"You've undoubtedly heard from highly knowledgeable wizards and witches that these demons are impossibly hard to slay, that they resist magic spells. Certainly our normal weapons, anti-tank guns, and missiles have no impact on the demons, other than perhaps annoying them or enraging them. And they are right. Yes, the wizards and witches are quite correct when they say these demons are highly resistant to magical spells and nearly immune to all of our conventional weapons. But dear people, there is hope. That hope lies in me!

"Why? I have discovered a way to terminate demons! Yes, kill them outright!" After the noise died down, he continued, "I've developed a special formula that will do just that. However, and this is a big however, humans are adversely affected as well. I asked myself, what good is it to kill a horde of demons attacking a city if I also kill off all the good people of the city? Nada. Nein! Thus, I set to work yet again. I had the way to terminate demons, but I also needed a way to protect us humans in their vicinity.

"Long has been my researches and studies, but I stand before you today to tell you that I have solved that problem! If you take a simple pill each day, and if you have the misfortune to be near a demon horde attack and if I am able to use my demon-termination method, you will suffer no ill effects whatsoever, while the demons and their evil jihadist supporters will perish! Both problems are solved! Bielfeld Pharmaceuticals is mass producing my formula pills for you. We've got plenty of supplies at this time.

"However, it is long, long past a time for change in the leadership of our magnificent country, mother Germany. Our corrupt and wholly ineffective leaders have now managed to bring us to the very brink of total destruction—indeed total annihilation of the entire world! We cannot look to the US for aid. Their government officials are now victims, morons at best. My friends, if we, you and I, do nothing, by the end of the year, we will all be under the domination and control of the demons, perhaps even sent down to rot in the Abyss itself! It is time for a new government, one which will lead us to total victory over these vile, evil demons, a government of the people and for the people, you, the people. Yes, I am talking about a new and glorious Fourth Reich!

"It is long past time for we, the mighty German people, the true Aryans, to rise and accept the leadership of the world in these the darkest times our world has ever seen. We should and we must lead. We must defeat the demons and the jihadists. No, I'm not calling on or supporting the Pope's Holy Crusade. Extermination of a people based solely on their religious beliefs, no matter how much we might find their religion objectionable, is not the answer. We do not stand for extermination, but for life, for families, for a future filled with prosperity and goodness for all!"

He knew from data gathered during Phase II that many people found the Pope's call for a Holy Crusade to wipe out all Muslims highly objectionable. Thus, he played into their point of view quite nicely. Dr. Menninger continued, lowering his voice strategically, "We know for a fact that women are the foundation of the entire human race. Without women bearing children, our future generations, we as a people will cease to exist! We should not and cannot afford to send our women into combat situations, unlike the policies adopted in the US and France, for example, and nearly so here in our country. Those countries might as well point a gun to their own heads, for they are heading for extinction. No, we must honor, cherish, and protect our women, those who bring forth new life, new generations.

"So I stand here before you this evening to announce the Fourth Reich, one in which our women will be treated as women should, the mothers of our future, our children.

We simply cannot allow our women to be endangered in any way whatsoever. It's simply not right.

"That said, tonight I ask you to support me, your Führer, and the Schutzstaffel. I and the SS will protect you and your families and loved ones. We will defeat and exterminate the demonic hordes. If I fail to do so, then you may toss me out of my position. I swear to you, my friends, that I possess the way, means, and will to destroy these demons and their jihadist followers. Join and support me and my protection pills will be provided to you at no cost to yourselves. Thus, if the demons attack near where you are located and I use my special weapon on them, you will not be harmed, but those who do not support me and choose not to take the pills surely will perish along with the demons. To them, I say good riddance. We must all work together. No man can stand wholly alone. Join us tonight and my special pills will be provided to you and your family.

"By joining, you also agree that the women in your life are precious and must be cared for, nurtured, and protected. Again, anything needed by the women will be provided at no cost to you, my supporters. Together, you and I, can and will build a new Fourth Reich. Our women will bring forth new generations. We will survive far into the future. The way that nations are crumbling as we speak, we may well find that we alone inherit the Earth. Trust in me and I will lead you forth into a brand new world, devoid of demonic hordes, filled with peace and prosperity. It is your choice. If you do not trust me as President Schmidt has done, then it is your right to take your chance, though I suspect you would prefer death to what has become of her or the now moronic men she had around her.

"Together, my friends, you and I, we will defeat this monumental threat to the very existence of human life on Earth. More importantly, we will survive, and through our women, we will create future generations."

He lowered his voice once again. "I know that there are those who believe that with my Schutzstaffel, my SS protectors, history is repeating itself. I'm referring to that ancient, insane man, Hitler, who led our country to near total destruction. I've no intentions, no plans to conquer the world. I've no army and I don't care to have one. We're not mobilizing for war, but we are preparing our arsenal to use against the demonic horde as it nears our beloved country. Make no mistake about this: if that demonic horde advances one inch onto German soil, I will not hesitate to strike and exterminate them. But as I have said, humans foolish enough not to join us and who are not taking the protective pill will also perish. My general claims such casualties are merely collateral damage and must be accepted if we are to exterminate the demonic hordes. I agree with him. That's why I am appearing before you tonight, long before that horde can reach our land, and am doing my best to encourage you to join us and take our offered pills, so that when it comes, and I assure you that it will be coming, you and your family will not be harmed while the demons perish, as they should and must.

"Please, please do not wait until the very last minute to join us. There might not be sufficient time to get the pills to you before we have to strike the demons dead. I know some of you are ready and willing to join up tonight. Please see one of the Schutzstaffel men in gray and get signed up. We'll get the needed pills to you as quickly as possible, along with all the things that may be needed for the women in your family to thrive and prosper as well. Yes, life for our women will be different, but they will be highly honored, respected, protected, and encouraged to bring forth our new generations as only they can do.

"If you need time to think about taking this fundamental step to ensure your survival and that of your family in these, the most perilous times ever recorded on Earth, then do so. When you have made your decision to join us and survive the coming holocaust of humanity, please contact any one of our Schutzstaffel, the men in the gray uniforms, and they will help you get signed up and your pills and your women's supporting needs filled. If you wait until the last moment, I have no sympathy for you. I've done my work to ensure the survival of my beloved

German people, but it is up to you to make an effort to ensure your own survival and that of your loved ones. Please don't wait until it is too late. Thank you for your time tonight. Remember always, that I, Der Führer, Hans Gotthilf, will not allow the demons onto one inch of German soil, not ever. I so swear to you."

He waved to the thunderous applause, smiling all the while. It took five minutes for the noise to die down. Only then did he walk smartly off the center stage. His SS men had hundreds of tables set up on the playing field. As expected, thousands came down from the bleachers to sign up. The men took down the specific details of each man and his family, cleverly cross-checking them against the "bad" list of those who were expected to be totally against the Fourth Reich. Those who tried to "get in" and were on that list found themselves being escorted out of the stadium, but were given ways and means of proving that they had had a true change of heart. Later on, wizards who could cast Detect Lie interviewed them and a few were allowed to join.

Each recruit who had one or more females in their families was told just what would physically happen to his women. The explanation given was this was the only way that the women could survive the weapon that was going to be used on the demons. Put that way, most continued with the sign up process. A few "had to think about it." That first night, over ten thousand signed up, but when one adds in the other members of their families that were also covered, multiply that by at least five.

By the time the demon horde reached the pivotal zone in Slovenia, the Fourth Reich numbers had swelled to well over two million, rising rapidly each day. The fear and chaos the demons instilled drove Germans into the Fourth Reich in droves, just as Dr. Menninger planned. Now, he moved on to Phase V, in preparation for the advancing hordes.

Now it wasn't implied that no one openly objected to his Fourth Reich. More than a few normals, wizards, and witches were quite vocal in their objections to his scheme.

Many claimed that he should give the pills to everyone, particularly if that was the only protection they'd have if and when he used his "secret weapon." Others demanded to know just what this weapon actually was. Still others demanded that he make it broadly available to all countries.

In one speech, he addressed a few of those issues. "Who has come to our aid, our rescue? No one. No country is helping us. It is up to us to protect ourselves and our families from the demon threat." After that, those who were considered the most threatening to his program simply vanished in the night. They were given the usual bio-genetic agent gas and genetically modified as those who lived in Rolla were. When they came out of their comas, they were quietly removed to remote assisted living complexes.

What of Gisella and Bella? Both were convinced by Dr. Menninger that all this was merely part of Gisella's Grand Plan to reduce and remove potential threats against her invasion force.

***

Mid-September came, and as the newscasts reported, the demon horde entered Slovenia; many began to seriously worry. Among such millions were Professors Heine and Wanda Walburg. Heine was a marginal wizard, never having mastered any spells beyond Grade 5, but he was a Professor of Math at the Berlin School of Magic. He loved to teach young people math skills. His wife, Wanda, was considered a powerful witch, having mastered six Grade 8 spells. Also a professor at the Berlin school, she taught Illusion Theory and all the more advanced illusion based spells. They had three children. Susanne was the oldest at fourteen and was about to start her third year at the magic school. Sofia was thirteen and ready for her second year, while Erich was twelve and terribly disappointed that he couldn't start his first year and learn proper magic.

Both professors and their children looked forward to the start of the fall term when in mid-August, the Board of

Regents ordered all magic schools to close indefinitely, due to the worldwide demon threat. For over a month, both professors worried about this, while their children complained bitterly about not being able to go back to magic school, none more so than Erich who felt somehow betrayed. Everyone else in his family could cast some spells, but not him. Hardly a day passed without everyone hearing his bitter complaints.

The SS men drove the streets of Berlin on a daily basis, advertising for the evening's meeting. By the middle of September with the horde entering Slovenia, Heine and Wanda finally decided that for the safety of their children, they should at least go to one of these meetings and find out what this was all about. Wanda had constantly reminded Heine that demons were resistant to magic spells and thus very hard to slay or banish. That the vile creatures were so close to Germany caused both to worry, particularly since they'd seen what had happened to their president and other government leaders and also had heard about the catastrophe in Washington, DC, crippling America. No help from that ally.

After the meeting, they watched as thousand flocked to sign up, but they were far more cautious. When they returned home, Susanne asked how it went. "Are we going to join up and be safe when the demons come, mom?" she asked.

"Dear, I just don't know. It's awful for us women," she shuddered.

"We best explain everything to the children. They deserve to know, no matter what we decide," Heine insisted.

"What's so awful, mom? We don't want to be eaten by demons," Sofia insisted, having heard rumors that the demons devoured those they killed.

"Well, this man, Hans Gotthilf, claims that he has developed something that will kill the demons," Wanda explained.

"That's good, right?" put in Susanne.

"Of course, dear. But whatever it is that he will be using will also kill any of us who are unprotected by his special pills."

"So we get his pills," Erich broke in. The solution seemed simple to him.

"We would like to but," Wanda continued, trying to find a way to explain the consequences, "we have to join his new Fourth Reich organization and support him."

"Well, that can't be so bad, if he's going to kill the demons," Sofia added.

"We aren't so sure, dear. You see, the pills will protect us and apparently there are no side effects on men, but for the women, the side effects are monstrous. There's no easy way to say this. If women and girls take these pills, we will lose our lower arms and hands. Our breasts will grow quite large and our feet will get changed somehow, forcing us to have to wear really high heels. We'll be pretty helpless like that."

"Oh! But will we still be able to cast spells?" asked Susanne. "That's what is really important, mom."

"Well, there would be a way. If Heine here casts his Morph spell on us, he could change us to what we look like now, with arms and hands. Then, we could cast spells. But one Dispel Magic spell and we're back to being handless and wouldn't be able to hold our wands," she explained.

"But we will be alive, won't we?" Erich interjected, "and the demons dead."

"That's what this man is saying, son," Heine said.

"Well, I want to be alive and go to magic school!" Erich declared flatly.

"But son, if we do this, you're going to have to be your sisters' hands around here. They'll need help with nearly everything, unless I can keep up with the Morph spells," Heine cautioned his son.

Erich frowned, turning up his nose. Heine admonished him, "Look, you help them around the house, and they can help you with your beginning spell casting. Now isn't that a fair trade, son?"

He looked at his sisters and then said, "Well, I

suppose so."

"No supposing, son. If we go ahead and do this, then there will be three of them who need our help with most everything, and there's only one of me. I need your solemn word that you will really help your sisters when they need it," Heine insisted.

"All right. All right, but I want to learn magic soon," Erich declared.

"So do we," Susanne added.

"All right, kids. Go play and let your father and I discuss this," Wanda insisted. After they ran off, she said, "Heine, I still don't think this is such a good idea. How will I be able to fix our meals?"

"Oh, I'm sure I can keep you going with a Morph spell. I'll have to take on more responsibility around the house, too. No question about that. No more ball games for me on Saturdays."

She grinned. He was a couch potato many Saturdays. "Well you certainly will have to do a lot more around here. Your Morph spells have a tendency to last less than a day. Still, they did say that they would be providing what we women will need, clothes and shoes."

Heine laughed, "That's a bargain! You women go through more clothes than I ever imagined!" Both laughed. After more discussion, they decided to play it safe and join. After all, they had to consider their children. Wanda knew that she alone could not fight off even one demon, should they invade Berlin. Heine would be nearly useless, almost as bad as a normal fighting a demon. For both, the safety of their children was paramount and ultimately the deciding factor. The next day, they signed on.

"Welcome to the Protection Squadron! I can assure you that when the demons come, you and your family will be safe. Now then, let's get the specifics down. I need the names and ages of everyone in your family," the polite man said. After that, he carefully noted the three female's ages, height, and weight. He asked for their current dress sizes and their shoe sizes as well.

He then retrieved five bottles of pills. "The system of

pills is truly a wonder of simplicity. You and your son, Heine, each take a green pill every morning. The pink pills are for Wanda and the girls. Get it? Green and pink—can't possibly make an error. Now it is important for you to take one pill every twenty-four hours. That's to keep the antidote at full capacity in your systems. We never know when the demons might attack, though it sure looks like it will be sooner than later!"

He went on, "Now Heine, you and," he paused to glance at the paper, "Erich will have no ill effects. In fact, you will likely not even know that you've taken the pills. However, a few hours after Wanda and the girls take their first pill, they will fall into what is called a mutation coma. It's perfectly harmless. They will be in a coma for about four or five days before they will wake up. It's perfectly safe. No woman or girl, not even a baby girl, has yet to suffer any complications or ill effects. Just make sure that they are undressed and tucked into beds before they fall into comas. Often, women take their first pill of an evening and simply go to bed. That's what my wife did. Here's a number to call if you suspect anything is amiss. But honestly, millions have undergone the process, and no one has yet to call. It's a perfectly safe procedure.

"Now during those four or five days, one of the SS men will drop by with new clothing and shoes for the women. Later on, you and they can visit any of the new apparel shops being setup around Berlin and acquire any additional clothing and shoes they desire, all free as promised."

Heine chuckled, "That will save us a bundle on our clothing allowance."

The man laughed. "You know, I feel the same way. My lovely wife spent more on her wardrobe than she did on groceries. Well, it seemed like that to me. Now we are saving a bundle, all thanks to the Fourth Reich."

Wanda asked, "Which reminds me, just how can this Reich afford so much clothing and shoes? With millions as you say needing them, it must cost them a fortune."

The man laughed. "We've a lot of very wealthy men

in the SS. They are kindly offsetting those costs. They recognize the incredible value of you women in our world and want to do their part. You see, everyone has a role to play in saving our country from the demons. Any questions? If you have questions later, don't hesitate to contact us. Again, welcome to the Schutzstaffel and the Fourth Reich."

The two headed home with their precious five bottles of pills. After supper and just before bed, the five took their first pill. After that, Wanda got each daughter nicely tucked into her bed, before turning in herself. "You watch over us, Heine. We're depending on you now and on Erich."

"I'll be here all the time. Now get some sleep. See you when you wake up. I love you and the kids more than I can say." Heine gave her a loving kiss, but wondered what the future would bring for this family of light blondes. They all had blue eyes as well.

Two days later, an SS man dropped by, leaving three outfits for each female in the house. He explained, "Deitrick's is the closest shop to you. Once your women get comfortable with their modifications, you should take them on a long shopping spree. I followed that advice with my wife. Let me tell you that made a huge, huge difference in her outlook. Now, I have to take her there at least once a week! Best part, it's free!"

"Thanks. I will certainly follow your advice. Not sure why, but my women do love to go shopping," Heine replied.

"Heine, this is vitally important. Included is a lengthy DVD on tips for the women. You should make them watch it many times, particularly when they first rouse. My wife has nothing but the highest praise for the DVD. You see, most believe that they are now helpless. The DVD shows them that they are far from helpless. It's just that my wife now has new ways to do the things she used to do. Make darn sure that they watch it at least a dozen times or more. By the way, my wife and I are now so much closer than we were. This has brought us together more than I ever expected. It also saved me big-time euros, because she had been hounding me to get breast implants you see. Now, she's more than pleased with her look and so am I for that matter. Say, once things settle down here, we could use more help delivering clothes to others. So many are now joining us that it's hard to keep up with the demand. Anyway, remember to visit Deitrick's soon. Best get going. I've got five more deliveries to make today. Glad to have you with us." They shook hands and the gray uniformed man left.

After sorting out the clothes and putting them in the proper bedrooms, Heine put the DVD in his player to satisfy his own curiosity. It was a huge collection of women who either had no arms at all or were missing most of them. Their videos demonstrated how they accomplished tasks of life, including vacuuming the floor. Heine was impressed and vowed to make all three study this video at length. Now, he could only watch over them and wait.

By the fourth day, the changes were readily apparent. Erich called out, "Hey dad, come look. Susanne's arms are falling off. Cool. Now she can't tickle me anymore."

Heine joined him and saw that they had indeed dried up and fallen off, leaving no scars at the ends of her upper arms. Quietly, he gathered up the six husks and disposed of them. He certainly didn't want the three to see them. Then, he sat Enrich down for a serious talk. "Son, when they wake up, they are going to feel terribly afraid and helpless. You must be strong for them and help them."

"But dad," he protested.

"Okay son. Lesson time." Heine focused, waved his wand, and Morphed Erich into Susanne as she now appeared in bed.

Erich screamed as the reality that his sisters would soon be facing struck home with him. "Dad, put me back. I promise. I promise," he pleaded. Heine canceled his spell.

"Good. If I catch you not helping them when they need it, I'll Morph you again until you learn. We have to respect them and be here for them. They are depending upon us, son."

"Okay, okay," Erich wailed, though he still wanted to figure out how he could avoid sister duties and not get on his dad's bad side.

Around noon on the fifth day, one by one the women woke from their mutation comas. As each awoke, their reactions hardly varied at all. Shock and panic reigned king for about an hour in the Walburg household, beginning with Wanda. "Heine! Help! Oh god! Help me!" she shrieked as she began to panic, moving her arms about trying to do what she'd always done with her hands as she awoke in the mornings, only they weren't there. Compounding the situation, she desperately needed to use the bathroom. Heine dashed to her side, helping her sit up and then stand.

Both Wanda and her daughters preferred longer hair and kept theirs trimmed just below their upper back. As she sat up, she saw her hair had grown significantly, now reaching her knees. Compounding her panic, she found it difficult to see over her bosom. When she went to bed, she had relatively small, but ample breasts. Now they seemed gigantic to her, somewhat obstructing her view. Further, as Heine helped her stand, she nearly fell. Her feet wouldn't lie flat on the carpeted floor, only her toes would.

"I have you. To the bathroom," Heine said, trying hard not to panic himself. After getting her situated, Susanne cried out in a similar panic.

"Go to her," Wanda whispered bravely. Heine dashed off to Susanne's room.

"I've got you. Bathroom, right?" he asked, wondering how both could use it at the same time.

"Dad, I'm really helpless now. And I have to. . ." she said in a rush.

He interrupted her, "I know, use the bathroom. Mom's on it, but let's get you there right away. Up you go, but watch your balance."

"My hair. Dad, it's so long now. Oh, I can't hardly stand. I feel so—oh!" Looking down, she suddenly noticed her new bosom and flushed. Before, hers had been just starting to fill out, a fact that she was very proud of, but now it was twice the size of what she remembered her mother's was, but she didn't dare tell him about that. Like Wanda, she could only just barely walk.

By the time they reached the bathroom, Wanda had gotten herself up and was leaning precariously against one wall. He sat Susanne down and helped steady Wanda, leading her back to her bedroom. They barely got there when Sofia began yelling, panic stricken as well. Heine dashed off to her bedroom. Sofia had much the same reactions as her mother and sister had. Heine was thankful that Susanne had the presence of mind to get herself up like her mother had, and he got Sofia on the toilet just in time.

A bit later, he went back to Wanda. "Now we have to get you dressed, dear. This pile is what they brought, but you are going to have to tell me what you want to wear."

"Heine, my bosom—it's, it's. . ."

"I know, huge, but we'll manage dear. Blouse, pants, dress?"

"Best try the dress. This is miserable. I can't get my hair out of the way for you."

"We will manage, dear. Somehow we will. Which shoes?"

"I don't see how anyone could walk in them. Okay, the ones that match the dress, the blue ones." After getting her new heels on, he helped her stand. "Oh, this is significantly better. I'll manage to get to the living room. Go help the girls."

Heine made sure that she was able to walk on her own before dashing off to Susanne's room. "Dad. I'll be naked. Oh well. There's no other way, is there? Oh no! Erich is going to see me naked, too! I mean when he helps us dress. Dad, can't you always be the one to dress us?" Susanne pleaded.

"We'll see, honey. I can't get you three dressed at the same time. Okay, there you go. Mom said she can walk much better. See how you do before I go to Sofia."

She wobbled wildly but managed to walk, so he

headed to the next room where Sofia was waiting for him. She was sitting on her bed, exploring what she could do with just her upper arms, unfortunately not much.

When those two joined the others in the front room, Erich finally joined them, staring wide-eyed at all three. "Erich and I will make lunch," Heine announced and Wanda nodded appreciatively. Purposely, he got Erich working on warming up the canned soup, and he snuck to the edge of the living room to see how they fared.

"Mom, look at us! We've really got boobs now! All the boys are really going to notice us when we get back to school, won't they?" Susanne gushed with a giggle.

"Yes, they most certainly will. I do hope we can manage in these heels, girls. I've never worn such extreme heels before, but we don't have much choice now," Wanda replied.

"Look at our hair, too," Sofia exclaimed. "Mine tickles my knees when I stand. I think I like it this long. Is that okay? Mom, who's going to brush it?"

"How do we turn the door knobs?" asked Susanne.

"I hope the fellows brush our hair. I rather like mine this long, too, girls. Door knobs? I don't think we can. I think we're going to find there are a lot of things that we can't do now, but we'll have to make the best of it. At least if the SS man is right, we should be protected if and when the demons attack. We are alive and that's what matters most to your father and me."

Heine heard enough and went to help Erich with the lunch. Erich and Heine had their hands full feeding the three their lunch. At least Erich didn't complain about it, for which Heine was grateful. All three women were in a fragile state at the moment.

Once they finished, Susanne said, "Okay, dad. We've had enough of this. Please Morph us now so we can cast our spells and send emails to our friends and chat with them."

"Not just yet." He saw three panicking women looking at him. "The deliveryman brought each of you a How To DVD. I looked at it and I agree. It is a bunch of videos that you three simply must watch many times. I know, some of the videos are probably centuries old, but they show some remarkable women who have no arms at all and how they go about doing almost everything. I even saw one young woman flying an airplane with her feet. So to the living room. It's video time for you three."

An hour into it, Wanda said, "Heine, this is incredibly valuable video. Girls, we are going to watch this and practice everything we see. Heine, you aren't allowed to cast your Morph spell on us until we each can do all the things we need to do by ourselves." The girls moaned, but Wanda was insistent. "Girls, we have to learn to be independent. What is going to happen to you at school when your Morph spell is dispelled? Susanne, you will soon be learning that spell, and I'm sure your teacher isn't going to keep on casting a Morph spell on you. We'll even practice using our wands with our feet. I have no idea if that will work, but we're sure going to try. We have to be independent."

Heine didn't ask why his wife had such a sudden change of heart, but liked what he was hearing. It made sound sense. During the afternoon, the three watched the DVD, fascinated with seeing women who often had no trace of arms doing everyday things, usually with their toes and sometimes their teeth. Late afternoon, Heine fixed a healthy supper. Surprisingly, the three made serious attempts to feed themselves using their feet.

After supper, they then retired to their mom's room and worked on brushing out each other's hair, chatting furiously about nearly everything. Once Heine tucked each daughter into bed for the night, he joined Wanda and discovered another effect of the mutations.

"Honey, I've just got to have sex right now. I'm so utterly horny that I can't stand it. This has never happened to me. Worse, the girls have already noticed it, too, and asked me what they can do about it," Wanda admitted.

"How peculiar. Well, you don't have to ask me twice, but the girls concern me."

"Let's do it first and then talk, please," she begged.

A half hour later, Wanda appeared satisfied, and they discussed what to do about these new overly powerful urges with their daughters. "It's driving them nuts," Wanda explained. "I guess they will have to pleasure themselves. Will they try to have sex with boys at school on the sly?"

"I hope we've brought them up better than that, but I see what you mean. Perhaps we should have another talk with them," Heine suggested.

"Dear, let me. They'll be too embarrassed to talk about such things with you. You know, something that we heard at the meeting is suddenly coming to mind. I think because of this overly powerful sex drives in us women, we're likely to have many more children than normal, adding to the numbers in their Fourth Reich. I'm beginning to smell a worm, Heine."

"Let me look into this whole thing tomorrow. Will you be okay with Erich here with you?"

"We better be."

Chapter 13—Fourth Reich Betrayal

Quite curious about this new Schutzstaffel (SS) group in Germany, Ericka attempted to find out more about the organization. An Internet search yielded very little information other than propaganda, which suggested this Der Führer of theirs had a unique way to stop and destroy the Iranian horde and the demons. Ericka found no hint about what that might be. Given what she knew, Ericka didn't believe the propaganda, not even remotely. She did discover that the horde was drawing close to the heartland of Europe, and thus people were getting desperate. She also knew that panicking people would grasp at anything that appeared to offer them safety and security.

Giving up her Internet search, Ericka decided that she needed more direct observation. Hence, she chatted with Katarine, looking to discover others still around the Bonn School of Magic whom she could contact. Unfortunately, the staff there had all fled to safety in other countries. Ericka couldn't blame them. She'd seen what had happened to Monica and her team. Such genetic changes would destroy wizards and witches.

Ericka brought up the worldwide list of magic schools on her computer. The SS headquarters was centrally located in Berlin, according to the propaganda online. The largest and most prestigious magic school was also in Berlin. Thus in Ericka's mind, Berlin was the place to go. She brought up the school's teaching roster and scanned down the list. She noticed the husband and wife team of the Walburgs. Something seemed familiar about Professor Wanda Walburg, but she couldn't place it.

"Have you found anything?" asked Katarine, who wandered in to chat, rather bored with so little to do.

"Not really. The internet only has the SS propaganda, no concrete data. I thought about checking with some of the faculty at the Berlin school. That's what I've got up now. Something seems familiar with Professor

Wanda Walburg, but I can't put my finger on it."

Katarine laughed. "Cousin, you are out of touch aren't you? She's also a Van Nie. Her mother was related to my mother, sisters. So that makes her also a distant cousin to the Van Nie's here in the States."

Ericka laughed. "Honestly, I've not tried to keep up with the homeland Van Nie relatives. I can barely keep up with those here. Well, I guess I should reach out to her. Thanks."

"Hey, if she's in trouble, could she come here, too? I'll help defray any expenses."

"Sure. We've always room for more. I simply have to find out more about this SS group. Something just doesn't sound right about it. Call me paranoid or something, but being around Monica all these years will do that to you." Both women laughed.

Unfortunately, Ericka didn't get a chance to follow up for several days. Orders for more enchanted bullets came in, and she and Tyler were hard pressed to fill them, even though another dozen helped them enchant the platinum slugs. Monica and her team returned with great news and wild stories of the destruction of the Dragon Hole. Even more so now, Ericka and Tyler knew their efforts were making a huge difference in the war against the demons and redoubled their efforts.
***

Gisella's Grand Plan was coming to fruition. Bella had the demon army in Slovenia, spending a few days there chewing up any humans still in the area. Why? She wanted to make the various countries in Europe worry and make mistakes. If Bella followed orders, which she often didn't, she was to strike overland into northern Italy on October 1, sweep up to Paris, and then on to Berlin, at which point, Gisella would announce that she was now the new leader of Europe. After that, she'd make new plans to conquer the US and then Russia and China. For the latter two, she knew that she needed far more demons than she currently had, either that or a new and diabolical plan.

As October arrived, every news station in the world

194

focused almost exclusively on the situation in Europe, so much so that the few other random attacks that Gisella ordered in the US and in Britain went almost unnoticed, except for those who were victimized and those few who responded to repel the attacks.

The morning of September 30, an emergency call roused Monica. Demons were again attacking St. Louis, this time in the Central West End's densely populated area, just north of the Cathedral Basilica. Worse, it was another debilitating bio-genetic agent gas attack. As fast as possible, Monica got herself prepared, as did her friends. Bergson and the team now stayed in guest rooms at her mansion, much better accommodations as far as Chrissy was concerned, because Monica had bathtubs. Satisfied that everyone was ready, Monica and her group teleported to the report in location, the Basilica. Demons hovered over the residential area north of the church and released the foul looking gasses.

Crystal suggested, "Gang, let's all cast as many blowing wind type of spells as we can. If we're lucky, we can disperse that cloud so maybe it won't be so devastating."

Nearly thirty wizards flew into action, while Bergson and crew did what they did best, blasting away with their enchanted automatic rifles. A half hour later, to everyone's great surprise, they succeeded in thwarting this attack. Their combined winds did disperse the gas cloud. While the final results weren't in for a week because the doctors wanted to make doubly certain, no one was seriously harmed, except the demons. Just as soon as Bergson and crew exterminated ten of their numbers, the rest fled.

After that episode, Crystal sent off many messages to her contacts across the country outlining what they did to avert disaster from the hideous gas attack. She hoped that others would follow her lead and prevent many more victims from ruined lives. Gisella ordered a similar attack on New York City two days later. The wizards and witches there did follow the advice of Crystal as relayed to them, averting yet more victims.

While in Europe, Bella decided not to follow the plan. *Hell, Gisella sits in her nice Washington mansion while I'm out here doing all the dirty work. Well, as soon as I get Berlin captured, the others will fall like dominoes.* "Today we march for Berlin. Northwards everyone!" The army of demons and jihadists marched into Austria and then on into southern Germany rapidly overrunning Salzburg and then Munich.

Naturally, via satellite feeds, the whole world watched the rapid advance of the horde! In her mansion, Gisella fumed and cursed. However, she resisted the temptation to teleport over there and attack Bella directly.

"Oh dear god, Heine!" Wanda exclaimed, "They really are invading Germany. Munich and Salzburg are under attack right now!"

"I had better go out and stockpile groceries. Things could get really bad! Erich, come on. Let's get going before the stores are stripped bare!"

"Make sure you get some bottled water, too," Wanda added.

Outside, Heine and Erich found the streets filled with panicking people, most of these had not heeded Dr. Menninger's suggestion to join the SS and Fourth Reich. As they reached their local grocery store, food riots broke out among the panic stricken people. Soon, he knew it was hopeless to even try to get groceries, and he cursed himself for failing to see this coming and to have already laid in a supply. Just as they turned around to head home, disaster struck. The mobs turned violent. Gunfire erupted.

Heine tried his best to protect Erich, but a stray bullet hit the youth in his head, and the boy collapsed onto the pavement. Heine got down to tend his son's wound and fired off a frantic Message to Wanda, telling her about the mob and Erich. Just as he sent it, the mob swung his way. Heine was trapped and trampled to death by the charging mob.

Back at their modest home, Wanda and the girls watched the news, terrified of what was happening around them. Gunfire rang through the air, and finally the local news began reporting on the riots in Berlin. Just then, Heine's Message scrolled past Wanda's eyes. She no more than finished reading it when she felt a pang in her heart. She tried not to think of its meaning, cursing the fact that she could no longer even cast a simple Message spell.

"Mom! What's wrong?" Susanne asked. She'd never seen her mother this pale.

"Heine said that Erich has been shot by the mob. I can't even cast a Message spell to Heine to ask more," Wanda wailed, her stomach knotting so tightly she thought she might faint.

"We can call him on our cells, Mom," Susanne declared, moving hers to the fore with her toes. "See, one number is fast dial. Dad's phone is ringing now. I'll put it on speaker phone, I hope." After some struggling, she got the right button pressed. No one answered; the call went to voice mail. All three began to panic, because Heine never failed to pick up. Even when he was in the middle of class, he would at least say, "I'll call you back." Now, Wanda knew what that terrible feeling she had was. Heine would not be coming home. Wisely, she didn't tell her daughters this, not yet. They were frightened enough as it was. Worse, she couldn't cast her Teleport spell to get them somewhere safe.

By late afternoon, even the girls sensed that something was terribly wrong. Susanne had dialed Heine's phone twenty times, ignoring the fact that each went to voice mail until she got a message saying his voice mailbox was full. At last, Wanda knew she had to say something. "Girls, I think that Heine is dead, too. I had a feeling right after he sent me word that a stray bullet hit Erich in his head."

"Mom! What are we going to do now? I'm starving," Sofia asked, trying hard to appear braver than she felt.

"We're going to practice what we've been learning on that DVD and fix ourselves something to eat. After that, we need to put our heads together. We'll think of something," Wanda suggested, though just what that bright idea might be, she had not the foggiest notion. "Girls, we can do this. Look, we have some arms and those girls on the DVD had none at all. So it should be easier for us. Let's work together, shall we?"

Two hours later with full stomachs, the trio had accomplished what they'd not thought possible. Once more, they sat before the TV catching up on the news. It was horrific. True to his word, Der Führer launched his deadly counterattack on the rampaging, chaotic demon horde and insane jihadists. However, the form of that attack was wholly unexpected by everyone except Dr. Menninger and his top three associates.

In secret, General Berend had been acquiring vast amounts of nuclear waste products from all types of commercial establishments, including hospitals and power plants. He concentrated the radioactive components by use of spells, storing them in lead containers. Each container was very carefully measured to ensure that the correct amount of gamma ray producing material was inside.

When Dr. Menninger gave his attack order to the general, Berend ordered a fleet of low flying crop dusters to take off, accompanied by a flotilla of loyal SS wizards. As they approached the locations of the demonic hordes, the planes released the radioactive material, now in a gaseous form and slightly heavier than air. The gas particles fell on the marching army of demons, humans, and innocent civilians, an invisible, but deadly rain.

The Cambion demons sniffed the air and looked about uneasily. Soon, they felt nauseous, but by then they had had a fatal dose. Within an hour, the human jihadists saw their demon companions dying around them, but couldn't see the actual cause and continued their attacks on the locals who had not yet fled the area. By nightfall, they were sickened and most didn't survive the night. Those that did looked awful the following morning and succumbed before noon.

Unfortunately, all the innocent civilians across much of extreme southern Germany and who were not SS members and on the special anti-radiation pills also perished as well. The last word Gisella had came from

Bella. "Something is making us quite ill. I'm vomiting. I'm sick, really sick." After that, Gisella couldn't make any contact with her fellow succubus. Like the rest of the world, she had to watch the newscasts to learn what had gone so very, very wrong with her foolproof plans.

The following day, Propaganda Minister Dirk Nordstrom held a news conference in Berlin. "Der Führer promised us all that he would exterminate the demons and jihadists if they set foot on German soil. Yesterday, they did so and he did as he promised. The bulk of the demonic army has been eliminated."

"However, there may well be other demons lurking around our country and some may have escaped the battlefield. Hence, we will continue to deploy our secret weapon across the rest of our beloved country, guaranteeing that absolutely no demons are here. I will have more news tomorrow at this same time. Thank you." He ended the conference abruptly, taking no questions, though hundreds came his way. Leave them craving news was his current agenda. Purposely, only a small area was going to be radioactive for years.

General Berend had the crop dusting planes in the air flying all over Germany during the next few days, though dropping a different formula on everyone. By October 10, Der Führer announced that Germany was free of demons, but wisely he didn't go on camera and had Dirk deliver that message. However, this was all a grand lie, but a lie that had several purposes.

First, he wanted to send an unequivocal message to Gisella that if she came anywhere near Germany, she would suffer the same fate as Bella had. She got the message. Second, he wanted total and absolute control over Germany. What was the lie? He used a modified version of his ordinary bio-genetic agent gas in the attack over nearly all of Germany.

He'd carefully formulated it such that those on any version of his five pills would be immune to the gas and its effects. Thus, the millions of SS who were part of his Fourth Reich were wholly unaffected and didn't even know

anything was going on. Those not on his pills were severely impacted. Men's IQs dropped into the mid-nineties, and they felt compelled to follow any SS man's orders. The women fared far worse. They ended up like all the women in Rolla, except they still retained their teeth. Slowly, the cadre of SS men made their rounds to every home, dropping off the supplies that would be needed by the women in that household. One way or another, Dr. Menninger ensured that every woman in Germany and every man was now a part of his new Fourth Reich. Further, they would all explicitly follow his orders.
***

Ericka followed the awful news on October 1. True the demons had been destroyed, but how? And why did so many innocent civilians also die? Everyone had many, many unanswered questions. Bergson took it upon himself as the leader of the top WIT group in the US to find out. "Consider this a massive crime scene. Let's get to the bottom of this. Monica, we'll need your help." The four set to work, commandeering many US satellites to spy on the impacted area.

Ericka decided that she'd best try to get a hold of her distant cousin in Berlin. Perhaps she could get needed answers that way. While the others took off to the FBI headquarters, Ericka focused and sent a Message to her distant cousin.

Hi Wanda. I'm Ericka Van Nie-Green, a distant cousin of yours in St. Louis, Missouri, USA. Katarine Van Nie-Stossel, who teaches at the Bonn School of Magic, has fled to my place for safety. She told me about you. I'd like to get together with you and discuss this business of the SS and the Fourth Reich. Can we meet somewhere convenient? Thanks for your time. Ericka.

Ericka waited patiently for her reply, but it didn't come. *Now that's weird. Even a wizard or witch who hates you will at least acknowledge Message Receipt. It's only polite!* She found Katarine and asked her more about her cousin. "She is not even acknowledging my Message."

"That's—that's not like Wanda at all. She always replies. After all, she is a professor at the Berlin School of

Magic. So is her husband, Heine. Something must be terribly wrong," Katarine explained, growing very worried about her cousin.

"Well," Ericka said, pulling slightly on her blonde hair and wrapping a few strands around a finger, "since the Message got sent, she must be alive. If she were dead, the Message spell would have failed. She could be unconscious or otherwise unable to cast a Message spell or even find a way to reply."

"Oh no! You don't suppose that she has become one of the victims do you? She could be helpless, and she's got two daughters and a son to care for," Katarine gushed, her worries having risen to actual fear for her cousin. "Try Heine. No, let me try Heine and Wanda," she declared. Waving her wand, she cast two Message spells in rapid succession. Her face paled.

"What?" Ericka inquired, her brows rising and with a crease on her forehead.

"Heine. It—the spell—it didn't work. Heine—Heine must be dead! And Wanda didn't acknowledge my Message either! Oh Ericka! Something must be horribly wrong with her. We have to help her somehow. I simply must!"

"We will. Let me get Tyler in on this one," Ericka insisted. She ran over to their workshop in the back of their small storefront where they sold magic items that they'd created. Interrupting him, she hastily explained what was happening.

"We must head over to Berlin now, but we're not going alone—too dangerous. We can't ask Crystal and the others. They have to be ready to respond to another attack here. I know. I'll get my brother to come with us. Let's plan on going, say around noon-ish. Let's go armed. I don't trust much right about now," Tyler declared.

Ericka kissed him and dashed back to Katarine, but she found the young woman wiping her eyes. "What?" Ericka asked.

"More bad news! It's mom and dad. They, they refused to join that new Fourth Reich thing. Now they are in a coma. A friend of mine who joined just sent me a

Message. I swear the world has just gone entirely mad! They've dumped whatever that stuff is—to kill the demon stuff—they've dumped it all over Germany. Got to kill off any demons that have infiltrated our country, but Ericka, it's turning everyone who didn't join this Fourth Reich into helpless women and moronic men. Mom and dad, they are in real trouble. If the food rioting and mob destructions weren't enough—oh, this is just too horrible for words! I've got to go to them!"

"Hold on! Is it safe for you to go right now? I mean, if the bio agent thing is still in the air, you could be infected," Ericka cautioned her distant cousin.

"My friend Bertha, she said the attack came yesterday and that the gas has dissipated now, but I've got to be there to help them. Whatever am I going to do now?"

"You have to go to them. Leave the kids here. We're going to check on Wanda at noon. Say, was Bertha affected? Is she helpless?"

"No. My folks have a small home outside Aachen, near the border with Belgium. Bertha and her family live just across the border in Heerlen, Belgium. Her dad is a good friend of my dad, so they stay in close touch," Katarine explained.

"Okay. Go. But keep in contact with me."

"I will. Why? Why would these people do this to fellow Germans? It makes no sense," Katarine wailed.

"Don't know, but I sure aim to find out, Katarine. Maybe it's all part of the demon's plan somehow. Well, you get going. Your kids will be safe here. Go. Go," Ericka insisted.

Once Katarine teleported away, she headed off to find her computer and mag-Google the address where Wanda and Heine lived in Berlin. It wasn't far from the prestigious Berlin School of Magic. One nice feature of the mag-Google site was that it gave excellent views of the locations, sufficient for anyone to use to teleport there. That was Ericka's purpose in looking up the address. She needed a good view of their intended destination for her Teleport spell.

After readying herself, she waited on Tyler. His brother Tim was thirty-five and had two sons, Bill and Len, fourteen and thirteen respectively. While Tyler was an accomplished wizard and highly skilled at making magical items with Ericka, Tim put his magic skills to an entirely different use and had already made a sizeable fortune. He helped design the new modern airliners and had been heavily involved in the design of the new giant Stratospheres. However, Tim's life had been turned upside down four years ago.

Thinking about this, Ericka sighed. His wife, whom she'd come to count as a close friend, and his daughter had been killed in one of those tragic, senseless car accidents. A drunk driver slammed into their car, crushing them both. Until Monica used her Trauma Erase spell on him, Tim blamed himself for not insisting the Janine and Sally always have the Skin of Stone spell on them while they were driving. Ericka pushed such memories out of her mind, just as Tyler and Tim came walking up to her.

"You're looking as ravishing as ever, Ericka," Tim complimented her.

She smiled. *Tim always had complimentary words for everyone.*

"Ravishing or not, we've a serious situation. Has Tyler told you what's up?"

"Righto. I've got your back—loaded with protection spells. He's even given me one of your automatic rifles with your fancy ammunition!" He swung the large gun around from his back to show her. "Got your back," he repeated. "Thanks for asking me. It's nice to be helpful. I know, Ericka, I'm not a powerful wizard, but I'll keep you safe."

"Tim, I trust you with my life, just as Tyler does. Power isn't everything and you know it. Okay, let's do this. I have no idea what to expect, so be prepared for anything. If it's really bad, we'll teleport back at once. Understood? We take no chances. We've all got kids depending on us," she stated dryly, making sure both men wouldn't suddenly "play hero" on her.

With a man's hand in each of hers, she cast her

Teleport spell, aiming high as a precaution, followed by a gentle descent from about fifty feet above the street. As they descended, they saw perhaps a dozen dead bodies lying scattered about the street, though gray uniformed men were picking them up, depositing them in a garbage collection truck. That image struck a chord in all three, who knew instantly that all wasn't right in Berlin!

Landing gently, Ericka double checked the address. "This is the right home. The question is: is Wanda here or someplace else?"

"Won't know unless you knock and all that. Look at them! Just tossing the dead away like garbage!" Tim whispered. Two men lugged a dead body over to a truck and tossed it in the bed on top of many other bodies. "What's going on here?"

Ericka knocked on the door and rang the doorbell. She heard a faint female voice calling out, "Help! Come in. We can't open the door. Help!"

Ericka didn't hesitate. She opened the door and let the three inside. She saw a young teen making her way slowly towards the door, but her appearance shocked all three. Fumbling slightly, Ericka said, "Hello. I'm a distant cousin of Wanda's. Is she here?"

"Oh hi! Mom's in the front room crying. We need some help. Dad and our brother are dead. We're alone. Can you help us? Oh, I'm Susanne."

"Yes, that's why we are here. Your Aunt Katarine sent us. Lead the way, Susanne. You are being a very brave young woman," Ericka praised her.

"I'm sorry! I'm such a wreck. Heine, my husband, he's dead and my Erich is too, shot in his head. That's the last Message I had from Heine. They went out to get groceries and never came back. The food riots, the mobs. It's been awful and now they are destroying everyone who didn't join that damned Fourth Reich and that Hans Gotthilf man! It's horrid," Wanda wailed. "Please, can you help us?"

"Yes, that's why we're here, Wanda. Katarine sent us. She'd be here, but she just got word that her parents were victimized and went to see what she could do to help them. Okay, let's get organized. Oh, I'm Ericka Van Nie-Green. My husband, Tyler, and his brother Tim."

"Very pleased to meet you, Wanda," Tim said cordially and shaking her right upper arm as though it was her hand. Their eyes met. He added, "You look far more beautiful than I imagined victims of this horrific mutation thing would look. Have you and your girls had any lunch yet?"

"Not really. Just a little cheese. There's not much left in the kitchen. That's why Heine. . ." Her voice faltered. She didn't need to say more though.

"Of course. Let me see what I can do. After my wife died, I had to raise my two sons myself, so I've learned to cook a little. Lost my only daughter. Car crash. Drunk driver. Ericka, you help them pack, and I'll rustle up what I can in the kitchen, unless you want me to stand guard at the door in case of trouble."

"No, I think we are safe enough inside. Food would be wise," Ericka replied. To Wanda, she explained, "We're going to take you and your girls back with us to St. Louis, Missouri. We have plenty of space at our mansion and lots of kids around your daughters' ages. Will that be all right with you?"

"Yes, more than all right. You are saving our lives," Wanda gushed. "It's utter madness here—all over Germany. Nightmare. Unspeakable nightmare."

"Indeed. We should start packing what you want to take with you," Ericka got her back on track.

"Of course. Girls, we must pack." To Ericka, she added, "We are doing our best to learn to become independent women again. They gave us an invaluable DVD. We have to bring it along with us. So many ingenious ways for us to do what we must. It's so crazy. You see, they provided absolutely everything women would be needing, clothes, shoes, the DVD—all free and all the clothes we want. And then they do this to those who didn't join. Monstrous betrayal. I just don't understand it."

"Mom's right. We are learning how to do things

ourselves—from the DVD of course," Susanne declared proudly. "Mom's a powerful witch. Once we're independent again, mom will let us get Morphed so we can cast our spells and go back to magic school. Will we be able to do that if we come live at your house?"

"Of course," Ericka replied. "You can go to the very same magic school that I and my friends went to—St. Louis School of Magic. It's a good one. Tyler, you help Wanda pack, and I'll go with the girls and help them pack."

Soon alone with Tyler, Wanda admitted, "Tyler, I feel so utterly helpless now. I can't even cast a single spell, not even the useful ones, and I was a Professor of Illusion Magic at the Berlin School of Magic."

"I understand, Wanda, but you are certainly taking the right approach to this disaster," Tyler said, hoping what he believed wouldn't upset Wanda further. "Learn to be as independent as possible. I'm sure somehow you'll soon be able to cast spells again, but being able to do things for your selves is critical, especially for your girls."

Wanda smiled.

His facial muscles relaxed. "Yes, that's precisely what I think too. Okay, can you get the DVD out of the machine? I guess I'd better start helping you with the packing. We've only a few outfits that will fit us, but I have to bring along our photo albums and keepsakes, oh and our hairbrushes. Seems we really need them now. Our hair has grown more than double its length." She relaxed and continued chatting. "So I knew that some of the Van Nie clan moved to America. We mostly lost touch with them. I wonder how Ericka and I are related? Katarine, she's my first cousin." The two chatted while she pointed out things to pack using her upper arms. Tyler shrank them and stowed them in bags.

"Soup's on," Tim called out cheerily.

When they all reached the dining room table, Susanne giggled. "Mom, he's used the good china."

"But of course, my dear," Tim said feigning a gallant style. "If this is your last meal here for a while, we should dine most elegantly. Don't you agree, Miss Susanne? Miss

Sofia?" he teased them both with a broad smile.

Both teens giggled and used their feet to pull out their chairs. However, Tim quickly moved behind them, helping them to slide up to the table, as though he was a waiter at a very fancy restaurant and they were his most special guests. The girls giggled again. "Thank you kind sir," Susanne replied, catching on to the game that Tim was playing with them. "I'll take the lunchtime special."

"But of course, madam," Tim replied, while Sofia giggled again. Wanda merely smiled appreciatively. "And what will the madam have?" Tim asked, continuing his entertainment and directing the question to Wanda, to bring her into the fun.

"Oh, what would you recommend?" she played along, much to her daughters' delight.

"I'd recommend the refined macaroni and cheese dish. The house seems to be rather short of more refined cuisine at the moment. I do believe the tea at this fine establishment is of the highest quality," Tim replied, uncovering the only large bowl filled with the last of the edibles in the kitchen. He'd used all three boxes. He had a teapot at the ready as well. In the background, Ericka could hear coffee brewing as well.

"Then I believe that I shall have the macaroni dish, please," Wanda said politely, her girls giggling away. Gallantly, Tim dished out a helping for her and the two teens in turn. He, like Tyler and Ericka, were prepared to feed the three, having positioned themselves between the three. Wanda explained, "We've been working on using our toes as fingers. I know it looks positively strange and downright weird, but we're sort of successful at it. With more practice, I think we can do it. Girls, let's show them how we manage this."

Sofia declared, "Mr. Tim, we're going to be independent again so we can cast our magic spells once more. Mom said so."

"Miss Sofia, I'm certain that is quite true!" Tim proclaimed.

Although awkward at it, the three did manage to use

their feet and toes to feed themselves, much to the surprise of Ericka and Tyler, though not to Tim, who instinctively realized the girls and Wanda desperately needed to regain their self-respect. By being as independent as possible, this goal was being met. He could see it on their young faces.

While they sipped their tea and coffee, Tim suggested, "You know Ericka, I've got plenty of room at my home. I'd love to have Wanda and the girls stay with me for the time being. I've got two boys their ages, and they've nothing to do since they closed the magic school." Looking at Wanda, he continued, "Ericka and Tim have so much going on around their place—they are enchanting the platinum bullets that everyone is using to kill the demons. Honestly, Ericka, Tyler, we need you both making as much ammunition as possible. I've got plenty of room at my place, and this way I can contribute as well. If you like, Katarine and her kids could move in with us as well. What do you think, Wanda, Susanne, Sofia?"

"Are you sure, Tim? We're going to be a whole lot of trouble—until we learn how to be independent again," she added hastily.

"No trouble. Besides, my boys will have something to keep them out of mischief. Bill was about to start his third year and Len was in his second year, that is, until they closed the school because of this demon threat."

"Can we mom? They would be in our class," Susanne begged.

"But Tim, think of the cost," Wanda protested slightly, knowing that she and her daughters were going to be a big financial burden, at least until she could somehow regain her spell casting abilities.

Tyler laughed this time. "You don't know my brother. He's independently wealthy. He's a big-shot airplane designer—worked on the Stratosphere airliner. But that doesn't matter. Ericka and I also do very well with our magic items shop. Money isn't going to be a problem either way. But Tim has a point. All of us around our place are heavily involved responding to demon attacks and such. Gets somewhat crazy around our place at times, but there's lots of children running around. Right now, Monica is off fighting demons. Crystal and the others are on standby in case we get another demon attack. Had one just a couple days ago, but Crystal's new idea of casting lots of wind spells dissipated the gas before anyone could get harmed by it."

Tim spoke up, "Look, they need peace and quite so they can practice and learn to be independent again. I know you mean well, Tyler, but your place is hardly peace and quiet. Besides, my place is within walking distance of your estate, just over the hill."

Ericka replied diplomatically, "Okay then. It's up to you, Wanda. Tim's got a point. If it doesn't work out, you simply must come stay with us." She saw Tim's point. The three didn't need a lot of distractions right now. They had to come to grips with their physical limitations, if possible.

"Well then, Tim, we graciously accept your offer," Wanda said, noticing her girls and their nodding heads.

"Excellent. Hey, I'll get to actually use the one new spell that I learned two years ago, Erase Trauma," Tim declared. "You see, I was an emotional wreck after my wife and daughter died. I blamed myself for not insisting and demanding that they always cast Skin of Stone on themselves when they took the car out. Heck, I don't even know if that would have saved them or not, but I blamed myself. Thank god for Monica. She cast that spell on me and via it, I was able to erase all that baggage. I felt so good, so relieved from that, that I went to the Magic School and learned how to cast that spell. I swore to Monica that one day I would pass on the precious gift she gave me. If you don't mind, I will help you three with it."

"I don't think anything can really help us now, Tim," Wanda replied, but decided that she better modify her harsh pronouncement and added, "but you are welcome to try."

"You finish your packing and I'll clean up the dishes," Tim suggested.

An hour later, the Walburg family took one last look at their home, making sure they weren't leaving anything important behind. Satisfied, Wanda nodded. Each took the upper arm of one of the three and teleported them to Tim's mansion, just across the hill from their estate and shops.

Tim had Messaged his boys, and they followed his orders, preparing bedrooms for the girls. Thus, both were in the living room, waiting impatiently for everyone to arrive. Suddenly, all six appeared.

"We have to learn to do that spell for sure," Bill whispered to Len, who agreed. Both boys then blinked and stared at the three newcomers. They were not what the two lads had expected.

Tim said, "Boys, this is Susanne, third year, and Sofia, second year. This is Bill, third year, and Len, second year—that is, whenever they reopen the magic school. This is their mother Wanda Walburg. You best watch it around her. She's a full professor of illusion magic at the Berlin School of Magic. So if you don't behave, I've given her permission to turn you into toads."

The girls giggled, but Bill declared, "But dad, you know that's not possible, but we'll behave, won't we, Len?" His brother nodded, still gazing at Sofia. "So Susanne, you look really pretty. I kind of expected the victims would, I don't know, look sort of weird or something. You look really good. I've cleaned up my sister's old room for you. I hope you like pink, cause we haven't repainted it yet. You are next to my room, so if you need something during the night, I'm right next door. Sofia, you are next door to Len, so dad, we've got the bases covered. Come on, Susanne. I'll show you the room. I suppose we can paint it any color you want. So you are third year too?"

She giggled. "Thanks Bill. Pink is good. Yes, but they closed our school, too. I was so disappointed. We're to learn the really powerful spells this year, like Ball of Fire. How many Grade 2 spells did you learn? I got all them except the necromancy ones. I found those distasteful."

"Same here. All but those kind. Who wants anything to do with dead things? Yuck. I know what you mean, balls of fire, bolts of lightning. I heard we would have gotten to use them on old pumpkins. Now that would have been cool!" Bill declared, walking slowly beside Susanne, while Sofia and Len followed along behind.

Wanda watched her daughters walking carefully in their tall heels with the two boys, chatting away. Smiling, she said, "Well, that's one thing that you can count on. Magic students at the same levels always have something to chat about. Tim, were we ever like that? Dying to learn to cast balls of fire?"

Tim laughed. "I admit it. Back then, I could think of nothing else, but I soon changed my mind. Flying took hold and it's never left me. Just don't ask me to use a broom though." Both laughed.

Ericka interrupted them, "Okay. We have to get back and enchant more bullets. If you need anything, just Message. If you need a woman's touch, let us know. One more thing, we need to have a long talk about this Fourth Reich, but first let's get you settled in and all that. Crystal and Monica will want to talk about that, too. Maybe tonight. Have to see what's up. Remember, just holler if you need anything. Katarine will drop by when she gets back from helping her parents."

"Ericka, thank you for everything. You have saved our lives. We owe you. Really we do."

"You would do the same for me, Wanda. Just keep on trying to learn to be independent and you'll come out all right. Bye for now. Tim, you be on your best behavior," she stared one last time at her brother-in-law. Then, she and Tyler vanished.

"This way. I'll put you up in my bedroom. That way, I'll be there to help you if you need something during the night. This has to be absolutely awful for you. I can't imagine how you are coping. I don't know if I even could. You are one strong woman."

"I have to be. I've got the girls to think about, Tim. Do you honestly think that we'll ever be able to cast spells again? Be realistic with me, Tim. Don't hold back. Are we just kidding ourselves?"

He helped her get her knee-length, wavy blonde hair to one side so she could sit down on the edge of the king-size bed. Tim sat beside her and took her upper arm in his hand, before answering. "Look, you've suffered enormous traumas. You've now got physical limitations that I can't imagine living with. If there is any hope, it must lie in as you have said learning how to become independent once more, as much as possible at least. As far as spell casting goes, as you said, Morph spells should make that work, if nothing else does. When I was in my sixth year, everyone was experimenting casting spells sans-wands and sans-words, though hardly anyone was actually successful at either. On the other hand, Monica Nicole Black is an expert at both. She can cast every darn spell without saying a word or using a wand. It's unbelievable. So if she can, then there simply must be a way to do it."

"That's—that's the Monica they were talking about? The Demon Hunter? That Monica?" Wanda asked, her eyes nearly popping out of her head.

"Er yes, that Monica. Why?"

"My goodness, Tim! She's famous. Everyone in Germany knows about her. Tim, maybe there is hope for me and my girls."

"Of course there is. Now let's get your things unpacked. Then, let's see that DVD of yours. Maybe I can be of use somehow."

Chapter 14—Adaptions and Data

After a delicious supper, Wanda and the girls retired to Susanne's new bedroom for their usual evening ritual of hair brushing and chatting. "Mom, Bill is really cool. I think he likes me. He's not like a lot of the boys at school. He thinks I am really beautiful. Can I be beautiful, like this?" she held up her two upper arms.

Wanda sensed she had to exercise extreme caution. "Dear, put your arms behind your back as though you were holding your hands there and look into the mirror."

"My hair is fabulous, isn't it? And my boobs are just terrific, but I don't know if I want them to get any bigger, like yours are mom," Susanne said thoughtfully.

"Yes, you look very pretty. So do you, Sofia. Just because we don't have the rest of our arms and hands doesn't suddenly make us ugly old maids, now does it?"

"I suppose not, Mom. How old do I have to be to kiss a boy?" Susanne came right out and asked what she'd been thinking about all afternoon.

"Yeah, Mom. How old?" Sofia interjected, not wanting to be left out. She too put her upper arms behind her and gazed into the mirror at her reflection.

"I think fourteen might be a bit young, dears," Wanda replied diplomatically, but she knew what all lay behind the question, and worse, it wasn't just normal teenage reactions. Their genetic mutations had definitely somehow made them far more aware of their sexuality. She too had felt incredibly horny most of the afternoon, but had wisely kept it suppressed.

Wanda added, "You both now look very much older than you actually are. Boys might think that you are seventeen or more and try to take advantage of you. I think you will know when it is the right time for you to kiss a boy. Now come on. This long hair is challenging enough."

"But Mom, our hair looks really, really cool," Susanne countered. "I don't want to cut mine, except

213

maybe split ends. It does make us look older doesn't it? When can we wear makeup? Lots of third year girls do, Mom."

The three chatted away, masking the extreme struggles to use their hairbrushes with their feet to brush out their wavy blonde tresses. Wanda thought, *I have to keep their attention off of how horrible this actually is.*

The next morning, Tim kept his long standing promise to Monica. He cast his Erase Trauma spell on Wanda, while the boys and girls checked out the home and later re-watched the DVD. He wisely cast a silence spell on the bedroom, dampening Wanda's cries.

An hour later, her traumas had been erased. "I feel so wonderful, light as a feather, Tim. I had no idea my body was in such pain as the lower arms and hands withered up and fell off."

"Of course not, you were in a coma. I'm glad I could do this small thing for you, Wanda. I'll do it for the girls next."

"Please! Thank you, Tim, thank you." She took a seat in the living room to watch more of the DVD while Tim took Susanne next and then Sofia. After that, he headed off to make lunch. Wanda followed him. "I wish there was something I could do to help."

"Sure is. See if you can set the table by any means possible," Tim suggested.

A bit later, Wanda grumbled, "This is impossibly hard, Tim!"

"But you're doing it, Wanda. That's all that matters. You are doing it and without using magic spells! Incredible, if you ask me. I don't think I could manage any of that." Wanda smiled, realizing Tim always said just the right thing.

After lunch, Tim suggested, "Why don't we take a stroll around outside the place? The trees are turning now and the colors are incredible this time of year. Kind of why we bought this place in the first place. Close to the city but yet with trees and hills. Come on."

"But we can hardly walk," Wanda protested slightly.

"I have your arm, madam. I shall not let you take a tumble," he played the role of a handsome knight. The girls giggled at his comic appearance, even bowing to Wanda. Laughing, Bill and Len emulated their father, bringing more gaiety. Soon, all three saw how much the women truly needed their support, but the three women fell in love with the scene that opened before them, gorgeous reds, yellows, oranges, and browns lined the surrounding hills, creating a magical scene.

"Over that hill is my brother's place," Tim explained. "We usually have a Halloween party there. I think Monica will still hold it this year in spite of the demons."

When they returned to the home, Tim said, "Wanda, you did very well walking in the heels. Practice is the answer, I think."

"You're right. I'm a bit more confident now, but Tim, we move so slowly compared to my usual speed," Wanda admitted.

Tim chuckled. "Say, Monica, Crystal, and Ericka often wear heels almost like these. So if they can manage, so can you."

"Yes, but what about the girls when they go to magic school? That has me worried. We can't move fast to dodge spells."

"I'm sure they will find other ways to adapt. They're quite brilliant young women. They will find a way, I'm sure. I should do some design work this afternoon. Will you be all right on your own around the house?"

"Of course, do your work, Tim."

After supper that evening, Wanda and Tim retired to the living room to catch up on the news. The four teens went into the basement to the game room, having decided that the girls could play Monopoly by using their upper arms. The four wanted to test that theory. Around 6:30, without any warning, all the lights and power went off, turning the entire house pitch black!

"What's happening?" Wanda cried out, taken by surprise and again ruing the fact that she couldn't cast a simple Light spell. Tim hastily did so.

"Power's out. That's weird. No storms around," he declared. Just then a Message scrolled past his eyes. "Damn. Ericka says demons attacked the main power grid downtown. They're on it. We best check on the kids. They went to the basement last I heard."

He helped her up in the dim light. At that moment, the four teens came rushing into the room, that is, moving as fast as the two girls dared, which wasn't much faster than a very slow walk for the boys. Susanne's face was positively radiant! "Mom! Mom! Look. I did it. A Light spell!" Sofia just nodded continuously, affirming it. Susanne had a Light spell moving along with her just out in front of her feet, illuminating the floor.

"What? You cast a Light spell?" exclaimed Wanda more than a little shocked.

"She sure did!" Bill enthusiastically backed her up. "The lights went out. Len and I forgot where our wands were at. She just did it! Susanne's going to be a powerful witch, isn't she? Hardly anyone can cast spells without a wand, can they dad?"

"Incredible. Very well done, Susanne," Tim praised her. "Right, other than Monica, I don't know any who can, except now Miss Susanne here."

The teen beamed. Wanda broke down and began crying, so happy was she to witness this, a miracle. There was real hope for the future, and two hours later, the lights came back on.
***

On October 20, Monica got a breather and with Ericka paid a visit to Wanda. After the introductions ended, Tim asked the kids to run off and play, which they were more than glad to do. Monica took charge.

"We've been monitoring the situation in Germany quite closely. Well, I haven't personally, but via some of my federal contacts. The situation is beyond grim. Let me explain what we do know at this point, and then I'll bombard you with questions, Wanda."

"Exact counts are not available and may never be," she continued while Tim quietly brewed a large pot of tea, suspecting this would be a long evening. "Estimates suggest a quarter of Germany's population fled to safety in various nearby countries. They are still there. Half of the remaining population joined this Schutzstaffel or SS group, at one time or another. As you know, the SS women all lost their lower arms and hands and are physically like you and your daughters. The other half that remained and who didn't join up were attacked, yes that's the only word for what the SS men did. As far as I and others can tell, they were attacked with a modified version of Dr. Menninger's biological-genetic agent gas."

"I say modified version because the men were not turned into exceedingly low IQ men, but rather just below average intelligence. That's had a drastic impact on affected wizards, naturally. The women look like you do, Wanda, but they have no voice boxes, confirmed by several doctors. At least they still have their teeth, unlike those who were sent to live in Rolla, North Dakota. For those witches, it's a total disaster. The governor of your school, the Berlin School of Magic—she's one of the victims. She can't talk or even cast a single spell. The Board of Regents had no other choice but to remove her from her position."

"Apparently, this Fourth Reich is working flat out to produce enough clothing and heels for the affected women. In a strange way, this has put a damper on the plans of the SS, at least I think that's the case since there have been no further actions, until this afternoon, late at night over there."

Monica went on, "This supposed Propaganda Minister gave a televised interview. Frankly, what he said or threatened has the international community up in arms, though as yet, no one is suggesting a viable countermove."

"What's he saying?" Wanda asked.

"It'll be all over the news in the morning, but the gist of his message was this. France, you have one week to join the Fourth Reich and the Schutzstaffel. Our SS personnel will distribute the necessary pills to those who join. After one week is up, the Fourth Reich will cleanse France, removing any demons that are hiding out in your country, just as we did here in Germany over a week ago."

Monica went on, despite gasps from Tim and Wanda. "Of course, we all know now what that means. Those who don't join will end up morons if they're men or helpless women who can't speak. Those who do join will end up like you are, Wanda."

"But how can they possibly do this? This is as bad as the demons," Wanda protested.

Monica replied, "It is exactly like the demons. I would have said that it's the insane Dr. Menninger at work, except that the demon horde was eliminated, thousands of them."

"But they can't do this to France, can they?" Wanda asked.

"By using wind spells, we've been able to thwart small gas attacks, but in the massive doses they dumped over Germany, that won't help at all. I'm afraid they will be quite difficult to stop if they want to drop that gas over large areas of France. And which country is next? Odds are on Belgium and the Netherlands, then Denmark and so on. Wanda, I've come by tonight to ask you to tell me absolutely everything you know about them, the Schutzstaffel, the leaders, everything. I'm hoping to get a clue or two from what you say. If we don't figure out something effective and soon, I'm sure that other European countries will not stand for this and launch an all-out war against Germany. Oh, one more thing. This morning, an agent captured an SS man and put him through an extensive medical examination and interrogation. What I find interesting is that he is under some form of Mass Charm spell, doing precisely what the SS asks of him."

"Heine and I didn't want anything to do with these people, at least not at first," Wanda began. "But we had three children to think of besides ourselves." She talked on for nearly two hours, broken by three rounds of tea, compliments of Tim, who also listened fascinated by her highly descriptive tale.

When she finally finished, Monica asked, "So this

Dirk Nordstrom fellow is their Propaganda Minister? He does all the talking it seems." She nodded. "General Berend Bettingdorf handles the actual bombing or gas attacks. That must mean the Dr. Fritz Bielfeld and his pharmaceutical company is supplying the drugs or pills. But who is this mysterious Der Führer leader fellow, this Hans Gotthilf?"

"Don't know. He seldom appeared in public meetings, not until very near the end. Even so, he's hardly ever seen by anyone," Wanda answered. "He sure isn't God's Hand! Try more like the Devil's Hand!"

"Curious choice of words," Monica replied. Until now, she'd seen no signs at all of any devil's handiwork and realized that she shouldn't discount their interference. "No one has a picture of this man. Just who is he? What does he look like?"

"Oh! Say, I took a picture of him when he addressed us. It's on my cell phone, which I can't really use well yet. Tim, can you get it for me, please. I'm way too slow to go get it. My password is Bellflower. I'll walk you through finding it. It's not the greatest. We were pretty far back in the audience."

A few minutes later, Monica stared at the fuzzy image of Hans Gotthelf. She cried, "Now it makes sense! That's really the vile, evil Dr. Menninger clone from the Abyss! He's in league with all these demons!"

After many gasps died down, Monica said rapidly, "Wanda, you may have just saved your entire country! I have to get this vital information spread out to the rest of the entire world immediately. Gotta run now. Thanks. More later." Poof. She vanished.

"She—she just teleported?" Wanda asked blinking her eyes.

Ericka laughed. "That's Monica. She never uses a wand anymore or even a staff of power. Shoot, she never even speaks the proper command words. But that's Monica. I best get going. I expect a run on our enchanted bullets yet again! Bye and thank for the tea, Tim."

Wanda watched Ericka closely and saw that she cast

the Teleport spell properly using her wand. Wanda smiled.

Not long after that, Monica fairly screamed to Deiter, "Yes, that Hans Gotthilf is none other than Dr. Menninger himself, the cloned doctor from the Abyss who works for the demon succubus. Now let the whole damned world know!"

"Yes, ma'am," Deiter replied, somewhat annoyed. Nothing was going according to plans anymore. The whole world was going crazy as far as he was concerned.

Later that evening, Monica and her entire group met to discuss this unexpected turn of events and its ramifications. Bergson grumbled, "As long as he has ample supplies of his bio-genetic agent gas, he can conquer any damned country he wants. What's to stop him? You join up and you become a charmed pawn if you are a man or a helpless woman if female. You don't join up and you become a moron if you are a man or a helpless woman who can't even speak. What's he up to? Controlling the whole damned world?"

Monica sighed. "I wish people would have listened to me nine years ago when he and a few others including the succubuses escaped our massive dragnet. I wanted to pull out every stop to find them, but no one would listen to me. Now look what we have? This is worse than the chaotic rampages of the demons. They impact only a few people, not millions upon millions!"

"We should track him down and fill him full of lead!" Kelly barked. Miller nodded in silent agreement with him.

"But we don't know where that man is," Bergson pointed out.

"Well, we know where the three henchmen are," Kelly suggested.

At that moment, Monica received a Message from Governor Lindsey. "Gang, Governor Lindsey wants us to come to a big meeting at Bradbury's at ten tomorrow morning. Bergson, guess you're going to get a peek inside of one of the most exclusive and expensive schools of magic in the world." He smiled.

***

At ten, Monica brought her team to Bradbury's, arriving before the main gates. Crystal, Ericka, and the others followed behind them. A solemn-faced Lindsey met them at the gates and welcomed them personally. "We're meeting in the main dorm cafeteria, since there are so many coming. Professor Pam Betts will show you the way. I'm on gate duty," she teased, but Monica knew precisely what she meant. Lindsey had erected numerous and extremely powerful protection spells on the school. Likely only she could lower them to allow others to enter.

Pam described the various building for the benefit of those who had never seen the school. Walking across the grounds and into and down to the cafeteria brought back very old memories to Monica, when last lifetime as Dominus, she'd been a student here. Pam brought her back to reality.

"As you can see, the place is crowded today. Folks are here from all over the US and from a dozen other countries—lots of big-wigs. The entire Board of Regents is here, too! Lindsey and Deiter certainly wield a whole lot of influence in very high places! You all can sit with me and the rest of our faculty here, though it's normally reserved for Yellow Hall, Monica."

That was a private tease. Her Dominus lifetime was spent in Black Hall, while her Monica time was spent in Red Hall. Pam, of course, knew this.

Bergson, Kelly, and Miller quickly saw that everyone seemed to know Pam, Amanda, Lindsey, Deiter, Ashley, and some others. What surprised them were the numbers who knew Monica. More than one impressive man or woman dropped by whispering a greeting to her. Many added, "I wish we would have followed your advice nine years ago."

Finally, with a packed room, Governor Lindsey appeared from nowhere and stood behind a table in front of the assembled group. "Thank you all for coming on such short notice. Everyone is here, so let's begin. Deiter will talk first."

She sat down and Deiter rose, clearing his throat. "As you all know from my many messages, we now know more about what is happening in Germany, thanks in no small measure to Monica Nicole Black. And let me just say this on behalf of everyone here today, Monica. We all wish that we had listened to you nine years ago. If so, we might not be here today facing this incredible crisis. All right, here's the situation as of 9:00 this morning."

He outlined everything that was currently known about the situation in Germany, how it developed, and as many details as he knew, including the various companies that the top three men owned. As he rattled off the list of companies, an overhead projector displayed their image. Monica realized that he'd gotten all this from Pam, the Sleuth. She smiled at Pam, who smiled back, knowing Monica knew he was relaying her findings.

When he finished, Juan Hildalgo from the Board of Regents rose to speak next. "We are facing a most confusing picture. It is a fact that the wizard known as Dr. Hans Menninger is a clone who was living and working in the Abyss for Prince Graz'zt, at least he was nine years ago. It is known that he was a cohort of the succubus Gisella, current whereabouts unknown. It is known that he has established this new Fourth Reich and the Schutzstaffel or Protection Squadron, declaring himself Der Führer. Several history professors have positively identified Dr. Menninger as having lived during the 1940's and was a scientific researcher of some renown in Hitler's infamous SS. So yes, this is a Dr. Menninger clone. To the history buffs, his attempt to resurrect the Reich makes perfect sense. How this plan ties into the demon plan is unclear at this time.

"What is baffling is that Dr. Menninger has apparently completely exterminated all the demons and Muslim radicals that were close to overrunning central Europe. He's literally wiped out the vast majority of the invading demons. And yet he is working for the demons. Thus far, the methods he used to exterminate the demons aren't fully understood. That said, apparently it had something to do with massive doses of radiation. Agents have confiscated samples of these special pills of the SS members and discovered one of the ingredients is a highly effective anti-radiation medication. Further studies are underway as we meet."

He went on, "Facts. We may never have an exact count from Germany. However, trusted estimates are as follows. Initial population: eighty-two million people. Number who have fled the country: twenty million. Number of people in the SS: thirty million. Number of recent dead: five million. Number of victims who are moronic men or helpless women who can't speak: twenty-seven million. By any standard, this is a calamity beyond description!"

"Every German female in the country has been victimized. Assuming half the population is female, that's twenty-eight million women who are helpless or who also have no voice boxes. Worse, these are genetically inherited traits, a fact proven by some two dozen births during the last two weeks." Several gasps echoed around the hall.

He continued, "Thanks to the work of Monica, Crystal, and her group, we know a bit more about these genetic mutations. With the women, the DNA is magically altered. If enough Dispel Magic spells are cast on the woman, her altered DNA can be restored to normal, meaning two key points. Her children will be quite normal. Monica's special Regenerate spell will regrow the missing arms and vocal cords. With the men, their studies show that their brain cells have degenerated to those of a hundred-year-old man who has severe dementia. A Rejuvenate spell will restore his brain cells—though I'm told they also need a bit of a jump start to get them functional once more."

"As long as I am talking about cures, let me be perfectly clear. There are one hundred six people in the world who can cast the Rejuvenate spell. If we ask these people to work their magic on the twenty-eight million men, at one spell per day for every day in the year, it will take three-quarters of a millennium to cure all the affected men. There is one person in the world who can cast the Regenerate spell, Monica of course, and at last count a dozen rings that can perform that action. The rings must be worn continuously for about a week. Thus, no matter how you look at the numbers, to cure the affected women will take far, far beyond a thousand years. In short, let's face reality. There isn't going to be any cures for those who have been genetically mutated, except we will try to Dispel the magic alterations in the women so they can have normal children. Beyond that, realistically there isn't any more that can be done.

"Just how terrible is this? Well, for a user of magic, it ends your career and probably all that truly matters to you—devastating. For normal men, their careers are over as well. For women, well, I won't even talk about that. When this is over, Germany is going to need massive assistance, no question.

"Last fact: the SS has issued an ultimatum to France. Either join the SS or not. Those who do will be given the pills whose effects we know. If they do not, then when the SS unleashes it gas, we know what the effect of that will be. Neither choice is acceptable to any sentient mind! The people in France have three more days to make up their minds.

"Representatives from twenty countries are here today to discuss what action the world community could take, preferably before it is too late for the people of France. Finally, the speculation: what is Dr. Menninger trying to accomplish? Is his actions part of this monstrous demon plan to take over Earth? Or perhaps he is acting on his own, going against the very demons he has been allied with for centuries? We can speculate all day. What must be done here today is to develop the best response possible. Thank you." He sat down.

Various people spoke next on various topics and ideas, but there wasn't any ideal plan yet. One man asked, "Do we want to capture these three top henchmen or just kill them?"

Someone else suggested they be captured. Another

called out, "Nay, we don't want another Dominus episode. Besides, he could well have many undetected supporters who might try to spring him from jail. Kill them. It's the only sure way!" Yet, there was no disagreement on Dr. Menninger's fate: kill the clone!

The group decided on the death penalty. They discussed ways and means for over an hour. One thing became clear. They believed the three henchmen could be located relatively easily and, with enough in the raiding party, terminally handled. However, no one knew where the elusive Dr. Menninger was located. Several believed they could torture that info from one of the three henchmen.

Finally, Deiter rose. "I would like to suggest that we take a break for some refreshments and hold private discussions. I have some ideas how we might proceed to get this notorious clone, but I must first speak with key personnel."

Lindsey agreed and in a flash of magic, food and refreshments appeared on all the tables, bringing many welcome smiles.

"Hey, that's cool!" Kelly declared, quite impressed. "Good magic," he added to Pam, who smiled.

No one ever asked Monica if she had a hunch that Deiter meant to talk to her during this break. In any case, he came straight over to her. "Can we and Bergson have a word in private?"

"Can I bring along a coffee?" Bergson asked, having just poured a cup.

"Sure. Ashley will be joining us, Monica."

Deiter took them down into the tunnel system and opened a secret door. They entered a storage room filled with old desks and junk. "I have an idea. I've had Ashley doing her thing for some days now, ever since you told me it was Dr. Menninger, Monica." To Bergson, he added, "She is a powerful Diviner. She is usually able to accurately locate nearly anyone, unless they have quite a few powerful protections on their person. Ashley," he ended.

"Well, Dr. Menninger has darn near every

protection against Divination on him and at all times as far as I can sense. He's one man who doesn't want to be found!"

Deiter resumed, "But I've thought of a way. I talked this over with Ashley and Amanda last night."

"Deiter! You can't do this!" Ashley pleaded. He ignored her.

"There is one way to draw him out."

"Okay, I'm listening," Monica countered.

"Look, you've heard everyone discussing how relatively easy it will be to go after the three henchmen. Suppose that in doing so, we make it widely known that this is wholly your attack on the SS and the Fourth Reich, Monica. You be the bait. If we know anything about what makes Dr. Menninger tick, it's revenge. He's going to be incredibly motivated to get revenge on you for destroying and bringing down his new Fourth Reich. He is certain to come after you!"

"Deiter, you can't do this. I told you why," Ashley protested. She turned to Monica since Deiter wasn't listening to her. "Monica, I've had a powerful premonition about this plan of his. If you do this, something very, very bad will happen to you. I just know it, horribly bad."

"Like what?" asked Bergson, growing quite concerned.

"Divination isn't so specific as that, Bergson. It would be really bad, that's all I can say. Deiter has no right to even ask this of Monica."

Deiter argued, "Well, Monica wants to get Dr. Menninger just as badly as the rest of us. Look, Ashley, he's already harmed eighty million people, ruining their lives at the very best. He must be stopped and I can't think of any other way to get to him without using Monica here."

"Go on, Deiter, I'm listening," Monica said flatly, curious what his plan involved.

"We make your location known, such as at a headquarters or something. Dr. Menninger will strike; he will lash out at you, once he sees your 'attack' has wiped out his Fourth Reich. We will be there with you, waiting.

He'll have to lower some of his protections. If he does, Ashley will divine his location, and we strike at once. If he doesn't lower his divination protections, he may use other ways to get to you. That's where Amanda comes in. She'll be able to track any magic directed against you, Monica. In fact, I'll take extra precautions and have others like Amanda triangulating his position. Then, we'll all charge in to your rescue. We'll have all the bases covered."

Ashley interrupted him. "Don't listen to him, Monica! He says he has everything covered, but things can go wrong, and they will! I just know it!"

"Monica, it doesn't sound like a good plan to me," Bergson spoke up. "Surely we can find other ways to find this fiend."

Monica bit her lip. "Yes, we just might, Bergson, but can we do it in three days or less? I doubt that. We need time and time isn't on our side. I can't sit back and do nothing knowing that in doing nothing millions more are going to have their lives destroyed. I feel just awful that I can't help all those women, but twenty-eight million women? Mind boggling. Tell me more about this crazy plan of yours, Deiter," Monica said, knowing well that Ashley was probably right, something terrible was going to happen to her. How long will I continue to pay the price for my past misdeeds, she wondered.

Deiter added, "Look, I don't necessarily trust everyone at this meeting. Lindsey has used her See True spell on everyone as they passed through the main gates, so none of us here is a demon in disguise and all that, but who knows where their loyalties lie. So we'll let them know that you've got this terrific plan to get them all and leave it at that. Those doing the actual three attacks will be the ones spreading the word that this is your plan, Monica, so word will get back to Dr. Menninger."

He continued, "Plus, we'll be on guard in case it really is Gisella and her group that is backing Dr. Menninger. No matter who comes after you, we'll get them."

A magical door suddenly appeared and Lindsey

stepped out, slightly annoyed. "So Deiter Cross, you have gone ahead and are trying to rope Monica in on your plan! Monica, has he told you the severe risks involved? Ashley's premonition?"

Deiter flushed. Apparently, he was going against Lindsey's advice. Monica answered her, "Yes, both have. The risks to me are obviously quite great. But Lindsey, doing nothing means many millions more lives will be crushed and ruined. Twenty-eight million women! I have a big heart, but I can't possible cure that many women. At least I can try to stop him from harming millions more, Lindsey. I have to try. Besides, maybe Ashley's premonition isn't totally accurate."

"Personally, I think we should try to find another way, which in part is why I called this meeting this morning. Alas, we're getting nowhere. Monica, if you do this, the world owes you big-time," she declared.

Monica stated her final declaration on the topic. "Find cures for all those women and perhaps the men. That would be payment enough. Okay Deiter. Let's do it. Let's not keep all those big-wigs waiting too long."

There would be no turning back now. She was committed. One way or another, the Dr. Menninger clone had to be terminated before he could wipe out France or portions of it.

When the meeting resumed, Deiter kept it short and to the point. "Monica and I have devised a plan to get these three henchmen and the Dr. Menninger clone. We will carry out the plan before they can harm France." He then asked some key personnel to stick around after the meeting, men and women whom he fully trusted.

After the meeting ended and most had departed, Deiter explained part of his plan to the assembled group. "Phase I will be to simultaneously take out the three henchmen. Ashley will try to get us their locations beforehand. If she can't, then we'll send parties to all known locations owned or frequented by them. Surgical strike, take out the three top men. Now this is vitally important. Make darn sure that at least one of the SS men there knows that this is Monica Nicole Black's plan in operation, to bring down the Fourth Reich. That's a critical detail so make sure that gets understood by the SS men."

"When do we strike?" asked Jim, Ashley's husband.

"Tomorrow. I'll let you know the time. There's quite a time zone difference between us and central Europe, like seven hours," he answered. "Make your preparations. We have this one chance to get them before they wipe out France and millions more fall victim to this vile creature."

Chapter 15—Action and Reaction

A very large group of very powerful wizards and witches assembled at Monica's mansion early the next morning. Fifty to be exact, not counting those who lived there. Michelle Folquet, the real Dominus' sister, had been invited, representing Marseilles School of Magic. She got quite a bit of attention, since she still had to wear ballet boots, walking on her toes. She looked much older than Monica remembered his sister, but there was no mistaking her. Monica felt a surge of pride in her sister from her last lifetime, even if he was back then a clone of her real brother. Also present were Tom Ryker, Emilio Lopez, Kathy Townsend, Audrey Lemon, Peaches Colt, Ahana Orondarka, Andy Rains, Orenda Orondarka, Fern Whitewater, and many others Monica didn't recognize.

Deiter tentatively thought the best time for an attack would be when the men ate their suppers. That meant they'd strike at around ten o'clock St. Louis time, that is, five pm Berlin time, assuming Ashley could locate the men. While the others milled around, some inspected the three shops—the magic items, the wands, and the potions shops. Ashley sat in Monica's bedroom with Lindsey and Monica on either side of her, watching over her as she focused solely and only on each of the three men.

After a time, she smiled. *The men are creatures of habit!* Around ten, she returned to the present. "Got them; let's tell the others," Ashley pronounced. As they stepped through Monica's Magical Door, she added, "They are creatures of habit, always dining at the same locations. Fools. They should know better."

Deiter assigned a dozen to each of the three men, and Ashley gave them precise directions using mag-Google references. Once more, Deiter reminded them of what they were to tell other SS men around the targets. Magical energies flashed and thirty-six were off. No turning back now.

"Where's Pam?" Monica asked, suddenly missing the Sleuth.

Deiter smiled. "In our secret location, waiting to cast Idiot Mind. Enough said in public." Monica smiled, realizing what Deiter had in mind, at least one of the things. "Okay, battle stations everyone. Ashley, as much of a warning as you can. Everyone ready here? Amanda? Wilma? A chorus of "yes" echoed.

Ashley focused and began a constant watch on Monica. Amanda focused and saw all the residual lines from the many teleport spells and memorized their pattern so she could eliminate them. She was looking for a new one. On top of one of the pyramids in Egypt and invisible, the Apache Tracker Monane waited for Amanda's signal. Monica had cast every protection spell she knew on herself and sat awaiting the reaction to come, hoping Ashley's premonition wasn't all that accurate. Surrounding Monica were Lindsey, Deiter, Amanda, Crystal, Ericka, Tyler, Jim, and a dozen more power houses of wizards and witches. Heavily armed, Bergson, Kelly, and Miller stood ready to be teleported into action. Now, they waited.

Five minutes after ten, Peaches and her group returned. "Damned easiest assignment yet, Deiter. Scratch General Berend Bettingdorf off your list. He's history. Left the message as ordered with ten SS men."

"Well done. Get out of here now. All hell might soon break loose," Deiter ordered. Peaches led her band just outside and then snuck back inside, unwilling to miss all the rest of the "fun."

A minute later, Michelle returned with her group, landing lightly on the tips of her toes. "Mission done. Dirk Nordstrom is quite dead." Deiter gave them well deserved praise and ordered them to evacuate. They appeared to do so, but soon saw Peaches and her group hiding and waiting and so joined them.

Another minute passed before Ryker's group reappeared. He reported that Fritz Bielfeld was now deceased, actually in many small pieces. After thanking him, Tom and his group headed out of the complex, but stopped beside the others.

"We're waiting to see what happens next," Peaches whispered. "Dr. Menninger is next, but we don't know how."

"It is so wonderful that you are doing this for my country," Michelle whispered. "All France thanks you."
***

In his secret hideout, a home along Eisenhartstrasse, just south of Alleestrasse, in Potsdam, Dr. Menninger sent a Message to Dirk asking if the next political message was ready for delivery at nine tonight. The spell fizzled and for a moment, Dr. Menninger sat at his table confused. He tried it a second time, before he realized what must have happened. Dirk wasn't alive. At once, he sent word to General Berend, asking him to look into what was happening with Dirk. Again the spell failed to activate, startling him even further. In desperation, he Messaged Fritz, but with the same result.

Stunned, Dr. Menninger merely sat in his chair for several minutes trying to grasp what was happening. His top three men—dead? How could this be? Trusted guards surrounded the three men at all times. The way he had set up his command structure, no one beyond these three men knew how to contact him. For sure, Gisella would be gunning for him with a passion. Well, he'd soon take her out of his equation, but now his whole plan was crumbling around him. He had to find out what had happened.

He lowered some of his protection spells and exited the house, teleporting into Berlin, specifically to his SS master headquarters. When he arrived around 5:45, the place was in total confusion. Men talked at once, but a sudden silence fell as they recognized Der Führer. "Sir, Dirk, Berend, and Fritz—they've been executed!" one man reported.

Dr. Menninger already knew they were dead. He needed details. More importantly, he would need to choose replacements for the three probably from these men here. "Do we have any eye witnesses? What happened to them?" he asked as politely and calmly as he could muster, considering he was in mental torment and felt a real rage coming on.

"A dozen wizards and witches showed up at the restaurant. I've never seen so many magical missiles fired at one time in my life. My god, sir, each one must have shot eight in a single volley. Dirk didn't have the remotest chance! Then, they cut his head off!" The man then went on to relay what one had said to the stunned SS men with him, that a witch named Monica Nicole Black had ordered and orchestrated the attack.

By 6:00, he'd heard similar stories from other SS men who had been with the other two. All told the same story, that Monica was behind the coordinated attacks. Her goal, they relayed, was to terminate the Fourth Reich forever. Hastily, he appointed three replacements and gave them the pass codes so they could access the three men's computers, which held all the data they would need to continue operations, or so Dr. Menninger hoped.

"You three, study the documents. Contact me in the morning and let's review where we are at with respect to France. They've only two days left, and we've have had only a very few of them join the SS and get their pills."

They saluted him and he teleported back to his secret home, totally infuriated, a seething, raging anger building in his mind. He had expected Gisella to attack him, but Monica? *That bitch! I should have had Sammy execute her when he had her there in Rolla! We still have no idea how she escaped the Paradise Fortress in the Abyss! She will pay and pay dearly for this! Kill her? That's not enough punishment! That's far too good for her. She needs to suffer each and every damned day for the rest of her life!* Mechanically, he brought out a cold beer and began downing it in gulps, steadying his nerves and lowering his rage slightly.

He had her handled nicely when she went to Rolla. She should have been completely helpless for the rest of her life and yet somehow she'd found a cure for herself and for the men with her. "It's her damned Regeneration spell. She must have somehow gotten it to work. I need her to be helpless forever, so there's no other way. I'm going to have to use my Wish spell and make my marvelous mutations permanent, but I damn well better work out the precise wording and not rush into this."

A half hour passed before he was satisfied the wording left nothing to chance. Wish spells were tricky things. Often they went awry because of a particular turn of phrase had more than one meaning. If so, Wish spells usually chose the wrong meaning, just to be contrary, he thought. *Okay, I want to see her face when I destroy her life forever. Summon. That's the ticket. Summon her here and cast the Wish. Oh how I will enjoy seeing her utter dismay as she realizes she will be utterly helpless for the rest of her life and that she can't regenerate anything!*

I wonder if I'm doing enough to her? He remembered how Graz'zt had fixed her up. No arms at all and fused feet that forced her to walk on the tips of her toes like a ballet dancer. For a time, he considered rewriting his Wish spell, but then decided what he had written was far better. *If she has only upper arms, they will be a constant reminder of what she doesn't have, quite visible, better than a total lack of something.* He scratched out his proposed changes, staying with his original script.

Next, he carefully prepared his Summoning spell. He drew out a perfect pentagram in the center of his living room, where she would be appearing. Next, he ran through the necessary preparatory steps, thoroughly testing the pentagram. Satisfied all was ready and with his scroll containing the Wish spell at hand, he cast his powerful Summoning spell, demanding that Monica Nicole Black appear before him. Brilliant magic flashed, but Monica did not appear!

***

Monica sensed powerful magic coming her way and instantly recognized the spell. She heard part of her true name being spoken and knew at once she was being Summoned, but also knew it wouldn't work. That wasn't her true name, thanks to Rob and an Indian god. "He's trying to Summon me right now!" Monica yelled, though she need not have yelled.

"On it!" Amanda cried, focusing and instantly zeroing in on the highly peculiar magical trace energy left by such spells. She sent a Message to Monane who also began searching for that trace energy likely coming from somewhere in Germany.

Monica felt more electrified than she ever had in her life. Every sense was wide open, examining every sensory perception she had. Dr. Menninger was after her. What would he try next? Whatever it was, Monica knew she had to be at the very top of her game. Dr. Menninger was a highly skilled wizard, not to be toyed with or not taken very seriously. She waited, trying to anticipate what he would throw at her next. Then it dawned on her.

As Dominus, she'd been in Dr. Menninger's shoes. He'd gone after his nemesis, Lindsey and Ashley. *A Wish spell. Well, two can play that game. If he casts a Wish spell, what can I counter with? Nothing. No, wait. If someone could kill him before he can complete the spell, I've a chance. But he will have all kinds of protection spell on his person. Even Deiter is going to have to break through them spell by spell, and I don't have that kind of time. I need almost instant action and an action that will stop him in short order. But what can that be? Oh! Right. It's going to be my only real hope. I do trust him with my life.* Monica relaxed, her plan firmly in her mind. She waited patiently, fully alert, fully in the present time stream.

***

Dr. Menninger said, talking out loud to himself, "Well damn. That must not be her true name. I shouldn't have expected it to be that easy to get to that witch! No time to mess around summoning other demons on the off chance they might know her true name. Let's go over this again. I know what I want done to her, but do I really need to have her right here with me just so I can gloat over her? God, how I would love that, but get real, man. That's not necessary. Time enough to look her up later on, once

you've got control of this miserable world. So all I really need to do is cast the Wish spell. Best recheck it. I can't afford the slightest mistake, not with this power house witch." He went back over his wording carefully and saw a potential loop hole and made a tiny revision.
***

Amanda called out, "We are close to having his point of origin. We've got it down to within a three block circle in Potsdam, Germany. You should send a bunch there now, Deiter."

"We'll go!" Peaches called out, surprising everyone. As they looked over towards her, they saw all thirty-six were still here.

"Okay go and thanks," Deiter called out, frantic with worry. *A Summon spell. What would he try next?* The man had power, he thought, and then had the nagging notion that perhaps Ashley was right—that this was a very bad idea. Too late. Things began happening, wholly unexpected actions, as far as he was concerned. At least the three dozen had just gone to Potsdam and were within three blocks of Dr. Menninger. He took some comfort in that.
***

Finally satisfied he'd covered all angles, Dr. Menninger took a deep breath, focused all his intention, all his will, all his determination, and began the lengthy preparatory chant. With that done and the proper but complex motions of his wand executed, ending in a brilliant, almost blinding flash of perhaps the most powerful magical energies of any spell, he said, "I wish the woman witch known to me as Monica Nicole Black to have her physical body permanently modified to be similar to my Sample Number Forty-two, in such a way that no form of regeneration or regeneration magic will restore her lost body parts."
***

Monica sensed the words coming her way, "I wish." She acted. Silently, she cast her Limited Wish spell. *I wish Bergson would be standing behind Dr. Menninger right now.* Lindsey sensed the coming of the power spell of Dr.

Menninger and alerted Amanda and Monane. At that instant, Bergson, who was standing guard just behind Monica, his large automatic rifle at the ready, suddenly and inexplicably vanished from sight, startling both Lindsey and Deiter and several others as well. Confusion occurred almost instantly.

Amanda added to it. "Got him. Latch on to me!" Without thinking, Deiter did so, as well as Kelly and Miller. Amanda teleported them to the intersection from where their triangulation had pinpointed Dr. Menninger's spell was coming. They arrived but bounced off a protection spell he'd placed on the exterior of his home. Jarred, Deiter headed for the front door, intending to bust his way inside, Kelly and Miller right behind him. Amanda stayed back, Messaging the others who were here within the three block radius. Within seconds, Peaches and the others arrived, just as gunfire erupted inside the home and as Deiter physically smashed down the front door.
***

Dr. Menninger carefully spoke the precise words as he'd written them down, going slowly and enunciating each syllable so as not to make even the tiniest mistake in wording, a mistake which could cause the spell to fail. He didn't care in the slightest that his body would age physically one whole year whether the spell succeeded or not. Revenge would be sweet no matter the personal cost. Monica had interfered once too often in his affairs. Just as he reached the last syllable, magical energies flashed behind him. It took all his will power to finish the spell and not stop and see what was there. If he broke his concentration now, the whole spell would fizzle! The ten million dollar scroll would be lost.

Bergson suddenly found himself standing behind a man sitting at a table in a strange home. The man was obviously chanting. Even from behind, he recognized Dr. Menninger. Bergson didn't hesitate. He pulled and held the trigger down. As fast as the automatic rifle could go, it spewed out a rain of enchanted, large caliber slugs. At this distance, two feet, he could hardly miss, but he did notice that the first several bullets bounced off of the man, although ripping gaping holes in his shirt. Then blood appeared and then internal body fragments began spraying out across the room. Bergson continued to hold the trigger down, but moved the aim about slightly, ripping, tearing new holes in the man's body, which began to slowly slump forward. Still Bergson continued firing. Only when his clip ran out did the gunfire cease, and he rapidly reloaded a fresh clip.

By then Deiter came racing into the room, followed by Kelly and Miller. Bergson didn't stop. He pointed the gun at the back side of Dr. Menninger's head and unloaded another full clip, spraying brain matter across the room as well as a good deal of blood. Only when that clip emptied did he stop and notice the others standing there staring wide-eyed at the grizzly scene.

"Got the bastard!" Bergson barked. He added, "That was a good move, Deiter, sending me here. You could have alerted me beforehand. I might have gotten a shot off sooner. I wasted a second or two before firing."

"Hell man, I had nothing to do with it! I'm as shocked to see you here as everyone else is. Wait, what's happened to Monica? Message Lindsey," he barked and magic flashed.

Bergson watched the man's face closely, as did everyone else who could see it. When his face muscles twisted, Bergson knew that he'd been too late.

"Crap! Lindsey said something has happened to Monica. Her body's been mutated or something. Let's clean up here. I don't want anyone to have any remote chance of using his DNA to clone another Dr. Menninger!"

Peaches said, "Darn it. We're a fraction too late. Okay, Deiter. You take them back and we'll clean up here."

Deiter needed no further encouragement. He took hold of Bergson and Kelly. Miller held onto Bergson as magic flashed. Deiter landed them perfectly not far from where they had been minutes before.

"Well I told you so, Deiter. Now look at the price Monica has to pay for your plan!" Ashley declared and then asked, "Did it work?" Deiter merely stared at Monica.

Also looking at her, Bergson said, "Menninger is quite dead. I cut his body into pieces. Put two full clips into his body and head. A hundred rounds to be precise. I'm so sorry, Monica, if I could only have been a couple seconds faster. I was disoriented, and I wasted a couple seconds getting my bearings before I opened up on him."

"It's okay, Bergson," Monica said. "I knew the risks. The main thing is that we've got all four and stopped them from harming many more millions of innocent people."

"Will somebody please tell me what just happened? None of it was my doing or my plan," Deiter cried out, terribly frustrated. Nothing had quite gone the way he'd envisioned, and Monica was paying a dear price.

Monica answered, knowing that Bergson deserved an explanation, not Deiter. "After he tried to Summon me, I figured what I would do next. Sorry Lindsey, Ashley, but I knew what I would do if I were him, and so I was prepared. I knew he'd be casting a Wish spell or a Limited Wish and that I would be alerted to it as he began the spell. I also know I'm a darn fast caster. I chose to cast a Limited Wish spell. So the very instant I detected he was casting a Full Wish spell on me, I cast my Limited Wish. That spell has severe limitations. I knew that and was careful. I wished to have Bergson be there with him right behind him. I knew that Bergson would recognize Menninger and not hesitate to take him out. My hope was that he'd get off enough rounds before Menninger finished the Wish spell. If he had, the spell would fizzle. I'm sorry, Bergson. I just wasn't quite fast enough. I gave it my best shot though."

Pam, who had dropped down from her half-teleport position, stood beside Lindsey. Both stared intently at Monica. Deiter's mouth dropped open as he heard what Monica had just done.

Deiter exclaimed, "Monica! Don't berate yourself, or you, Bergson! Do you realize what you actually did? It took perhaps ten seconds for him to rattle off his wish. In those ten seconds, you cast a very powerful spell, got Bergson there behind the creep, and he fired almost at once."

"Wasted several rounds," Bergson lamented. "They sort of bounced off his back, but then they penetrated and began ripping his body apart. Wasted too many seconds, Monica. Sorry."

"Good god, Bergson! No one could have done what you two just did," Deiter exclaimed growing more and more animated. "You two are almost super human!" He calmed down. "But Monica, why didn't you send me there? I'd of gotten him."

Monica roared with laughter, rather embarrassing him. "Deiter, the man was loaded up with protection spells. How long do you think it would have taken you to get through all of those and take him out? I bet Bergson's first kill shot that penetrated was done maybe three seconds at most after he got there. It was a matter of seconds. I knew no magic user could possibly prevent the Wish spell from activating. With Bergson, I knew I had my very best shot at it. Still, I guess he and I did a whole lot in just ten seconds. Bergson, you and I are going to have to practice some and get it down to seven seconds."

Bergson stared at her for a second and then began belly laughing. Kelly joined in as well as Miller. Finally, everyone else got the joke.

Pam then spoke up, "So Monica, what's the damage? Is it permanent? What can we do to help?"

"He wanted my body to be like some experimental test subject, so what you are seeing with me must be what that woman looked like: no lower arms and hands, big boobs, and screwed up feet. If I am not terribly mistaken, I must look like the regular SS women victims. Have to see myself in a mirror. However, he put in two clauses that make this permanent. No regeneration and no magical regeneration of the missing parts. So yes, I'm more or less screwed."

Kelly grinned, "I'll help you with that tonight, if you like."

Monica roared, "I bet you would like that!" Again, everyone had a good laugh, as Kelly wisely broke the tension. Monica noted just how observant these three normals actually were and how considerate Kelly could be, when he chose to. He'd definitely lightened the very somber mood of the whole group.

When the laughter died down, Monica said, "Deiter, you and the others should let the world know what has happened. Make damned sure whoever is left in the SS doesn't try to continue down his path. Do it fast before more French people decide to join and take those pills. Also see if you can get all stocks of them destroyed and the formulas, too."

"We'll get some samples in case the doctors can figure out some cures from what's in them," Pam modified Monica's suggestion. "But we best get on this pronto, Deiter. Time is not on our side."

"Later, we should meet and discuss what to do next," Lindsey suggested.

Monica added, "She's right. While there could well be other isolated demons about, for sure we've still got one succubus to find and those she still has with her. It's not over yet. Please, gang, don't fail me this time. We have to get rid of all the demons and not let some slip through the cracks."

Bergson interjected, "I'd like a forensics team to go over that home, but we've no authority in Germany. Still, I believe we should thoroughly search his private home."

"I'll leave someone guarding the place all night. Tomorrow, you can search all you want," Deiter advised him. Bergson nodded.

Everyone promised to continue the demon hunt, and then after thanking Monica for her sacrifice, they teleported away.

"Well, I'm off to clean up. Got back-splatter on me clothes," Bergson declared.

Crystal added, "And we'll take Monica and get her clothes adjusted and so on. Enya, how about some tea in a while?"

As soon as the men left, Monica exclaimed, "Get me out of this top! It's crushing my boobs! And get these boots off. My feet are throbbing fiercely!" Crystal and Ericka quickly did so, much to Monica's relief.

They levitated Monica and floated her along to her bedroom. As they did so, Crystal added, "We thought about undoing your top right away, but we thought that would give the fellows too much to look at."

Monica chuckled. "Big distractions." All three laughed at her pun.

In her bedroom, the women stripped Monica, and all three examined her body form carefully, Monica via her full length mirror.

Crystal declared, "Everything looks as it should, all things considered, but I'd like a full medical checkup. Enya can draw some blood and check for anything magical, like last time."

Ericka added, "I doubt she'll find that, Crystal; this was a Wish spell. But you're right. We should explore every possible avenue."

"What's it now, an H-cup again? At least they are perky and not droopy," Monica asked looking her now large bosom over carefully.

"Looks like that's about right. You wanted them large once, remember?" Crystal teased. "Let's see if I can make them smaller." She cast her Shrink spell. All three laughed as the spell fizzled. "Can't be magically altered, I see. Well, let's have a close look at your feet. Can you move your toes?"

Ericka added, "Wanda and her daughters are working on using their toes as fingers. Is that an option here? Wiggle them some." Again, after careful checking, her toes were unaffected, but her arch right after her heel was bent sharply, almost at a ninety degree angle. Only her toes could rest flat on the floor.

After trying on her usual six-inch heels, Monica sighed. "Even these are going to hurt some to wear. Guess I am going to need more extreme heels than these."

"On it, love," Ericka volunteered.

"Meanwhile, I'll get your wardrobe magically altered for you, unless you want to do it," Crystal volunteered.

"Go ahead. I just want to relax a moment and

recover. That was really stressful, maintaining the attitude that I'm a-okay when obviously I'm really screwed."

An hour later, Ericka returned with a suitcase full of new heels and boots in many colors and styles. "Try on one of these. I think the fit will be absolutely right for you."

"Heavenly. How high?"

"Seven inches. Small steps, but then you already know that. Wanda and her girls are still learning that bit," Ericka stated. "Oh by the way, the other night when they knocked out the power grid, her eldest daughter, Susanne, she cast a Light spell. Sans wand. Wanda was shocked and pleased. Isn't that interesting?"

"Indeed. I'm going to have to spend some time with them soon," Monica replied.

"Say, your hair is longer, isn't it?" Crystal inquired, finally getting around to the finishing touches on Monica's wardrobe.

"Haven't paid attention to that yet. Let's see where it falls when I stand. Cool heels, Ericka, quality leather. Perfect. Right. It is longer, about eighteen inches I'd guess, maybe a bit less. Down to my knees instead of my rump. Have to be a bit careful with it or get it cut. It's been a while since I had it this long. I think I'll keep it this long for a time. Looks about the same otherwise. Okay, let's get the medical stuff done. Might as well know all the bad news at once."

A bit later having teleported to St. Anne's, Monica, Crystal, and Ericka walked into the large hospital. "Well, spells still work fine," Monica commented, "but I'm walking with even smaller steps than I'm used to and slower, too."

"To be expected in those heels. On the bright side, you aren't going to be punishing your knees since your feet are properly shaped for the heel height," Ericka pointed out. Monica though of saying "great," but then decided against sarcasm just now. She'd agreed to be the bait and knew the risks. No sense whining about it now that it had happened.

An hour later, most spent waiting, the scans were

finished. The doctor explained, "Miss Black, all looks perfectly normal. However, we do have your old DNA on file and will compare that with yours now. That way, we can tell if the modifications will be genetically inherited by your future children. Also, we'll review everything. We'll call you in a few days if we find anything unusual. Thank you for choosing St. Anne's."

Monica couldn't help tease the doctor, so she added, "And your bill will be in the mail shortly." The doctor chuckled as he departed, while the two women quickly redressed Monica saving her from having to use magic to do so. That done, Monica teleported them back home, again checking out her spell casting.

Lunch was waiting on them. Enya had kept it warm, though it was now going on two o'clock. Monica found Rob was there waiting for her. "Hi Mom. They said that I could see you when you got back from the hospital. Are you okay? You look different."

"Wish spell. Got my arms, breasts, and feet. Other than that I'm perfectly healthy or so the doctors told me. I'll be all right, Rob. Might need your help now and then. Now run off and play. I bet school will start up fairly soon."

"Okay. Love you," Rob said, giving her a quick hug before dashing off.

"Want us to feed you?" Ericka asked.

"No, you go back to work. I know how much those enchanted bullets of yours mean. I'll be fine. You go, too, Crystal. You've got things to do as well. I'll be fine."

"Okay then, but holler if you need something," Crystal insisted. Both women left and Monica sat alone in the large, empty dining room. She was hungry and hastily began casting Move Object spells, as she had to do some nine years ago. After eating, she tried to use her hands to move her hair out of the way, but nothing happened. Annoyed, she tossed her head about until her raven tresses slipped off to one side. Carefully, she rose. Keeping her balance was far more difficult in these heels, she had already noted, but now that she was wholly alone, it was more shocking to her. The gorgeous spiked heel was not even an inch from the back of the soles that lay flat on the ground. Slowly, she made her way back to her bedroom and sat down on her bed.

Alone at last, her emotions swelled, and she began to cry softly. She knew she was stuck like this. Her spells couldn't regenerate her arms or even her feet, let alone reduce her large bosom. She lay back and allowed herself to cry, letting all her pent-up emotions run freely. She'd been suppressing them ever since the Wish spell activated. Now she could let them run freely. After a time, she felt better and began experimenting a bit, seeing if she could do more things with just her upper arms. Soon she realized that they were pretty well useless, except for a few things such as helping her with balancing. *Well, I'm paying the price, but I've stopped him and saved millions of other women from becoming like this. That's something. But what about the estimated twenty-some million women who are like me?* She had no answer.

Just then, a refreshed Bergson knocked and entered her room. He'd bathed and put on a clean shirt and pants. "Hi, there."

"Hi there yourself," she replied.

"So, I wanted to check and see if you really are okay," he said uncharacteristically gently. "You aren't okay. What the heck am I saying? They told me that not even magic can undo what that bastard did to you."

"I'm okay, mostly, Bergson. We almost beat him, too. My spell casting is not affected in the slightest, but in these heels, while impressively sexy, I walk even slower than I'm used to walking. I'll need a hand on rough or soft ground, that's for sure. I hope I don't hold you up with my pathetic slow gait."

"We'll manage, Monica. We always do. And yes, they are impressively sexy as is the rest of you. I keep wondering if I could have somehow been just a few seconds faster, Monica."

"And I keep wondering if I could have cast the spell seconds faster. No, Bergson, we both did our absolute best. What we must keep in focus is what we accomplished.

Think of it, Bergson, we prevented millions of other women from sharing this fate and millions of men from becoming barely able to even function in life. No, we done good, kid, we done good."

"Points taken, Monica. Still I just wanted to let you know that I'm here for you. Whatever you need. I've never met anyone quite like you. Oh, I always meant to tell you that I loved your long hair, but now it's even more impressive. It's rather difficult for me to say such things, but I'm trying. Say, did you really mean what you said back there to Deiter, that you trusted me more than him?"

"Big boy, you betcha. Deiter's a powerful wizard. No question there. But if we were to have any chance with that man, it had to be you. Bergson, you are a most impressive man. I'll be honest with you. I've never thought much about normal men before, but you've changed my opinion completely around. You're damned impressive yourself, the kind of fellow I'd like to have around me, along with your big gun, too."

He smiled. "I feel the same way. I've never though much of any wizard or witch before. Kind of like they were cheating in life, doing everything the easy way, but being around you these months, I've seen you're just like me, a regular person, only you take on far more risks than anyone ever should."

"Just like you do, you mean," Monica countered.

"Touché. We make quite a pair, Miss Black . . . Monica."

"You know, Bergson, Alan, we certainly do make quite a pair." Acting on pure instinct, Monica leaned over and gave him a passionate kiss. She felt his body melt. His arms slipped around her, pressing her tightly to his body, returning her passion. *Wham.* Monica suddenly experienced the final modification to her physical body, an overly powerful sexual urge.

Alan sensed something happened and gently pulled back, believing he'd overstepped propriety somehow. "I'm sorry."

"No, Alan, it isn't you. I, I wanted that, badly

actually. No, it's another change in my body that I hadn't noticed yet. Alan, I am so utterly horny I can't sit here. I know others have mentioned it. I think Ericka said Wanda mentioned something about this happening to her. I'm slipping. I should've paid a visit to her sooner. Too many other things have kept me from it. Anyway, I'm going absolutely nuts over here—how very weird."

"Hey, does it have anything to do with what we learned about the SS and their goals? Didn't they say something about women having lots of children?" he asked.

"Bingo. That's it. He put this modification into the mix just so that women would crave far more intercourse than they might normally desire!"

Bergson finished her thought, "Thus, more babies and more people in their Fourth Reich. Brilliant strategy, though."

Monica chuckled, "You can say that again, brilliant. Only don't do a Kelly on me and say it again," she teased.

"We seem to finish each other's thoughts sometimes. Kind of spooky," he suggested.

Monica smiled, recalling that they did. "You're right. We do, particularly when solving cases." Their eyes met again. Once more, she leaned over and gave him a passionate kiss. Again, she felt a huge sexual urge, but this time, she wanted it, she wanted him. As their lips separated, she whispered, "How much of an invitation do you need? I want you now, big boy."

"And I want you, sexy woman! Oh, should I undress you? I have no idea what you can and cannot do now," he said gently.

"I'm going nuts, so you undress me. Unzip the back. It's faster this way."

"No bra?" he asked as he helped her slip out of her satin, red dress.

"I don't think they make them for knockers this big. Besides, I would have a difficult time putting one on. Now shut up and kiss me!"

Their lips met again, and Monica allowed her greatly exaggerated urges to run free. Why suppress what she desired in the first place? Sometime later, she cuddled up on his broad shoulders, recalling how she used to do this with Rob. Somehow, this felt right. "Thanks, I truly wanted that, Alan. I'm greedy, too. I want more, lots more."

"Now?" he asked a bit surprised.

She giggled. "No, I'm fine now. How about tonight?"

He chuckled. "You're one heck of a woman. Perhaps more than I can handle."

"And you, big boy, are almost more than I can handle. We make quite a pair, don't we?"

"One fine pair, Monica."

"I guess I should use the bathroom and then let you get me dressed again. We should see how Deiter is making out with ending the Reich," she whispered.

"Not before this," he said softly, giving her another passionate kiss.

"Keep that up, and you're going to have to do it again. My motor is starting to rev."

"I figured that it was. Now I have your number," he teased her.

"Rats! Found out. Well, I'm going to have to find your ignition switch, too," she replied playfully.

He responded, "As if you didn't already know what that is." Both chuckled. A bit later, he fumbled around but got her dress back on and zipped. "Don't see how you can even walk in them," he commented as she slipped on the new heels that matched her dress.

"Can't walk much without them. They do help a lot, but you're correct. We can barely walk in them. See my arches? That's why." She slipped a pump off, and he very closely inspected her foot.

"Wow, that's really bent. Now I do understand, Monica. I didn't before, but I do now."

"Hey, tonight give my feet a rub, will you?"

"I'll rub whatever you desire," he teased back.

Both grinned. She tossed her hair about until it was off to one side and then rose carefully to her feet. "I don't know what help you need. So please ask or whisper or something."

"I will. Come on. Let's start with the news. Tomorrow we have to search Dr. Menninger's home," she reminded him.

Chapter 16—Changes

"Changes are happening rapidly in this country of some eighty million people," the reporter talked rapidly. Many people had turned on the news to hear what had happened in Germany and to the Fourth Reich. Word had quickly spread that something major had just occurred. Monica and Bergson turned on her set in her study next to her bedroom and were in time for the top of the hour latest reports. "Unidentified sources told us that at dinner time—that would be approximately six hours ago—unidentified wizards and witches appeared at three dining establishments in central Berlin and brutally killed the three top men of the new Fourth Reich. Propaganda Minister Dirk Nordstrom, General Berend Bettingdorf, and Dr. Fritz Bielfeld were executed as they were eating. Security guards, that is to say other SS members, were present with them at the time of these brazen attacks, but were unharmed by the assailants."

He continued his summary reporting, "Approximately an hour later, Der Führer, the self-appointed head of the Fourth Reich, Han Gotthilf, appeared at the central SS headquarters in downtown Berlin, where our inside man reports that he was appraised of the situation. In turn, he appointed three SS men to replace the fallen trio. After giving them the necessary security clearances and orders to get up to speed on the issues, Herr Gotthilf told them he would contact them shortly with further details."

"Der Führer was also told by witnesses at all three crime scenes that a witch by the name of Monica Nicole Black had orchestrated the assassinations of his key personnel. As Herr Gotthilf departed SS headquarters, he was heard saying that he would take care of the witch. All that was about six hours ago and much has changed since then."

"Herr Gotthilf failed to contact the three new

replacements at the top of the SS command structure. Their attempts to send a Message to Der Führer failed, not once, but repeatedly, according to our inside source. We talked to Mage Alberto Fernando about this apparent anomalous spell failure. He pointed out that there were only two reasons a Message spell would fail: the recipient was deceased or the recipient was not on Earth."

"Reporters on the scene and who are risking great bodily harm in doing so are reporting mass confusion within SS headquarters and in many local branches. We replayed video taken inside SS headquarters in Berlin for Mage Alberto. His response was. . ."

The news broke away to a short clip of the white bearded wizard, who said, "Ah, vell it looks to me like they are just now coming out of a Mass Charm spell." He started to tell them about an experience he had long ago at a magic school, but they edited the clip, stopping it here rather abruptly. The reporter reappeared on the screen.

"Mass Charm. Other wizards are confirming this conclusion. This brings up a major, as yet unanswered question. Were all members of the Schutzstaffel somehow under a Mass Charm spell?"

"Considering the magnitude of that question, we've sent many reporters out into the field to find out, and I must add at great personal risk to their own safety, what with the biological-genetic agent threat looming now just hours away. Uniformly, they are reporting the SS members in the local offices that they visited are also displaying similar confusions. Every man they interviewed expressed shock and disbelief that the women in their lives have been so horribly mutated, but they also were thankful that the demon horde was exterminated. We all are thankful for that. Still, the SS men interviewed were appalled at the physical condition of their wives and children. One reporter likened the men's reaction as that of someone who had only just now seen the physical effects on the women in their lives."

"Mass Charm, pills that cause incredible physical changes—one cannot help but recall a similar situation some ten years ago in the United States with its National Health Care Program, a diabolical plot by the notorious Dominus Malefic. Some are asking if somehow, someway Dominus is back? Resurrected from the dead? We put this very question to our Mage Alberto. Here's his response."

The old wizard's white bearded face reappeared, "Yes, of course such a thing is possible, but one would need his DNA to construct a clone of him. I would point out that this Hans Gotthilf fellow doesn't look remotely like Dominus, though admittedly what we see could be the result of a Morph spell."

They cut away to the reporter again. "Shocking news, is it not? We explored this further and came up with some incredibly shocking new evidence. Hold on to your seats, viewers! An anonymous source tipped us off to this."

Suddenly two images appeared on the screen. The reporter's voice explained, "On the left is an archival, antique image of the notorious Nazi scientist known as Dr. Hans Menninger, wanted for countless crimes against humanity committed during his genetic experimentations on captured human prisoners of war, and under Adolf Hitler's orders. At the end of World War II, Dr. Menninger mysteriously vanished. For over fifty years, many have searched for this butcher to bring him to justice, all to no avail. On the right is the best image we currently have for Der Führer, Hans Gotthilf, otherwise known as Dr. Menninger."

Now the reporter reappeared. "Yes, there can be no doubt about it; the two are nearly identical, down to the thick black glasses he wore! Given the terrible effects of his SS pills on his supporters and the effects of his secret weapon that presumably exterminated the demons, one could be led to believe that the two are the same. How could this be? The real Dr. Menninger was around forty years old in 1940. This is 2200, making him two hundred sixty years old! That, my friends, is utterly impossible. So we are left with two possibilities."

"One, our Dr. Hans Menninger is actually a clone of the original, or two, Dominus has been revived and is using a Morph spell to appear as that ancient war criminal Dr. Menninger."

By now, Monica's face was burning. She wanted to scream: Deiter! What have you done to me? It took all her will power to remain calmly watching the newscast beside Bergson, who was watching it intensely. She had been that evil Dominus last lifetime, but she was a different person today.

"We sent reporters to interview the Colorado Department of Justice. Officials there confirmed that they did record the death of Dominus Malefic. He was shot by a still unknown long range sniper, a single large caliber shot through his head, removing half of his face. Upon further questioning, officials there verified that Dominus was buried in an unmarked grave in the Denver Memorial Gardens. At this time, we are pursuing a court order to have that grave dug up and its contents verified as the remains of Dominus Malefic. However, this just in, our investigative reporters have interviewed an old caretaker at the Denver Memorial Gardens who recalls once discovering that his grave had been dug up by persons unknown, but that was many years ago. Based on this, it is expected that we will soon have a court order and see just what lies in that unmarked grave.

"So while the mystery surrounding the true identity of this Dr. Menninger remains, we will continue to investigate and bring you the latest discoveries in this, the most shocking mystery of the century. Turning now to the explosive situation in Germany and France, new developments are happening as we speak. To bring you the latest, here is Mr. Deiter Cross of the US States Department of Justice."

Deiter appeared on the screen. "The Fourth Reich has been terminated. The members of the SS were unwittingly Mass Charmed by Propaganda Minister Dirk Nordstrom. At this time, that spell is broken, and the men are displaying confusion and dismay over what has been done, particularly to the women of Germany. Forces have already raided and seized existing stockpiles of both the five types of pills and the bio-genetic agent gas that has been used to mutilate men and women.

"Thus, there will be no attack on France. I repeat. The Fourth Reich is history. There will be no gassing of anyone in France. So do not, I repeat, do not take any further pills handed out by SS members. I encourage anyone who is in possession of any of these pills to destroy them at once. Do not take any more of these pills.

"At this point in time, Germany is leaderless. Worse, much of its male population is nearly unable to function, while the women are nearly helpless. We know that approximately a quarter of Germans fled the country. I would appeal to those to return to your homeland and take charge. Free and open elections must be set up soon. Now is the time for honest Germans to step up and help lead your nation out of the disastrous state that it is in.

"Further data on the genetic mutations: the initial scientific chemical analysis of the pills and the gas and earlier demon gas attacks are finished. I can report the following facts. The gas used in the many random demon attacks, the gas used by the SS to exterminate the demon horde, the gas used by the SS to 'eliminate' any possible demons who fled into Germany, all five types of SS pills are all derived from the same basic formula! This has been proven chemically. I'm told that a key active ingredient differentiates the physical effects on the person based on the presence or absence of the Y chromosome. Hence, the extreme difference between the effects on men and women. There is only a slight difference between each of the five types of pills distributed broadly by the SS personnel and between the various gaseous forms unleashed upon the world at various times and locations.

"Further, initial analysis of the gas that was used to exterminate the demons has shown very high levels of radiation were in it as well. The pills that the SS distributed that protected consumers contained high levels of the most commonly used anti-radiation poisoning drug, widely available at your local pharmacy. That is why those who were on these pills and in the area of the attacking demons were able to survive. Thus, there is no mystery behind all these. They were invented by Dr. Menninger himself.

"Back in the US, he carried out his initial experiments on some of our citizens. He cleverly converted a small town to hold the resulting victims, moronic men and helpless women unable to speak. They are being humanely looked after at this time. Dr. Menninger was in league with the demons, helping them restore an ancient and long disused portal to the Abyss, buried for centuries under desert sands, called the Dragon Hole. It was through this portal that Dr. Menninger and his succubus associates were able to funnel thousands of demons from the Abyss into our world.

"I am very pleased to announce to you today that this portal, the Dragon Hole, has been located and destroyed. Miss Monica Nicole Black and her associates, the top Homeland Defense Force-World Investigation team of the United States and a number of wizards and witches destroyed it several days ago. That funnel has ceased to exist, though many demons and at least one succubus are still at large in our world.

"The reports that Miss Monica Nicole Black was behind the assassinations of the three top SS men are partially true. She and many others worked together to put an end to this heinous group that has already destroyed the lives of more than sixty million Germans and many others, as well as preventing similar destruction of countless lives of those living in France. Yes, Dr. Menninger is dead. Steps have been taken to prevent any possible future cloning from his DNA.

"At this time, the international community is ready and willing to help surviving Germans rebuilt their devastated country. Full cures are impossible. Yes, that is the saddest note about this entire situation. Let me be more specific. Men. In their case, studies have shown that the bio-genetic agent has prematurely aged their brains to that of a hundred-year-old man as well as installing forms of dementia. In the most severe cases, the man's IQ has been lowered to barely fifty. In the case of the SS men, their

IQ has been lowered to the normal range at best. Can it be cured? Miss Monica Nicole Black and her team have discovered a way to cure the men. First, a full Rejuvenate spell must be cast on the man, followed by a severe emotional jar. After that, they experience a full recovery. The problem we are facing is that there are only one hundred six people in the world who can cast the Rejuvenate spell. Considering there's an estimated thirty million or more men who have been victimized, millennia will be needed to cure them all."

"In the case of the vastly worse female victims, Miss Monica Nicole Black has also found a cure. There are two critical aspects involved here. First, these women's DNA contain magical energies, which if not handled, will guarantee that their physical deformities are passed down to their female children! This is intolerable. After a sufficient number of Dispel Magic spells are cast on the victim, all traces of these magical energies in their DNA are gone. Thus, their physical deformities will not, I repeat, will not be passed down to their children. Today, I am asking the international community of wizards and witches to step forward and lend a hand. Millions of women simply must have this much of a cure, because unless this magic is dispelled, their children will be as debilitated as they are.

"Second, their missing voice boxes, lower arms, hands, and feet can be restored via a Regenerate spell. Unfortunately, with all the resources on Earth that can cast or emulate this spell via magical rings, it would take a millennium to cure so many millions of women. Thus, looking at the reality of the situation, realistically, beyond dispelling the magic in the women's genetic structure, there isn't likely to be any cures forthcoming. Again, I call upon those Germans who wisely fled to return and begin rebuilding your country. The international community will also do what it can to help the millions of victims.

"One final matter. As you may be aware, Governor Lindsey Barron and myself along with our Rodents were the ones who captured Dominus Malefic and his Death Stalkers. I would like to state in no uncertain terms that

Dominus is dead. He has *not* been resurrected and pretending to be this criminal Dr. Menninger. In fact, we know absolutely that Prince Graz'zt of the Abyss had many Dr. Menninger clones working for him in his Abyss complex. One of those clones managed to reach our world some nine years back and managed escaped the dragnet that rounded up most of the invading demons at that time. I can assure you unequivocally that Dominus and Dr. Menninger are in no way one and the same person. Both are quite dead. I urge you to focus on assisting Germany to recover and to help the millions of innocent victims of these diabolical demons and insane doctor. Thank you."

Just then, Enya entered, looking very worried. "Monica, there's a host of reporters outside demanding an interview with you, something about your role in the killing of the SS leaders. What should we do?"

"That's the last thing I need to do—give them an interview. If I do, I'm likely to do something I would regret! I'll handle them." Monica focused and cast an illusion.

Outside their complex, a giant banner scrolled before the dozen reporters and their camera crews. It read: Focus on the millions of women victims and how you can help them.

One reporter cried out, "Did you get that?" Her cameraman nodded. "Okay. Go live with it."

A bit later, Monica was surprised to see her Illusionary banner on the newscast. Bergson merely laughed his head off. Miller smiled.

***

The next morning as the WIT team assembled their many bags filled with assorted equipment they planned to use in their thorough search of the doctor's home, Miller noticed that Bergson seemed far more relaxed than normal. In fact, he was actually quite civil to her and to Kelly. Curious, she decided to keep an eye on him. Something certainly had changed with her boss.

"Okay, we got everything? We don't want to have to make Miss Black have to bring us back here to pick up something we forgot," Bergson said politely.

Uncharacteristically of him, Miller thought. *Perhaps, he's being considerate of her because she's now a victim that can't be cured.*

It was three in the morning in St. Louis, but ten in Berlin when the team arrived, compliments of Monica's Teleport spell. Bergson commented, "You know, I could get to like this mode of transport, though I miss the accommodations of our Stratosphere. Okay, let's go over everything in this place."

"Allow me to check for booby traps first," Monica advised.

As they walked up to the door, a sleepy-eyed Fern Whitewater stepped out. "Oh, you're here. Good. Place is secure. We found a dozen traps, but they're now disarmed. A few were poisoned, but those are neutralized. I'm heading home now. If you need the place guarded when you leave, send word to Deiter. Bye."

"Thanks, Fern," Monica replied, just as the Apache vanished from sight. The four entered the home, unpacking their gear near the front door, which had already been repaired. Deiter's crew had been thorough.

"Miller, search the place for electronic bugs. Gang, anything electronic that we find, get it to Miller."

Monica added, "And anything with writing, send it to me. I'll set up in the front room by the couch there."

The group fanned out, though Chrissy held some device in her hand and began moving slowly about the room, before moving deeper into the home. Fifteen minutes later, she declared the house had no eavesdropping bugs installed. One bedroom had been converted into his study. Because so many books and papers littered the room, Monica changed plans and decided to park herself there. Using Move Object spells, she began sorting through the papers, while Bergson found his computer and took it down to Miller.

Time slipped by. Bergson and Kelly went over the entire home. Nothing escaped their scrutiny, just as Miller did with his cell phone and laptop. They found many dates and locations where the various agents were manufactured and these were quickly relayed to Deiter. What surprised everyone was Professor Pam Betts, who sudden appeared.

"Hi ya. Deiter asked me to do my sleuthing here. He's paranoid we'll overlook something significant," she explained, anticipating at least a growling reaction from Bergson, particularly since Deiter hadn't bothered to notify him that she was coming. Besides, she expected top investigators to likely resent her butting in on their work.

"You are most welcome to lend a hand. Miller's working the electronics. Got some leads already. Monica's in his study going over—well I don't know what all. The books and papers stuff. Place is clear of bugs. We're now looking for concealed safes and such," Bergson explained politely.

A surprised Pam joined Chrissy first. "What's with him? He didn't take my head off or even complain. I know, Deiter should have let him know he was sending me."

Chrissy smiled, "He's acting really strange today, all nice like. Weird. Don't know why. Well, I've got a lengthy list of the agent production sites and where they got all their radioactive materials. As far as I can tell, he was letting his rich German SS men fund the entire operation. He doesn't even have a bank account that I've found."

"No cryptic accounts? No special passwords?" Pam asked.

"I cracked those right away."

"Looks like you are spot on here. I'll go check with Monica. How's she managing?" Pam asked.

"She's a trooper. But it's hard for her."

Pam headed into the study.

"Oh hi, Pam. Lots to go over here. Glad you're here."

"What are you doing? Those his spell books?" Pam asked. Monica was doing some strange page flipping. It looked rather random to her.

"Yes. I'm trying to find the most worn pages," Monica replied, "darn hard without hands though."

"Hey, cool idea. Those would be the ones that he referred to the most. Honestly, with all the spells we can cast, it's nearly impossible to remember the details of every one of them," she chatted.

"Indeed. Look this one over, will you? See if you come up with the same thing I just did," Monica asked.

Pam took the heavy book from the table. She waved her wand over it and commanded, "Frequent." The book opened to one specific page.

"Hey what was that one?"

Professor Pam smiled, "A teacher's special spell. Really simple, actually. It shows me what pages in a book a student looks at most frequently. Useful and keeps students on the up and up. 'But professor I was up all night on that spell.' I cast Frequent and their book opens to an entirely different spell. Keeps them honest." Monica chuckled. "I'll teach it to you before I go. Really simple. But what have we here?" Pam suddenly got very interested in the spell on the page.

"Ah, my crude way and yours agrees. He's spent an awful lot of time on this page with this spell: In Case Of," Monica said. "Now this is an obvious spell to have enforce. In Case I get badly wounded, teleport me home—that sort of thing. Dr. Menninger wasn't stupid. From what Bergson said happened—his first few bullets bounced off his back—he had Skin of Stone on himself. So we know he had protections. He would have been a complete fool not to have had an In Case I get badly wounded spell also on himself."

Pam broke in, "I see where you are going with this. Excellent sleuthing, by the way. Precisely so. Odds are great that he did have this spell on himself when Bergson shot him. And yet Bergson splattered him all over the room. You should have seen the mess they had to clean up! Glad I got there late. So if he had that spell on him, which he most likely did have, why didn't it work?"

"Or if it did work, why didn't they see it happening?" Monica suggested an alternative.

Pam bit her lip. "Vitally important data. One we must answer, that is, if we're going to be thorough this time. Don't worry. I'm on your side. Thorough we will be, period. Too bad Deiter got there after the man was dead.

He might have seen what happened. Look here; he's also paid a lot of attention to the Clone spell. Well that makes sense since he was a clone himself."

"By the time Deiter got into the room where he could see what was going on, Alan had already put most of a clip of slugs through his body. Even if a few first bounced off, he was likely long dead before the fiftieth slug hit him, and Alan stopped to reload—probably dead after the first couple went through his chest. Alan was using large caliber rounds and centered on Menninger's chest. A couple of those and his major organs would have been destroyed."

Pam grinned and teased her, "So he's Alan now and not Bergson?"

Monica flushed.

Pam added quickly, "I'll keep my mouth shut. He's rather handsome. Big and strong. Anyway, he would be the only one who would have seen Menninger's In Case Of spell activating. Wish he wasn't a norm. Darn."

"I know. There's one way we might get an after the fact look at what happened, but it's, well it's going to be very personal. He might not be willing," Monica hinted.

"If anyone could convince him this is a key point, it's you," Pam suggested.

"All right. I'll go speak with him." Monica rose carefully, trying hard not to wobble wildly in front of Pam. Meanwhile, Pam dove into the pile of papers, looking for additional clues.

"Bergson, a private word with you?" Monica asked.

He and Kelly were moving a bookcase out of the way, checking for a hidden wall safe. He nodded to Kelly, who continued their search, and he followed Monica into the hall.

"Alan, I want to ask something of you that you might not like. Feel free to turn me down." She explained about the In Case Of spell.

"So you're saying that he could have cast one of them? But he died. His body was right there in the chair, rather what was left of him."

"I know, Alan, but if he did have that spell on him,

then we could well be missing something that is vitally important here. This man was a survivor to beat all odds. Look what he's been through. It doesn't make sense that he wouldn't have had that protection spell on his person. All powerful wizards use it. You know, in case I get badly hurt, teleport me home or some such thing."

"I see where you are going with this, Monica. So where do I fit in? I know nothing about magic," he reiterated the obvious.

"We've a spell that we can use. We can't legally use it without your permission. We can join our minds to yours, but that will allow us to read the most private thoughts of the other person. It's kind of like a mental rape, unless the person is very willing to share their intimate thoughts. What Pam and I are proposing, but only if you are truly willing, Alan, is to cast it on you and then have you very carefully recall everything that you saw from the moment you found yourself behind him in that room until Deiter arrived. Go over those few seconds in your mind very slowly and let us see what you saw. I promise we won't look at anything else but that."

"Holly crap! You wizards can do that? Wow! I never knew that. Yeah, mental rape is the right term for it. Illegal you say?" he asked, quite startled.

"Yes. The Department of Magical Misuse will jump on anyone doing that with a sledge hammer. Doing it once will land you in major, major trouble," Monica answered honestly. She added, "I've seen men who have done that thrown into jail for years for that offense. We've got to enforce that law in a big way or the trust factor between users of magic and those who can't would be shattered, probably beyond repair."

"You can say that again!" Bergson barked.

"We've got to enforce that law in a big way or the trust factor between users of magic and those who can't would be shattered, probably beyond repair." Both broke into a loud laugh.

"Okay," Bergson said. "I can see I could well have seen something absolutely critical to this whole investigation, though I know that I wouldn't know that I had seen it. Just don't look at my private thoughts."

"We'll swear that we won't, Alan. Professor Betts is a Sleuth and best qualified to observe."

"Okay then, let's do this. We're not finding a lot of useful stuff here, except leads on where the plants are located that have been pumping out his biological agents." The pair walked back into the study. "Hello, Professor Betts."

"Hi ya, Bergson. I take it he's agreed to let us do this?" Pam inquired, looking at Monica.

"Yes, but we must swear we won't look at his private thoughts, just his memories as he shows us what happened during those initial few seconds before Deiter came charging into the room," Monica explained.

Both swore and Monica cast the spell on Bergson. She and Pam found themselves seeing what Bergson was seeing, thinking what he was thinking, feeling what he was feeling. All three blushed for a second before he began recalling the event.

The pair watched the few seconds pass by. *Show us again*, Monica placed her thought in his mind. Three more times he recalled those seconds, grizzly and bloody though, before Monica canceled the spell.

"Well?" he inquired, adding, "That was spooky!"

"I think so," Pam declared, biting her lip. After a pause, she asked, "Monica, did you see that tiny flash of magic there just after that first shot sent blood and stuff flying out across the room in front of him?"

Monica looked at her memories she now had of his memories. "Right! Something did happen, and it happened when that first bullet tore through him. Rather looked like that slug might have taken part of his heart with it. Something definitely happened there."

Pam declared, "Precisely. His In Case Of spell triggered. He had something in mind when Bergson shot him. But what? Now that *is* the question of the day!"

Monica declared, "Well, the most logical things one might use didn't happen. He didn't teleport to a safe house.

He didn't step through a Magical Door. Other protection spells didn't activate. In fact, other than the magical energy flash, I didn't detect anything. Could his spell have failed?"

"Definitely not. Trust me on that one. I'm something of an expert in this area. Sleuth and all that," Pam said, speaking rather slowly and thoughtfully. "He made use of that spell in some unorthodox way. Monica, we must find out what he did. I'm sure it is more than vital in this case. Whatever he did, it was his dying command, and it wasn't trivial!"

Monica began thinking aloud, "We know this fiend has a tenacious hold on life. He was a survivor on more than one occasion. Sensing he was about to be killed, which he was, he would have wanted to cast something that would ensure his continued survival in some way. Could he have Jarred himself into a special container, allowing his physical body to die?"

"Magical Jar? Well, that's a possibility, but then what? Spend eternity waiting for someone to come along and then take over their body?" Pam spewed a stream of thoughts as fast as she was thinking them.

Bergson looked quizzically at Monica, and she picked up his unspoken question and proceeded to answer it. "Yes. That would be the person himself. We have a body. We have a mind. But who was looking at those memories of yours a bit ago? You were. That's you the person, the personality, or in some religions, the spiritual being. It is possible to cast a spell that slams the person out of his body and into a special magical vessel, a jar for lack of a better name, like a genie in a bottle. Pam's speculation is that he did that and is now residing in just such a jar. What that means is that when someone with a body he likes comes close to the jar, he could slip out and take over that person's body, slamming them into the jar that he was in. Rather like body snatching."

"Holy crap! Did he do that? Is he around here? What's this jar thing look like? Could he already have taken over one of us? Kelly? Miller? Me?" Bergson barked, growing very worried indeed.

"If you can ask those questions, then absolutely you haven't been body snatched, Bergson," Pam answered. "No, I would have detected him if that would have happened to any of you four. After all, I'm the Sleuth here. I suggest we look over absolutely every object in this house and make darn sure it isn't a magical jar vessel!"

A half hour later and after Pam and Monica had cast countless Detect Magic spells throughout the house and after Bergson and Kelly had smashed every conceivable jar, glass, cup, and vase in the house, they were convinced there was no magical jar vessel here.

"Well, back to the drawing board," Pam declared, annoyed that this obvious solution must not be the right one.

"So now what? He did something," Bergson growled.

"That's what we have to figure out," Monica explained. "You two keep on with your search. Let us ponder this further. He did something, and we have to figure out what that was!"

Bergson declared, "Don't know nothing about all this magical mumbo jumbo stuff, but if I knew I was about to get hit, I'd have an escape plan ready. I'm gonna find it my way."

He left them rummaging through the man's spell books in search of another idea, while he headed off to find Miller. "Find anything?" he asked.

"Only what I expected to find—stuff about production of the bio agent things. Here, have a look. There is only one minuscule datum that doesn't compute. Here, take a look yourself." She moved her monitor around and zeroed in on one transaction in a list of thousands.

Meanwhile, Pam cursed. "I've been a dope. An idiot. I should be using my Sleuth skills on this one. Give me a minute."

"What do you mean?" a curious Monica asked.

"Oh, a Sleuth can tell what spell was cast or get a good idea from the magical energy traces left behind, the ones we saw though Bergson's eyes. I should have done that at first. Silly me. I'm getting old."

"Hardly." Monica watched as Pam closed her eyes and concentrated for a few minutes before she opened them. Now her face looked more confused than ever.

"Now that is strange, Monica. I can recognize a lot of spells just from their magical residue. But this one has me baffled. It's not like any that I have ever seen, and mind you, I've seen a lot! Whatever it was, it was very short range only. The energy never left the room. He did something to something in the room where Bergson shot him, but what? Now that is the question we must answer. Come on. Back to the scene!"

Pam raced into room where Bergson shot Menninger. Kelly was still tapping and pounding on the walls, looking for a concealed safe. "Excuse us, Kelly. We need to search this room, too," Pam declared before realizing that she'd left Monica far behind her. Turning around, she saw Monica making her slow way into the room. "Er sorry. Carried away. Kelly, he did something magical to something in this room. We have to find what that was."

"Well, all the books and computer were removed from here," Kelly explained. "We've tossed just about everything else. Even took the desk apart. That's why all the junk is on the floor in a mess. What are we looking for?"

"We will know it when we find it," Pam declared.

Monica added, "We don't know what, only that there has to be something critically important in here."

"Like I said, just a pile of junk. I'm still hunting for a secret safe in the wall." He resumed his tapping search.

Monica felt pretty useless, and let Pam do the sifting through the debris littering the floor. She merely looked at all the objects. After a time, she saw what looked interesting. "Pam, what's this thing?" she pointed her right toe towards it.

"Oh, that's one of those ancient transistor radios. Probably a hundred fifty years old or more. Rare, but not valuable," Pam rattled off her analysis. Suddenly, she stopped and picked it up. "Could there be more to this than meets the eye? Kelly, got a screwdriver?"

"Yeah, over there in my bag. Just put it back when you're done with it. Can't afford to lose it. Handy sometimes."

Pam pried the back off. "Now what do we have here? This isn't an antique radio at all, but what is it?"

"Hey Miller!" Kelly yelled. "In here. Need you."

Shortly Chrissy walked in, "What's up? More electronics?"

"Over here, Chrissy. We found what at first look appears to be one of those antique transistor radios, but when I opened it up. Look," Pam showed her the device.

Chrissy knelt down beside Pam. "Now this *is* interesting! It's a modern signal transmitter. Range, probably several hundred miles. Operates on one very specific frequency only. I'll have to get my test gear to find out what frequency. But this little part here is some strange kind of switch. Never seen anything like this before. Here, when these two copper pieces touch, the transmitter turns on. Probably an automated signal, kind of like a distress beacon. What's this doing here?" she explained and asked.

"Monica, I'm a real idiot!" declared Pam, slapping her forehead with her hand. "Duh, how about a dodo? The In Case Of spell—it was Push. Nothing more than a ridiculously simple Push spell, which anyone knows! I was looking for all manner of really powerful, useful spells, you know such as Magic Jar, but it was Push. Duh! I can see I need to get out into the field more. I'm losing my touch!"

Bergson entered and overheard much of the exchange. He broke in, "Professor, what does Push have to do with this case? I don't understand. And what's he doing with the transmitter? No one came to his rescue."

Pam stood up, lending a hand to Monica. "When you shot him and the first slug actually ripped through his body, his In Case Of spell triggered. It was a localized spell. Without a doubt, the Push was directed to those two small copper wires. Show him, Chrissy."

"Right those. They made the electrical connection, which then turned on the transmitter, which then sent out its unique signal. Somewhere out there, a receiver received that signal."

"Makes sense so far, but then what?" Bergson inquired. "No one came to help him. No rescue. No aid. Nothing. We didn't see any counterstrike happening elsewhere. Just nothing at all."

"I know, sir. That is what is most peculiar and intriguing. We have only half of the puzzle in our hands, sir. We have the origin point. We need to find out what was on the receiving end to know what Menninger had in mind. However, given his mind, it has to be extremely important, vital to his long term survival, somehow. I know, he's dead, but he went to extreme lengths to send that signal. We have to get to the bottom of this mystery for sure!"

Pam was now highly animated. She felt ten years younger, as she was when she was hot on the trial of Dominus Malefic! "I'm on your team now. You can't get rid of me, not until we solve this one. If you won't let me, then I'll work alone. This is really a cool one. Wow. Dr. Menninger really had something going here, but what? I, Sleuth Betts, will find out. On that, sir, you can count!"

Bergson suddenly roared with laughter. "Professor Betts, I wouldn't dream of excluding you. We've learned more today than we knew for months about this insane man. I've relayed the biological agent data to Deiter. He can see to its confiscation and destruction. My team, we must absolutely pursue this. Hard evidence, as I always say. Miss Black, this is hard evidence that Dr. Menninger set some failsafe thing in motion. And we have to find it before it can trigger or activate or whatever it is supposed to do."

Pam visibly relaxed and calmed down. His reaction was the opposite from what she had been led to believe it would have been. Perhaps Deiter got everything wrong, she thought.

Chrissy looked quizzically at Bergson. He too was acting strangely. She'd expected him to flat out reject her joining them, and yet he welcomed her, another witch, without hesitation. Something was wrong with her boss, but what?

Chrissy spoke up, changing the topic to one which interested her. "Look. The battery in this device is depleted. The first thing we need to do is put in a fresh battery and let me figure out the frequency it's using to broadcast. From that, I should be able to analyze what data stream it is sending out. That should give us more clues. Also, I can get a better determination of its range."

"Make it snappy, Miller," Bergson barked.

Chrissy smiled. Now that was her boss. She dashed off to fetch her bag of tricks.

Pam said, "We should let her do her work. We could speculate all day on what message this device sent and where it sent it to—even why it was sent. Let's continue our searching while Chrissy works her magic on it."

"Sorry," Chrissy broke in, having returned with her large bag, "no magic in it, just simple electronics. I should have some answers in a half hour, maybe less if I am lucky and its signal frequency is within the range of my portable signal detector here. Even if the message is encoded, I believe I've enough software here to decode it. Just give me space, fellows."

Kelly was leaning over her shoulder peering down at the small device. He flushed and backed away. He grumbled, "I'm going to be pissed if there isn't a damned wall safe somewhere in this house!"

Meanwhile, Monica and Pam returned to the study where all the papers and books had been deposited. "We've tons of documents on his genetics research," Monica said. "I suppose I ought to collect them together. Perhaps Deiter can find some competent geneticist who can make some sense of them, maybe even find more cures."

Pam said didactically, "Wise move. Do it. I'm still going to ponder his spell books some more. I wonder why he spent so much time on the Clone spell? Was he going to use it? On whom? Certainly not himself. After all, when a clone finds out it is a clone of another, the two usually engage in mortal combat until only one is left alive. Was he going to clone some world leader? Ah, speculation again.

Bergson's right. We need more hard facts."
some world leader? Ah, speculation again. Bergson's right.
We need more hard facts."

Chapter 17—Hot on the Trail

The team of five returned to Monica's complex for dinner, bringing with them everything they'd found. Already Deiter had dropped by to pick up the genetic research documents, and Pam had made a quick trip home, returning with her bag, explaining to Monica that Lindsey and Professor Cho Lin would substitute for her, if the Board of Regents opened the school while she was away.

After eating, Chrissy explained to everyone what she'd found. The last of her tests just finished. "Okay, the transmitter has a maximum range of two hundred miles. Point of origin: Potsdam, Germany. The signal sent is what I find perplexing. I was expecting to discover an encoded secret message or something like that. Instead, it just sent what you could call an electronic beep, rather like someone turning on a light switch. Apparently, it sent this same signal over and over until the battery ran down. Somewhere within a two hundred mile radius of Potsdam, there is a receiver tuned to this frequency and which picked up that signal. My current theory is that the signal activated something. What? Who knows."

She went on, "So this is a pretty big area to search. Could be as far north as Copenhagen, maybe as far west as Cologne, but that's pushing its range a bit, as far east as perhaps Lodz, or as far south as Prague or a bit farther."

Kelly exclaimed, "Duh! Doesn't that include most all of Germany and half of Poland, too? Needle in a haystack, Miller, needle in a haystack. Gotta do better than that," he teased her playfully.

"Oh, I'm just warming up, Kelly," she retorted playfully. "While I was going over Menninger's records of all his business transactions, I found one anomalous entry. Deiter and his group are running down all the other ones, but I kept this one for us. He made one shipment, quite small compared to all the other shipments. In fact, compared to them, this one was minuscule. It went to

Prague." She smiled at Kelly, as if to say, "so there!"

Bergson spoke up. "Okay. Before we head off to Prague, tonight, I want everyone to go back over all his records and make sure we've not missed anything else that could point us towards this mysterious receipt point of his transmission. Miller, you get on that location in Prague. Usual treatment. We won't go in there blind."

While Miller knew what he meant, the others didn't. Curious, Pam followed her to her room, where Miller had all her portable systems set up on a relay going back to the giant Stratosphere still parked at Lambert. "Impressive," Pam commented. "I'm quite good with such things," she added.

Miller looked up at her, smiled, and whispered, "I know, Madam Fingers." Pam flushed; Chrissy knew her secret hacker identity! Hastily, Chrissy added, "Weasel Worm here."

Pam relaxed, recognizing a fellow hacker with whom she had chatted online more than once. "I always like to really know whom I'm dealing with," she added. "Come on. Lend a hand. See if you can find out who owns this place and what's there. I'm commandeering a satellite feed now. Bergson wants to know how many people are at this location and anything else I can find out. Probably we can get an IR image later tonight."

An hour later, Pam commented, "This is a tough one. The address is in what's called the 'Old Town.' It's a maze of tiny, wandering streets and buildings at all angles and shapes. Only a mini-car can navigate the streets there, so mostly foot traffic. Quaint shops though. It's got a series of apartments on the upper floors. This one's a fourth floor apartment. The name of the occupant is a Dr. Fritz Wilhelm. Rent is paid by the year. Not due until 2202, so he must have already paid next year's rent."

Chrissy added, "Bergson isn't going to like this. That area is crawling with people, even at night. And with so many apartments there, I can't tell how many people are in the one we're after. We're going to have to use spy tactics, stealth and all that. I'll let him know. See if you can find out more about this Fritz fellow."

"Of course," Pam replied, typing away, quiet bothered about what she wasn't finding. That is, there seemed to be no record of this man's existence in any Czech database or any of the dozen others she'd already tried. By the time Chrissy returned, she'd changed tactics entirely. Obviously, this man didn't want to be recognized and had gone to great pains to hide his true identity. For Pam, that was nothing new.

Already another approach popped into her mind. When Chrissy returned, she saw that Pam had hacked into the street cams around the building in question. "Clever," she commented.

"Don't look at what I'm doing next. Kind of illegal," Pam whispered. Chrissy laughed and turned her head.

"Okay. I'm setting up a long running program now. The way I figure this, Dr. Menninger must have paid a visit on this Dr. Fritz fellow at some point in time. So I'm using the FBI facial recognition software to do just that. I've entered the best photo we have of Dr. Menninger, and the software will run through every image from those dozen street cams over the last two months, since that's how long the video is kept online. Older stuff is archived in the cloud, making it more difficult to gain uncontrolled access to that footage. But if I have to, I can get into the cloud. Hopefully by morning, I'll have some hard evidence as he keeps saying." Chrissy chuckled and said good night.

After tucking Rob in for the night, though he did all the work, Monica kissed his forehead. He said, "Mom, are we still going to get to go trick or treating next week?"

"Sure we are. Got any ideas for your costume?"

"A ghoul. You know, a creepy thing," Rob replied. "Enya says she can make me a costume since you can't now. That's okay, isn't it, Mom?"

"Sure thing. Make it real creepy. Night. Sleep. Mommy will keep the ghosts away," she whispered, stifling the lump in her throat. That she couldn't make his costume as she had done for the last eight years sent a wave of unexpected and conflicting emotions through her body. As

Dominus, she never had such emotional reactions, but this female body seemed hypersensitive to all kinds of emotions, and she still had not gotten used to just how suddenly they could appear and with such ferocity.

When she reached her bedroom, she found Alan waiting for her. "What's wrong?" he whispered.

"Is it that obvious?"

"Wet streaks on your cheeks," he replied. Monica tried to wipe her face with her upper arms, but with poor results. Alan stepped up and dried her face. "There. Want to tell me about it?"

"Oh, it's utterly stupid, Alan. Not important," Monica attempted to dismiss it.

"Let me be the judge of that, Monica," he said gently.

"Something that Rob just said," she sighed and told him what had happened.

Somewhere in the back of her mind, Monica desperately wanted to see just how Alan would respond. She couldn't have said why if asked, though.

He put his arms around her and whispered, "That means you're a good mother, Monica. Come on; we've a busy day tomorrow."

When Bergson and Monica made their slow way into the large dining room the next morning, already most had eaten and dashed off, particularly the many kids who were eager to get outside and play. Fall was here; the rain and cold wasn't far away. Kelly was sitting drinking his second cup of coffee and monitoring the news channels on his ten-monitor, portable tablet. "Oh morning, boss, Miss Black. Betts and Miller are off looking over their surveillance program. I've been monitoring the news. Chaos is growing."

Without asking, Bergson fixed two plates and sat down beside Monica, assisting her with breakfast. "How?" he asked as the two began eating, though he did check his watch. 8:00. He'd overslept again, but it was well worth it.

"Germany is a disaster zone, damned nearly wiped out. It's just like news reporters, that was yesterday's news.

Can you believe this? Not even one small mention of the situation in Germany. Oh no. Everyone is reporting on the attacks on Muslims here in the US, how the Pope's Holy Crusade against Muslims is about to go into action, and some crap about that long dead wizard, that Dominus fellow. Must be Halloween time. They can't let the dead rest in peace. Of course, that one isn't likely to rest in peace," Kelly teased.

Monica choked slightly. After swallowing, she asked carefully, "So what are they saying about that dead wizard?"

"Something about having gotten a court order to exhume the body, only the coffin was empty. No body. Now the reporters are having a field day with this tidbit. Dead men rising from the dead on Halloween. The new headless horseman, except he didn't own a horse when he was alive."

Bergson griped, "Crap! Germany's is in a terrible condition and the news reports on a missing dead body! What's the world coming to?"

Pam had entered and overheard much of what was being said. She saw Monica's worried face and quickly spoke, using her didactic, professor voice, "Of course, helpless women and a country of forty million people on the brink of collapse isn't headline news. Empty coffins and senseless murders of innocent people make news, Kelly. What do you expect from the news? Sensationalism attracts viewers. These are all over Twitter2200 and other social media sites today. Everyone feels sad for the Germans, but local murders and the Holy Crusade are hot topics. Mag-news isn't any better either, Kelly. Anyway, as soon as you are done eating, Chrissy and I need you in her room. We've got highly disturbing video. Dr. Menninger is alive again."

Bergson swore, ignoring the rest of his breakfast and rising at once. Monica swallowed hard and very carefully got up as well, trying her best to "act normally," though her physical situation was anything but.

"Darn it! We killed him once! How many times do

we have to kill him?" Kelly swore angrily.

"Interesting, Kelly, that was Chrissy's response, too. Well, come on then. You're not going to like what we found," Pam replied, leading the way back to Miller's room, filled with her electronic monitoring equipment.

"Hi all," Chrissy said softly as the four entered her room. "Pam's idea worked. I've cued up some video. First clip. Last month." As the twenty-second clip played, they could see the late Dr. Menninger entering the white stone building in Old Town, Prague. The streets were narrow and filled with people, though one mini-car attempted to navigate its way down the narrow street, pretty much filling the entire width of the street. Jilska was the name of the street, but the buildings were anything but regular in shape. This one appeared to only have one right-angle corner, though on closer inspection, that was the norm in this Old Town. The second clip showed Dr. Menninger departing from the building.

"Apparently," Chrissy continued, "that was his last visit, unless he arrived without being caught by any street cam. Now watch this one. It was recorded the morning after Bergson killed Dr. Menninger." Chrissy's voice was surprisingly soft and unemotional, considering what the group then saw on the twenty-second clip! "I spliced this from the inside and outside cams."

The five watched as a slightly younger Dr. Menninger wearing a completely different suit, a modern one, stepped out of the top floor apartment door. Monica gasped. Beside him was a fabulously gorgeous young woman, wearing a bright red dress and matching five inch pumps. Her long, rich looking, wavy black hair flowed down to the small of her back, bouncing slightly as she walked. Her fingernails were at least three inches long, painted the same shade of red as her dress. Monica recognized the woman instantly. As Pam saw Monica's reaction, she also suddenly realized who the woman was.

"Oh heaven help us! We're in even deeper trouble," Monica gushed. "That woman. She's Glasya, a devil, a Princess of Hell and the Consort of the Arch-devil

Mammon! We are so screwed!" Monica cried out.

Pam's heart sank. Now that Monica recognized her, so did she, though she cursed herself for not having remembered the devil from nine years ago.

"Devils? Devils are real?" Kelly asked aghast. Nightmares come true filtered through his mind.

"What the heck is going on here?" Bergson barked angrily. "Demons *and* devils? Whatever happened to simple crimes? And how do you know this is a devil princess?"

"Met her nine years ago. Hey, she's not like the demons. Devils follow a precise set of codes or laws, particularly when dealing with us humans, wholly unlike the demons," Monica began, wondering how she could explain all this without going into her own personal history back then.

Pam said, "I'll alert everyone, Monica, but what could Glasya possibly want with Dr. Menninger?"

"But we killed him," Chrissy protested.

Simultaneously, Bergson and Monica said, "Clone." After a chuckle, Monica continued, "He's a clone copy of Dr. Menninger. We first should go search that apartment. Perhaps, we'll find some clues about what's going on."

"Is, is our world coming to an end? Is this the Apocalypse or something?" asked Chrissy, growing more frightened by the minute. "Should we pray or something?"

"Don't worry, Chrissy. I know Glasya. It's not the end of the world, though for Germany, it could well be, unless the international community steps in and fast. Come on. We should check out that apartment. We need more clues," Monica suggested, rapidly changing the topic. Now wasn't the time to divulge her entire life story! Besides, that was the last thing that she wanted to do just now.

The WIT team was efficient, amazingly so Monica and Pam both thought. They had their gear packed and ready to go in less than ten hectic minutes. As they were preparing for the Teleport spells, Bergson ordered, "Okay. Lots of civi's around. So tread lightly. Clandestine all the way. Don't attract attention to ourselves. We don't have

Czech authority to investigate in Prague."

"Got it, boss," Kelly replied. "Door mouse here," he joked. No one laughed though.

Seconds later, they arrived in a side alley close to the white, five story building. Even so, a dozen people saw them apparate on the cobblestone alley. Smells of open-air cooking stalls greeted their noses, while voices chatting in the local language filtered into their ears. Quickly, Pam cast a few spells, and all suddenly found that they were understanding Czech. "Whoa, this is cool!" Kelly exclaimed. "Am I speaking Czech, too?"

Pam smiled, "Simple Comprehend Language spell, Kelly. Yes, until I cancel the spell, you are speaking the local dialect. Now what?"

"We enter the building and find an elevator," Bergson barked, but softly. He decided to keep an arm around Monica, steadying her. Her tall heels and the relatively uneven cobblestones didn't mix at all well, a fact that he noticed at once. Monica whispered a hasty thank you to him.

Old world charm. That's how Pam described the lobby of the building. Quaint and yet with an elegance of a bygone era greeted their senses. Unfortunately, there wasn't an elevator in sight, just a marble stairs with an ornate, wrought iron railing. Up they went, as Monica whispered to Bergson to keep her steady, which he quietly did. Several others passed them in both directions, but no one paid them any real attention, except for Monica, who received numerous stares and whispers about her massive bosom, missing lower arms, and her extreme heels. She did her best to pretend that she hadn't heard them.

When they approached the apartment door, Miller stepped forward, lock picks and a detector in hand. With a practiced motion, she reported, "Alarm system installed. Give me a minute." She played with her hand-held device until a tiny green light appeared. "Disarmed." Working her lock picks, Miller had the door opened in fifteen seconds.

Monica whispered, "Stand back. He could well have traps installed." She and Pam both cast their Detect Traps spell, though Pam used her wand while Monica cast hers silently.

"I'll disarm them, Monica," Pam whispered and moved slowly into the room. Five minutes later, she called out, "Clear." The other four entered and closed the door, staring at the pile of equipment that filled one bedroom where Pam was standing.

"What is all that stuff?" Kelly whispered.

"Cloning machine. Chrissy, there's lots of electronic things in here. See what you make of them," Pam suggested.

"Right. Rest of you, fan out. Search this place from top to bottom. We need clues and hard evidence," Bergson growled in a low voice.

Thirty minutes passed as the four went from room to room, gathering up anything that might provide any kind of clue. Chrissy finally joined them. "Well, I found the receiver. I was right. Dr. Menninger's device sent a signal here, where this receiver picked it up and turned on all this equipment, which I haven't the faintest idea what it does or did."

Pam added softly, "When the machine activated, it awoke the cloned Dr. Menninger. He must have created the clone some time ago and kept it unconscious until the machine roused him when he sent that signal. Dr. Menninger definitely doesn't want to die!"

Monica spoke, "But gang, it isn't the same Dr. Menninger that we killed, at least not completely. He appeared younger. So this new version doesn't know what all our dead Dr. Menninger did or planned or what happened since the clone was made. I suspect the new Dr. Menninger is at least one or two years younger, so he's definitely totally ignorant of what our dead Dr. Menninger has done for at least the past year or two."

"But will he still be as nasty as the version we killed?" Bergson inquired, knowing this was what was truly important.

"He'll have the same knowledge and spell casting ability our Dr. Menninger had at the time he made this new clone," Monica explained. "So yes, he'll be just as dangerous and formidable as before, but he won't know what our Dr. Menninger has done since the time of its cloning. We have a small break there."

Pam added, "I'm not too sure of that, Monica. There is a lengthy journal outlining his actions and plans in the other room. So if the clone had time to read it, he knows conceptually what the dead Dr. Menninger did and planned." Several cursed.

"Trouble is, the bastard hasn't left us any hard evidence," Bergson barked, "except for all this medical-like equipment. We've got nothing, nothing at all, and the new bastard is on the loose!" That sobered everyone.

"Square one!" Kelly griped.

"I'll start up my comm monitoring program again, boss," Miller volunteered. "Maybe we'll get lucky and pick up some clues that way. Surely, someone will recognize him and post about it."

That was one aspect of social media Miller could always count upon. People tweeted about all kinds of silly things, in her opinion, but often a tweet gave her a clue about the location of a person of interest to one of their investigations, though quite by accident.

Monica had been silent for a while, as the others gathered up what they wanted to take back with them. At last she reached a decision and said, "Maybe there is another way. I know Glasya. Why don't I contact her and see what she is willing to tell us about Dr. Menninger? It can't hurt."

"You can really trust one of these devil beasts?" asked Kelly, scarcely believing what he just heard.

"A demon, no. A devil, sort of. If I do this, whatever you do, don't make any wishes or bargains around her or any devil! That's suicide," Monica explained.

"No way would I do that!" Kelly barked.

Monica grinned, "Princess Glasya can be incredibly persuading, Kelly. She's one hot devil, charming and seductive beyond all imagination. Hold on to your pants, Kelly." Miller laughed; Pam grinned, but the men looked very sober.

"Go ahead, Monica, if you think it will help," Bergson suggested. "We've hit a dead end here, and we have to get something, anything on this Dr. Menninger before it's too late yet again."

Monica focused and sent a Message, though she wasn't surprised to find the spell worked. Had Glasya not been on Earth, her spell would have failed. That Glasya was still around came as no surprise. Obviously, there was far more going on than just this demon invasion. Almost at once a Message scrolled past her eyes. "Okay. She will meet us at Dusana's Kiosk, some kind of open-air diner here in Prague."

"I'm on it," Miller called out, typing swiftly on her laptop. "Got it. Dusana's Kiosk. I'm sending the location coordinates to everyone's phones now. I think it's about ten blocks from here. Still in Old Town."

"Going down is harder than going up," Monica whispered to Bergson, who again quietly slipped his arm beneath her hair and around her waist as they approached the stairs. The others moved on ahead of the pair, who brought up the rear. Once more, Miller thought Bergson's behavior was off. He always took the lead.

Some twenty minutes later, they arrived at the open-aired eatery, where the odors drifting through the air invited one to sit down and dine beneath the shade of the many multi-colored canvas umbrella-like covers above the many tables. Glasya stuck out like a sports car among the mini-cars. Moving around the some dozen widely scattered tables, the group soon joined her and the doctor. Their table sat only four, so Monica and Bergson took the two remaining seats, while Miller, Kelly, and Pam sat at the next closest table. At least they could overhear everything being said.

"Ah Monica. You are slipping. I expected to see you a half hour ago," Glasya said, very politely and friendly-like. "My, I do so like your new look. Your hair is just fabulous, dear."

"Dr. Menninger used a Wish spell on me, but you

probably already know that," Monica replied. "We've got quite a lot of questions about this mess. I was very surprised to see that you are involved, Glasya."

"Ah Monica. No kind words for me? Haven't you missed me? I missed you. Ah well, all business. You and Mammon. Doesn't anyone just want to play and have fun anymore? How about you, Bergson, or you, Kelly? Little romp in bed to start our meeting off on the right foot, so to speak?" Kelly flushed but said nothing.

Bergson growled, "What can you tell us, princess? Time is pressing."

"So business-like. All right then. Once again, you humans have made a complete mess of the playing field! Correction: the worst disaster in millennia to be more precise, and I always prefer to be precise."

Bergson looked confused, so she added, "The situation as you've allowed it to become here on Earth is so intolerable that even Mammon is threatening to intervene. Already the demons have stolen over a hundred of our people, the ones that have struck up bargains with us devils—stolen and taken away to the Abyss no less. Both Mammon and Dispater are furious. I've never seen either one as angry as they are right now."

"But it's far worse than that. Within Germany alone, we have several hundred others who are now victims of the demon's biological-genetic attacks, as you call them. Mind you, this is extremely serious, since each of these people had already made bargains with us long before the demon attacks came. Now, they are claiming breach of contract. Devils never, ever breech any contract. That's against our laws. Mammon and Dispater find themselves having to make numerous visits here to try to rectify the broken agreements with men and women. They are forced to use all kinds of spells to return men's minds back to what they were, to say nothing of what they have to do to restore the women, all in hopes that the victims will re-honor their earlier contracts. Not all do, mind you. This is a very serious situation indeed, one which you humans seem to be unable to solve yourselves.

"And it is only getting worse. This new Holy Crusade is just getting started. Millions will be murdered in the very near future, not only in Africa and the Middle East, but nearly everywhere there is a substantial Muslim population. Left alone, the carnage will make what happened in Germany look like nothing at all. Do I need to spell this out for you? Incredibly bad for business, and that is putting it mildly! But then," she softened her tone, "that is the way of demons: create maximal chaos and destruction, while gathering in recruits with promises of invulnerable bodies with super-human strengths and magic abilities, none of which does them much good down in the Abyss.

"Both Dispater and Mammon were just about to send in an army of their own to clean up this mess, but a couple days ago, they sent me here to check on the exact situation before they take direct, positive actions. Now I have to hand it to the deceased Dr. Menninger. His plan worked beautifully, but with rather nasty side-effects. Those are what have so irked us devils. True, he managed to destroy nearly all the massive demon army, but that also killed hundreds of thousands of humans from the Middle East, five of whom had contracts with Dispater, who was forced to intervene and personally recover them from the Abyss. He is generous and is willing to overlook that, but not the hundreds of others whose contracts have been broken, most of whom are in Germany."

Bergson looked confused, and Glasya allowed him to interrupt her and ask, "But why? Why would Dr. Menninger kill the demons? He was in league with them. I don't believe you, princess or whatever you are supposed to be called."

"Glasya. Glasya will do admirably, Bergson. Why? Simple really. Would you like to answer that one yourself, Dr. Fritz? He calls himself Fritz now."

The new Dr. Menninger adjusted his glasses. "Two hundred fifty-five years I've been held virtually a prisoner by Prince Graz'zt in the Abyss! True, his minions did rescue me just as they were overrunning my experimental laboratory, but I didn't ask to be taken to the Abyss. He cloned me countless times. The only way I could stay alive was to do his bidding, creating new genetic mutations of women to help him breed his massive army of Cambions intended to one day retake the Earth. At long last, I was finally allowed to return to Earth, supposedly to help his succubus Gisella carry out his plot. Well, when everything went south, I, Gisella, General Franco, and a few others escaped."

"No way was I going to let them take me back to the Abyss! I put the seeds of a new plan into that succubus' mind and she bought it. After that, I played along with her, bidding my time until I could activate my own counter-plan, which was working perfectly until you came along and destroyed it! At least that is what was in his log and what Glasya has shown me on the newscasts of late. I wanted out from under the thumbs of those insane demons forever and very nearly succeeded until you killed him."

Glasya retook control of the discussion. "I've shown Dr. Fritz here that his predecessor's grand plan for a new Fourth Reich has almost completely destroyed his beloved homeland, just as Hitler once did. To his credit, Dr. Fritz has signed a contract with Dispater, his only way out of this mess. As soon as the demons discover the existence of the new Dr. Menninger clone, they will come after him with everything they have. He's too valuable to their cause, you see. Now, he is under Dispater's protection, and the demons won't be able to touch him—"

"Why Dispater and not Mammon?" Monica interrupted Glasya. Bergson's mouth opened, shocked that Monica had the balls to interrupt this devil. In fact, her four companions all looked surprised at Monica's nerve.

"Well, that's a number's game. More of Dispater's contracts are victims than Mammon's. The two reached an agreement, though I'm not privy to those details. Suffice it to say that Dr. Fritz here has an iron-clad contract and must uphold his side of the bargain or he'll be personally delivered to the demons by Dispater."

"And just what does this contract require, Dr. Fritz?"

Monica continued to interrupt Glasya's meeting.

He didn't answer, but Glasya did. "He'd rather not talk about that, but I will because it concerns you. I know you want to execute this clone—right now if you think you can get away with it."

Bergson and Kelly flushed. She'd read their minds! "Don't try it, unless you wish to depart this world. Now then, the bargain. It seems Dr. Fritz might be able to completely cure all those victims who were recently subjected to the biological-genetic agent in gaseous form, but not those who took the pill versions."

She continued, "So if he succeeds in doing so quickly before too many of those who signed contracts give up, then he will be guaranteed protection from demons for the rest of his natural life and have his fondest wish come true."

"Just so we are clear, what is this fondest wish, Glasya? If he wants to make even worse genetic mutations, we obviously won't stand for that, devil protection or not," Monica declared, startling the other four who stared at her, wondering how she could be so bold with this powerful devil princess.

Acting as though Monica was merely chatting with her, she replied, "He is acutely aware of that aspect, Monica. He's pledged not to do such things in the future. To answer the rest, if he is successful, then Dispater will see that he gets married to the woman that he's fallen in love with. You see, during his nine years of roaming the world as a mostly free man, he's fallen victim to the commonest human emotion, love. He'll get his Elise and a small country home and live happily ever after. That's the third most common thing they make contracts for on this world."

Monica smiled, adding, "Third only to money and power?"

Glasya smiled demurely, "Astute as ever, Miss Black. So you see, it's in all our best interests that Dr. Fritz here and I be allowed to pursue his theoretical cure for around twenty million German victims, including I might add,

Miss Betts, all of those who have been listening in on our entire conversation via your spell!"

Pam's face turned bright red. As soon as they had approached Glasya and the cloned doctor, she'd cast a Hear What She Hears spell allowing Governor Lindsey and her entire Rodent pack to hear every word that was said thus far. Until this instant, Pam believed she'd gotten away with her sneaky spell. Obviously, she hadn't.

Bergson didn't see Pam's face nor did he realize the significance of Glasya's words. He was more concerned about the Menninger clone. "But we can't allow this beast, this mass murderer to go free. Crimes against humanity must be punished."

Glasya smiled disarmingly, "Ah, my good Lead Detective. Hard evidence. I ask you, just what crime has this new Dr. Fritz committed? He isn't the man that you killed, you know. Do you charge a man's son for crimes the father committed?"

Bergson flushed, "But he's a clone of Dr. Menninger, a vile beast if ever there was one."

"Of course, he was," Glasya said with a coy smile. "And you doled out justice. I call your attention to the simple fact that Dr. Fritz here is not that dead man."

Pam spoke, having cooled down some and regained her composure, "Bergson, she's right. Dr. Fritz here is a different person. True, he has all the knowledge and such that Dr. Menninger had, but he's not the one who actually committed all those atrocities against humanity. At this point, he's innocent, unless he's done some crimes since he was roused by that signal from Dr. Menninger."

"But Pam, there's no end to the damage this man could do," Bergson declared. "Okay," he said trying to sound as agreeable as possible, "point taken. However, we will keep close tabs on this doctor. We don't trust him in the slightest. One wrong move and we'll come gunning for you. That's a promise!" Kelly nodded.

"I'm sure he knows that," Glasya said sweetly, adding a veiled threat to Dr. Fritz, "and if he doesn't keep up his side of the contract with Dispater, he'll welcome being shot by you, for that'll be far more pleasant that enduring Dispater's wrath. We devils tend to get very angry with those who break sworn contracts with us." Dr. Fritz did look a bit pale at this point, he noted.

"Okay then," Monica agreed with Glasya's assessment, "so who is this Elise? Where does she reside? I can't say that I would like to be forced to marry someone against my will."

"Dr. Elise Gottendorf, a microbiologist at the University of Hamburg. Dispater will not be using magic on the doctor. Rather, she will see him as her knight in shining armor coming to her rescue, as your people often still say, though it's been centuries since there were such men roaming the French countryside. Dr. Fritz claims that she holds the key to the cure for millions and speaking of that, we must be heading to Hamburg shortly. The cure is most urgently needed. Oh, and one more thing, Miss Black. If I were you, I would go into hiding immediately. Foul things are afoot on this world at this time, many directed against you."

"I say," Bergson finally shrugged off Glasya's aura of charm and broke in, "I think we should go with you and see what we can do to get this cure found and implemented."

Smiling disarmingly, Glasya surprised him by saying, "I had anticipated you would, Bergson. While I can protect myself quite well, when heading into a hornet's nest, it's wise to bring along some protections. I'm not a fool. However, send Miss Black here into hiding some place where she can't be found and then we'll be off to Hamburg."

"Glasya, I'm certainly *not* going into hiding! This is my world, and I will do my utmost to keep it safe and free it from this demon threat," Monica declared. "Besides, they call me the Demon Hunter," she added in jest.

Glasya broke into a broad smile. "Point taken, but don't say I didn't warn you. All right then, we're off to Hamburg to find Elise and the cure."

Bergson barked, "Fritz or whatever you are calling yourself, goof this up, try anything, and I'll kill you as I did

Dr. Hans Menninger."

Poor Dr. Fritz looked extremely pale. Demons wanted him, probably to subject him to eternal torture for what he'd done to their mighty army. He'd bargained away his soul to stay alive, but he was with those who had executed his original clone and who certainly would do so again, given any excuse. Monica realized the man's tenuous position, but had no sympathy for him. He'd cast his line and how had to live with what he reeled in, good or ill.

Chapter 18—Adventure in Hamburg

Late morning of October 26, the party of seven arrived in Hamburg, Germany, arriving in the center of one of the two ornate tiled circles facing the fourteen sets of ornate, dual white columns supporting the portico facade at the main entrance of the centuries-old university. The eight similar pairs of white columns sat above them on the second floor, giving an impressive appearance to the institution.

Noses rejected their arrival. The stench of decaying bodies greeted them and a quick glance around them showed a number of dead men and women lying at crazy positions in the streets and along the sidewalks. Chaos had already found its way here. In the distance, they did spot two gray uniformed SS men wearing face masks slowly removing the bodies.

As soon as they landed, Miller got a Wi-Fi signal and promptly Googled Dr. Elise Gottendorf, a microbiologist. "Here's what she looks like," Miller said softly, trying to also keep from inhaling the foul odor. She showed them the doctor's photo that was on file along with her faculty listing that gave her office number. Elise was probably in her mid-thirties, Monica guessed, with light brown hair, cut short, and blue eyes. She wasn't all that physically attractive and for a moment didn't see what could have possibly caused Dr. Menninger to fall so in love with her.

Just then, two men carrying lugers came rushing up to them. One barked, "Give food. Now. Food. Give." He seemed terribly confused though.

The other added, "Yah, food. Give food. Now. All food."

Obvious to everyone, these men were victims of the gaseous form of Dr. Menninger's bio-genetic agent. Their combined IQs, Monica guessed, might not even be that of a moron. However, the reason for the dead bodies was apparent. Low IQ men found ways to stay alive, none good.

She acted, throwing up a Force Wall between the men and themselves. Pam merely cast her Sleep spell on them, and they dropped to the street sound asleep. In doing so, their guns went off. Thanks to Monica's quick reaction, the bullets bounced off her force screen, ricocheting harmlessly into the street.

"Thanks, Monica, I hadn't considered that aspect," Pam admitted, then explained what she and Monica had done.

"So how do we find her? We need some protection spells," Dr. Fritz asked. Hastily, many Skin of Stone spells were cast, while Glasya said a brief chant. Shortly, a weird looking creature appeared. First, a black cat walked up to the party from a nearby bush. As it approached, it morphed into a devil creature. It stood nine feet tall and was quite skinny with a monkey-like head and face. In its hands, it carried a wicked looking bone weapon, pointed and barbed. A scorpion-like tail arched over its head, stinger at the ready. Monica later identified it as a bone devil.

"Ah, this is my assistant, Sammy. Sammy, these people are with me," Glasya introduced the arrival.

The devil bowed to his princess. "I have located the human as you commanded, My Princess. It is too bad I'm not allowed to join the street battles. It is so exciting to see so many fighting it out over mere scraps of their food when there are warehouses filled with food not far away. Never, My Princess, have I encountered such stupid creatures as these humans here are."

"Yes, they have been genetically altered to be this way, Sammy. So where is this woman? We need to meet with her now," Glasya commanded.

"She is in an apartment complex, Number 304. It is at Feldbrunnenstrase 31, only a few blocks away. Shall I take you there, My Princess?"

"Yes, please. Thank you, Sammy." At that, the bone devil morphed back into that of a black cat and began scampering down the street. "A bit slower, please. Miss Black cannot keep up with you," she added.

Tall trees, whose leaves had nearly all fallen, lined the streets. Piles of multi-colored leaves littered the grounds, pushed into piles by the varying winds. No one had the intelligence to rake them, thanks to the biological-agent gas. However, before they got to the apartment building, they were assaulted twice more by starving men looking to rob them of whatever food they had on them. Pam simply put them to sleep for a while.

After a short walk, the group stopped before at the locked door of Elise's apartment. Before any could cast an Unlock spell, Miller quickly brought out her lock picking tools and had the door open in less than a minute, pleasing Kelly and Bergson. Monica noticed that Glasya didn't mind allowing the humans to pick the lock, instead of her or Pam or Monica or Dr. Fritz casting a spell to do so.

Then Glasya took control. "Allow Dr. Fritz to enter first. We wait here for his signal. Knight in shining armor thing," the devil explained, smiling seductively at Kelly, batting her long eyelashes at him and running her long talons over her lips. Such had the effect she desired, Kelly moaned slightly, fighting hard to resist her charms.

Five minutes passed before Dr. Fritz called to them. "My friends, come on in now. Please, can you see if there is some food you can prepare for my Elise? She hasn't had anything to eat for days. I've gotten water in her, and she's bouncing back now."

Her apartment was a two-room efficiency, with a small kitchen-dining room combination and a bedroom-living room area. She had stacks of papers piled high on the floor in the latter room just in front of tall bookcases crammed with books. Her bed lay against the opposite wall. Her minuscule bathroom was part of the kitchen area, and Pam headed there to see what she could find to fix for Elise to eat.

"Oh Dr. Fritz," Elise whispered, "I thought you were dead, too. Betrayed, we ver all betrayed by dat Dr. Menninger. So many dead. I took your advice, but now I wish that I had not and was dead. I'm so helpless."

"But you are alive, my love. That's what matters

291

most. I'm here, and I'll look after you, I promise," Dr. Fritz declared. "Elise, these are my associates. They've come back to Germany with me to help you and me find a cure for some of our people."

"But Fritz, I'm helpless. You best go off and leave me," she whispered.

"I'll do no such thing."

"So how did you two meet?" Glasya inserted herself into the conversation, knowing that was what Pam and Monica wanted to hear or perhaps she had another motive entirely.

"We met at the Microbiology Conference five years ago. I teach—used to teach," Elise corrected herself, struggling to keep herself from breaking down, "microbiology at the university here. We fell in love, and he came by nearly every weekend when he could." He gave her another sip of water and Elise continued.

"Here at the university, we refused to go along with that awful man, his SS men, and visions of a Fourth Reich. Well, I did too until the very last minute, when Fritz convinced me to accept their pills. See what the pills have done to me! I'm a helpless invalid now."

"But you are alive," Dr. Fritz pointed out.

"Yes, perhaps I am lucky. Dr. Helene, she and her husband live next door. They told me I was a fool for giving in and taking the pills, but when the gas attack came, they were horribly changed. She's as helpless as I am, but can't even speak. He checked on me and told me so. He went out for food, but never came back. That was days ago now. Fritz, perhaps one of your friends could go next door and see if Dr. Helene is still alive and help her some. She's a history professor—well she was. Now she can't even speak, Fritz. Is this the end of our country? What's going to happen to us all?"

"I'll check," Miller volunteered and headed off to do that.

"Elise, remember what we were talking about the last time I was here?" Dr. Fritz asked gently.

"Why yes. You said you were getting close to a cure.

Have you found any? I think it is hopeless."

"Actually, I believe that I have come up with a cure for those who were recently gassed. I'm still working on one for those who took the pills. That one is much more difficult, but perhaps one day I will find it. Dr. Elise," he said using her formal title, "I desperately need your help with the cure I've found. The solution requires the use of your talents in microbiology. As soon as we get your strength back, you and I, we simply have to try to work out this cure. If we can succeed, my love, we can save at least twenty million of our people."

"But Fritz, I'm completely helpless now," she protested weakly.

"Didn't you get the supplies that all those women on the pills were supposed to get?" he asked glancing around the cramped room, noticing a large box sitting unopened just inside the door, but off to one side.

"There's a box that came while I was unconscious. I have no way to open it. Hermann did when he came by before he headed off to find food. He said there were clothes in it."

"Soup's up," Pam called out, bringing a large bowl into the room. Fritz took it from her and began spoon feeding Elise.

Miller popped in, saying softly, "She's alive, barely. Little help next door."

The soup worked wonders on Elise. She brightened up considerably. Glasya suggested the men step outside and discuss what needed to be done next, while the women cared for Elise's personal needs. Reluctantly, Dr. Fritz agreed.

"So just what is this cure of yours?" Bergson demanded to know when the three men stepped into the dark hallway.

"I've got it formulated, but I need Elise's help to create a way to aerosol the cure. Microbiology is the answer. Just need some time with her and her expertise in her lab and we'll have it. Trust me," he explained.

"No can do that," Bergson barked, "not with your

track record." Then, it dawned on him and he added, "Say, you and I both know that you don't need her help to turn that cure into a gas form. You already have such skills, having wiped out your entire country with it."

Dr. Fritz's face turned quite flush. "Please, don't say anything about that. I'm trying to save Elise, in more ways than one. Please, don't say anything."

Kelly looked confused, but Bergson understood the man. "All right, Fritz, we won't say anything as long as you deliver the goods."

"Of course I will deliver the goods as you say. My survival depends on it, if you hadn't noticed," Fritz barked back, slightly hostile to Bergson. Then, the man's demeanor softened. Lowering his voice, he added, "I don't like this any better than you do. I didn't make this bio-genetic agent crap. He did. If those cursed demons find me, I'll be back in slavery again, if not tortured for centuries. Dispater is my only hope for avoiding them, and his protection is wholly dependent on my curing of those he gassed." Glancing around to make sure no one else was listening in, he whispered, "If something does happen to me, go to 24 Ruestrassa. The cure is stored there. Just give me a few days with Elise and we'll carry out the cure. A couple of days, man, that's all I ask, for Elise's sake, please," he begged.

"Okay then. I can understand why you are doing this with Elise. Makes sense, especially since there's no cure for her and the others who took his damned pills," Bergson replied.

"Okay boys, you can come back in now," Glasya finally called out in a teasing voice. Fritz dashed inside, while Kelly held Bergson back.

"What was that all about, boss?" Kelly whispered.

"Self-respect. He knows as well as we do that Elise will be like she is the rest of her life. He's trying to give her back some self-respect by letting her think that she's helping to restore the lives of twenty million men and women. I'll give him credit for that move. We'll give him a couple of days, but at least we know where he's stored the cure, Kelly. I'll tell the others about that when there's an opportunity. It makes me wonder just what else Dr. Menninger had planned before we exterminated him. Was he going to miraculously cure all those he victimized with the gas attack? What about all those trusted SS personnel on the pills? There's more behind all this than we currently know, Kelly, so keep your eyes and ears open." The two then entered the tiny apartment.

"Here she is," Glasya said proudly, sweeping her arms around as though pulling aside a curtain that was hiding Elise. The women had gotten her cleaned up and dressed in the fancy satin dress from the box of clothing. She wore matching pumps, nearly identical to those Monica had to wear. Her bosom matched that of Monica's, but they had trimmed her hair back some. Wavy light brown tresses now fell just to the small of her back. Though she'd wanted it cut quite short again, Glasya persuaded her to take it back in stages, seeing if she might like it longer, hinting that Dr. Fritz might like it long. And she'd agreed.

"Incredible, Elise! You look stunning, my dearest, beautiful beyond words," Fritz exclaimed, getting his first view of her all dolled up.

"Oh Fritz, be reasonable," she protested. "Not with these," she raised her upper arms and added, "these monsters." She meant her huge breasts. "At least I can sort of stand on my own now, but I'm not so sure about walking."

"You still look stunning to me, beautiful Elise," Fritz continued to declare.

Whatever else Elise might be, she wasn't a dope. "Fritz, if you've got a cure, and if you truly do need my help, then we must get started on it at once. People are desperate out there. I keep hearing sporadic gunfire. That can't be good," Elise stated the obvious. "So where do we begin?"

"All right then," he answered, "we need to go to your lab. That's the starting point, Dr. Elise. You heard her. We're off to her lab. Please, will someone bring along that DVD so when she has time she can watch it?"

"Got it," Pam stated.

"Where is her lab?" Glasya inquired.

"Just across the bridge. Hamburg University of Applied Science," Elise answered, "but I don't think I can walk that far. Are the taxis running?" Fritz shook his head no.

"I'll teleport us all there," Glasya countered, adding, "some of us are witches you know." That brought a smile to Elise's face. She was a normal. Monica had already determined that fact as soon as she first met the woman.

The building was deserted. Fritz entered her pass code and they entered without mishap. "There's a lounge with cots down the hall from my lab. Probably still has some food there, too. Some of us spend long nights here and sort of camp out, while our experiments are running," Dr. Elise explained.

After seeing the pair into her lab and listening to their rapid-fire tech talk of which they understood not a word, "got to find a binding agent to attach the microbes to your bacteria," everyone but Glasya headed to the lounge to see what was there. The princess sat quietly in the back of the lab observing the pair.

Monica guessed she was under orders not to let the man out of her sight. Once in the lounge, Bergson quickly related what Fritz had told him about where the cure was being stored, "Just in case this all goes south," he added.

"Well, there are enough cots here for all of us. Their small fridge still has stuff in it," Kelly stated the obvious.

"I suppose I should head home for a bit, bring everyone up to date and all that. I can bring back some better food, if you're going to be stuck here for a few days," Pam suggested.

"We could use more of our gear. I sure miss our Stratosphere!" Bergson declared.

"You can say that again," Kelly piped up.

"Boss, I could go back with Pam and bring it to the Hamburg airport," Miller suggested. "According to Google, it's about seven or eight kilometers due north of here."

Bergson rubbed his face. "Okay. You know how I

dislike being utterly dependent upon magic for travel. Let's hedge our bets. Go bring our liner here, Miller. You should be safe enough driving the armored rover back from the airport."

"On it, boss," she replied, thankful he'd agreed. She longed for a good night's sleep and a good hot shower, if not a clean set of clothes or a bath. True, Monica had cast Clean spells on their clothes from time to time, but it didn't feel the same to her as putting on freshly laundered clothes. Perhaps it was the smell that was different. "Back in around eight hours."

"Hey, bring me back a thick steak, will you Miller?" Kelly requested. Miller merely smiled back as Pam teleported her away.

"Hey guys, can you get this TV going? We should see what's on the news," Monica asked.

". . . wild theories. Personally, I believe that someone resurrected Dominus and that he is once more walking among us, recruiting a new batch of Death Stalkers. Considering the world upheaval, he should be able to find many supporters this time. Of course, the real question is would Dominus accept a jihadist fanatic as one of his henchmen? From my extensive research into Dominus, he definitely had no religious tendencies, so it is this educated wizard's professional opinion that he would reject them."

The news switched back to the studio reporter. "There you have it. Our latest polls are just in. Well look at that! Fifty-three percent believe that Dominus once again walks among us, compared to forty-three who do not. Ten percent remain undecided. Of course, this leads to the question on everyone's mind, what are the Department of Justice and the Department of Magical Misuse doing about it? We tried to interview them, but they all declined to go on camera. Several suggested that we are being ridiculous, that he's quite dead. But in this reporter's view, if you haven't got a body, how can you declare him dead? After this break, we will go live to our cameras on the streets of downtown LA, where witnesses claim to have seen

Dominus murdering a group of Muslims. Stay tuned for the details." A commercial began running.

Kelly griped, "Next they'll be saying that Dr. Menninger has risen from the dead, the one you killed boss, not this Fritz fellow. Honestly, people are so gullible. I saw the photos of Dominus. No one can survive having half their head blown off. Most of his face was gone. He'd be unrecognizable if he was alive."

"I agree, Kelly," Bergson replied, uncharacteristically solemn. "Large caliber rounds through someone's head most definitely kills them. Period. End of story. Darn it, not a single word about the ongoing disaster here in Germany. It's as though the world has forgotten about their desperate plight."

"That's the news industry, merchants of chaos and death," Monica said. "They specialize in spreading word about such things; attracts viewers. Raises fear and worry levels in folks so they continue to watch the news tomorrow. Still, maybe they will say something about the situation over here."

"But why raise old wounds?" Bergson asked. "I know plenty of older people who were harmed one way or another by that evil wizard. All this is only rubbing salt in their wounds."

"Attracts viewers," Monica replied tersely, wishing this whole thing had not ever come up, but she knew it was a byproduct of what Deiter had done. "I guess people needing help isn't going to make news," she added.

"You can say that again," Kelly griped. So she did just that, and he cracked a smile, adding, "Good one, Miss Black, good one."

They listened to the news for a couple of hours, but heard very little about the ongoing situation in Germany. Worse, the news station was in Paris. Around dinner time, Glasya, Elise, and Fritz joined them, he holding onto Elise much as Bergson had done for Monica.

"We have an experiment running now," Dr. Elise explained, "but it will take a couple of hours to complete. Have you found anything we can eat?"

"Pretty bare bones," Bergson answered, "but Mrs. Betts is due back soon with dinner. Later, Miller will be landing with our Stratosphere. Our airliner is well stocked, plus she'll be bringing the armored Rover with her so we should be safe from the random gunfire."

Not long after that, Pam returned bringing a hot food with her, including steaks for everyone, pleasing Kelly. After the group finished, Monica suggested, "Will someone put in that DVD that Elise was supposed to watch? I'd like to see it too, since I'm in the same boat as she is."

"I'll do it," Pam replied.

The men decided it was time to take a stroll around the entire building, checking on security. If they were going to sleep here, Bergson needed to know if someone had to stand guard duty while the others slept.

"This is incredible," Elise exclaimed. "Those poor women don't have any arms at all and yet that one is flying a plane!"

"And she's driving a car," added Pam. "I guess the purpose of this DVD compilation is to show you two how you can do normal things in life. That woman is using her feet to gesture with and that one is using her toes like fingers to sip coffee and feed herself."

"Wanda did say that they were told that the DVD was designed for them to learn how to do everything," Monica explained what she'd heard from her.

"This is really a useful DVD," Elise declared. "Though I think I'll have to watch it hundreds of times to figure out how they are doing everything. Monica, maybe there is some hope we'll be able to sort of be independent again."

"I think you are spot on, Elise," Monica validated her, knowing that Elise had finally admitted that she had some hope for the future ahead of her. Then, something struck her. "Pam! Can you replay that last minute or so? I just realized something vitally important."

Pam did so, but saw nothing but the woman sipping her coffee, holding the cup between her toes.

Monica declared, "Look, it's function that is

monitoring physical structure and not the other way around. Structure doesn't dictate function, but just the opposite!"

Pam said, "Huh?"

Elise said, "Monica, you're right! This has enormous potential!"

For Pam's sake, Monica explained, "Pam, look at her toes. See how they are wide spread and almost looking like fingers? Function, the purpose and goals are changing the actual physical structure of her toes, making them more like fingers in that woman's case. The purpose, the function of her toes is to act as fingers, and over time her toes are looking more like fingers than toes. I know my toes certainly can't do even a fraction of what she's doing with hers. Yet, Elise, I bet if we start using our toes as the women in this DVD are doing, in time our toes will begin to look and operate more like fingers."

"Precisely, Monica. Function is monitoring structure. Now it is so clear to me. How could I ever have missed this in my microbiology? The purpose of the tiny organism is in no small way determining the physical structure that it has. This is incredibly powerful. I wonder if Dr. Fritz knows this? I'll ask him later on. Keep on playing the video, Pam."

Later, the men returned along with Glasya, who still had not let Dr. Fritz out of her sight. Glasya explained for Monica's benefit and for Pam's, "We've installed some additional protective spells."

Around eight that night, Miller called up Bergson on his cell. "Boss, I've safely landed here at Hamburg Airport. I'm going to stick around the plane tonight. I've got my systems monitoring all kinds of activities that aren't being covered by the news people. They seem stuck on beating the dead issue of that long dead wizard. Have someone teleport you all here if you want."

Bergson was hesitant to bring the devil princess and Dr. Fritz onto his Stratosphere, but Glasya overhead Miller's voice. "Oh tell her that we would be delighted to spend the night on your big liner, Bergson. Oh please," she feigned begging, batting her eyes and smiling coyly, though Monica noticed she refrained from using her special powers of seduction. She knew Glasya only had to turn on her special charm to have all the men falling over themselves to please her every desire. She had seen the princess do just that once before.

Minutes later, the group joined Miller on the giant ship. Bergson ordered Kelly to give Pam, Glasya, Elise, and Fritz a tour of the non-secure locations and to get them situated in the guest rooms, while he and Monica joined Miller in her communications center. She'd been quite busy.

"I've ten different monitoring projects going," she explained, mostly for Monica's benefit, since Bergson recognized her set up, one she'd often used before. "These two are rendering IR images so we can get a better picture of just how many are on the ground moving towards the battle zone developing in the Middle East," she explained and continued on for several minutes.

Later, after the tour finished and guest rooms assigned, they met in the now cramped dining area for a late evening snack. "So which one of you big boys will be joining me tonight?" Glasya asked rather seductively, though still not enforcing her will on the three men. "Ah come on, fellows," she begged. "Not many men can claim they've slept with a Princess from Hell."

"Glasya, you are one hot chick," Kelly admitted, "but only a fool would do that."

"Not even if I promise to be a good girl?" she pleaded, girlishly.

Bergson barked, "Do devils even know what it means to be a good girl?" Kelly roared, while Fritz looked petrified, waiting for Glasya to turn the loud mouth into a worm or something equally disgusting.

Glasya smiled. "Okay. Have it your way, boys. But Monica, you should explain to them that we devils do play totally fair, unlike demons. Night all."

Later alone in their shared room, Bergson said, "Glasya—is she as powerful as I'm thinking?"

"And then some, Alan. Her powers dwarf mine, and she's got some of the most powerful allies in the entire universe at her instant call. But she was serious about sleeping with someone, meaning there would not be any strings attached, at least not at this moment. Still, I'm glad no one accepted her offer. Now get me undressed. I need satisfying badly." He complied.

***

Around eleven the next day, Drs. Elise and Fritz came out of her lab, huge grins announcing their success. "He's done it!" she exclaimed.

"No, it was Elise's micro-binding agent that has done it," Fritz countered. "We've got a cure, at least for those who were attacked by the gaseous version."

"Has it been tested? How will it be mass deployed?" Bergson barked immediately, still not trusting the Menninger clone.

Glasya ambled out, looking amused at something. "Oh, I give you my word, Bergson, that it is ready and will work. If you will kindly escort Elise and the others back to your big plane, Dr. Fritz and I will see to its deployment all over Germany. We should congratulate Dr. Elise and Dr. Fritz for their efforts. In days, at least twenty million Germans will completely recover."

"If you say so, but I reserve judgment for when I can see hard evidence that it has worked and with no ill effects," Bergson growled back.

"Of course," Glasya replied demurely. "I wouldn't expect less than that from you, big boy. Oh, Monica, once more I urge you to go into hiding somewhere, for your own safety."

"Don't be ridiculous, Glasya. I'm here doing my job, doing my best to help everyone. If I run away and hide, how could I ever retain my own self-respect?" Monica countered.

"Point taken. While you are on your plane, let them watch the DVD as much as possible," Glasya added. "Now, armed with their solution, it's time for positive action." The two teleported away.

With nothing else to do in the lab, Pam and Monica teleported Elise and the two men back to the Stratosphere, where Miller was still going over all the recordings she'd made during the night and thus far during the morning.

"Guys, come check out these recordings, will you?" Miller asked quietly, once Elise and Monica were situated and watching the DVD again. Pam paid close attention to the images, which looked somewhat strange to her. "This is their main government offices, where their leaders used to run the country from—right here, this building," she pointed out. "Until six hours ago, the place was completely empty, well at least for the last five days anyway. I have to access the Cloud to go back any farther. Now, you can see there are dozens in there."

"So have some Germans who fled returned and are now taking control of their country?" asked Bergson.

"I thought so at first, but then you know me. I trust nothing—hard evidence and all that. I brought one of the US IR satellites online, positioning it over the building. Here's a rapid series of what I call key shots." She played back excerpts that she'd painstakingly assembled, in hopes that it would be quite clear to the others who hadn't stared at these monitors nearly all night.

After sufficient video demonstrated that several dozen forms were now continuously occupying the building, she zoomed in on several of the reddish forms, using maximum magnification. Bergson gasped. Kelly cursed, and Monica carefully got up to come see what was going on.

"Demons!" she cursed.

Some images definitely displayed horns on the tops of their heads. Others had tail-like appendages, while several arms ending in what appeared to be giant claws.

"Yep," Miller said quietly. "Demons are in control of the main government offices right now, but I think it might be worse than that."

"How can it be worse, Miller?" griped Kelly.

Miller said nothing, but moved her video stream along, focusing in on the floor beneath the building's giant, ornate dome. Unmistakable, there was the outline of a glowing pentagram. Monica cursed again. "That's a permanent Gate to the Abyss. They can use it to bring as many demons up here as they want to. Pam, best let Deiter know about this."

"Already have," Pam whispered, just as shocked as the others were with this discovery.

Monica stepped back, biting her lip. "So we know the demons are here, probably attempting to control Germany, likely using the surviving SS men, I'll wager."

"I agree with your assessment, Miss Black," Bergson said formally. "I suppose you should contact Glasya, if you can."

"On it," Monica replied, sending a hasty Message to the princess.

At the same time, a Message scrolled past Pam's eyes. She announced, "Deiter says not to worry. His contacts have already found and destroyed the voluminous supplies of the Dr. Menninger's pills and gasses, so the demons can't use any more of that on people. He also said not to take action until he brings in reinforcements later today. I told him we would wait, right? We're not going up against those demons ourselves, are we?"

For once, Pam was unsure of herself. Would Bergson order them to attack the demons right away? From his dossier, she believed he would do just that. Again, Bergson surprised Pam.

"Okay everyone. Time to gear up. We must hold this Stratosphere at all costs until Deiter arrives. Miller, if we get attacked, get this plane airborne as fast as possible. I'm sure Glasya can bring Fritz to us safely."

He glanced at the worried face of Elise when he said that last. She sighed, slightly relieved, though obviously growing worried about the safety of Fritz.

Monica's mind raced down many paths. Had this been part of Dr. Menninger's plan all along? Denude Germany of its key personnel so that the demons could come in and take over the entire country? Or perhaps was this the demons' response to Dr. Menninger's betrayal of their plans? Would they be going after the new Menninger clone? Where did the demons come from? From other parts of the world or just the Abyss? Was the US now free of its clandestine demons? What did the demons hope to achieve by controlling Germany, when the vast majority of its population was incapacitated? Was this a diabolical attempt to have incapacitated humans begging to be taken to the Abyss for new and powerful bodies, that is, a massive recruitment project?

Monica was both confused and baffled by this startling news and returned to her seat beside Elise, slumping dumbfounded into the chair. She had nothing but unanswered questions racing through her mind, distracting her completely when it happened again.

Chapter 19—Attacked

Monica pondered the myriad new questions flashing through her mind when it happened. Although she was later asked about it, she knew if she hadn't been distracted, the results would have been the same. The casting of a Wish spell is nearly impossible to prevent if one isn't in the presence of the caster. In Monica's case, the caster was thousands of miles away from her when he did the deed.

Bergson, Kelly, and Miller just started to rush out of the room to gear up in case the demons discovered they were here in their Stratosphere when it happened. Elise and Monica were sitting on a couch watching the special DVD. Pam sat on a chair off to one side. All five were in her field of vision when the spell triggered. Although distracted, Monica definitely heard the wording of the spell as its powerful magic slammed into her. She heard a man's voice speaking. "I wish that whatever physical form Dominus Malefic now has be altered into a physical form duplicating what he did to my Lisa's body, and with the same poison capsules to prevent their removal just as he did to my Lisa."

Pam blinked from the flash of magical energies encompassing Monica for that brief instant of time. The flash caught the attention of Elise, and the three who were preparing to dash out of the room to don their protective gear. All eyes turned to Monica, who suddenly began gasping for breath! Her arms were entirely gone as was her clothing, revealing breasts that were twice as large as they had been before, almost basketballs in size. She gasped for air because a tight laced, wasp-waist corset constricted her waist down to an unimaginable twelve inches in circumference, but the heavily steel boned corset was somehow beneath her skin, melded into her body, just as Dominus had done to many women years ago. Her feet were encased in knee-high, black ballet boots that fit as tightly to her feet and lower legs as though they were a second skin. Worse, the boots could not be taken off her feet, since they had no visible laces or zippers.

"Can't. Breathe. What's. Happened. To. Me," Monica said between panicked gasps for breath. Each shallow breath was just enough for her to get out one word before frantically gasping once more. "Poison. Can't. Take. These. Off," she added, primarily for Pam's benefit, praying she'd understand the magnitude of Monica's distress.

"What the hell just happened?" yelled Bergson, rushing to Monica's side.

"Good god!" exclaimed Miller.

"Wish spell," Pam declared. "Someone else just cast a Wish spell on her. Bergson, don't try to pull those boots off her feet. There are poison capsules in them. Any attempt to remove them will release the poison, killing her."

Shocked with what he was seeing, Bergson barked, "What the devil is that around her waist? It's killing her!"

"Bergson, trust me," Pam took charge. "I've seen this many times before, but not for many years. Back in the days of Dominus Malefic, he used to do this to women, making them into his sex dolls. That's a super tight corset that's been melded into her body, just below her skin. It's also booby trapped with poison capsules. Try to cut it out of her and they'll explode, killing her. We've dealt with this before, Bergson. We can do it again, trust me."

Monica's frantic gasps ended. She fainted. Bergson caught her and carefully carried her to the guest bedroom where she'd been sleeping, and Miller followed after him. "What can we do?" Kelly barked at Pam, while his boss left carrying Monica.

Very worried, Pam ordered, "Get geared up to protect this plane. I'll let the others know and see what I can do for Monica. Meantime, we can't let the demons get us."

The situation had suddenly become disastrous, if not outright perilous. Pam had no idea who had cast the Wish spell, but presumed it was one of the nearby demons.

Elise just sat on the couch, shocked speechless. Pam rose and followed after Bergson and Miller. "Good. Lay her down. I'll tend to her til the others get here. Bergson, you better get geared up. We could be under attack any moment."

"Will she live? She can't breathe," he stammered, obviously quite shaken up.

"Yes, takes some adjustments, but she'll be fine in time. The demons must be about to attack us," Pam theorized the only thing that made any sense to her at the moment.

"Okay. Just get her to safety if we get boarded! That's an order!" he barked angrily.

Now that's the Bergson I was told to expect, Pam thought. "I promise. Go. Protect us." Bergson nodded, rose, and ran out of the room, Miller right behind him, her face as pale as a ghost. After firing off a slew of Message spells, Pam roused Monica. "There. Shallow breaths. Easy does it. Give yourself time to adapt, Monica."

"Thanks. So. Hard. Shallow. Got. It," she said between inhales. Silent for a moment, she sent a Message to Senator Bart Marton telling him she forgave him. "I'm. Okay. Now. Got. To. Get. Up. Help. Fight. Til. Others. Come," Monica fought to tell Pam.

"Okay then, but easy does it, Monica. I know we need your spell casting skills. I just hope we can hold out until the others get here. I've got you," Pam explained, holding her securely upright.

"Been. Like. This. Before. I'm. Okay," Monica continued to attempt to explain to Pam. Surprisingly, she found she was able to walk fairly well, since she'd been through something like this before with Prince Graz'zt. By the time they reached the others near the rear of the giant Stratosphere, Monica was walking acceptably well, though she constantly gasped for air. She also knew that in a week or so, her body would have adjusted to the intense compression and pressure, and she'd be able to get by fairly well. "Can't. Bend. Much. Can't. See. Feet," she added.

Bergson, Kelly, and Miller had on their bullet-proof vests and were slinging their assault rifles over their shoulders, along with bags of clips containing the enchanted bullets, when it happened again! Only this time, all five were not only taken by complete surprise, they were shocked! Monica sensed yet another Wish spell being cast, but the words being spoken were in a language she did not understand, though it reminded her of what she'd once heard being spoken by natives of the Abyss.

Magical energies flashed as brightly as before, alerting Pam that something terrible was happening. After blinking, Pam stared at Miller. She again appeared as she once had when she'd been a victim in Rolla. This time, she retained her teeth and voice, but her lower arms and hands were gone, her breasts were the size that Monica's had been and that Elise's were, and her feet were malformed just as before. She was stark naked, except for the seven-inch pumps now on her feet. All her gear now lay on the floor behind her.

The men were even more shocked than Chrissy! They too were naked, but now had breasts the same size as Chrissy's. Likewise, they had no lower arms and hands and their feet were identically malformed. Like Chrissy, they were standing naked, their gear behind them, and wearing identical tall heels.

Monica, on the other hand, found the changes rather beneficial. Her basketballs shrunk back to their previous H-cup size, the same size as the others. More importantly, the ballet boots vanished, replaced with identical seven-inch heels that the others now wore. This second Wish spell had partially undone what the first Wish spell had done to her body. Rather minor, all four now had hair that fell to their knees.

Pam rubbed her eyes in complete disbelief! Bergson managed to scream, "What the hell?"

At the same instant, Miller cried loudly, "Not again!" Kelly just screamed, unable to grasp what had just happened to his body.

Once more, magical energies flashed, and Monica recognized the spell at once, Limited Wish. Whoever was behind this had immense powers. Pam blinked and all four vanished from sight!

Pam seldom if ever cursed, but the shocking events of the last few minutes overwhelmed her. She cursed loudly. Sleuth Pam knew she likely only had seconds before they came after her and Elise. She raced back to the viewing room, grabbed Elise's upper right arm, and cast her Teleport spell, arriving at the main gates of Bradbury's School of Magic. Only then did she frantically Message Lindsey. Seconds later, she opened a Magical Door and stepped out into Lindsey's office, dragging the speechless Dr. Elise along with her.

"Good grief! They got them all!" Pam screamed wildly.

Governor Lindsey had never, ever seen Pam this distraught, this upset, so out of control! Silently, she cast six Calm spells over Pam, before Pam finally eased herself into one of the plush chairs, having forgotten all about Elise, who managed to get herself into another chair on her own. "There now, Pam. Take a deep breath and relax. What just happened?" Lindsey asked softly.

Before Pam could even begin to formulate an answer, many other Magical Doors opened and six others entered the room, including Deiter, Ashley, and Professor Cho Lin.

"First Monica got it. Then all four got it. Then they just vanished! Lindsey, it's too horrible for words!" a highly emotional Pam blurted out, far from calm.

"Okay, Pam," Deiter declared, "we are ready to go into action right now. Just what's happened?"

"I told you so!" Ashley declared testily. "Deiter Cross, I tried to warn you, but did you listen to me? Oh no! Calm Pam!" She cast yet another spell on Pam, who again visibly relaxed once more.

Pam swallowed, took a deep breath, and slowly let it out. "Okay. I'm in control again. Wish spells. A whole lot of them. Just barely got Dr. Elise and me out of there before they got us, too. First, it was Monica," Pam began explaining what she'd witnessed.

As she began relating the events, Professor Cho Lin kept casting Calm spells on her, though Pam didn't realized that she was doing it. That's how engrossed the sleuth was in accurately describing what she saw and what hints Monica had given her.

"So yes, poison capsules. Can't remove the melded corset, just like Dominus did to all those women that we rescued, Deiter," Pam continued. "But that's only the beginning." She then told them how in spite of everything, Monica insisted on getting up and joining the others by the rear doors to help defend the plane. "They were all geared up and ready to defend the plane when the next Wish spell detonated," Pam explained.

She outlined just what physical changes she'd seen in all four. "So Monica got a break. Her bosom is back to where it used to be, still damnably large mind you, and the boots with the poison in them are gone, replaced with the same tall heels that she had been wearing, just like the other three and Elise for that matter. Conclusion: since all four look pretty much like Elise and the other female victims, it has to be the demons who are behind this second Wish spell. But that's not all," Pam concluded and continued to describe what she believed to be the third Wish spell that caused all four to suddenly vanish.

"So obviously, they're now in the hands of the demons, probably being tortured and worse," Pam finished up. "I got out of there with Dr. Elise as fast as I could run! Maybe we are so far away that they won't get us."

"Or maybe they didn't know you two were also there," Professor Cho Lin speculated.

Ashley put her hands defiantly on her hips. "Deiter, I told you this was not the right plan before you went ahead and took out Dr. Menninger's three henchmen and then the mad doctor. Now look at where that's led to! We've probably lost all four forever!"

Deiter's face turned red. *How could my plans work out so utterly wrong?* This he simply couldn't fathom and that bothered him. Why the world was now worried about Dominus Malefic when the demons were the real threat totally eluded him.

Governor Lindsey knew she had to act, and while Pam was telling them what had happened, she silently cast her own Limited Wish spell. When Ashley finished her condemnation of Deiter, she spoke decisively. "I've some news. All four are alive and still in Germany, but yes, they are captives of the demons who now are in control of Germany. We have a break there."

"How do you know that?" asked Pam, who'd recovered her senses and resumed being a sleuth. "Limited Wish?" Lindsey nodded.

Pam smiled, thankful that she'd not lost all her observational skills, just most of them.

At that moment, a Message scrolled past Lindsey's eyes. She cracked a smile. "Well, you'll never guess who is asking for permission to enter Bradbury's."

"Who?" Pam asked, beating everyone else.

"Princess Glasya. She's got Dr. Fritz with her and wants to chat with us. I've granted her permission and lowered the barriers. Ah, here she comes now. This should be interesting."

"Good grief! A devil? On Bradbury's grounds?" gushed the shocked Professor Cho Lin.

The Magical Door opened and Glasya, still wearing her crimson outfit, stepped into the room, bringing a very worried Dr. Fritz with her. "Hello everyone. Thanks for letting me come in. Mind you, Professor Cho Lin, I didn't need Governor Lindsey's permission. The school's protections are trivial for me to dispel, but it is only polite to ask. May Dr. Fritz go to his fiancé? We need to chat."

"Of course, Princess Glasya. Please, have a seat," Governor Lindsey replied, motioning to her.

"Oh just Glasya among friends. We are all friends here, at least right now," she replied, taking the offered seat, though she kept an eye on Dr. Fritz, who ignored everyone else and rushed over to Dr. Elise's side, whispering to her and then holding her tightly.

"Professor Betts has just informed us about what has happened to Monica, Bergson, Kelly, and Miller," Governor Lindsey explained. "Three Wish spells, I believe. Demons, we presume. I know they are alive in Germany and are prisoners of the demons."

"Two disparate Wish spells and one Limited Wish spell, to be more accurate," Glaysa corrected her. "What I find utterly fascinating is that Monica Nicole Black has already forgiven ex-Senator Bart Marton for what his Wish spell has done to her. She did so before the second spell detonated."

"What? I don't understand. Who's Bart Marton?" asked Deiter, growing more confused than ever. Absolutely nothing was now going according to any plan he'd ever dreamed of.

"Men. You have such short memories," Ashley chided him. "Don't you remember Dominus' sex doll toys that we rescued? Lisa Marton, his daughter. We got her out of that house of ill repute in which Dominus kept her and the others. Wait! Glasya, Monica has forgiven him?"

Glasya smiled, "Indeed so. She sent him a Message right after Pam brought her around after she fainted. I must say, her Message has rather stunned that old man. But that's a red herring. We've bigger problems. Dr. Fritz simply must fly over Germany and release the gaseous cure that he and Dr. Elise have developed. The cure will restore all those who fell victim to Dr. Menninger's gas attacks. Unfortunately, it will not cure any of those who took the man's pills. Still, it is a good start. However, he and I cannot do that when the demons control the country."

A frustrated Deiter burst out, "But he's Dr. Menninger, well, his clone anyway."

"Yes, that is true, Deiter. Perhaps you should think of Dr. Fritz here as you do Miss Black. Neither are the person they once were," Glasya explained. "But come; we have far more important things to discuss here. I'll be quite blunt. Humans, you have one more chance to remove these demons from your world before we devils take matters into our own hands. Let me explain just what is going on and why something must be done immediately."

Once more, she outlined the devil's position, as she had previously done with Monica and the WIT team. However, she added some additional details. "Mammon has recently learned Gisella's successes here on Earth have finally come to the attention of several demon lords. They are now observing the events with watchful eyes. If this succubus succeeds much farther in her Grand Plan, almost certainly they will join her. And that, my friends, simply cannot and will not be tolerated by the devils. Dispater and Mammon will send forth their armies of devils to Earth to battle the demon hordes. Alas, when they finish, the world as you know it will be likely uninhabitable."

She continued, "Mammon's spies told him that as of this moment, the demon lords have not made any decisions. As they see it, the scorecard is heavily in your favor, what with the extermination of the vast majority of the invading demon horde by Dr. Menninger. However, should Gisella succeed in taking Germany and in defeating the coming Holy Crusade, then it's a certainty the demon lords will move in for the final kill."

Pam swallowed hard. "We, we should have listened to Monica nine years ago and not let her search for the escapees slide."

"Told you so," Ashley added, feeling vindicated after nine years. Glasya merely smiled demurely.

Deiter spoke up defiantly. "Hey, this is our world. We'll take care of this demon problem and soon. You keep them devils of yours off our world."

"Don't worry. If the worst happens, remember, you only have to call out our names. I assure you that Dispater, Mammon, and I are always ready to make bargains for your souls, especially powerful ones such as yourselves. Dr. Fritz here has done just that. He's under our protection now," Glasya put in a bit of promotion for her cause.

"So are you going to help us fight the demons?" Governor Lindsey inquired.

"Sorry. My task is to see that Dr. Fritz here completes his side of his bargain. We must get his cure spread out over Germany and soon. I'm afraid you're on your own, that is, unless you are ready to make a bargain right now," she answered.

Governor Lindsey laughed. "Hardly, Glasya, hardly. I was just checking. Let me get this straight. You're waiting until we get the demons cleared out of Berlin so you and Dr. Fritz can spread his cure over that country."

"Precisely. And do hurry up," she added. "In the mean time, I'll take Dr. Elise with us, since she's also under our protection. One less person for you to have to worry about."

Deiter swallowed and declared, "Well, we were just about ready to go attack them when all this happened. So if you don't have anything more to say or advice to give us, we best get on with it."

"I'm done," Glasya replied. "And I did warn Monica to go into hiding several times these past couple of days. Of course, I didn't expect she'd heed my warning, which of course she didn't. Now there's a soul worth obtaining! She'd make a superb sister-princess but a dangerous rival if Dispater got to her before my Mammon. So I suggest you do get on with it, Mr. Cross. Now, if you will excuse us, please Message me when it is safe for Dr. Fritz to begin dispensing his cure."

With that, she rose, took hold of the pair, and vanished in a puff of multi-colored smoke, despite all the protections Governor Lindsey had around Bradbury's that prevented teleporting in or out of the school.

Deiter broke the sudden silence. "Well, you heard her. Let's get this attack and rescue underway. To the dining hall; everyone's there waiting for us. Peaches has a dozen of their fancy automatic rifles with silencers, just like the ones that Bergson's group uses, and plenty of Ericka and Tyler's enchanted ammo. Time to kick some demon butt!"

Ashley replied sternly, "Deiter, you better not mess this one up!" He gave her a rather dirty look and stepped through his Magical Door, arriving in the dining hall below the five dorms, where forty others were waiting, including nearly everyone from Monica's group. Misty stayed behind to watch over their dozen children. Tim and Wanda joined her, bringing their four children with them. Both wanted to help, but Ericka convinced Tim that he could best assist by helping to look after the many children.

Peaches handed out eleven of the large caliber rifles to those who claimed they knew how to fire a gun, but kept one for herself. After what she'd witnessed at the Dragon Hole, she felt far more confident holding onto the big gun than she did with all her powerful spells. In fact, many of those assembled who had participated in the attack on the Dragon Hole now had an enormous respect for the WIT team and their big guns. Ericka and Tyler were also two of the eleven who carried them, prepared to use their own enchanted platinum shells.

"So Deiter, what did that devil woman have to say?" Peaches asked, when Deiter stepped into the room. She was by the Black Hall tables, checking her ammo clips.

"No time. Later. Is everyone ready?" he asked. Many heads nodded.

"So what's the plan this time, Deiter?" Lindsey asked. While the two had discussed this at length before Glasya appeared, she felt that everyone should be reminded.

Deiter stood tall and answered so everyone could hear. "Nothing fancy this time. We arrive at the front entrance to the building and charge inside, guns blazing. No time for fancy plays. We strike and strike hard. Lindsey, Ashley, Pam, you three are in charge of finding Monica and the WIT team. Don't join the battle unless you have to, just focus on finding them and getting them out of there. Hey, Peaches, don't I get one of those big guns?"

She laughed, "No. You have to stay focused on controlling this attack." Several laughs echoed around the large room. That wasn't what he was expecting for an answer, but he was wise enough to understand why. She'd handed out the guns to those witches and wizards who were more vulnerable or who didn't command as much magical power as he did. Ericka and Tyler, for example, were definitely not the types to engage in magical battles, whereas his Rodents most definitely were.

"Okay, Deiter, I've got the mag-Google image of the building up on the giant monitor," Ashley interrupted. "Everyone, take a good look. Here's our teleport destination."

When everyone was watching the big screen, Deiter barked, "Okay. On three. One. Two. Three." Magical energies flashed and forty wizards and witches vanished from the dining hall, arriving in a loose group just before the main entrance to the Executive Mansion in downtown Berlin, where the local time was around six that same night. The WIT team had been abducted five hours before.
***

Monica was still fighting for each breath. The unrelenting compression and intense pressure of the extreme corset permitted only a slight amount of air into her lungs. Worse, the steel boning prevented nearly all motion of her back. Between both effects, Monica knew that focusing on casting a spell would be neigh onto impossible. When the third round of magical energies flashed, she and the WIT team were transported into the main entrance hall of the Berlin Executive Mansion, arriving totally disoriented. Worse, the WIT team members were confused beyond all rational thought.

"Well, well. Look what we have here," the snickering voice of Gisella broke the silence. The four wobbled and flailed their upper arms about, as they got their balance on the inlayed marble floor, whose designs were spectacular, emulating ancient designs used in some of the Holy Roman Emperor buildings centuries ago. She added, "Our Public Enemies Number One have arrived."

Gisella wore a seductive blue satin gown and appeared in her human female form, though she wore an SS armband around her left shoulder. Two dozen Cambion guards wearing the gray Schutzstaffel uniforms and carrying automatic rifles milled around in the background.

A very tall Cambion wearing a general's uniform stood to the succubus' right. Monica and her team immediately recognized the Cambion Baron Jamal, who had escaped the battle at the Dragon Hole by diving into its waters. However, even more shocking, to her left stood Jonellith!

This incredibly beautiful and shapely demon didn't try to hide her six arms and giant snake body. Her hair was longer than before, draped seductively over her naked breasts. She held an automatic rifle with grenade launcher in each of her six arms. Beautiful and shapely applies to what is seen from her bosom upwards. Based on that point of view, she could easily be a top beauty model, as long as one didn't look any further down her body.

Jonellith spoke. Her voice sounded positively angelic. "Mistress Gisella, it's done as you asked. Now I want my super-hero man."

"Oh I assure you, he'll be coming soon. Now then, don't you four look positively stunning. Impressive knockers, Bergson. Don't worry. I'll have you on display so that everyone can see just how fine you and the others now look. Guards, escort them to the two bedrooms for now. Lay them on the beds. Mind you, take them in pairs— Monica with Bergson—Miller with Kelly. Don't let them join forces. We don't want Monica trying to teleport them out of our grasp. You four, I strongly recommend you engage in sex. Your bodies crave it now. Besides, it'll be the last time you'll ever be able to enjoy such. Take them now."

Several guards moved next to the two pairs, nudging them forward. In their tall heels, they had to begin walking, either that or fall down on the cold, hard marble floor. Gasping for each breath, Monica focused solely on not fainting, knowing she dare not lose consciousness. She needed all the will power she had to prevent that from happening as they were escorted down a long, dimly illuminated hallway to a row of private bedrooms. She and Bergson were pushed into the first one, while Kelly and Miller were forced into the second one.

A plush queen sized bed nearly filled the small chamber, though the small desk and chairs were of the finest quality, suitable for state guests. The covers had been pulled down, indicating that their abduction had been planned in advance, a fact not missed by either Bergson or Monica, though the terrified and shocked Kelly and Miller didn't make that connection, not yet.

"Have at it. Gonna be your last," the Cambion guard spoke up, before turning and leaving the room, closing and locking the door behind him.

Gasping, Monica stood still for a minute, trying to recover from the exertion. "God. This. Is. Bad," she finally said between gasps. "Can't. Bend. Have. To. Sit. Down." She did so on the edge of the bed. Watching the shocked Bergson joining her, she realized this bedroom interlude was also part of the Wish spell, though the reason for it completely defied all her logic.

"Monica, I can't help myself! I've got to do it with you. I've been fighting against it since this happened to us," Bergson wailed, in obvious distress.

"Okay. I. Can't. Fight. It. Can't. Bend," she replied and more or less just fell backwards onto the bed. "We. Have. No. Choice. But. I. Want. It," she added.

"Me too, Monica." Bergson awkwardly got into the bed beside her, but they found it easier to maneuver while lying on their sides. "God, what's happening to us?" he whispered frantically, before their magically enhanced passions took over.

"Okay, all is prepared. Go fetch our prisoners," Gisella commanded.

"This is positively brilliant, Gisella," Jonellith declared, smiling broadly. "I have to hand it to you. I thought the whole scheme was wiped out at the Dragon Hole, but this, well, this is simply brilliant!"

Shortly, the guards returned, escorting the four satiated victims back into the Grand Entrance Hall of the Executive Mansion. As the four walked slowly into the hall, they saw four new three-foot tall white marble blocks with embedded colorful swirls arranged in a row and centrally located. Each block was square, a foot on each side. Rising from the back of the tall blocks were steel poles. As the four reached the demon women, Gisella ordered, "Put the collars on them. Carefully, mind you."

Other Cambion guards walked to them, carrying what looked like simple dog collars, but each had a ring attacked to it. At least the men were gentle putting the collars on their necks, especially with their knee-length hair, which had to be moved out of the way.

That done, Gisella ordered, "Now lift them into position and adjust the poles." Strong hands lifted the gasping Monica up onto the tall marble block, turning her to face the entrance. She heard the steel pole sliding some and felt it being inserted into the ring on her collar. Monica grasped what he was doing. The pole was raised high enough so she had no way to push herself upwards to get the ring off of the small hook at the top of the pole. She and the others could only stand still, permanently atop these marble blocks, unable to get themselves down.

Well, Monica thought, I can still levitate us up and get us down; just wait for the right time.

"Excellent. Now lower the bell jars," Gisella ordered. The four heard noises above them and twisted their necks upwards enough to see tall, thick glass jar-like constructions being slowly lowered down over them. A couple minutes later, the bell jars rested on the marble floor, totally sealing them inside and while standing on their pedestals. Magic flashed and etchings appeared in the front face of the marble pillars. "Public Enemy Number One," Gisella explained, "that's what the inscriptions read. You see, from now on, when anyone enters this, the Executive Mansion, they will first see you four, helpless enemies, standing naked before them. Oh don't worry. You won't need food."

She chanted in her own language, but the constriction and pressure kept Monica from hastily casting a simple spell to understand what Gisella was casting. Magic flashed. Monica couldn't see anything different, not immediately.

Then, she and the others began seeing the world around them moving at some kind of super-high speed.

Cambion demons entered, stared at them, and departed. It was as though someone had made one of those time-lapse movies covering a day's worth of time and then shown the movie at high speed. Suddenly, Monica realized what had happened to them. They were now contained in some kind of stasis field, where one second of their time translated to hours of real time. No wonder they wouldn't need to be fed. By the time they got hungry, days of real time would have passed, if not more.

As this realization struck home, Monica realized her true peril. While she could still cast spells, even a simple Message spell would arrive many days after she sent it. Gisella had effectively nullified Monica's impressive command of magic while not actually harming her. Worse, she was now on display, totally helpless to do anything about it! Monica panicked and nearly fainted again. She used every ounce of will power to keep from fainting!

Outside her bell jar, the figures continued to move like high-speed ants. Then, brilliant magical energies detonated, like some July 4th celebration speeded up such that the entire display occurred in a couple of seconds. That display was followed by someone canceling the Stasis spell. In real time, Monica saw the jars being lifted off of them. *Lindsey! She is here!* Monica relaxed and fainted, exhausted from her efforts to keep going.
***

The forty wizards and witches suddenly appeared before the mansion's entrance around six that night. Street lights provided substantial illumination, and Deiter yelled, "Charge!" The group raced up the marble steps and into the building where they came up short, staring at the four naked prisoners standing motionless and erect on the marble blocks, all of which was inside rounded, glass bell jars. They couldn't help see the inscriptions etched into the marble bases, "Public Enemy Number One."

Their momentary pause ended seconds later, when dozens of Cambion guards wearing the grey SS uniforms and carrying automatic rifles burst into the giant entrance hall. The battle began; bullets rained around the hall.

Lindsey hastily cast a Force Wall, putting it between the bell jars and the oncoming demons. Pam and Ashley quickly cast additional walls, slowly surrounding themselves and the four prisoners, protecting them from stray bullets. Magical energies flashed wildly, as suddenly there was light and then there was total darkness and back to light once more, as though some kind of flickering lightbulb about to burn out.

Jonellith spotted Deiter among the attacking group and focused her efforts on acquiring her super-hero. "You are mine, Deiter Cross!" her voice bellowed, carrying across the huge room, attracting his attention towards her. Magical spells flew back and forth between them, as both completely ignored the large battle going on around them.

"Take that, bitch!" Deiter exclaimed, arcing a giant bolt of lightning at her. Jonellith ducked in time; the bolt knocked out a chunk of the ceiling behind her, which came crashing down upon a luckless Cambion, whose body turned into a gray ooze as he was jerked back into the Abyss from whence he came. She returned the favor. A similar nasty bolt shot towards Deiter, but he stood his ground, knowing that his protection spell would work. The bolt seemed to arc around him, though it also jarred loose a chunk of granite in the wall behind.

Deiter countered with Lindsey's favorite spell. A giant boxing glove appeared close to Jonellith's head, threatening to pound her senseless. Her innate magic resistance kicked in and the glove moved off and pulverized another luckless nearby Cambion, turning it into gray ooze. After that, the Cambions hastily moved quite clear of Jonellith.

Laughing, Jonellith cast the same spell back at Deiter, who knew his protections wouldn't help him with this one. He dove out of the way of the glove, but it pounded him senselessly until Lindsey cast her Dispel Magic at the glove, whereon it vanished. Dazed, he got back onto his feet and shook his head, trying to get a grip on the situation. A bullet tore through his left shoulder, knocking him to the ground. Jonellith's laughter could be heard over the deafening din. Smoke came from one of her six rifles. Deiter cursed, but Peaches returned her fire, enchanted bullets ripping into Jonellith's body. Then a protective spell of Jonellith's activated.

The silver-lined giant pentagram cut into the center of the hall began glowing. Jonellith dove into it, vanishing from sight. The glow promptly vanished and the gunfire ceased. "Got them all!" Peaches yelled as loudly as she could.

"Darn it! I'm hit," Deiter called out. Many others yelled that, as well.

Lindsey barked, "Peaches, stand guard. Pam, Enya, dole out the healing potions immediately!" She rushed over to Deiter who was lying on the floor, holding his bleeding arm, grimacing in pain. "Drink this," she demanded. Deiter didn't object, gulping it down and reaching up for another. Lindsey handed him two more before moving onto the next fallen person. Only ten of the attacking party were uninjured, but fortunately with the rapid guzzling of the many healing potions, everyone survived, though a bit shaken up by this new tactic the demons used.

"They are using our own weapons against us," Ericka declared. "That's not fair."

Lindsey smiled and said, "Who said demons play fair?" Several chuckled.

Peaches called out, "Deiter, all clear. We've searched the rest of the place. No more demons. We're destroying the Gate now. Are the four alive?"

"Good. Destroy that vile pentagram. I'm okay, Lindsey. Come on. We have to get these four back to Bradbury's pronto before anything else happens to them," Deiter ordered, still favoring his shoulder, though already it had begun to heal rapidly. What looked strange to him was seeing the lead slug popping out of the wound.

Enya saw his look and smiled. "Little something we added to the potions."

"Way cool. Gotta get us some of your potions, Enya," he replied.

Meanwhile, Lindsey, Pam, and Ashley began to examine how the four were affixed to the poles, since they remained almost motionless all this time. Pam declared, "Just undo their collars. Simple enough. There, I've got you Monica."

"Thanks. Can't. Breathe," she said between gasps. A minute later, the four were teleported back to Bradbury's, arriving in the Infirmary.

Chapter 20—A Goof and Successes

Monica and the team rested on cots in the Infirmary, covered with warm sheets and blankets. A half hour after they arrived and were quickly helped by Lindsey's medical staff, a Magical Door opened and Lindsey, Deiter, Pam, and Ashley stepped out. Deiter held a scroll in one hand. He'd changed his bloody shirt, Monica noticed.

Lindsey spoke first. "Well, we've taken care of the demon infestation in Germany. Several of their more powerful wizards have just returned to Berlin from exile and will see to the reconstruction of their country. I've alerted Glasya and she claims that she and Dr. Fritz are beginning to spread his cure over Berlin right now. Time will tell on that one. Thanks to you four, we got the warning just in time to prevent an even worse mess. I'll tell you about what Glasya told us in a bit. Deiter, you are up."

Ashley chided, "Deiter, don't screw this up!"

Unrolling his scroll, Deiter declared, "Ashley, stop worrying! I've got this. I'm going to Wish that these four are restored to just the way they were before they were attacked with those Wish spells." Magic flashed, startling everyone, none more so than Deiter, who had prepared for this—his gallant rescue—for nearly a week, intending to impress absolutely everyone. "Wait! I wasn't ready! That wasn't my wish, not exactly!" He produced another paper from his pocket on which he'd carefully written out just the right words to say.

Pam commented wryly, "I think you just used it, Deiter."

"God! Hands. I've got hands!" cried Bergson, pushing himself up into a sitting position. The covers fell away revealing his normal chest, although he felt it to make certain the soccer balls were gone. His hair was back to being quite short.

"Wow. I'm me again!" Kelly cried out. "That was a nightmare! Humiliating beyond words! Cursed demons! I swear I'll never play a joke on anyone ever again!"

"Me, too. I'm okay now," the soft voice of Chrissy contrasted sharply from the loud exclamations of the men. "That was a nightmare all right, Kelly, but honestly, I do prefer you with big boobs."

Kelly turned to her, aghast. Seeing her teasing grin, he realized he'd been had and broke into a hearty laugh. Even Bergson managed a smile.

Deiter relaxed. His spell had worked. "So Monica, how are you doing?" he asked, turning his attention to her. All eyes focused on her. She was still lying down, though the other three were sitting up. Chrissy held the sheets over her chest however.

"That's a relief, Deiter. I can breathe now. Yes, that was one incredible nightmare, Kelly. For the first time, I admit I was petrified. She found a way to make all of my magic utterly useless!"

While she was talking, Pam moved to her side. Noticing the raised soccer balls, she realized Monica wasn't back to normal, long before the others did. She gently raised the sheet a bit. "Well, Deiter, she hasn't got that melded corset on and that's something, but she's like she was before, no lower arms and the rest, like Dr. Elise and Wanda."

"I told you, Deiter Cross, you'd just mess it up!" Ashley chimed in. "Again, you didn't listen to me. Monica's not okay and you've wasted that Wish scroll."

"What happened to us? How are we now back to normal? What's she talking about?" barked Bergson, demanding to know what had just happened. Worse, Monica wasn't back to normal and that truly bothered him, now more so than ever.

Deiter's face crimsoned. "I—I bought a Wish scroll so I could get Monica back to normal. After all, we owe her so much, but I also wanted to get you three back to normal, too. I had it all written down, just what I had to say to get everyone fixed up just fine."

"And you blew it, Deiter," Ashley interrupted, "just as I predicted you would. Why don't you listen to me?"

Lindsay laughed, "There went twenty million bucks, Deiter. Still, no one's going to complain. The WIT team is back to normal and Monica is mostly alright. Bergson, we owe you and your team for helping save the whole darn world. This is the least that we can do for you and your team, undo the awful effects of magic on your bodies. As you probably saw, we've made use of your field-proven tactics when we rescued you and took out the demons holding Germany hostage. You see, normals and magic users can work well together. We really aren't any different than you. Each of us just has different skills. Now then, much is happening, and we do need to hold a conference to discuss what is going on and what must still be done. There's not much time. So let's get your clothes back."

"They are on the Stratosphere parked at the airport," Monica stated.

"Good. Pam, you go fetch their clothes. Probably I should send along a pilot who can fly the plane back to Lambert. Let's get them their clothes and back to Monica's place. That's a better place for us to meet. I don't want to put the kids here at the magic school in any more danger than I have to."

Monica suggested, "Lindsey, "I'm really exhausted and it's late, our time anyway. We could fly the plane back and sleep on the way. Could the meeting wait until morning?"

"Yes, I think that is wise, Monica," Ashley said determinedly. "We all need some sleep. Look, their bodies have undergone massive changes. They need physical recovery time to be at their best."

"Okay, that's settled. How about meeting at eight tomorrow morning?" Lindsey went along with her Diviner's support. "Wait a second." A Message scrolled past her eyes. A broad smile appeared. "It seems Glasya has already moved your Stratosphere to Lambert field for you. Interesting. Let's get you back to your plane so you can get some needed rest."

***

An hour later, Monica and Bergson quietly retired to her cabin on the Stratosphere. They'd returned to St. Louis and their plane, gotten dressed, paid a quick trip to the mansion to assure everyone and Rob that they were just fine, dined a good meal, and were now retiring for the night. After helping her get undressed, he said, "I wish Deiter hadn't messed up whatever he did so you could be back to normal, too."

Monica sighed. "I know, but I'm a million times better now that I was. Come on. I really want you with me tonight, Alan. I've never been so scared as I was in that bell jar of hers. Helpless, Bergson, completely helpless."

He crawled in beside her, pulling her gently over to his side. "Oh, I'm sure you could have gotten us out of there somehow."

Monica smiled. "Well, that's also true, but so much time would have passed us by before I could. For us, time was slowed way, way down. Now stop talking. I need loving, big boy," she whispered, moving her upper arm over his chest, touching him ever so gently.

In the galley, Kelly and Miller were fixing some hot cocoa. "It will help you sleep, Miller," Kelly insisted. "I've got to take good care of you."

"Thanks."

"That has to be the freakiest thing that's ever come our way, Miller. Eye opening, too. I had no idea how awful it was for you and Monica and all the other female victims. Hell, I could hardly walk. And so helpless. That's a feeling I can do without. Crap, Monica's still stuck like that."

"I know, Kelly. No one should ever have to suffer like that."

"Right. Say, I'm sorry for doing it with you, there in that bed. I don't know what came over me. I couldn't stop myself," he admitted.

"Me, too, Kelly, but I don't think it would have been so overwhelming if we didn't already have feelings for each other," Miller said softly.

Kelly flushed slightly, admitting, "Yeah, that's true. I can't tell you how many times I've wanted to do that with you, but I was. . ." His voice trailed off.

She finished his thought, "scared that I would reject your advances?"

"Yeah. I don't think I could handle that, Miller."

"Well, Kelly, I've wanted you that way, too, but I'm too shy to say anything. I am much better with women."

Both smiled, staring into each other's eyes. He said, "Say, did you mean what you said back there—that you preferred me with those soccer ball boobs?"

Miller chuckled. "Well, actually Kelly, you did look incredibly sexy to me that way." He gave her a playful punch and she laughed. "Seriously, I did like to see you like that, but it's not natural. Come on; let's do it right this time. My bed or yours?"

"You kidding me?" he replied, unwilling to trust his own instincts after this nightmare day. She gave him a gentle kiss in way of reply. The two headed off to her bedroom.

***

"Breakfast is up. Come on; rise and shine you sleepy WIT grunts," Bergson's uncharacteristically cheery voice roused Kelly and Miller. The smells of bacon and eggs seeped into their room.

"What's with Bergson?" Kelly asked, dressing quickly, though keeping an eye on Miller as she followed suit.

"Dunno. He's been acting strange for days now. When was the last time he made us breakfast?" she asked.

"Duh, never. You're right. The boss has been acting, well different," Kelly replied. "Come on. I'm not about to turn down breakfast."

"Hey, me either. For once, I don't have to make it, but goodness, I hope the coffee is drinkable!" she declared.

"Hey, I don't make coffee," he replied.

"I know, I know," she teased him.

The two headed to the galley and found Monica was also there, dressed in a red gown and matching heels. She was watching Bergson preparing breakfast. "Hi, you two. Bergson's volunteered to make breakfast today," Monica said. "Is he any good at it? Should we stop by the Arches instead?"

"Oh yea of little faith," Bergson replied, turning his head towards her, a smile on his face.

"Don't know, Miss Black," Kelly answered, "Boss has never fixed us breakfast before. I think his brain's been muddled."

"I heard that, Kelly. Watch it or you'll be on KP duty all week," Bergson teased him. Kelly laughed.

After he filled everyone's plates, Bergson sat down beside Monica. "I best feed you. Can't have you using up all your magic on this."

"Okay. I really should sit down and watch that DVD and figure out how to use my feet to do this, but other things are more pressing. Thanks," Monica replied.

Later, Chrissy volunteered to brush out Monica's hair for her, while the two men cleaned up the mess in the galley. Back in Monica's guest bedroom, she spotted some of Bergson's things tossed onto the floor. She smiled. "Monica, can I ask you something privately? You don't have to answer if you think I'm out of line or something."

"Sure ask away. Thanks for doing my hair. I'd have to resort to using a bunch of spells to do it myself. I wonder how Wanda is managing to do it? I really do need to spend some time with her."

"It's about Bergson and you. Is he sleeping with you?" Miller asked, her voice barely audible.

Monica grinned. "Is it that obvious? Yes, we are. I hope I'm not violating any rules."

Chrissy giggled. "No, nothing like that. It's Bergson. He's been acting different for some time now. More thoughtful, less, well less barking at us. I think you are good for him."

"You know, I've noticed that, too. What about you and Kelly?"

She flushed. "Well, we slept together last night. I needed someone sleeping with me to feel safe again, but I do like him. I think we're both too shy about such things. Oh, I hear them. Mum's the word. Come on. If I know Bergson, he'll want to get to this meeting on time."

***

"Monica, you're looking good today," Crystal declared. Monica and the three just arrived at her mansion where everyone there greeted the four, welcoming them home. After receiving hugs and well-wishes from the kids, the children headed off to play and try out their Halloween costumes. The big night was only three days away. Enya fixed a large pot of tea and the group sipped tea in their large dining area, waiting for Lindsey and her group to arrive.

"I feel tons better, thanks to Deiter and a good night's sleep. You know, we're fighting demons who can cast Wish spells. Frankly, I'm beginning to be scared, Crystal. Gisella managed to completely nullify my spell casting abilities!"

"Hey, and they're adopting our own tactics," Crystal added, "and I've a bullet hole scar to prove it."

Just then, they were interrupted by the arrival of the Rodents pack. After a bit of hustle and bustle, everyone had a seat and some tea or coffee. Lindsey began the discussion. "Glasya paid us a surprise visit right after the four of you were attacked." She described in detail just what the devil princess had told them, sobering everyone present. Many of Lindsey's group hadn't heard directly what Glasya had said, though by now they all knew of her visit.

Next, Lindsey asked Monica to describe what had happened to them yesterday. Monica sighed. She didn't want to go into the gory details of her last life, not in front of all these people. Yet, she had to tell them what happened. "The first attack on me was a Wish spell. It took me by complete surprise. I don't believe it's directly related to the demons, though. I managed to send the caster a Message that I forgave him for doing that to me. It must have been a mistake." She knew several here would know that it wasn't a mistake, per se, but she also knew they would understand.

She added, "The man has suffered enormously from the evil that Dominus Malefic caused. He just wanted his own brand of justice. Now I guess he is satisfied. Anyway, then we got hit with a Wish spell cast by someone with the demons. I don't know who did it. That was followed by a Limited Wish that took us physically into the Executive Mansion." She went on to describe what happened after that.

"So you can see why I am really, really scared. That's saying something. Gisella managed to find a way that completely nullified my magical abilities, all them, though perhaps if I could have been breathing properly I might have been able to do something before we were put into that Stasis environment. I'm very worried about these demons. We are going up against full Wish spells and that's not good at all. In fact, it's terrifying." When she finished, utter silence followed. That Monica admitted she was utterly helpless gave everyone present pause to think hard about the situation, for most believed she had almost as much power as Lindsey.

Crystal broke the silence, "You know, I'm not so sure about that Monica. Demons are not noted for knowing that spell, the full Wish spell. From our research, it's likely that the demon lords Demogorgon and Orcus can cast it. Certainly, many devils can, but demons, not so much. We've not found any references that suggest a succubus or a Type 5 demon can cast such a power spell. Certainly no demon who was there last night could cast it, but then Gisella and Baron Jamal weren't there. Jonellith was, and she certainly would have cast it if she knew it."

Monica interrupted her friend, "So what are you saying, Crystal?"

"Just that I don't think these demons have that spell in their native arsenal. Greg and I have another theory. Look, they've managed to take control of some forty million Germans, some of whom are wizards and witches. We think it more likely that they got one of those people who could cast the Wish spell to make them some one-use scrolls with that spell on it."

"Ah ha. Just like I did," Deiter spoke up. "I bought mine off the Internet. Glad I did. So you think they have a bunch of these Wish scrolls?"

Crystal answered, "To my way of thinking, Deiter, I believe so. I wouldn't put it past these demons to have gotten a hold of someone who could cast it and then forced them to write out a large number of Wish scrolls, draining the writer of all the remaining years of his or her life. In any case, Monica has every right to be terrified. A handful of Wish spells can create incalculable damage to Earth. And yet, if we don't stop them, as Lindsey has said that Glasya said, the demon lords could well pay us a visit. Then, things could only get much worse."

"Wish spells or not, I'm going to continue going after the demons until there are no more on Earth," Monica declared.

The meeting was interrupted. A Message scrolled past Monica's eyes and one scrolled past Deiter's eyes.

He spoke up, "Hey, good news. I've just received a brief word from a contact in Berlin. Those people who were victims of Dr. Menninger's gas attack have fallen into comas. We should know the outcome in a few days."

Ashley commented, "I think I will be a good outcome."

Monica added, "That was from Katarine. She says her parents are also in comas. She took them back to their home to get some keepsakes when the gas cure was dropped over the city. She's fine, as are those who were taking the pills, but everyone else who became victims of the gas version are in comas." Again, she was interrupted by another Message spell.

"How curious. That is Katarine again. She said she finally understood her father's rather moronic ranting. Apparently, he was given a Wish scroll over twenty-five years ago by a close friend, Dietrich Von Eberhardt. Her father was trying to tell her that he needed to go back to their home to get it and use it to cure them. She found it and used it. Her parents are now back to normal, but her dad told her that Mage Dietrich did know that spell and urged her to go check up on her dad's old friend, who lives in Aachen. She's there now and just told me that the sixty-five year old man looks to be ninety at least and has died of old age. His wife is currently in a coma, and Katarine is taking her back to her parent's home for now."

"Ah ha!" Deiter exclaimed. "So we've found the source of these Wish spells."

"Don't jump to conclusions, Deiter," Ashley cautioned him. "Pam, you should pay that home a visit and see if you can sleuth what may have happened to the man."

"Tom and I'll go right now," Pam volunteered. "This is something I should be able to determine in short order. Just don't leave Tom and me out of whatever you're going to do next." With Lindsey's assurance, she and her husband teleported off to Aachen, where Katarine agreed to meet them.

Bergson spoke next. "We should go to our plane and see what all we can dig up on this Holy Crusade of the Pope's. I'm afraid with all that's been happening, we've rather lost touch with what they are doing."

"Right," Deiter declared, "and I'll see what contacts I have over there and what the current situation is. Someone should monitor the mag-news and regular news. Something might show up there."

"I'll take the news," Peaches volunteered. Several others joined her, monitoring several different stations.

She tuned to KMAG. ". . . claim that the victims of the demon gas attack will be cured. When asked what that meant, the spokeswoman said that, and I quote, 'both male and female victims will be restored to their original physical state.' At this time, millions in several areas of Germany are in comas once again. Doctors suggest they will be under for a number of days, presumably as their bodies regenerate. No one is claiming responsibility for developing the cure at this time, though rumors suggest a microbiologist may be involved."

"Meanwhile," the reporter continued, "back home, this Dominus Malefic fiasco continues to explode. Despite officials claiming the evil wizard is long dead, reports of Dominus sightings continue to flood into many news stations, some as far away as Singapore. We do know Dominus did travel extensively around the world, as many wizards and witches often do, so one should not be surprised at the myriad sightings."

"Today, we have a special guest with us, ex-Senator Bart Marton. His daughter, Lisa, was one of the many victims of Dominus. Senator, good to see you again. Retirement seems to suit you."

"Good to be here, Bob."

"So tell us, how has this surprising development, the reappearance of Dominus Malefic affected you? It was your young daughter who was so badly mistreated by that man. How is she taking this terrible news?"

"Angry, Bob. There's no other way to put it. We depended upon our departments to take care of this vile man, and they let us down. So yes, I'm angry. I urge every parent to let their anger out as well. I'm not going to say anything about Lisa, for her own protection. Lord, he might go after her again. I'll say this, my daughter has married, has a good job, and given me several delightful grandchildren. But that's not why I agreed to be on your show, Bob."

"Why then?" the reported asked his follow up question, knowing full well what Bart would be saying. They'd carefully rehearsed the interview.

"Some of us have the means. I cast my own Wish spell on him."

"What?" exclaimed Bob, feigning total surprise.

"Yes, I purchased a Wish spell and used it. I assure you the magical spell detonated. You all know what that means. Dominus exists or the spell wouldn't have activated!"

"Incredible, Bart, just incredible. What did you wish for, if I can be so bold to ask?"

Bart smiled covertly. "I asked that he appear just as he had my Lisa done up. So now you're looking for a male wizard with those giant breasts, long hair, no arms, and wearing those exotic ballet type boots, bedroom boots I believe they are called."

"Wow," exclaimed Bob, "so you gave Dominus a taste of his own medicine."

"Indeed I did. But Bob, we both know some of his followers can also cast Wish spells. Some of them may go ahead and try to undo what I've done to him, so I'm here to ask other parents of his victims who have the means to purchase a Wish spell and use it to make Dominus pay for his crimes." The camera zoomed in on Bart's face as he said, "Don't Wish him dead. That's too good for him. Make him suffer as our daughters were made to suffer." The camera pulled back, a sure sign this interview was staged beforehand. Bob now appeared alone on the screen.

"Well, there you have it. You heard it first here. We contacted the Missouri Department of Magical Misuse to get their reaction to this startling revelation from Senator Bart Marton. Here is Leslie Traub, the head of the Missouri Department of Magical Misuse."

The face of Leslie appeared on the screen. She looked as stern as her voice! "Yes, Bob, we've all heard the revelation of Senator Bart Marton during your interview late last night. While we can sympathize with the Senator, we cannot and will not condone the misuse of magic. As we speak, he is being arrested and will face severe charges involving the misuse of magic. Let me be perfectly clear. Vigilante justice is not and never will be condoned in our country. Anyone who does what the Senator has done will be tracked down and arrested. Using a Wish spell in this manner is not only a terrible and illegal misuse of magic, it also lowers the caster to the same evil level as Dominus was!"

She continued, "Look, Dominus is long dead. True, what has happened to the physical remains of Dominus is unknown at this time. Authorities are investigating the grave robbing incident, and those responsible will be apprehended and tried." Once more, the camera zoomed in on her, a sign she'd gone over this interview carefully beforehand. "I'll let you in on a very little known fact, Bob. The thing we knew as Dominus was actually a clone. The real Dominus, who continues to remain entirely anonymous, is and always has been a valued, productive, honest member of society, who had absolutely nothing to do with and no connection to this raving, insane clone. He had no part in the clone making process, and the man who did is long dead as well. As you should know, Bob, clones have been known to go insane. Further, given this vital fact, any attempt to use his DNA to re-clone him is doomed to failure because of the fact he was a clone to begin with. Clones of clones almost never survive the process. So Bob, all this talk of Dominus rising from the dead is simply Halloween gossip. It is a physical impossibility. If you doubt me, check the spell details in your Grade Spells books, under Clone Spell."

As the camera zoomed out, she wrapped up her interview, "So let me remind your viewers, anyone using a Wish spell as Senator Marton has done will be subject to the fullest prosecution under the law for misuse of magic."

Bob returned full-screen. "Now that is quite a revelation. Dominus Malefic was a clone! And yes, I did check my spell book as Leslie suggested. Her point is valid. So if someone stole his body and re-cloned it, the results must have been far less than they had hoped for. Stay tuned next hour. I'll bring in several authorities on the Clone spell and discuss what may have happened if someone did try to re-clone the Dominus clone. Also, I'll have several authorities who will discuss this surprising new detail, hopefully casting more light on just what caused this clone to go so berserk. All that and more next hour." The station flipped over to commercials. Cleverly, Peaches managed to record most of the report and sent an email to Monica, attaching the MP4 file to it.

Just then, Ashley sent her a Message.

Turn to the Vatican Channel. They've some key news. Ashley.

Peaches did so, but quickly cast her Understand Language spell, since she didn't speak Italian. She got in on the tail end of the broadcast.

"So in summary, Pope Pius is asking all those who have volunteered to join his Holy Crusade to eliminate all Muslims everywhere to join the mass blessing to be held on October 30, 2200 at Stadio Euganeo di Padova, just north and west of downtown Padova. He will give each recruit his personal blessing. The Holy Crusade will be launched from Padova on the 31st. This announcement will be repeated at the top of each hour until then." Once more, Peaches made a recording of this, sending it to several others, including Monica.

***

Meanwhile, Pam and Tom met with Katarine just outside an apartment complex on Altdorfstrasse just off Kapellenstrasse and not too far from one of the local hospitals. After hasty introductions, Katarine explained, "He's still inside. I've notified the city morgue, and they will take care of his body, but who knows when. They're still collecting bodies from the riots days ago. This way."

Dietrich Von Eberhardt was more of a recluse, collecting all kinds of books and papers. He didn't own a computer or a cell phone, which Pam thought highly unusual. Katarine led them into the main living room, where his body still sat in a chair at a work table. Papers and books lay strewn about the place. Quills and ink sat atop many papers, but Pam recognized them immediately as just what one needed to create a scroll to hold a magical spell. The most important ingredient, the paper, was not present. One glance at the man verified Katarine's statement. He looked ninety not in his late sixties.

"Okay, sleuthing time," she declared.

Tom ushered Katarine out of the room, "We best leave her do her work undisturbed. She's the best at this."

Pam focused and began perceiving the residue of magical energies in the room along with the physical details present. Had Bergson been present, he may well have attempted to hire her as a WIT team member. She was that thorough and good. A long half hour passed before she sat back from her squatting position on the floor and got up. "You can come in now. I've discovered much and even some mysteries."

As soon as the two joined her, Pam explained, "You're correct. He was forced to write Wish scrolls until his body aged so much that it died. I believe that he wrote twenty-three of them before he died, though the last one might not have been successful. I found traces of demon presence here as well. Look here; he scratched out a couple of words. Das ist nicht richtig. Translation: this isn't right. I think partway through his ordeal, he realized what he was being forced to do wasn't right. Here, he scribbled 'fehler,' which means error. If I'm not mistaken, he's telling us he introduced some error in some of the scrolls, probably designed to ensure they will fail when used."

"That's not all. I think he was trying to tell us something as his body failed him. Look at this, barely legible, probably hadn't the strength to dab the quill into the ink bottle. I've enhanced it with my cell phone. It's a phrase, I think. Heilige Nacht des Dämons Steigt. Translation: Holy Night of Demons Rising. I'm pretty sure that was the very last thing he wrote. Question is, what does it mean?" Pam declared, firing up her computer.

Tom beat her to it, calling out, "Mag-Googling it now, dear." Katarine looked over their shoulders, watching the husband and wife team tracking down the lead, chatting between each other, oblivious to her presence. After a half hour, he said, "Agreed?"

"Yes. Agreed. This must be what he's trying to tell us," Pam declared definitively. "We have to let the others know about this at once! Back to Monica's now!"

After Pam and Tom returned, Lindsey gathered everyone together to hear what the duo had uncovered. Needless to say, no one was pleased to hear that there were potentially twenty-three Wish scrolls in the hands of the demons. However, that some may be booby trapped went over well. Presuming they had already used two or possibly three, that left twenty of them out there, any one of which could prove disastrous.

"Now what is really vitally important is his dying message to us: Holy Night of Demons Rising," Pam explained.

"But what does that mean?" asked Lindsey.

"We asked that question immediately," Pam continued. "Tom and I split the searching up so we could figure it out faster. We believe we have worked out what Dietrich was trying to tell us. There's a very rare alignment of planets and stars of a certain constellation that occurs around every three thousand years or so, but because of stellar movement, the star pattern of the alignment does vary slightly. We aren't sure just which planets or star constellations because the ancient documents are in pretty bad shape. Many have put forth their suggestions and most don't agree with each other. Anyway, what is important is that in ancient Babylon, they called this alignment the Holy Night of Demons Rising, a time when the ether connecting the Abyss to Earth is at its thinnest, allowing faster and easier travel between the planes. It is calculated to occur again on October 31, 2200, beginning around 7 am, GMT, that's Greenwich Mean Time, the local time in England. The event lasts twenty-four hours."

Tom concluded, "Gang, I'll bet anything the demons know this and are planning something really big on Halloween!"

Peaches spoke up, "How weird is that? Pope Pius is launching his Holy Crusade on the 31st! Weird or what?"

Bergson added to the discussion, "Well, there certainly is a huge army gathering outside of Padova! Satellite imagery shows perhaps a million on the ground. The place is densely packed. The stadium parking lot is wall to wall people, as are many local farm fields in the area. Chrissy has been able to pin point the tent where Pope Pius is scheduled to bless the Holy Crusaders. It's smack in the middle of the stadium grounds."

He continued, "I just don't understand why the leader of my church, Pope Pius, would order the extermination of an entire people, just because they have a different religious view. Mind you, I'm not a devout Catholic, but my folks were. This is like something out of the Dark Ages, not the twenty-third century. Yet, there it is right before my eyes: millions ready to swarm into the Middle East with murder as their objective."

Kelly griped, "And we can't stop millions of well-armed fighters and wizards. No way. So Deiter, what's the plan now?"

Everyone glanced around, looking for Deiter, but he wasn't there! Lindsey called out his name and then fired off a Message. A second later, a breathless Deiter popped into the room. "Er, sorry about that. I was, well sort of on a spy mission of my own. Took a look see inside the Vatican, peeking from above." He added that last phrase so that his Rodents would understand what he had been doing, a half-teleport and peering back into the world from above, something he and Pam had discovered when they were in magic school.

Lindsey, looking annoyed with her husband, stated dryly, "I hope invisibly so."

He cracked a smile. "Of course. No one saw me. It took a long time. That place is huge, but I found their battle planning table. They're going to launch a three-prong offensive. One group will land in Morocco and sweep across North Africa, wiping out every Muslim as they go. The second group will land in Egypt and sweep across Arabia and on into Iran. The third group will start at Istanbul and sweep down through Turkey into Syria and so on. The date of the initial sweep is October 31. Not a bad piece of sleuthing, if I do say so myself." He sat back with a proud look on his face.

Ashley spoke up, "We already know that and why he's chosen that date. You missed the most important part of the meeting, Deiter Cross."

His smug look vanished. "Okay, someone bring me up to date, please? I'm sorry I was late."

At that instant, magical energies blazed, taking everyone by surprise. Monica heard the spoken words,

341

unfortunately. "I wish this new Dominus Malefic's body be permanently modified to look like what he did to my daughter, Melissa Blackhawk." Monica's world turned utterly black. Nevertheless, she felt the tight restriction of a corset around her waist, felt her dress vanishing, and felt suddenly very top heavy. Instinctively, she tried to rub her eyes with her upper arms, but felt nothing. Then, she heard gasps from those around her.

Amanda's voice called out, "Call Leslie. I'm tracking now." The Apache's wand waved and she vanished from the room.

"Not again!" That was Pam's voice. "Get her covered up."

Monica cast See Through Another's Eyes and saw herself through Pam's eyes. "Well, someone please get this corset off of me. I'm fine otherwise. Can't see. Probably glass eyes."

"I've got you," Bergson put one arm around her while his other held her dress in front of her body, hiding her somewhat. "Damn those demons!"

"Does this make nineteen Wish scrolls left?" Peaches asked.

Monica also heard Ashley whisper to Deiter, "This is all your fault. I told you, but you didn't listen. It's happened again and is likely to happen even more times."

Now, Monica understood. Ashley had probably had a Diviner's premonition that by making the demons and the world believe that taking out the SS men and Dr. Menninger was Monica's idea, a connection to Dominus Malefic would arise, just as it had. That one of his devout followers, Mr. Black would dig up his dead body and try to resurrect him would certainly come to light, opening old wounds. Some would go to any means to get what they believed was justice. Hence, Monica's predicament.

"Honestly, I'm in much better shape than I was the last time. The upper arms weren't much use. I can see through other's eyes so I won't be blind all the time. But Bergson, we should get me to my room and find some clothes that'll fit. Back soon. Don't do anything without me." *I have to sound brave for everyone's sake, especially Bergson's!*

"You sure you can walk?" he whispered.

Monica changed her spell's target and used his eyes. "Yes, I'm seeing through your eyes now. Keep looking ahead so I don't trip. Yes, bring my dress with you. I can magically alter it or Crystal can. Really, I'll get by okay, dear." She sensed his intense worry for her well-being and did her best to keep him calm.

Crystal followed right behind them. Once in her bedroom, Crystal said, "Well, Bergson, I hope you like giant knockers. Monica, I'll try to reduce them, but with a Wish, it might not work."

"I know. It didn't last time, but give it a try before you alter my dress. And Bergson, see if you can undo this corset. It's not as bad as the other one was, but I certainly don't need it or the black nylons."

Ten minutes later, Crystal had Monica's dress magically altered to fit her much larger bust. Her attempt to reduce their size failed completely. "There, how's she look to you, Bergson?" Crystal asked.

"She looks beautiful, but Monica, I swear if I ever get my hands on one of those Wish scroll things, I'll wish those damned demons were dead!" Bergson swore angrily.

Monica smiled, "Dear, that's the one prohibition about Wish spells. You can't wish someone were dead, but you can wish for anything else. Well, there's also some arcane prohibitions about wishing across planes of existence and wishing harm to gods. So if you do, careful what you wish for. Me, I'm not into Wish spells, because frankly, I don't want to prematurely age. I've grown very fond of this body and this life, dear. And don't worry. I've already cast my Regeneration spell on myself. With luck, in a few days, I'll have eyes again. Don't think I'll miss the upper arms all that much."

"But I will. Damn it, this isn't right. No one should do this to anyone," Bergson griped.

Crystal reminded him, "Remember what Leslie said in her interview. She'll track the perp down and see he's severely punished. This is a gross misuse of magic, Bergson. Come on; let's get back to the meeting. I don't want to be left out of this either."

Bergson frowned, evidently not satisfied. "You go on ahead, Crystal. I'd like a private word with Miss Black." Crystal gave him a hard look, but decided not to interfere in Monica's personal affairs. She left the two alone in the bedroom.

"Miss Black," he said formally, "Once, perhaps an accident, but twice? That's not a coincidence. Why are these magic-using people going to tremendous expense to cast these debilitating Wish spells on you? What is your connection to that vile, evil Dominus wizard? Is he really dead?"

Monica sighed. *I knew this day would come.* Thanks Deiter, she thought sarcastically. "Karma, Alan, Karma. Please don't tell anyone besides our team what I'm going to tell you. I don't really have proper words to explain this, but I'll try. The best I can do is say that last lifetime, I was that evil wizard. And yes, everything you've probably heard about him is true and much more. The things I did, especially to women, are unforgivable. And yes, I was shot by a still unknown person. Hit me in the back of my head and exited to the front, taking most all of my face with it. That body died instantly. Some follower dug up the corpse and tried to resurrect it. Long story, it failed miserably and I ended up with this body. Karma got me. I've paid for my crimes with my life. People can change; I have to believe that. This whole new lifetime, I have devoted myself to helping others, to do the right thing for everyone."

She went on, "If I could go back in time and undo all the evil I did last lifetime, I'd do it without any hesitation, but we both know that once you do something, it's done. You can't undo it. Yet, you can stop doing the bad actions, do what you can to repair the damage done, and move forward along a better path.

"Alan, I already told the Senator I forgave him for what he did to me, just after he cast the spell. When he comes to trial, I'll appear and plead for mercy for him. I've no idea who just cast this one on me, but I think Leslie will discover who did. When I know who did it, I'll forgive them and also plead their case when it goes to trial. What I did to those women isn't forgivable, and I accept that Karma is biting me in my ass, but I'm not about to let that interfere and make me veer away from who and what I am now or from my goals of helping everyone on Earth.

"So Alan, I can understand if you want to divest yourself from me and have nothing more to do with me. I can accept that. No one will think less of you for dumping me from your WIT team as the hot potato that I am. It was those damned demons who threw us together in the first place."

She sighed and concluded, "Just say the word and I'll disappear from your team and life immediately. However, I certainly will not stop my attacks on these cursed demons, not until every last one of them are back in their infernal Abyss where they belong. I would appreciate it if you wouldn't tell others beyond the WIT team about this. Otherwise, I'll have many more Dominus haters gunning for me before I can help get rid of these demons."

Bergson asked politely, "So who all knows about this?"

"Lindsey and her group and my friends at my mansion estate. And yes, it was Deiter and Pam who captured me last lifetime, ending my insane, evil rampage."

"We should tell Kelly and Miller all this," he declared. "As for the rest, don't be silly, woman. I've never run across a more honest, ethical person, so devoted to helping just causes as yourself. I don't know anything about Karma—raised Catholic. God forgives. Perhaps that is what has happened. Heck, I don't know and don't care. I'm not about to dump you from my team, unless you think you can't handle the action any longer. Seriously though, are you going to be able to continue? As you are now?"

"I can handle things, just going to be a bit more challenging, that's all. Come on. If you aren't going to dump me, we need to join the others. I'm worried about Deiter concocting another plan."

Bergson chuckled. "Okay then, Monica, let's see what they've in mind. I have some ideas, too. We need to stop this Holy Crusade before it destroys us all."

Chapter 21—The Holy Crusade

"It's so awful I can't even describe it!" Ashley shrieked. She'd had another of her premonitions. Deiter wondered what would happen if they did nothing and just allowed this Holy Crusade to sweep across the Mideast, wiping out jihadists and demons alike, more or less ignoring the fact that they would also be exterminating anyone practicing the Muslim faith. Ashley had done as he'd asked, but her blood-curling shriek got everyone's instant attention and recognition that the results would be beyond "bad."

Both Lindsey and Pam cast Calm spells on Ashley, but several were needed before she recovered her senses. At last she was able to say, "Deiter, we can't let that happen. If we do, the Earth will become one monstrous battlefield, filled with hideous demons and worse devils. We won't survive it."

Deiter, clearly frustrated and rubbing both hands through his hair, didn't know what could be done. "How? How are we to stop them? Miller's crowd estimating program suggests there's already millions around Padova ready to start the crusade. We can't take on that many."

"Well, have we tried to talk with Pope Pius and get him to cancel his crusade?" asked Pam, who believed fighting wasn't the answer to all problems. Reason was, if only someone could hold a rational discussion with this holy man. Obviously, the imminent threat to Rome was gone, thanks to Dr. Menninger. Perhaps, he would see reason.

"Tried that, Pam, a dozen different ways," Deiter lamented. "He's not taking any calls and rejects all Message spells. He won't take visitors either. Even my half-teleports failed. I triggered their alarm and protection spells, but being also invisible, I was able to get quick peeks around before they almost spotted me. We're really screwed."

Bergson spoke up, "Why not take the direct approach? He is supposed to give his personal blessing to the recruits. Miller's located where that's taking place, the center of the Stadio Euganeo di Padova. So we go there, finagle our way to the front of the huge mass and meet him directly when he gives us his blessing. Might have to talk fast though."

"But we don't have any authority in Italy," Peaches pointed out the obvious. "What do we do if he still won't listen to reason? We can't fight a million people."

"We certainly don't want to fight them," Lindsey interjected. "They are just doing what their religious leader has asked of them. We'd be no better than Dr. Menninger, if we harmed them."

Crystal tossed in her latest discovery. "Gang, I checked with my federal contacts. If you recall, I developed a way for them to identify demons using specific IR scans. I've just learned that somehow the demons who have been around these past nine years found a way to bypass that test and remain undetectable that way. However, they also tell me they have been going back over their satellite feeds, and all these new arrivals were picked up. Hindsight. Guy told me that the two large hordes so lit up the screen with images that he couldn't count them. He's confirmed that Dr. Menninger's attack has wiped out all traces of them in Slovenia. There are still some in Iran, though. I've asked him to check on northern Italy, but I've not heard back yet."

Lindsey queried, "So your older method only works on the new arrivals?" Crystal nodded. "I see. If the IR scans show nothing in northern Italy, then that's not to say demons are there, but that there could be some demons who have been on Earth sometime."

"That is correct," Crystal replied.

"Okay then, if the latest IR scan shows demons in northern Italy, we know we have to do something fast. If it shows nothing, we're merely in the dark and shouldn't assume there aren't demons there. Does this help any?" Lindsey asked.

"Yeah," Deiter replied, "we need the IR scans now. Come on, Crystal. I've some federal influence. Let's see if we can get realtime access right now! The rest of you, keep thinking of what we can do. Come on, Crystal; let's do this."

After he left, the group more or less disbanded. No one had any real notions of how to stop the coming Holy Crusade. Monica and the WIT team found themselves apart from the others.

"You know," Monica suggested, "I would like to go to this Padova stadium and check it out. See what is really there, besides a mass of people intent upon starting a holy war."

"But you can't see," whispered Chrissy.

"I'm seeing through Bergson's eyes right now. I'll get by okay. We need hard evidence, something irrefutable we can use to get through to these people who want to fight this crusade. We're not going to get it sitting around here," Monica answered.

Bergson took charge, "I agree. We're doing nothing by being here. Ordinarily, I'd say let's take the Stratosphere there, but that's a very long flight, and with all those people there, we'd be hard pressed to land anywhere near this stadium. I think we'll have to rely on Monica to get us there this time."

"But boss, she can't see, hasn't got any arms, and still has to wear those impossibly high heels," Chrissy stuck up for Monica.

"Chrissy, I can do this. I'll morph into another form, but I'll still be blind and need to see through your eyes. We have to get hard evidence and soon," Monica countered.

"Okay, you heard her. Gear up," Bergson barked his decision.

"You're doing what?" exclaimed Lindsey. Monica hastily told Lindsey where they were heading and why. Just in case something happened to her, others could come and bring the WIT team back home. "You can't see and haven't even upper arms now, Monica. This is foolish."

"I'll get by. I always do. I'm seeing through others eyes right now. I plan on morphing into a man to compensate for everything else except sight. I'll be fine. We need to find hard evidence," Monica explained.

"But I can't even get a Message through to you. You can't see it to read it," Lindsey cautioned.

"Point taken. Nothing I can do about that. I'll keep you up to date on what we find, if anything." With that, Monica turned to leave. Unfortunately, her world went utterly black again. The spell had ended. Hastily, she cast another one, using Lindsey's eyes to more or less find her way out of the room. Of course, then she was once more in the dark. *Maybe I can't do this.* She fought down the wave of panic threatening to sweep over her. *Silly. This is my home. I know every inch of this place. I just have to find the wall.* Taking tiny steps, she continued to move until at last she bumped into a wall. Feeling a bit more secure, she kept moving with her side just brushing the cold wall.

"Ah there you are," the friendly voice of Bergson entered her ears. At once, she cast her spell and saw herself. She was going the wrong direction. "You sure you can do this, Monica? I think you were heading to the kitchen."

"Alan, this is damned scarey. I won't pretend otherwise. Until you came, the world was blacker than black. Now I'm using your eyes. At least where we're going, there should be millions of eyes that I can use. I've got to do this, Alan, I can't quit now. Come on. A steadying hand would be really welcome."

***

"Incredible! Just look at the throng! I've never seen so many people packed so close together before. Damned near everyone is packing weapons!" Kelly exclaimed.

Monica had teleported them onto the Padova stadium grounds. What once was a parking area was filled with people chatting about the coming war. Carefully, the four maneuvered their way inside and were now standing on the grass playing field.

"One bomb and they'd all be taken out," Miller pointed out both softly and worriedly. "Boss, this isn't good at all. What if someone starts firing? Could be a bloodbath and a mass stampede."

"I'll get us out immediately, if trouble comes. The protection spells I put on you should keep a few stray bullets from harming you," Monica whispered back. "Come on. We should get closer to the golden tent."

Monica had morphed herself into a burly looking man, but still couldn't see, though she could walk normally and had hands. Of course, a simple Dispel Magic spell and she'd be back to being nearly helpless once more. This, she tried desperately to keep in the back of her mind, focusing on the job at hand.

"Look, there's a dozen Vatican guards there by the tent," Miller whispered. "I recognize their uniforms. If my data is right, the pope is supposed to conduct his blessings inside that tent.

"Hey, this is as far as you get. Line forms here. No cutting," a rough voice interrupted their slow forward progress toward the tent. The man was taller than Bergson and heavy set. He carried the latest in assault rifles and another combination grenade launcher. Dozens of ammo clips were strapped to his body, but from the thickness of his chest, Bergson surmised he was wearing a protective vest.

"Just getting a good look," Kelly pipped up. "Pope's going to bless us, right?"

"Yeah, you got that right. Then, we're off to kick some ass! Damned Arabs and Muslims. Heck, they kill each other nearly everyday in Iraq and Afghanistan. They suicide bomb folks trying to bury their dead. They even got kids blowing up themselves and anyone around them. I heard they blew up a market in Kabul yesterday. They ain't any better than the damned demons, if you ask me. They should have called for this Holy Crusade fifty years ago! Get rid of these vile beasts, these Arabs, these Muslim fanatics, these insane jihadists. The world don't need their kind. The only good Muslim is a dead Muslim. The only good Arab is a dead Arab, that's what I say. Most everyone here says so, too. Come tomorrow, it's time to exterminate all of them filthy cockroaches. Make the world a better, safer place to live."

Kelly couldn't help playing along with this opinionated man. "Yeah, that mad Dr. Menninger, he sure wiped a slew of them out."

"You can say that again! He's our hero around here. Hope they catch whoever murdered him. Worlds needs more like him, someone not afraid to kick these insane radicals' asses! 'Course, it was a good thing he killed all them demon creatures. Now me, I can't wait to unload this baby into one 'o them demon bellies. I hear they are fat bellies, too. I heard they turn to goo or something when you kill them. That's a good thing, cause you don't have to clean up the mess when the battle's done. I heard we're supposed to leave the dead cockroaches for the hyenas and vultures so they have something to eat. Now that's fine with me, cause these pitiful excuses for a human aren't worth the effort to dig a hole to bury them."

"Hey, they do turn to goo when they get killed. You're right about that one," Kelly continued to play along. "I know, cause I shot one. His foul body turned into some gray ooze. Smelled bad, too. At least I didn't have to bury the remains."

"You got one? Hey, that's great!" the burly man patted Kelly on his shoulder. "Ya gotta tell me all about it."

Bergson realized what Kelly was doing and took advantage of it. While the man was entirely distracted, he, Monica, and Miller studied the tent and guards.

"Oh crap!" Monica whispered. Bergson realized she'd uncovered something critical and moved the three of them back from Kelly and the fighter. "Those guards, the Vatican guards, they're demons, Cambions, morphed into human-looking bodies! I better Message Lindsey about this one. Something is rotten here—I just know it."

A bit later, a surprised Monica heard Ashley's voice inside her head! *Monica, Ashley here. Lindsey wanted me to tell you that Deiter and Crystal have discovered around twenty demons are near the center of the playing field of the stadium. Oh, Lindsey just told me that you already discovered that. Cool. Bye.*

Not long after that, Ashley's voice again rang in her head. *Monica, Deiter and everyone are on their way to you now. He's going to want to outright attack the demons, but please don't let him do that! He's not listening to me. That would lead to a bad reaction.*

Monica Messaged back, suggesting another approach. After ten minutes, Ashley appeared in her mind once more, *That's a whole lot better Monica. I'll relay that to the others. They are getting ready to teleport there now. Bye.*

Just then, something invisible bumped into Bergson who bumped into Monica and Miller, startling them. Deiter instantly became visible. "Er, sorry about that. Finding you four was a bitch! This crowd is impossibly dense. Is that them? The demons?" He didn't wait for Monica's answer, but cast his own See True spell. "Yep. That's them. Come on; let's attack them now. Help is coming."

"Whoa, Deiter. We're doing nothing of the kind just yet," Monica barked in a very commanding tone. "Look, you want to start a mass panic? Here's what the WIT team is going to do and what we need *you* to do, what with all your international connections." She whispered her plan to him.

"Heck, Monica, that's a far better plan. Okay. I'm on it. This had better work!" Deiter replied, promptly vanishing via a Teleport spell.

Monica, still looking like a burly fighter, moved up to the still chatting Kelly and the tough fighter. "Hey guys, what would you two do if you got up to that tent and found demons had infiltrated the Vatican guards?"

Kelly was about to take a stab at what he thought Monica wanted to hear, but the other man named Sam beat him. "Heck, I'd let everyone around me know and we'd open fire, filling them with lead!"

Kelly added, "Yeah, and try not to hit people, just the demons."

"Right. Aim for the filthy demons," Sam added.

"Well, I just heard some demons were going to raid us tonight when the pope begins his blessings. Spread the word. Tell everyone to be on the lookout for demons," Monica whispered, as though this was top secret information.

"You got it! Come on, Kelly; we have to let everyone know." He and Sam moved off a bit, whispering the news to many others. Monica smiled. So far, so good.

A half hour passed. Already, the crowd around them was buzzing. Her hinted message was spreading as rapidly as women's gossip, precisely what Monica counted upon happening. Ashley's voice again appeared in her head. *Okay. Everyone's all set. When do we do it?*

Monica replied with a simple Message.

Wait until we go into the tent to get the pope's blessing. If the pope isn't a demon, we must protect him. Can't have him getting injured. Monica.

Now they could only wait. Twice, bottles of water were handed out and passed around, along with wrapped foot-long sandwiches. Monica couldn't help but wonder who was providing the food. At last, the Vatican guards began ushering people into the tent. Loud cheering broke out spontaneously. The Holy Crusade was about to start.

Kelly and Sam rejoined the trio. "Hey we're next," Sam pointed out. Those in line in front of them had already been ushered into the golden tent. They spotted glimpses of the blessed recruits exiting by one of three ways out the rear of the tent. Slowly the line progressed until the five were at the tent's entrance, closely guarded by two Vatican guards, well armed.

Inside, a voice said, "Next," and the five entered. Ahead of them, a dozen other men toting all manner of automatic weapons stood in line before the gilded throne on which the purple robed Pope Pius sat, blessing each fighter as they approached him. Now they could hear him speaking. "Take the door on your right." The men obeyed, leaving by the right exit. "Take the door on your left." The next man made the cross sign, bowed, and headed out that way.

Monica cast her See True spell. It took all her self-control not to gasp aloud. The pope was a Cambion demon!

354

Baron Jamal in fact! Monica sent a one word Message to Lindsey, "Now." Then, she cast her powerful Dispel Magic spell. She felt an unknown power boost, one that greatly aided her spell's effectiveness.

"What the bloody hell?" exclaimed Sam. He saw the gray skinned demon sitting on the throne wearing his pope's robes. He saw the two guards to either side were also Cambion demons, as well as the two at their sides! "Demons! The demons have killed our Holy Pope! Die fiend! Die!" Sam screamed and opened fire.

The WIT team acted. Miller and Kelly fired at the two guards at their sides. From two feet away, the guards had no chance to avoid the enchanted bullets that tore through their bodies. Bergson fired at the guard on the right side of the pope, while Monica shot her giant volley of Magical Acid Missiles at Baron Jamal. Once more, she felt a surge of unexpected power behind her spell. The noise inside the tent was deafening, but Sam unloaded his entire clip at the three demons in front of him.

Outside, Lindsey cast her Dispel Magic at the many Vatican guards. Like Monica, she experienced an unexplained power boost to her spell. Instantly, the eighteen guards now appeared in their true forms, Cambion demons. Deiter, the Rodents, and Monica's friends opened up on them, joined within seconds by hundreds of others. Lindsey and Monica only just barely got protective walls of force up preventing the spray of bullets from entering the tent proper, though the front side was shredded by all the gunfire.

The combat lasted barely two minutes before the last of the demon bodies turned into the grey goo. Monica and Ashley knew this was the critical moment, and they prayed that Deiter wouldn't mess this one up. Considering there were millions around here, all about to panic, and all armed with powerful weapons and spells, the situation could well degenerate into the worst disaster imaginable.

Deiter did a Deiter. He was known for slightly goofing up a spell. For example, when he used the Disarm spell to help capture the pack of Death Stalkers, instead of adding the name of the person he wanted disarmed, he left that out, resulting in what others jokingly named a Mass Disarm spell. His friends called it "Doing a Dieter."

Deiter cast a Mass Dispel Magic spell, again aided by an enormous power boost that came from a source unknown. Monica's body returned to her true form and the world went utterly black again. Hastily, she cast another spell so she could see out of Bergson's eyes.

Then, Deiter cast a Magnify spell. A giant Deiter now towered two hundred feet tall, dwarfing everything and very visible to the millions pack in around the large stadium. Even his voice was magnified, so that those close to him heard his voice at a comfortable volume, while those nearly a mile away still heard him as though he was standing beside them.

"I am Archmage Deiter Cross, States Department of Justice, USA. The demons have long ago killed Pope Pius and have been impersonating him. Cambion demons took the form of Vatican guards. The demons here in Padova are now dead. Please remain calm." He cast a Calm spell, but his team members who were scattered around were already doing so as fast as they could.

"This whole idea of a Holy Crusade has been a sham, a demon plot to get you all killed or worse, abducted into the Abyss. I know that you came here to fight demons and you still want to fight demons. So let's go fight the demons. All of you who wish to continue the fight against the demon invasion are to report as soon as possible to the Italian Department of Magical Misuse in Rome. They will give you your marching orders as we head into the Middle East to eliminate any remaining demons on our world. So time to either go home or to Rome. Let's have an orderly evacuation in case the demons retaliate on us. We're packed in like sardines right now, sitting ducks, as a friend of mine just said. Get going. Get to safety or to Rome. Let's carry this fight to the demons!"

With that, he canceled his spells, returning to normal size where he was standing some fifty feet from the golden tent. "Okay Ashley, how was that?" he asked.

She replied, "That has the best chance of working, Deiter, as I said. I hope it works, but get ready to get the heck out of here if it doesn't! Oh, Pam's Messaging me." Pam was invisible, flying high above the stadium. "She says the crowd at the edges are starting to disband and leave. Good sign."

Inside the tent, Bergson kept a secure arm around Monica. Sam came up and gasped, "What the hell happened to her? Is she blind? No arms?"

"Demons got me. I'm fine, Sam. Good shooting. Did you get your demons? Did they turn into goo?"

He puffed up, "Damned right I did! Turned to goo, just like you said they would. 'Course had a lot of help. I'm heading to Rome as soon as I can get out of here. Say, I wonder what happened to the others who went out the back three doors?"

"Don't know. Why don't we go see?" Monica suggested. "Lead me, Bergson, please."

The five checked the back exits. "Hold on. I sense magic here," Monica suddenly cautioned them. She cast a spell and three glowing arches appeared. "Gate portals. I've heard of them. I bet one of these leads straight into the Abyss, but perhaps the others lead to where they planned to assemble the crusading army. Man, I hope they haven't laid a trap for them there! Let's find Deiter at once."

Outside the tent, they found Deiter surrounded by over a hundred witches and wizards. "Yes, I'm from the States Department of Justice. Brought along lots of extra support. We found out about this diabolical plot thanks to Miss Monica Nicole Black and the best WIT team in the US. Oh, here they come now."

"Deiter, a word with you, privately," Monica whispered. He backed out of the swarm to her side.

"Look, they were sending the recruits through magical Gate Portals at the rear of the tent. I'm worried that it's a trap. You should take some and see what's happening at those three assembly sites for the planned three-pronged attacks."

"Oh crap! Okay, on it. Got lots of help now." He turned back to the large group of compatriots. Shortly after that, three large groups vanished, heading off to check out the three sites.

Just then, magic flashed and Glasya appeared, wearing her most seductive red satin gown, matching low heels, and long nails. "Hi ya. Looks like you've got the explosive situation under control."

Monica said, "I suspect you had a hand in it."

"Caught! Guilty! Honestly, I just could not resist. So exciting, so entertaining," the devil princess replied coyly.

"So it was you who boosted my Dispel Magic spell?" Lindsey asked.

"And Deiter's and Monica's. Look at it this way, I have everything to gain from seeing the demons defeated here. Now after such an exciting time, I wonder if there are any men who want a hot time with me tonight? You up for a romp, Kelly? Bergson? Rats, Deiter's off again. All well, perhaps another time then? Keep track of Dr. Fritz. See ya. Good job, by the way." With that, she promptly vanished, leaving behind a faint trace of sulfur.

"Well, I'm willing to accept her power push. How about you, Lindsey?" Monica asked.

"Ordinarily, I want nothing to do with devils, but this time, well, she has a point. It was in her interests to help out. Oh, Pam says the crowd is rapidly departing. I think it is safe for us to head home."

"Grab a hold of me, and I'll take us home," Monica suggested. A minute later, she was back in the safety of her own mansion home.

"I need a long, hot bath!" Miller declared. "Kelly, come wash my back."

"You don't have to ask twice," Kelly replied, following after her.

"Come on, big boy. Thanks for helping me tonight. I don't think I could have done it on my own, not like this. Crap. Spell's gone again. Bergson, you can't imagine what it is like to see nothing but utter blackness."

"I have you. I'll be your guide. You've done more than your share tonight, Monica. Want your back scrubbed?"

"You bet and a whole lot more. I seem to have misplaced my hands." Both chuckled.

Chapter 22—Halloween Treat and Trick

"Wake up Mom! It's Halloween," Rob jostled her, ignoring Bergson beside her. "We're still going Trick or Treating, right?"

Bergson sat up, keeping the covers over his lower body and all of Monica's. "Yes, yes, but not until we have supper. I know, early supper. Don't want you on a sugar high, buddy," she replied. "Oh, my eyes are regenerating. I can see tiny bits of light this morning."

"Monica, that's good news. So Rob, you ready to go out tonight?"

"You bet! Misty has made me the coolest ghoul costume ever. Mom, wait til you see it. Oh, Mandy wants me. Gotta run. Get up. The day will go faster." Rob scampered out of her bedroom.

"Best help me up a bit. Kind of awkward for me now, Alan," she whispered.

A half hour later, the pair joined the throng for breakfast. The dozen children chatted about which houses to visit and whose costume was the best. Eating in gulps, they soon finished and dashed off.

Without any warning, magic flashed and Monica heard, "I wish what I did to Monica was undone." Suddenly, Monica's eyes and upper arms were restored. Pam spoke up, "Good. Leslie and Amanda tracked down the man who used the Wish spell on you, Monica, and made him undo it. Looks as though that worked."

Raising her upper arms about, Monica said, "Yes, just fine. Please tell them thanks from me. I'll chat with them later on." Pam nodded and fired off some Messages, before sitting down to have breakfast and relay some news.

"The Padova crowd is totally gone, but the mess they left behind will take weeks to clean up. Someone found the dead bodies of Pope Pius and two dozen guards down in the Holy Crypts area. Guess now they have to elect a new pope. Deiter says that all those who were gated to the three staging areas are A-okay and on their way home. He doesn't know if that was a trap or not, only that no demons showed up. He's in Rome now, helping them work out an effective strategy to pursue the demons remaining in the Middle East and likely Iran. More later, he says. Ashley has a good feeling now; she thinks we have averted the coming disaster. I guess after tonight, we'll know for sure. Now I personally don't believe in such magical conjunctions and all that, but we'll see." Pam felt very talkative this morning, and Monica enjoyed listening to her chat and seeing the world around her again.

Kelly asked, "Boss, how about the day off? Miller and I, we want to visit this pub in downtown St. Louis. She says they are famous for their Halloween parties."

"Go, you two. Take the day off. If anything critical comes up, I'll get a hold of you. We all need to catch our breaths. I don't think this is over, but we'll see," Bergson replied, pleasing the pair, who left shortly after that, taking the armed Rover.

He turned to Monica, "I wondered how long it would take for those two to get together. I'm shocked that it took three years. They are well-suited, don't you think?"

Monica laughed. "You are asking the wrong person. I'm about as ignorant of such things as anyone could be."

"Here you are," Misty interrupted the two. "I just heard from Kelly that you're taking the day off. Is that right?" Monica nodded. "Well then, could you please watch the dozen kids around here today, at least until supper? We're having it a 4:30 so the kids can get ready and be out the door by five."

"Sure. You have been extremely generous watching them these many days. It's long past my turn. Bergson, we're on kid patrol today. Where are they at now, Misty?"

"Playroom, where else? I swear they've got some candy horde hidden around here and are bouncing off the walls on sugar highs right now," she teased and then hurried off to get some more wand orders filled.

"Lead on. This should be interesting, but I should warn you, I'm not particularly good with kids, especially ones using magic," Bergson cautioned her.

The pair entered the large basement playroom filled with game tables, consoles, doll houses, and many toy boxes. A dozen boys and girls whose ages varied from six to fourteen stopped what they were doing and rushed over to Monica.

"Hey, it's Monica and Bergson," Rob called out.

Kathy asked, "Does it hurt if I touch them?" By that, she meant Monica's upper arms.

"No, go ahead and feel them. They are just like yours, only the rest of my arms aren't there."

"Just like Susanne and Sofia," Rob pointed out. "Misty said you're with us today."

"Yes, it's way past my turn. So what should we do?" Monica asked.

Kathy suggested, "Teach us how to dance. You know, the formal kind, because we're going to have to know how when we go back to school. I don't want to look like a fool on the dance floor at Thanksgiving. Neither does Rob or any of the others. Besides, the littler ones can learn and get a head start on it for when they to go to school. I know, they are supposed to teach us that in PE class, but we really don't want to be embarrassed in front of the whole class, as if we're bumpkins or something. So please, you've just got to, Aunt Monica, please. We all want to learn, don't we?" Thankfully, she finally came up for air, and many other older heads nodded. The smaller children looked bored with it.

"Okay, Kathy. That sounds like a perfect thing to do today. All those who want to learn formal dance, over there to the open area. Those who don't, go back to having fun, just no running around the mansion. All right?" Heads nodded and four smaller children dashed back to their own games.

"Wait. The girls need to go put on their heels. It's much harder to dance in heels, isn't it, Aunt Monica? We should be practicing like we will be when we actually do it," Kathy insisted.

Rob complained, "But you already look really pretty, Kathy."

"She's got a point, Rob. Give the girls a few minutes to get their heels. Yes, it is more difficult to dance in heels. Meanwhile, Rob, get the boom box, please." Turning to Bergson, she asked, "You do dance, don't you?"

He flushed. "Two left feet."

She chuckled, "Well, it's time you learned. The kids will appreciate you learning with them."

"What have I gotten myself into this time? Can I go fight demons instead?" he jested. Monica batted him playfully with her upper arm.

When the girls lined up, proudly wearing their first somewhat tall heels, Monica reminded the boys, "Remember, the girls take smaller steps in their heels. The higher the heel, the smaller their steps. When they're as tall as mine, steps are very small. So boys, pay attention to your partner."

Time flew by and early dinner came, leaving the older children wanting more lessons. Even Bergson enjoyed himself, especially once he got the hang of leading. They watched the excited children gulping down the food only to dash off to get into their costumes. Around five, Tim arrived, bringing Wanda, and their children with them.

"Wanda, you and I need to have a long talk, as soon as I can get free," Monica whispered to her.

"And we need to talk to you," she replied.

"Look at me," Susanne interrupted. "I'm going as a princess and Bill is my Prince Charming. I have to wear these heels so I might as well be a princess, since she would wear them, don't you think so, Monica?"

"Me, too," Sofia added, not wanting to be left out. "Len is my prince. This way, we won't look so weird, right?"

"I think you both look fabulous and being a princess is a brilliant idea. Well done, both of you," Monica replied, pleasing the girls. Bill and Len, with their arms around their princess, led them off to find their friends.

"Honestly, Monica, do you think we and my girls will be able to walk well enough to do all this trick or treating?" Wanda whispered, hoping Tim wouldn't hear.

"As long as we have a supporting arm, I think we'll be fine. We'll try to avoid going down steep hills." Before long, the army of creatures appeared en mass, along with parents following behind. Enya stayed behind to hand out candy at the mansion.

"Are my princesses ready?" Tim asked.

Both girls giggled. He'd rigged up a collection bag for each girl, slinging it over their shoulders so it couldn't fall off. Smiling, off they all went. As they walked out of the mansion by the circular flower garden, Monica was surprised to see Susanne and Sofia casting Light spells. Sofia said, "See, we can cast spells any way. We're providing the light so we all can see where we are going, but we'll turn them off when we go up to a house."

Monica commented to Wanda, "Amazing. Your girls are incredibly mature for their age."

"This whole mutation thing has actually forced them to grow up faster than I might have wanted. It's as if they didn't have much choice. Still, I'm very proud of them."

"Are we going to go to a hundred houses this year, mom?" Rob asked as they approached their first one.

"We will see. We don't want to be late for Enya's big party at eight, do we? You know she always makes the greatest cupcakes."

"Oh yeah, right. Forgot about that. Say, maybe we could dance after that, like we learned to do today." Rob rang the door bell. "Trick or treat."

Later, Rob called out, "Hey slow down guys. We're leaving our beautiful princesses behind." His thoughtful concern pleased Monica.

"Observant boy you have there," Bergson whispered to her. She smiled.

Time passed as did houses, while candy bags slowly filled. Part way through the long night, Bergson asked, "I meant to ask you if your feet are okay. I've heard that wearing really high ones hurt your feet."

"We put in these gel pads. Without them, you bet you would be carrying me about now. I let Wanda know about that tip when I first met her. Sent over some samples. Still, by the end of tonight, I could use a good foot massage, since I'm rather hard pressed to do that myself now, big boy."

By eight, the children were pooped and more than ready to be teleported home to sort out their candy haul and to dive into Enya's cupcakes. Enya had the large dining area decorated in Halloween decor, pumpkins glowing, and colored leaves in banners turned the rather sterile room into something akin to a banquet hall. After wolfing down several cupcakes, Rob took charge, "Party time! This year, we're going to have our own fancy dance. Miss Susanne, may I have the first dance? Mom, put on the music!"

Misty got the music started and soon even the adults joined the youngsters on the dance floor. Bergson whispered in Monica's ear, "The boys are all going after Susanne and Sofia."

She replied, "I see that. Their genetic mutations make them look much older than they really are, more fully developed. Still, I think it is doing wonders for their self-esteem. At least with all this dancing, the kids are burning off some of their sugar highs."

"Party pooper," Alan whispered back, a wry smile on his face. "I used to go trick or treating when I was their age. How about you? Go as a princess?"

"Nope. I missed out on all that. I sort of ended up with a twelve-year-old body this time. I'll have to tell you about that one day."

"Deal. Say, it looks like Tim has really taken a fancy to Wanda. They've not missed a dance yet."

"Interesting observation. Tim lost his wife and daughter a couple years back. He's not really gotten over it and hasn't dated since then, but now perhaps that's changing. From what I know of Wanda, she would be a good match for Tim. She is or was a magic school professor."

Bergson became serious, "With Wanda, is this the end of her magic using career? Or is it possible she can somehow compensate? I couldn't help notice that nearly all of your kind use wands, except you and Lindsey, but she also has that big pole sometimes."

"That's her staff of power. Lindsey is better than I am casting without saying the words aloud or using the energy boost from the wand."

"Energy boost?" he asked, growing curious.

"Nearly every user of magic must use a wand with very precise motions to funnel in the magical energies to make their spell work. It's a combination of intention plus proper sequence of command words plus proper wand action to combine them into what you see as a spell activation or detonation. Rare indeed is Lindsey who can cast every spell she knows just with her own intention and innate power. I've learned how to do that from her. During the sixth and last year of magic school studies, equivalent of a senior in high school, all students make an attempt to cast without using their wand or without verbally speaking the proper words. Hardly anyone is ever successful at it. And yet, Sofia and Susanne are able to cast a few of their spells this way."

"Incredible. Yes, their Light spells came in very handy tonight. Can anyone learn to cast spells? Is it like a professional musician in that they have to start learning as children or can adults dive right in and pick this stuff up?"

"Best talk to Lindsey about the first question. I simply don't know. I do know that adults have gone through magic schools, but I personally only know of one case who did."

Crystal called out, "Okay, kids. Last dance. Boys, let Bill and Len have the last dance with Susanne and Sofia. You can go over to Tim's place tomorrow and see them." Several boys grumbled, including Rob, but allowed the two grinning boys to have the last dance with the two girls.

Monica whispered to Alan, "Keep an eye on the older girls around here tomorrow. I bet you see sudden breast growths." Both stifled laughs.

"Boys will be boys," he added.

"And girls, girls," she added. They laughed once more.

***

After tucking Rob in for the night and kissing his forehead, Monica and Bergson headed to her giant bathroom and tub. "Allow me," he said softly, filling the tub. "Time for your foot massage."

"Heavenly, Alan, heavenly. You've my permission to do this every night!" The bath lasted an hour followed by a romp in her bed, after which both got an extremely good night's sleep.

In the morning, Monica struggled to sit up. "Well, the world is still here. I guess the demons haven't come flooding into our world after all. That's a positive sign."

"We're making progress," he replied. "Let me get you dressed. Then, I need my coffee."

When they joined the others at breakfast, already the kids had eaten and dashed off. While they were eating, Chrissy and Kelly joined them; both looked very alive this morning. "Morning, boss. What's on tap for today?" Kelly asked.

Bergson didn't get a chance to answer. Magic flashed and a tired looking Deiter appeared before them. "Back from the Middle East. Did an all-nighter."

"Sit down and have some breakfast, some coffee," Monica suggested.

He did. "Well, we can relax a bit, I hope. I have the Italian forces the task of coordinating the mop-up operation in the Middle East. No sign of Gisella or Jonellith anywhere and that has me plenty worried. We took care of their new baron who pretended to be the pope, but those two are still at large. Worse, they probably still have twenty Wish scrolls they can use. I really did expect they would have used them against us when we disrupted their Holy

Crusade. To be honest, I didn't think we'd come out of that one in one piece, but we did—"

Monica interrupted him, "So now you're wondering just what their plans for the Wish scrolls are, if not to prevent us from stopping the Holy Crusade."

"Astute observation, Monica. Precisely so. Granted, Pam believes some of the Wish scrolls will fail to work, but still with even ten scrolls, the damaged they could cause is enormous. And we have no idea where they are at. Scarey," Deiter admitted.

Bergson added, "And Crystal's detection method won't work on them since they've been on our world far too long. Right?"

"Right," Deiter said definitively. "We've no way to locate them. Shoot, they could be right here in St. Louis hatching some new and terrible plot, for all we know. Monica, can I ask you something?"

"Sure, what?"

"Glasya. Do you suppose it would hurt to ask her for a little more help? I mean without selling away our souls and all that."

Monica bit her lip for a moment before answering, though everyone around her paid very close attention to her. "Well, I do like Glasya as a person, that is, when she is just being a normal woman, if that can even be said of a devil. However, right now, she is definitely on a very critical mission. She did covertly aid us when we went after the Holy Crusade tent. Notice it was covert aid and not overt aid. I'm pretty sure she is still working constantly with Dr. Fritz to get his cure spread across Germany. From what little we've been hearing back here stateside, they still have about a quarter of the country to go. So I think it would be prudent not to bother her right now, Dieter."

"I kind of figured that, but I had to ask. Seems the powers that be are trying to promote me to the new head of the entire Justice Department. I don't know if I want that much responsibility. I'm more of an action sort of person," he admitted.

"I know what you mean," Bergson spoke up. "Same with me. Give me a good case to solve and I'm happy."

"Right. You get it. Well, I'm heading home. Maybe a bright idea will somehow enter my head while I sleep. Frankly, Monica, I'm scared of those Wish spells. Just one of them—well you both know better than most of us what one could do," Deiter explained.

"Get some sleep," Bergson agreed. "My team will put our heads together and see if we can find out where the remaining demons are at." Deiter thanked him and quickly teleported home.

"Guess that's our assignment for today, WIT team," Bergson announced. "Ideas?" No one had any. Just as they were preparing to get up and head to their Stratosphere and their equipment, Misty stomped in, looking rather infuriated.

"What's the matter?" Monica asked.

"Oh those girls. They are using their spells to grow their bosoms and then altering their dresses, trying to look like Susanne and Sofia. Honestly, Monica, can you put a stop to such nonsense?"

"I could try, but we both know it wouldn't do any good. Let them play around. It's part of growing up a witch. Just be glad that they aren't making their hair neon green or orange or purple."

That brought a laugh to Misty. "You're right. We did do dumb stunts like that when we were in school. Still, just to get the boys' attention? Honestly." She rose and headed back to her wand shop.

Smiling, the WIT team rose and headed for their Rover, which Kelly parked just outside their front entrance when he and Chrissy returned from the pub party last night. As the four were just getting into the Rover, Monica vanished completely! "What? Where did Monica go?" exclaimed Kelly, not amused by her antics.

"Maybe she forgot something," Bergson suggested. "Give her a minute."

Five minutes later, the very concerned trio headed back inside to look for her. "I thought you were off," Misty stated when Bergson entered her small shop. A second later, Misty sounded the general alarm, sending frantic Messages to everyone. Her Message spell to Monica failed to activate, meaning either she was dead or she was not on Earth.

Just as the entire group at the mansion gathered together to attempt to figure out what had just happened, a pale-faced Lindsey suddenly appeared near them in the dining room. "Guys, Deiter has vanished! I can't get a Message through to him! He just vanished while we were having tea and discussing what to do next!"

"Monica's vanished, too," Crystal took charge, "vanished while they were getting into the Rover. I can't reach her either. What the heck is going on?"

Lindsey slumped into the nearest chair, fighting back tears. She had so hoped that Monica could somehow help her find Deiter. That she was missing as well only meant one thing. Fighting to control her wildly swinging emotions, she said, "Wish spells."

"Oh crap!" Bergson gushed. "What can we do about that?"

One by one, they all slumped heavily into nearby chairs. Crystal said in a soft voice, "Not much, I'm afraid. I'm really worried we've lost both of them this time. Our spells only cover Earth. I'll bet anything they have been abducted and are somewhere in the Abyss."

Ashley suddenly appeared. She looked very distraught! "No word?" she asked. "Monica, too?" She slumped into a chair. "I did my Divination thing. It's—it's not good—bad really—no, awful, terrible. I can't even tell if they are alive anymore."

The petit potion maker, Enya commented, "Well, Deiter and Monica did lead all the disruption of the demons' many plans, so I'm not surprised the demons have used those Wish spells to take them out."

Professor Pam Betts suddenly appeared, white as a sheet. "Lindsey, I just heard! This is terrible. Oh no. Monica, too?" she added. Many nodded. "Darn it. At least, the demons can't use the Wish spells to wish them dead.

You can't use a Wish to kill someone. Some hope there, I think."

"But by now, they could have already just killed both of them, once they got them into the Abyss," Lindsey countered, expressing her worst fears, and doing her best to keep from breaking down entirely. She felt completely helpless to save her loving husband. While he often went off half-cocked, she knew he could usually take care of himself, but against these powerful demons and in the Abyss, he had no chance at all. Worse, he had no way to get home, even if he could somehow get free.

Pam knew she had to say something. "Look, if it were those powerful demons who took Deiter and Monica, then it's not too likely they want them dead. Last time, they incapacitated them and put them in the stasis bell jars on public display. I'd think they might be doing something like that this time."

"But how can we rescue them?" asked Bergson.

"I can open a Gate to the Abyss," Crystal volunteered, "but that's no good. We don't know where they are being held. It would be like someone arriving on Earth and looking for a friend—a needle in a haystack. I could try summoning up some lesser demons whose true names we know and see if they know anything about them, but the chances of that working are virtually none."

"Well, we know one thing for sure. They aren't on Earth at the moment," Pam declared.

***

Halloween night, a pair of dejected demons sat atop one of the pyramids in Egypt. Gisella griped, "I just don't understand how my plan went so wrong, Jonellith. I had every eventuality worked out on paper. Nothing was supposed to go wrong."

"Ah but it certainly has, Gisella," Jonellith replied, reluctant to speak sarcastically to the succubus. "Those two interfered again, hero Deiter and that infernal Monica woman. Jamal should have suspected someone would try to disrupt his Pope Pius act. He should have had hundreds of demons there, not just a few dozen. But I did see his point: the more demons present, the greater the chance of discovery. Still. . ." her voice trailed off into the night.

"Think there is any chance of salvaging this mess?" Gisella asked her best friend. "Be honest with me. Should I ask Demogorgon for his help and take a very back seat again?"

"Salvaging? To be honest, love, you're realistically back to square one, except that this time we have Wish spells. Speaking of Demogorgon, what are you going to do about your promise to him? After all, you made him a promise to deliver two million new recruits by tonight. Only a handful got sent before they disrupted Jamal's sorting at the stadium in Padova. You dare not go back on your promise. Heck dearie, he'll do unspeakable things to you for breaking your promise to him."

Gisella's body shook slightly and not from the cold atop the tall pyramid. "I know, I know. The only thing I can do, Jonellith, is to use a bunch of the Wish spells to get him his promised quota. At least then I will be on his good side."

Jonellith laughed, "Good side? Gisella, he doesn't have one!" Both laughed, though bitterly.

"Well, I better get started on the wishes," Gisella finally decided. She and Jonellith had split their precious scrolls evenly, though both had already used some. She opened one scroll, focused, and cast her wish. "I wish that a hundred thousand of my recruits in the Middle East and Iran were now at the Pleasure Fortress in the Abyss." Powerful magic flashed. "Well, that's working. Good thing I researched the quantity the spell could handle. I best give them time to move that group out. I bet Demogorgon is smiling now."

Jonellith grinned, imagining the scene in the Abyss, regretting she wasn't there to absorb the intense emotions these hundred thousand radiated upon arriving there.

An hour later, she cast the next spell. By one in the morning, she'd cast seven such spells, procuring seven hundred thousand hardline jihadists for Demogorgon. Only three more spells to go. She took out the next scroll and began casting once more. Unknown to her, Mage Dietrich Von Eberhardt realized these demons wouldn't let him go and would make him write Wish scrolls until he died of old age. Thus, partway through his ordeal, he began inserting small booby traps. Unknowingly, Gisella just triggered a particularly nasty one.

When the magical energies flashed, both Gisella and Jonellith knew something had gone very wrong! All traces of Gisella's large wings and horns vanished! She felt really funny, somehow different. "What's happened to me?"

"Gisella! Your wings—they're gone. Horns, too! What's happened to your body?" Jonellith asked, very much surprised, though not as much as Gisella.

"I don't know!" she exclaimed, feeling her head where her horns had been and then struggling to feel her backside where her lovely wings had been, only to feel absolutely nothing there. "They're gone!"

"Maybe if you morph into something and then back again, they'll reappear," Jonellith tried to suggest something positive. Without her wings, Gisella couldn't fly.

"Oh no! Nothing's happening!" Gisella shrieked. She knew a fair number of magical spells and attempted to cast each one. With each failure, her panic rose exponentially. At last totally desperate, she attempted to open a Gate to the Abyss. Even that failed utterly. Gisella fainted.

"There, there, it'll be all right," the soothing words of her friend roused the succubus.

"Jonellith! I've lost all my casting abilities and my wings! I'm doomed! I'm cursed! That damned Dietrich Von Eberhardt—he did this to me! I just know it!"

"He must have sabotaged the Wish scrolls. Heavens, don't use any more of them! Let's see if we can find out what he's done to you," Jonellith suggested.

For a succubus to lose all her spell casting abilities and her wings was unheard of anywhere. Worse, Jonellith began to think, she might not even be a demon any longer. She sniffed Gisella, trying not to attract her attention to what she was doing.

Gisella was too bright to fail to notice. "Smelling me? Oh gods, Jonellith. What? What?"

Jonellith swallowed hard, distancing herself from her once friend. "Your, your body—it's human. You smell just as the humans do. I'm *so* sorry, Gisella!"

Gisella shrieked. "What am I going to do now? Human? Oh gods, no! I'm helpless."

Jonellith knew their friendship had just ended. She wanted nothing to do with humankind, except to torture them and kill them. Gisella had now become a genetic enemy! "You still have your youth and great beauty. Perhaps, you can find a wealthy man or a powerful wizard who can cast a Wish spell and get him to give you the money to buy the spell or even cast it on you. We're close to Cairo. I think it best if you head into the city right now. Heaven help you if one of the Cambions comes by. If they see you, you're a goner!"

"Gods, Jonellith, you're right! Beautiful. Yes, I'm still quite good looking, I hope. Good idea. Give me some time to find and charm the right man and I'll get this undone. Whatever you do, don't use any more of those cursed scrolls!"

With that, Gisella hastily began climbing down the pyramid, cursing with each step. Flying up had been trivial, but going down like a human was both horrible and embarrassing.

Now alone on the pyramid and with all of the remaining scrolls in her possession, Jonellith pondered her next move. It was obvious this entire Grand Plan failed miserably. Only a few Cambions were left, mostly commanding the rag-tag armies of the jihadists and Iran. They wouldn't last long. Something stirred deep within her snake half. "Oh! It's time again. She was fertile and her clutch of eggs were primed and ready for fertilization. Sensing this, she opened a Gate to the Abyss and her solitary dwelling place.

Jonellith's dwelling was more like a cavern, but with walls that looked like some ancient gray stone castle walls. Quite long lived, she loved the stone castle appearance and constructed the inside of her cavern to look like a cosy dungeon, with numerous rooms. Her private bedroom or nest rivaled some exotic hotel's penthouse suite, luxury bedding, king-sized of course, blue satin sheets with a golden canopy over head. Other rooms contained centuries of accumulated objects, primarily from Earth cultures. She hung her new six automatic rifles in her trophy room, replacing the older swords and axes from that bygone era. She slithered into her study and dumped the remaining Wish scrolls onto her work table.

One by one, Jonellith studied each detailed marking that Dietrich made on the expensive paper. "Ah, this one is spoiled," she muttered and caused it to burst into flames. Casting the burning paper in the trash can, she picked up the next, sorting out the obviously damaged scrolls. That done, she compared the remaining ones in minute detail. She tossed out six more she couldn't trust, though she couldn't tell with any certainty if they were booby trapped or just flaws. After what happened to Gisella, she took no chances with these.

When she finished and felt confident the remaining Wish scrolls were the real thing, she had four left, a fact that pleased her significantly. *One for each of them and two for future needs. Now to make use of two wishes.*

She did a bit of housecleaning, making sure her bedding was ready for the breeding impregnation, which her body demanded happen soon. Next, she returned to her desk and began sketching out just the proper wording for her two wishes. Like any magic user, she knew full well the dangers of not being precise in the wording of a wish. If there was anyway for the wording to be misinterpreted, that was certain to happen.

Finally satisfied, she picked up the first scroll, chanted aloud the written script, then said decisively, "I wish Deiter Cross, my hero, be brought here to my soft bed in my sanctum room in the Abyss but with his arms and legs no longer attached to his body and with his body fully healed from the four separations." Magical energies flashed. She heard Deiter screaming from the next room and called out, "I'll be with you in a moment, Hero Deiter.

"Trouble is this time my hero is Monica Nicole Black and not so much Deiter Cross. Who would ever have figured that could happen? Well, she can't fertilize me, but she's such an incredible fighter that I simply have to have her here, too." Discarding the burned out scroll, Jonellith picked up the next one, unrolled it, and placed the paper with her second precise set of words next to it.

Again, she focused, ignoring Deiter's continuous screaming from the other room as best she could, and began the lengthy chant, slavishly following the written script. She then said just as decisively, "I wish my true hero, Monica Nicole Black, be brought here to my soft bed in my sanctum room in the Abyss but. . ." She was slightly interrupted by an even shriller scream from Deiter, though she tried hard to ignore his outburst, and continued, "under the influence of the Idiot Mind spell." Magic again flashed brilliantly and the scroll was burned out. Discarding that one, she slithered out of her study and into her sanctum room, quite pleased with herself. She had her new hero companion, albeit a woman, which she could perhaps make some adjustments to such a relationship, and almost a hero to impregnate her clutch.

Jonellith saw the head and torso of Dieter lying on the soft bed. His arms and legs lay in a heap on the floor beside the bed. Nearby the bed, Monica stood looking quite dazed and confused. Upon Monica's arrival, Deiter mostly stopped his panic screaming. As the naked, gorgeous, six armed demon moved silently into the room, Deiter turned his head and saw her. Above the waist, she looked like an extremely beautiful woman with firm but large breasts. Her brown straight hair draped over her upper shoulders, just barely hiding them. However, the additional four arms extending from her sides detracted from her "beauty" by human standards. Below her waist stretched a very long snake-like body some fifteen feet to its tip.

"Monica! Save me!" screamed Deiter.

A rather silly expression formed on Monica's face when she looked at the demon woman. "Oh how pretty. Nice arms. Can I have more arms, too? Good bed. Like beds. Deiter like bed?"

Deiter moaned. Instantly, he understood what the demon had done to Monica. He and the Rodents had made excellent use of the Idiot Mind spell on many occasions. He moaned because in that instant he realized Monica would be of no help whatsoever. Her mind was that of an idiot, super low IQ at best, wholly incapable of casting any spell or even thinking rationally. And he was completely helpless.

Chapter 23—The Nightmare

Jonellith slithered into the room, a huge grin on her face. "My heroes. Calm down, Hero Deiter. Act more like your companion Hero Monica. See, she's doing well. Yes, Monica, you may sit down on the bed."

"Just kill me, you sadist, you fiend!" Dieter yelled.

"In time, Hero Deiter. First, it's time for my eggs to be fertilized. So soon, Hero Deiter, we will mate, and you will fertilize my clutch. I always find a hero to breed with, always, though I admit it's been over a century since I last had a clutch. Once we've bred and my eggs are fertilized, then I will put your head on my wall so you can join your fellow other heroes, who have bred with me these past many centuries. Stop screaming. You don't need your arms and legs to breed. I'll do the work."

"You fiend. I'll die before I breed with you," Deiter shrieked, but he knew it was an empty threat. He couldn't even move, only turn his head slightly.

Monica spoke up. "Not die. Deiter. Pretty woman. She pretty. You breed her. Eggs come. Must be made whole. Women give new life. She very pretty. You be nice head. Can see hero heads, too?"

"Certainly. You both must see my collection of weapons and hero heads. Mind you, it's a very impressive pair of collections," Jonellith replied. "You should feel highly honored, for very few have ever seen my incredible collection of heroes. They are perfectly stuffed, and some are thirteen hundred years old. Monica, you'll have to walk, since I must carry my Hero Deiter."

Monica rose carefully on her toes. "Hard standing. Heels too tall." She wobbled about, her upper arms wiggling around.

"Ah, but they do look so good on you, Monica. You should always wear them. You look very sexy. After all, once Hero Deiter fertilizes my clutch and I stuff and mount his trophy head, it'll be just you and me. I so want you to look beautiful for me, and I know you want to look beautiful for me."

"Oh yes. Want be pretty. You pretty. Me pretty. Always wear them."

"Good." Jonellith bent over and slipped her top right arm beneath Deiter, lifting him up. He tried to squirm and perhaps force her to drop him on his head, breaking his neck, but bobbing his head about did nothing.

She adjusted Deiter in her arms, holding him such that he could see well, and then slithered along gracefully, but going slow enough that Monica could manage to keep up with her.

"Monica, you walk so beautifully," she praised the witch. Monica smiled, rather stupidly though, as she took her tiny careful steps, trying to see and to keep up.

"Ah, here is my weapons collection. Some of these are almost two millennia old, but all are magical, some highly magical."

The pair gazed at the three walls. Weapons of all types were skillfully arranged and properly labeled. "This one is my finest sword. Its enchantment is five times powerful. It belonged to Hero Jamal of Babylon. His clutch turned out to be the best. Many fine offspring from him. Maybe Hero Deiter, your offspring will be powerful, too. We'll see, won't we Monica. Sorry Hero Deiter, you won't be able to see them. As you can see, I've now added six of those new automatic rifles with the enchanted bullets. I admit when Gisella hired me, I didn't expect to be adding new weapons, but Hero Deiter surprised me."

"Gisella pretty. She demon," Monica tried to put together an idea.

"Well, she was, but she's not a demon any longer. She used a defective Wish scroll, which turned her body into that of a normal human woman. She's not a demon anymore, nor can she cast any spells, but she's still pretty, Monica. Now, these weapons over here came from Genghis Kahn, a present for me." She continued moving along, showing them various weapons, anyone of which Deiter could have used to slay this demon, if only his body was whole.

"Pretty weapons," Monica muttered.

"Now this way," Jonellith said, leading them out of this room into the hall once more. "No, that is my laboratory, Monica. The head trophy room is this next one."

They entered another similar sized chamber, probably thirty foot square. This time, male heads hung on the wall. Each was affixed to a wooden placard and hung about six feet above the floor, right at perfect eyesight for both Monica and Jonellith. Had Monica been in her right mind, she would have noticed that each head was perfectly preserved. Jonellith had done an incredibly fine job of taxidermy. Below each wooden placard was the hero's name and a date.

Monica tried to count them, but got confused when she reached two heads. Deiter counted fifteen heads, but saw a placard with his name burnished into the wood: Deiter Cross 2200. He swallowed hard and wondered if he could use his teeth to bite her to death, but realized that it took magical weapons to harm a demon. He sighed, giving up that notion.

"Deiter go there?" Monica asked, pointing to the empty placard with her right upper arm stump. It took a Herculean effort on her part to get that thought expressed.

"Very observant, Hero Monica. Yes, Hero Deiter's head will go there."

"Where Monica head go?"

"Sorry, Monica. You will have to be happy just living with me. I only put breeding heroes on the wall. We can't breed. We are both female, so you'll just keep me company."

"Okay."

Deiter finally broke. He knew he was helpless to prevent any of this from happening. He began softly crying. *Soon, she'll forcefully breed with me. Then, she'll at least be merciful and kill me. While I sure don't want my head up there, I'll be dead and won't care any more. But poor*

Monica. She's going to be trapped here for half a century or more. I guess I'm going to luck out. "I'm sorry, Monica. I got you into this," he sobbed.

"Deiter is hero. Not sorry," she replied stupidly, causing him to sob all the more.

Jonellith merely smiled. They had all cried in the end, some sooner than others, as they accepted their fates and the simple fact that Jonellith was more powerful than they were. "It is good to cry, Hero Deiter. We will breed soon."

She then took them back to the bedroom, laying Deiter down in the middle of the large bed with the silky sheets. "Now, I have to go prepare myself for the breeding, Hero Deiter. Later I'll come back and we can breed. Don't worry. I'll handle the details, since you don't have arms and hands now."

With that, she slithered out of the room, leaving Deiter sobbing on the bed. Knowing no better, Monica followed after her, but Jonellith slithered along very rapidly, leaving her far behind. Monica moved slowly along the hall. "See in here," she said aloud, thinking the demon could hear her, but Jonellith was far from her location. Monica entered the demon's laboratory and began marveling at all the items and work tables, though with her 40 IQ, she had no idea what she was seeing. Still, curious, she looked around.

Then, her eyes fell on the two remaining Wish scrolls. At that instant, the Idiot Mind spell dissolved away! In fact, Jonellith had been distracted enough by Deiter's screaming that she'd made a tiny inflection error in her casting, one that only implemented that spell for about an hour. In a flash, Monica's mind cleared, and she grasped what had happened and where she and Deiter were located. She looked down at the Wish spells written on beautiful scrolls. If only she still had even one hand, she could unroll it and cast a Full Wish spell.

She knew she had to act. It was now or never, particularly for Deiter. Any moment, the demon would slither back and breed with him. Once done, she'd kill him, remove his head, stuff it, and add it to her trophy wall. Monica knew what to do. Silently, she cast a very simple spell, Invisible Helper. She directed it to stuff one of the scrolls into her enormous cleavage. Then, she had the invisible hands unroll the remaining scroll. Hastily, she read the words, calling up the powerful magical energies, and barked, "I wish Deiter Cross who is in the nearby room would have his arms and hands back on his body, just as they were before Jonellith cast her Wish spell on him."

Magical energies flashed and the scroll disintegrated before her eyes, but she had already begun her slow walk back the twenty feet to the bedroom. As she entered, Deiter nearly knocked her over. He'd gotten up, discovered he was somehow whole again, and was making a mad dash to get a weapon from her trophy room. "Oh!" he exclaimed, grabbing her and preventing her from falling over.

"Quick, grab onto my back and don't let go," Monica whispered.

"If I can get one of those swords, we can fight her," he protested, but mechanically did as she asked.

Just as soon as she felt his arms around her waist, holding tightly, she began walking, ignoring his silly comment. She focused and began her extra-planar travel, using her PSI powers, powers that Rob, once her husband and now her son, had taught her how to use. The grey castle-like dungeon walls gave way to a stinking swirling dark landscape, somewhere deep within the Abyss. Monica continued to keep her mind clear and focused on the next step and the next, ignoring the vomiting Deiter behind her. The stench of the land about him caused him to gag uncontrollably. He was just thankful his stomach was mostly empty.

Soon, the hideous grey land grew lighter. In the distance, Deiter could see shadowy images of giant, ugly demons, but their bodies seemed almost transparent, just as the land they were apparently walking over was. Suddenly, a warmth spread over his body; they left the topmost layer of the Abyss behind them, entering more neutral lands. On they walked, albeit very slowly. Deiter thought he saw Monica's home ahead of them. Slowly, the thin image grew both closer and more solid, until at last, he heard her seven-inch, tiny metal heels clicking on the concrete of their walkway.

"You can let go now, Deiter," Monica whispered and then collapsed, totally exhausted.

While he was about to let go, he felt her slipping down, and he kept her from falling, lying her gently on the ground. By then, the many Alarm spells around the mansion activated, bringing a rush of wizards and witches rushing out of the PIWIP complex—Protections, Investigations, Wands, Items, Potions—the one-stop magic store and residence.

Crystal yelled, "Deiter? Is that really you? Monica, what's happened to her. Oh move over silly boy and get some clothes on."

Only then, did Deiter realize he was standing there naked. His feet were bleeding and covered with grey filth from the Abyss. This, Enya noticed as she rushed out. "Abyss?" she asked. He nodded. "Come with me. We have to get that filth off your feet and some healing potions in you before you get terrible infections. Abyss slime does terrible things to human bodies. Come on. Oh, someone has Messaged Lindsey for you."

Dumbly, he followed the short potion maker. As they approached the main doors, Enya levitated him and pushed him along. "Look, we don't want to contaminate our place, so I'll just float you along."

Several of the many children poked their heads out of the playroom to see what was going on. "Look, it's Deiter. He's naked!" Several young teens ran out and giggled, though putting her hands over their mouths. Still, they all looked, much to his embarrassment.

Bergson raced out with the others, but had beaten everyone else to her body.

"She's just used too much mental energies," Crystal pronounced. He cradled her head, while Crystal examined her. "She's basically asleep, Bergson. Why don't you carry her to her room. If she wakes, get her cleaned up and tucked into bed. Deiter can tell us what happened."

He needed no further orders. Gently, he picked her up and headed inside, just as Lindsey apparated close to the doors. Crystal said, "Don't fret. He looks fine, just a bit dirty. Enya's getting the Abyss filth off his feet. I'll take you to him. Monica is asleep. Used too much mental energy, I suspect."

By the time that Enya had Deiter cleaned up, enough cleansing potions down him, and dressed—Lindsey had made a quick trip to Bradbury's to fetch him some clothes—Monica joined them; Bergson had a secure arm around her waist. Her hair was still wet though. "How's Deiter?" she asked.

He replied, "Humiliated beyond words, but alive and whole. Again, I owe you my life, Monica."

Purposely alerting everyone, Monica said, "Okay then, gang. We need to be alert for Jonellith's retaliation. She was trying to breed with Deiter when we escaped. She'll likely come gunning for us again."

Several hastily cast protection spells, before they headed to the kitchen and dining room for tea. "Okay, so what happened?" Lindsey asked. "You both just vanished."

Deiter's face reddened. "I've never been so helpless or humiliated in my life, dear. You best tell them, Monica."

"Gisella used some of these Wish scrolls. Apparently, she tried to use a defective one and it backfired, changing her body into that of a human woman. She's lost all her spell casting abilities. So we don't have to worry about her any longer. Jonellith then took her share of the Wish scrolls, discarding the defective ones, leaving her with four. She used two of them to Wish Deiter and me into her Abyss chambers. Deiter arrived, but with his arms and legs no longer attached to his torso. He was lying naked on her bed. Apparently, her eggs or clutch is ready for fertilization, and she only uses heroes to breed with, hence Deiter's abduction. Once he'd fertilized her, she would have cut off his head, stuffed it, and mounted it on her trophy wall, along with a lot of predecessors."

Deiter butted in, "Fifteen of them."

"Right. I was under an Idiot Mind spell and couldn't count how many heads were there—"

Lindsey interrupted, "But if you were, how could you undo that spell, Monica?"

"Deiter's doing, I think. When she was casting it, he was screaming rather loudly, distracting her slightly, causing her to make a mistake. While she was off preparing herself for breeding, I wandered into her lab and saw the remaining two Wish scrolls. At that moment, the Idiot Mind spell fizzled out. I cast some spells, bringing one Wish scroll back with me and used the other to Wish Deiter back to normal. I knew I could planar walk us home, but he'd have to have his arms and legs back to hold on to me, since I couldn't carry him. Her chambers are deep within the Abyss, many layers down. I thought I'd never get out of there, but we made it."

The others asked questions of the pair for another half hour. Then, Bergson spoke up, "Monica, can you use that remaining Wish scroll now and get your own body fixed up?"

Monica sighed. "While I'd like to, I'm saving it to help find a cure for all those who took Dr. Menninger's pills. If I can use it to save millions of other women's lives, that is far more important than my own body. I need to sleep. I am so tired it's not funny."

Crystal answered, "You should know that the cure seems to be working. Those who entered the recovery coma first have woken up. Their bodies appear normal, especially the women. So we believe about half of them are going to recover. Still no ideas about how to repair those who took his pills."

"Okay," Monica sighed. "After I sleep, I'll use the Wish scroll and see what I can do. We simply have to find a cure for those twenty million or so. Bergson, help me back to my bedroom, please."

As she rose, Lindsey moved up beside her and gave her a solid hug. She whispered, "I owe you big time, Monica. Thank you."

Chapter 24—The Cure

Monica rose early the next morning. She smiled down at the sleeping Bergson. Yesterday's tension and worry lines had melted during the night, and she knew the man truly loved her. Silently, she cast her Morph Me spell and then dressed. She fired off a lengthy Message spell and headed to the kitchen to make some tea and wait on the outcome. Monica felt strongly this was a critical decision she alone had to make and thus sought Ashley's advice.

As she sipped her tea, a sleepy-eyed Misty wandered into the kitchen. "Oh Monica. Oh, Morph eh? So are you going to fix breakfast today?" She was teasing, for Monica rarely cooked any meals.

"Yes, Morph. Time I take some responsibility for myself. I'm waiting for Ashley's reply. I don't think you want me to make breakfast, do you?"

Misty laughed. "Hardly. Sometime you should take cooking lessons. So are you and Mr. Bergson a thing?" she asked curiously. Many were speculating about the pair.

"Could be. Not sure yet. Ah, hold. Here comes her reply." Monica read the scrolling message as it moved past her eyes. "I thought so," she sighed and sent Ashley a thank you. "Time to use the Wish scroll. See you later, Misty."

Seeing and hearing this, Misty became even more curious. "So are you going to use the Wish to get your body fixed up? You deserve it, if anyone does." She hoped this would fish a bit more out of Monica. It did, sort of.

"No. Not with twenty million others whose lives are ruined. Back in a while for breakfast. Thanks for making it, Misty."

Monica carried her tea with her and headed for her own study lounge. As she walked, she Summoned the precious Wish scroll to her. Once at her desk, using her Invisible Helper, she spread the lengthy scroll out and studied it, looking for any flaws. While she'd only read that one Wish scroll down in the Abyss, she was looking for physical damage to the scroll during the transport here. Finding none, she set about working out the wording she intended to use, knowing well that she could leave nothing ambiguous in her phrasing, for the Wish spell would surely implement the wrong meaning.

Satisfied she had the wording correct, she began the lengthy chant, reading off the scroll's words. Then, she barked with conviction, "I wish that Simone Folquet and his Folquet Enterprises would soon develop a cure for all those who took one of the five types of pills that the Schutzstaffel and Dr. Menninger distributed to people protecting them from their attack on the demons, pills which caused women to lose their lower arms and hands, grow enormous breasts, and distort their feet." Magical energies flashed. The sheer volume of energy released was similar to that released when she cast her own known topmost Grade 9 spells. Thus, she knew something happened. Now all she could do was hope for the best.

Misty had told Crystal about Monica's uncharacteristic early rise and Message to Ashley, the Class IV Diviner. Thus, Crystal paused at the door to Monica's study. She saw the Wish scroll laid out and heard Monica reading the written words. Wisely, she remained utterly quiet, though intensely curious about just what Monica would wish for. Once the magical energies flashed, both women saw the scroll turn into black dust particles and vanish from the desk.

"Wow Monica. You didn't use it to fix your own body up," she exclaimed.

"I don't know if I could have resisted everyone else begging me to use the scroll to fix myself up. After all, there's something like twenty million men, women, and children who need a cure far more than I do. Lord knows I want to be whole again, but they need it a million times more than I do. Perhaps later on I can purchase another Wish scroll, as Deiter did."

"Well, that was magnanimous of you, Monica. Damned generous beyond all expectations. Come on. Misty has breakfast ready. Bergson is looking for you, too. I think he's smitten."

Monica flushed. "I know. I never thought I could love again, not after Rob, but. . ." Her voice trailed away as those painful memories reappeared.

When the two entered the dining room, the tables were packed, though the children were gulping down their pancakes and eggs, eager to get outside to play before the cold and snow came again. Monica sat down beside Alan. Seeing his confused look, she whispered, "I used a Morph Me spell. Time I started being responsible, Alan."

He chuckled. "My goodness, woman. I've never met anyone who is as responsible as you are!"

Once the children dashed off, Crystal spoke up. "Just so everyone knows, Monica used the Wish scroll this morning. Are you going to tell us what you wished for or should I?"

"I wished that Simone Folquet and his Folquet Enterprises would soon find the cure for those who took their pills." Only a few knew the significance of the man and his company, though everyone knew this French company had developed a cure for the nasty pills Dominus had unleashed on the world as part of his health care attempts to take over control of the US. Monica knew Ashley would let Lindsey and the other Rodents know about her wish. Further, she knew they would appreciate why Monica had chosen him and his pharmaceutical companies, for it was Simon's father who had cloned Simon, making and unleashing the Dominus clone on the world.

Bergson asked, "So if they do find a cure, will it help restore your body, Monica?"

A hush swept around the room. All eyes turned to her, including Miller and Kelly.

"What?" Monica asked, her face reddening slightly.

"Well, will it?" Bergson repeated.

Monica sighed. "Darned if I know. My body has been the recipient of so many wish alterations that I've no idea if such a cure would restore my body or not. Once things settle down some, I'll try my Regenerate spell, but not until the millions of others are handled first. Meanwhile, I'll use my Morph Me spell, my Invisible Helper spell, and Move Object spell. So what's on the agenda today?" She cleverly attempted to deflect the conversation elsewhere but on herself.

Just then, Deiter apparated in the dining room. "Hi everyone, Monica. Ashley just told me what you did with your Wish scroll, Monica. So I wanted you to know I was going to buy you another Wish scroll so you could get your own body fixed up. But right now, I can't. With some twenty million others in equally bad shape, the few sellers of Wish scrolls have jacked their price up tenfold. What's more, they're getting it! Can you imagine spending two hundred million for one scroll?"

Monica smiled. "Thanks Deiter. Yes, I can imagine how desperate those people are. Unless a cure is found soon, their lives are destroyed, though maybe in time they can adapt to their severe limitations. Hence my wish."

"Well, I just wanted you to know that I tried. Maybe later on the prices will come back down," Deiter suggested.

"Twenty million for a Wish spell? Deiter, save your money," Monica advised. "There is so much more good that you could do with that kind of money."

He didn't respond to that, but quickly many others asked him what the current situation was. At once, the conversation changed, for which Monica was grateful.

"I'm going to visit Wanda, Tim and her girls today. Have someone Message me if you need me, Alan," she explained. He agreed, but was actively engaged with Deiter.

A few minutes later, Monica's Teleport spell landed her just outside Tim's home, over the hill from her place. Out of respect for Wanda and her girls, Monica cancelled her Morph spell. Now she looked much as they did. Shortly, Tim opened the door. She noticed he seemed very alert, flushed, and happy.

"Monica. Great to see you. Come on in. We've wonderful news for you, really wonderful." He led her into his living room, where Wanda was waiting for them.

"Monica! We've got wonderful news to share," Wanda exclaimed. "Tell her, Tim."

Bashfully, he said, "I've asked Wanda to marry me, and she's agreed."

"Congratulations!"

"Yes, we're getting married Sunday, because Monday, I start my new job." Wanda's grin was catching. "They've hired me—St. Louis School of Magic. I get to teach illusion magic theory and beginning casting. It's what I was teaching in Germany. I just love teaching the youngsters."

She grinned again and added, "But that's not all, Monica. Watch." Wanda focused and magical energies flashed, bringing her Invisible Helper into being. She'd cast the spell silently and without a wand. As Monica watched, invisible hands picked up Wanda's wand from the mantle, and the witch cast her next spell using the wand. Much stronger magical energies flashed. Suddenly, Wanda's body appeared whole, as she had looked before taking the terrible pills.

Wanda explained, "You see, once I could prove to them I could manage on my own, the governor offered me the job. I have to be able to have my hands back so I can cast all manner of spells. I know it's a bit of a bootstrap, but it works. I can cast the Invisible Helper just as you do, Monica, and via it, I can cast Morph Me. And now I can cast all the spells I know. It's a miracle, even if the spell isn't permanent."

Wanda was quite excited. "Plus, the girls and I have been practicing casting by using our wands in our toes. That's also working well. I know the girls have been working hard on learning how to cast their beginning spells without using their wands, and that's working as well. Tim thinks it's necessity that is driving us to succeed. I don't know about that, but it is working. And the girls have been accepted into the St. Louis school, too; they will be joining Tim's boys Monday when classes resume. They're cutting next year's summer vacation down to just August, so we can make up the two months we've lost this term."

"It's amazing though. Susanne and Sofia are now able to cast nearly two dozen spells without their wands. Tim's boys have been working with them every day, coaching them. But there's one serious problem."

Monica smiled. Hearing such good news instead of the next disaster resonated with her. "That's amazingly wonderful, Wanda, but what's the problem?"

"It's the intense sexual drive that the pills imparted to us. Tim understands and has been just incredible with me, helping me over it, but the girls. You see, their bodies now look as if they are much older, mature young women, and yet they're only fourteen and thirteen. However, their bodies are craving sexual stimulation, too. I'm afraid that they might—well, you know what I mean. I doubt any of us would have any self-control left if someone kissed us passionately."

"I know. It's really tough to resist those impulses," Monica admitted.

"Plus, both girls really do love how their bosoms have developed far beyond what they should be at their ages. Makes us look older, mom, Susanne told me. And both girls claim the boys really do gawk at them, especially in their heels. Both feel grownup, but they aren't, not yet anyway."

Monica chuckled. "Wanda, didn't we use our spells to alter our appearances when we were their ages?"

Wanda flushed. "Well, yes, but we didn't have this incredible sex drive back then, not as we all do now. And one more thing. Both girls have asked me about a cure, especially since the cure has been found for those who inhaled the gas form of the biological agent. While they would like their arms and hands back, they aren't so sure about the rest of it." She laughed. "They'll change their minds later on, when they get a little older." Monica chuckled along with her.

"Well," Monica said, "I came over to chat with you and find out how you and the girls were managing. I guess I've my answer on that one. How is it going with being independent?" She finally asked what she desperately wanted to know. Was it really possible for women to be independent in life with their bodies so modified?

Wanda glanced at Tim and laughed. "He wouldn't let me cast Morph Me until I could handle everything on my own. We still haven't morphed the girls yet. In fact, they've asked me not to do it. How surprising. When we first took the pills, they begged us to morph them all the time. Now, they are very pleased with their appearance and casting skills. So Tim and I are honoring their request, since the more spells they can cast without using their wands, the better. I hope we're doing the right thing."

"Oh, I'm sure you are. Well done, Tim. I bet it's been ripping your heart out to not cast morph spells on Wanda and the girls."

Tim visibly relaxed. "Spot on, Monica. It felt as though I was dying or something, but I resisted the temptation to morph them. Now, I'm incredibly glad that I didn't. All three of them can do most everything for themselves, something I couldn't imagine was possible. Well, the DVD has been a Godsend."

"Practice, Monica. That's the key, that and allowing plenty of time to do something. As long as you are patient, you can do it. The women on the DVD show you how, but it takes a lot of practice. I'm so thankful that Tim resisted his natural urges to morph us. I know I'm terribly slow, but I can take care of myself and the girls now. Don't get me wrong, I'll welcome the cure; it's just now I feed myself and am not wholly dependent on others."

Monica agreed. "Well done, both of you. I've been so darn busy with this demon thing that I've not had the luxury of studying the DVD, let alone practicing doing much with my feet. I hope things have calmed down so I can."

"Tim, can you make her a copy of the DVD on your computer?"

"You got it, dear. Only take a few minutes, Monica."

"Thanks, Tim. I really do need to practice myself."

"You won't regret it," Wanda declared. "Eventually, you'll get your own confidence and self-respect back—once you figure out how to do the things you used to be able to do."

Monica spent the afternoon in her bedroom watching the DVD and experimenting on her own, trying to emulate the way the women carried out their daily tasks. Slowly, she began to see that it was possible. While it wasn't desirable or wanted, she could manage if only she took her time. "It's taking me ten times longer to do something, but I'm doing it," she muttered, suppressing her frustrations.

Bergson wandered in and overheard her. "What's taking so long? Oh, I see, getting your hair brushed out. Looks good."

She sighed. "Yes, thanks, Alan. I've decided to follow everyone's advice and learn to use my feet as much as possible. I can't believe how well Wanda and her girls are managing. I'm determined to follow their example."

"I'd think much less of you if you didn't, Monica."

"So what's new today? I hope everything has finally quieted down."

"Today's news? Well, Kelly and Miller—they're getting married. Arnold actually proposed today and Chrissy said yes. I gave them my blessings. They're going to tell you when everyone gets together for supper."

"Great. They make a good pair." *What about us?*

"Monica, I've been thinking about us. I don't want to spoil what we have going, but I'm going to ask anyway. Would you marry me? It's all right if you don't want to. Maybe both of us need more time to get over our own losses."

Monica rose to her feet, pushed her bosom into his chest, and said, "I thought you'd never ask. Yes, I'll marry you, but we have to agree on who wears the pants."

Alan put his arms around her, lifted her off her feet, and twirled her around, before passionately kissing her. Not to be outdone, Monica silently cast Levitate and Move Object, lifting them both off the ground and twirling them around. Both began laughing heartily.

"So who gets to wear the pants?" he asked.

"We both do," she replied. "I should make sure Rob is okay with this, since you'll be his father, sort of."
***

Three weddings were held on Sunday. Crystal and Ericka decorated the mansion's living room and helped make the long dresses for the three brides. Today, no morph spells were in use. Wearing their new gowns, proudly, Susanne and Sofia took their slow steps down the aisle, escorted by Tim's boys, Bill and Len respectively. Then, as Tim and Wanda said their vows, Ericka's eyes watered fiercely, though there were few dry eyes among the women.

Once the new couple walked back down the aisle amid clapping and cheers, Arnold Kelly and Chrissy Miller were married. Lastly, Alan Bergson and Monica Nicole were married. Then, the reception party began.

Crystal commented to Monica, "It's wonderful to have good things happening here at our place, instead of all the terrible things we've been reacting to. I hope the demons stay in their Abyss."

"What's amazing to me is that I'm married to a normal. I would never have predicted that," she replied.

"You've matured, Monica."

"Don't know about that, but I feel so light, so happy, so wonderful."
***

"Well, Monica, you got your wish," Crystal said. It was early December and light snow coated the landscape. "It's on the news."

Everyone gathered around the TV in the living room to hear the official announcement. "Yes, it's official. Folquet Enterprises has announced that they've created a cure for all those who took one of the five pills handed out by the SS and Dr. Menninger. They are gearing up production of the antidote as we speak. They anticipate the production of a million cures per week. Official estimates suggest that twenty weeks will be required before all victims receive their cure. By next April, everyone should be cured and back to normal. Folquet Enterprises will announce the distribution procedure later this week."

The reporter then changed topics. "And this just in. Dominus Malefic has been spotted in Singapore. . ."

Crystal turned off the TV. "When will they stop such silliness?"

Ericka commented, "Probably never. It's like the old western Jessie James or the Bonnie and Clyde thing. The legend lives on."

"Well," said Monica changing the topic, "I'm just happy that Amos stepped up to fill the power vacuum here, until elections this spring. Without a president and Congress, our country is rather in limbo land."

Bergson added, "I'm just glad all is quiet. We need a break from criminals. Besides, Monica and I have to go on our honeymoon soon."

The ringing of Monica's phone interrupted the small group. Enya answered it for her, but hastily put it on speaker phone. "It's the President!" she whispered.

"Hello. This is Monica."

"Hi there Mrs. Black-Bergson. I'm Acting President Amos Slaughter, Head of the States Justice Department. Congratulations on your recent marriage. As you've heard, we're working to bring order back into our government and country. I can't begin to thank you enough for what you and the WIT team has done, not only for our country but for the whole world. In line with this, I would like to offer you a full-time position in the Homeland Defense Force-World Investigation Team. You would be assigned to Alan Bergson's team, naturally. Your country needs your help at this critical time. Once new leaders are elected and the situation is under control, you could resign, if you prefer."

"I'd be delighted to help the WIT team and be an official member, Mr. President. Thank you."

"No, it is we who must thank you. Off the record, do you think the demons have all been eliminated this time? Or have we left some behind? We should have listened to you nearly ten years ago. Whatever your response is, we will listen. I promise you."

Monica thought for a moment before answering. Her entire group listened intently to hear her reply, including her WIT team. "Well, this time, I think we got them all. Last time, I know several slipped through, but I believe we got all the leaders. Deiter Cross can give you a better picture of any that might have escaped the roundup in the Middle East."

The End.

A Favor to Other Readers

How about helping other readers? Many readers rely on reviews to make the decision whether to buy a book. You can help them make their decision by leaving your opinions and viewpoint in a short review of the positive things of this book. Writing the review and expressing your opinion only takes a few minutes, and other readers will appreciate your efforts.

Click this link: Lindsey Barron Series Volume 8 Down the Dragon Hole
scroll down to Customer Reviews; click on Write a Review, and enter your review. Thank you.

Author Information

Visit My Amazon.com Author Page
Vic Broquard Author Page

Follow My Blog
Vic Broquard's Blog

Follow Me on Social Media
Facebook
Google+
LinkedIn
YouTube

Other Books by Vic Broquard

Without Warning (fantasy)

The Trident Series: (fantasy)
>   Volume 1 The Trident and the Book
>   Volume 2 The Trident and the Scepter
>   Volume 3 The Trident and the Resurrection

The Adventures of Elizabeth Stanton Series: (science fiction)
>   Volume 1 The Evolution of the Path
>   Volume 2 The Great Messiah
>   Volume 3 Of Kings and Queens and Troubadours
>   Volume 4 Chaos in the Aftermath
>   Volume 5 Power Plays
>   Volume 6 Age of Exploration
>   Volume 7 Abducted
>   Volume 8 The Emperor and Empress
>   Volume 9 A Job Worth Doing
>   Volume 10 Degradation
>   Volume 11 The Second Crusade
>   Volume 12 When Worlds Collide
>   Volume 13 Dark Ages

The Lindsey Barron Series: (fantasy)
>   Volume 1 The Rod of the Apocalypse
>   Volume 2 The Board of Governors
>   Volume 3 The Crown of Moses
>   Volume 4 Dominus for President
>   Volume 5 The National Health Care Program
>   Volume 6 States Justice
>   Volume 7 Cross and Double-cross
>   Volume 8 Down the Dragon Hole

Zoran Chronicles Series: (fantasy)
>   Volume 1 A Dragon in Our Town
>   Volume 2 Dragons, Power, Courts, and War

Planet of the Orange-red Sun Series: (science fiction)
Volume 1 When Kingdoms Fall
Volume 2 Dark Ages
Volume 3 Age of the Towers
Volume 4 Difficillis Exitus
Volume 5 Age of the Lords
Volume 6 The Renegade Tower
Volume 7 Rebellions
Volume 8 The Aliens Return
Volume 9 Power Struggles
Volume 10 Guilds, Genetics, and Gods
Volume 11 Magi, Witches, Swords, and Superstitions
Volume 12 The Voyage of the Eagle's Seed
Volume 13 Eagle's Seed and Origins
Volume 14 Justifications
Volume 15 Responsibilities

The Return of the Wizards: Twelve Companions – The Making of Wizards (fantasy)

Slow Comes the Dark Series: (science fiction)
Volume 1 Creeping Darkness
Volume 2 Serendipity
Volume 3 Darkness Descends
Volume 4 Perversion Incarnate
Volume 5 Extermination Wars

Reclamation Series (science fiction)
Volume 1 For the Want of a Pill
Volume 2 Organ Donors

Dragons, Magic, and Me (fantasy)
Volume 1 The Box